Harlequin Books is proud to offer
classic novels from today's superstars
of women's fiction. These authors have
captured the hearts of millions of readers
around the world, and earned their place on
the *New York Times, USA TODAY* and other
bestseller lists with every release.

As a bonus, each volume also includes a
full-length novel from a rising star of series
romance. Bestselling authors in their own
right, these talented writers have captured the
qualities Harlequin is famous for—heart-racing
passion, edge-of-your-seat entertainment
and a satisfying happily-ever-after.

New York Times and *USA TODAY* Bestselling Author

ELIZABETH LOWELL

Dark Fire

HARLEQUIN® BESTSELLERS

Recycling programs
for this product may
not exist in your area.

ISBN-13: 978-0-373-60581-1

DARK FIRE

Copyright © 2010 by Harlequin Books S.A.

The publisher acknowledges the copyright holders
of the individual works as follows:

DARK FIRE
Copyright © 1988 by Two of a Kind, Inc.

EXPECTING HIS CHILD
Copyright © 2000 by Leanne Banks

Printed in U.S.A.

HARLEQUIN®
www.Harlequin.com

CONTENTS

DARK FIRE

New York Times and USA TODAY Bestselling Author
Elizabeth Lowell

ELIZABETH LOWELL

first started her romance career in 1982. Just three years later her novel *Traveling Man* was voted Best Intimate Moments by *RT Book Reviews*. In 1994 she received a Lifetime Achievement Award from the Romance Writers of America.

She has several million copies of her books in print, and since 1992 she has had thirty books on the *New York Times* bestseller list.

Prologue

"You want me to do *what?*" Trace Rawlings asked, raising dark eyebrows.

The man called Invers sighed and rubbed his palm over his thinning hair. "You heard me the first time."

"I've been back in Quito for less than an hour," Trace pointed out. "That damned Polish orchid hunter you sicced on me was the genuine article. He was after orchids, period, and he would have taken on hell with a bucket of water to get to them."

Invers tried to look sympathetic. He failed. He needed Trace too badly to be diverted by something as useless as compassion.

Trace swore under his breath and glared at the small passport photo Invers had given to him. A woman's face stared back at him. Cynthia Edwinna Ryan McCall had black hair, midnight eyes, skin as fine as expensive porcelain, a remote expression and a father who could make highly placed American embassy officials sweat bullets.

"Hell," Trace muttered. He looked up, pinning Invers with a jungle-green glance. "After this, we're even."

Invers let out a rushing breath. "We'll be better than even, Trace. I won't forget this, believe me."

Trace grunted.

"She'll land in a few minutes, so we'll have to be quick. The passport is issued in the name of Cynthia Ryan. She won't tell anyone who she really is. Also, she doesn't know that her father has been in contact with us."

"Does it matter?"

Invers rubbed his palm over his head again, a sign of his unhappiness. Silently he wondered just how much of the story he could tell Trace before the other man would throw up his hands and back out. To anyone who didn't know Big Eddy, the whole story would sound preposterous. To anyone who did know him, the whole story would sound like what it was: preposterous but all too true.

"You ever meet Big Eddy McCall when you were in the States?" Invers asked cautiously.

"No."

"Um. Well. Ms. Ryan doesn't get along with her father. Not surprising. Nobody really *gets* along with Big Eddy. You *go* along with him or you go under.

Nothing personal, you understand. That's just the way he is. A real steamroller."

Trace grunted again. "What about her?"

"Ms. Ryan? Oh, she must be at least as stubborn as he is. More stubborn in some ways. Every man her father has picked out for her has been thrown back in his face. He's finally given up on marrying her off." Invers paused as though struck by a new thought. "By God, that's quite an accomplishment. I think she might be the first human being ever to say no to Big Eddy and make it stick."

"So?"

Invers rubbed his head again as he gave Trace a sideways glance. Everything Invers had said so far was technically true. Big Eddy had given up on marriage for his daughter. He had not, however, given up on the idea of grandchildren. He wanted an Edward Ryan McCall IV to be born as soon as possible. One of his sons had produced a grandchild. That wasn't enough. Big Eddy wanted about a dozen other grandkids as backup for life's nasty little surprises. That was where his daughter came in. Big Eddy had finally figured out that a woman didn't have to be married in order to have children.

Invers didn't think Trace was ready to hear about that part of Big Eddy's proposed deal. In fact, Invers doubted if Trace would ever be ready to stand at stud for Big Eddy, much less to find out that it had been Raul's idea in the first place. It was the better— indeed the only—part of valor to tell half-truths to Trace and to let Big Eddy believe what he wanted to believe about the man he had ordered Invers to hire. And never to mention Raul at all.

"Um. Well. Big Eddy's daughter goes by the name of Cindy Ryan and is in business with a woman called Susan Parker. That's where you come in."

Trace arched his eyebrows again. It wasn't like Invers to loop around a subject eight times before getting to the point.

"Ms. Parker comes to Quito several times a year to buy cloth," Invers continued. "This time her native buyer didn't show up, so she hopped a bus over the Andes to go looking for him."

"Did she find him?"

"No. She won't, either," Invers added with uncharacteristic bluntness. "When he wasn't buying cloth he was smuggling emeralds out of Colombia. He stiffed one of his connections and hasn't been heard from since."

Trace shrugged. "It happens."

"Yes. Well. Ms. Parker hasn't been heard from for ten days, either. Not officially, that is."

Green eyes focused on Invers with startling intensity. "And unofficially?"

"Unofficially she is the pampered guest of Señor Raul Almeda," Invers said. "*Señor* Almeda would like her to remain for a while longer. That's why his shortwave radios are all on the fritz."

Trace hissed an obscenity that Invers chose not to hear.

"From all indications, Ms. Parker isn't burning down the house trying to leave," Invers said.

The left corner of Trace's mouth kicked up slightly. Raul was a good friend as well as a connoisseur of elegant women. Raul was also very well connected to the government of Ecuador, which was why Invers looked so unhappy at the thought of displeasing him.

"So what's the problem?" Trace asked. "Is Ms. Parker's family worried about her?"

"She has no family, but apparently she's rather close to Ms. Ryan, who is flying to Ecuador to find out what happened to her partner."

"I still don't see the problem. Just tell Big Eddy's daughter that her friend is shacked up with every woman's dream lover."

"I suggested a similar solution to Señor Almeda."

"Raul didn't go for it?"

"No. He can be rather, um…"

"Autocratic," Trace said flatly. "He was born too late. He should have been an emperor."

Invers, being a diplomat, chose not to point out that Raul was descended from French, Spanish and Inca royalty, and ruled his immense land holdings like the tyrants his ancestors had been. A benevolent tyrant, granted, but a tyrant nonetheless.

"In any case," Invers said smoothly, "we all want to avoid any suggestion of an, um, incident. We can't have Ms. Ryan running around raising an embarrassing hue and cry for Ms. Parker. If we tell Ms. Ryan that Ms. Parker is quite happy on the Almeda hacienda, Ms. Ryan will want to talk to her. Then we'll have to tell her that the radio isn't functioning at the moment and won't be functioning in the near future. I don't think Big Eddy's daughter will find that explanation, um, acceptable."

Eyes closed, Trace went over all that Invers had said. And more importantly, all that he had not said.

"You're quite certain that Raul's latest captive is a happy captive?" Trace asked, focusing on Invers with an intensity that made the other man long to be elsewhere.

"As of five days ago, yes."

"Do you have any indication that Ms. Parker or Ms. Ryan are involved in smuggling of any kind?"

"No, thank God," Invers said fervently.

"Then what is it, precisely, that you want me to do?"

"Allow Ms. Ryan to hire you to 'find' her friend. Take your time getting to the Almeda *hacienda*, and—"

"How long?" Trace interrupted.

"Four or five days. A week at most. Señor Almeda isn't known for the duration of his, um, enthusiasms."

Trace smiled slightly but said only, "Stalling shouldn't be a problem. That early storm made a mess of the mountain roads."

"It disrupted communications, too," Invers added without missing a beat. "Be sure to point that out to Ms. Ryan."

"No problem. Hell, it's the simple truth."

"There is no such thing as a simple truth," Invers muttered beneath his breath.

Trace smiled rather grimly. "Anything else?"

"Don't reveal that you know Ms. Ryan is Big Eddy McCall's daughter. And be very, very certain that Ms. Ryan doesn't know you have been hired by her father. Otherwise she'll walk out on you and try to hire another guide. That would make things exceptionally, um, difficult for the embassy."

"Have I been hired by Big Eddy? I thought I was just doing you a favor."

Smiling blandly, Invers offered Trace one half of a very complex truth. "Big Eddy requested of the embassy that we hire the best man in Ecuador to guide and protect his daughter while she's here. She would, after all, make a tempting kidnap target. You'll be paid one thousand American dollars a day for your, um, efforts."

Trace's green eyes narrowed. "That seems excessive."

"Big Eddy is excessively rich. Think of it as combat pay," Invers added, smiling thinly.

"Are you really expecting someone to grab her?"

"No. But face it, Trace. I'm not sending you on a picnic. Any woman who can stand up to Big Eddy could teach stubborn to a Missouri mule."

"I'm hardly known as a pushover," Trace pointed out.

"Yes. I am well aware of that fact."

Invers smiled and silently wished that he could go along with Trace and Cindy Ryan. It would be worth considerable inconvenience to find out who taught stubborn to whom.

Chapter 1

*G*ood work, Invers. It saves a lot of wear and tear on the hunter when the prey walks right into the trap, Trace thought sardonically as he watched the tall, raven-haired woman weaving through the smoky bar toward him.

At that moment Trace was ready to accept any break Lady Luck was passing out. He had left Invers less than twenty minutes before. No time to shower, shave, change clothes or do anything else in the way of recovery from the past six weeks of trying to keep J. Ivar Polanski, orchid collector extraordinaire, from killing himself or someone else while pursuing living baubles to adorn spoiled rich women such as the one crossing the crowded room right now.

Not that Cindy Ryan needed any decoration, Trace decided as she came a bit closer. The face-only photograph hadn't done her justice. She had the kind of figure that made a man…restless.

"Mr. Rawlings? I'm Cynthia Ryan."

The voice was a husky contralto that made every one of Trace's masculine nerve endings stir. His physical response irritated him. So instead of responding immediately, he sipped at the fine Scotch that the waitress had put in front of him a few moments earlier. Without saying a word he let the smoky, intimate taste of the liquor expand through him like a kiss from the kind of woman he had always wanted and never found. Only after the taste on his tongue had dissipated to a shimmering echo of heat did he look up.

At that moment Cindy found herself hoping she was mistaken and that this man was not Trace Rawlings. It was all she could do not to step backward when his cool green eyes focused on her. The man lounging at the small table with his long legs stretched in front of him wasn't what she had expected to hire. She couldn't believe that this man with his stained khaki bush clothes, scarred boots and a dark, three-day stubble on his heavy jaw, was the guide the American embassy had enthusiastically recommended that she hire. Could this be the bilingual backcountry genius who had no peer in Quito, Ecuador, or anywhere else up and down the South American Andes?

"Trace Rawlings?" Cindy repeated, knowing her

voice was too husky, too skeptical, and unable to do anything about it. The man was frankly unnerving. He radiated the kind of relaxed, clearly undomesticated presence that people associated with cats stretched out in a patch of sunlight. Big cats. Black jaguars, for instance. Dangerously handsome, dangerously powerful, dangerously sleek, dangerously…*dangerous*.

"That's me."

Trace's voice was a perfect match for his appearance. The resonances were deep, predatory and compelling. Nerve endings Cindy didn't know she had stirred and shivered in dark response.

"Do you have any identification?" Cindy asked finally, frowning as she looked Trace over once more.

Her opinion hadn't changed since her first glance at him. There was nothing reassuring about Trace Rawlings, and Cindy very much needed reassurance right now. Susan had been missing for ten days, and Susan, whatever her quirks, was not the type to vanish without leaving so much as a note for her friend.

Trace felt his irritation turn into a razor edge of anger at the dubious looks he kept getting from Big Eddy's snooty daughter. Coolly Trace gave Cindy precisely the kind of once-over she had just given him.

"ID?" he asked softly. "Sure thing." He turned and called to the bartender in machine-gun Spanish and instantly was answered in the same way. "Anything else?" Trace asked indifferently, reaching for the Scotch once more.

"I beg your pardon?"

Someday, you'll do just that, princess—and mean it, Trace thought with a surge of purely masculine emotion as he sipped the aromatic golden liquor. *Snotty rich girls who go slumming in the wrong places tend to get men knifed in back alleys.* And beneath that thought was another: *God, if Cindy's partner is half as sexy, no wonder Raul wanted to sabotage the radio, lock all the doors and drop the keys into the nearest sacred well.*

"You wanted ID. Paco vouched for me," Trace said carelessly. "We've known each other for years."

"But I don't understand Spanish."

Trace shrugged. "Tough taco, princess. It's the language of the day around here."

Cindy's black eyes narrowed. When Trace focused his attention once more on his Scotch, she fought a sudden, sharp struggle with her temper. Normally she would have been the first to find humor in the situation confronting her, but nothing was normal for her right now. She was tired, had a screaming headache from Quito's ten thousand feet of altitude and was worried about Susan.

In no way did Cindy feel like catering to the ir-rational male whims of a lean, dark, down-at-the-heels American who had gone native.

"Well, Tarzan, put this in your taco," Cindy drawled. "Invers at the embassy told me that a man called Trace Rawlings has been known to hire himself out…if the price is right. So I guess I'll just have to start naming figures. When the price is right, Trace Rawlings will stand up and be counted."

Only the fact that Cindy had been raised by a
steamroller disguised as a father, and had an older
brother whose temper was frankly formidable, gave
her the courage not to turn and run when Trace
looked up at her. There was a long silence while she
returned him stare for glare.

Slowly Trace smiled.

Cindy felt tiny shivers chase up and down her
spine. If she had believed she could outrun Trace, she
would have sprinted for the door right then. But she
knew she couldn't outrun him, so she didn't even try.
Trace was acclimatized to Quito's staggering
altitude, but lack of oxygen would bring her down
before she had taken thirty steps. There was no
choice for her now but to dig in right where she was
and brazen it out the way she had always done with
her father.

Besides, Susan was somewhere out in the wilds
alone, and this was the wild man who could find her.

"One hundred dollars a day," Cindy said, her
voice too husky, almost breathless.

Trace's cold green eyes looked Cindy over again
in a very leisurely manner, admiring all the velvet
curves and alluring shadows, noting with a kind of
distant surprise that she had made no effort to
enhance or even to announce the feminine bounty
beneath her clothes. The off-white suit she wore was
loose and wrinkled. The belt around the waist of her
pants could have been tightened several more
notches without cutting into tender flesh. She wore
flat sandals rather than heels, which would have em-

phasized the sway of her shapely hips. Her toenails were bare of polish. So were her fingers. If she wore makeup, it didn't show in the bar's dim light.

Maybe that's why Big Eddy keeps picking out men for her—she's so rich she's never bothered to learn all the little tricks and traps poor girls use to get men interested.

"Two hundred."

Trace flicked another disparaging glance over Cindy and went back to his Scotch. *The most important thing I'll teach her is that there are some things money can't buy—and Trace Rawlings is right at the top of the list.*

"Three hundred."

Angrily Trace wished that he had told Invers to go spit up a rope. But Trace hadn't been that smart. Instead he had promised to keep an eye on Big Eddy's obviously spoiled daughter. In order to do that Trace had to appear to be hired by her…which meant she would think she had bought him.

Combat pay. And I'll earn every nickel of it.

Trace shrugged again. His pride could take it. He had suffered far worse blows and survived. And he owed Invers.

"Four hundred."

Trace stretched, bringing his long arms and large hands high over his head. Cindy measured his size and length and realized with a sudden curious weakness in her knees that she was within his reach.

"Five hundred," she said in a rush.

"Princess, you just hired yourself a guide."

Cindy looked at Trace and wondered how Red Riding Hood would have felt if she had hired the Big Bad Wolf to guide her through the terrors and traps of the forest.

She would have felt the way I do now. Scared!

"All right." Cindy took a deep breath, telling herself she was relieved to have hired a guide, wishing she believed it. "My friend and business partner, Susan Parker, came to Quito to buy native weavings. But she doesn't speak Spanish so she has a native buyer who meets her in Quito and turns over all the cloth from the various native villages on his circuit. You see, we have clothing boutiques on both coasts of the U.S., and Susan is a designer, and we…never mind, that's not important," Cindy said, realizing that she was babbling but unable to stop completely. Trace was too unnerving. She wanted to run but she couldn't, so the next best thing was to finish hiring the jungle cat, find Susan and get the hell away from those disdainful green eyes.

"Susan arrived in Quito ten days ago," Cindy said quickly. "Pedro, the native buyer, didn't show up. She called me and said she was going to check the villages on Pedro's circuit. That was ten days ago. I haven't heard from her since. She hasn't checked out of the hotel, but she hasn't been in her room since she asked directions to the bus. The clerk wrote them for her in phonetic Spanish so she could say them correctly."

Trace reached for the Scotch. "Bus? Phonetic Spanish?"

"She doesn't drive or speak Spanish. She was born in Manhattan."

Trace grunted. "Let me see if I have this straight." He finished off the Scotch and looked at Cindy with heavy-lidded eyes. "Your friend doesn't speak Spanish, doesn't drive and is somewhere out in the boondocks looking for a native known to her only as 'Pedro.'"

Scarlet stained Cindy's cheekbones. Put that way it made Susan sound as though she had the IQ of a toothbrush. That wasn't the case.

"I assure you, Mr. Rawlings, Susan is an accomplished traveler. She speaks neither Arabic nor Chinese, yet she has traveled extensively—and alone—in the Middle East and China."

Trace grunted. "Then why are you worried about her?"

"She always leaves me an itinerary. When that isn't possible she calls every few days. Never less than once a week. It has been ten days since her last call."

"Maybe she found Pedro or some other native and holed up with him for a little slap and tickle." Trace let his glance rove over Cindy's body again. "It happens, you know."

"Not to me," Cindy retorted instantly.

"But you're not the one who's lost, are you?"

"Mr. Rawlings—"

"Yes, Cindy?" he interrupted.

The casual use of her first name didn't escape Cindy. Trace was flatly stating that he was in control of the situation and she was not.

"For five hundred dollars a day I expect a little less insolence, *Trace*."

"Say it again, princess," he murmured.

"What?" she said scathingly. "Your name?"

"No. Insolence. You put just the right amount of nose into it," Trace added, brushing the nail of his index finger beneath his nose in a mocking gesture. "You learned that at a fancy finishing school, I'll bet. Pity they didn't teach you something useful, like good manners."

Cindy felt another wash of heat over her cheek-bones and made a desperate attempt to get a grip on her fraying self-control. She told herself she was feeling emotional because of the altitude, the worry, the lack of sleep…anything but the fact that she hated seeing masculine disdain in Trace's cold green eyes. She closed her own eyes, hoping that the stabbing, screaming pain of her headache would be calmed by darkness.

No such luck.

"Mr. Rawlings, I don't have the time or energy to play word games with you." Cindy opened her eyes. "My friend is missing. I was told you were the best man to find her. I have met your price. Could we just get on with it?"

"Oh, you've got plenty of time to play games," Trace said, signaling for another drink. Against his better judgment he used his right foot to shove out a chair for Cindy. "Sit down before you fall down."

Trace spoke over Cindy's shoulder to the waitress, who was approaching with his Scotch.

Cindy understood just enough of the Spanish to be irritated by what he had ordered for her.

"I'm old enough to drink," she said.

"Dumb enough, too, I'll bet."

"Is that the voice of experience speaking?" she asked, looking pointedly at the Scotch Trace had just picked up.

"You'd better believe it, princess."

The whiplash of Trace's voice snapped Cindy's attention back to his face. Not for the first time she realized that he was not a man whose looks inspired a gentle glow of comfort in a woman. Without glancing away from Cindy's pale, strained expression, Trace raised his voice and called out again in rapid Spanish. Two more rounds of Scotch materialized with dazzling speed, accompanied by a warm bottle of Coke.

"Drink up," Trace said, gesturing to the liquor and simultaneously snagging the bottle of Coke in one big hand, taking it out of her reach.

Cindy looked warily at the Scotch. "Why?"

"Right now your head feels like someone buried a hatchet in it, your stomach has a sour disposition and walking across the room is like going up a flight of stairs. It's called altitude sickness. If you want to make it worse, have a shot or two of liquor. Have it on me. The sooner you drink, the sooner you'll know that I *am* experienced in this territory. You aren't. I may be a peon, but you need me, princess. The quicker you get that straight, the better off you'll be."

Cindy sat down and looked away from the jungle-green eyes staring at her, labeling her, dismissing her. The pain in her head doubled suddenly, making her breath catch. The airline flight attendant had warned the passengers that altitude sickness wasn't uncommon for the first few days in Quito. The best advice was to rest as much as possible, eat lightly, drink juices and take aspirin for the headache. If you didn't feel better after a few days, you were supposed to go to a lower elevation.

And stay there.

Sighing, Cindy put her elbows on the table and massaged her temples. "Sorry to disappoint you, Mr. Rawlings. I like my headache just the way it is. No additives necessary. So drink up. My treat." When the silence had stretched to the point of discomfort, she grimaced. "The first village on Susan's list was Popocaxtil. Do you know it?"

"Yes."

"How long will it take us to get there?" Cindy lifted her head and unflinchingly met Trace's green glance. "Don't try to talk me out of going with you. If Susan is hurt or needs help, I want to be there for her."

"Is she your sister?"

"No."

"Your lover?"

Cindy's jaw dropped. She tried to say something but no words came out.

It was Trace's turn to sigh. There went the obvious explanation for the fact that a woman who looked like Cindy—and was rich into the bargain—

was neither married nor, if Invers were to be believed, interested in men at all.

"Women have been known to prefer women," Trace pointed out calmly.

"Having met you I'm beginning to understand why!" Cindy pushed the two shot glasses of Scotch away from her with a sweep of her slender hands. "How far is it to Popocaxtil?" she demanded.

"It depends."

"I'm waiting breathlessly. On what does it depend?"

"The weather," Trace said succinctly.

"When I landed an hour ago, the weather was just fine."

"You were lucky. The rainy season is early this year. The area around Popocaxtil had a hell of a storm four or five days ago. Part of the main blacktop road washed out. As for the last fifteen klicks of the dirt road to the village…" Trace shrugged. "It will be two, probably three days before the road will dry out enough to be passable."

"Klicks?"

"Kilometers."

"Oh. Fifteen kilometers is about seven miles, isn't it?"

"Close enough."

"That's not very far."

Trace's very dark eyebrows were deeply arched to begin with. When he raised one of them in a silent show of skepticism, he appeared almost diabolical.

"That depends," he said.

"On the weather?" Cindy retorted.

"You're learning."

"We'll just have to tough out the weather. I can't sit around here waiting for—"

"Princess, I just got back from six weeks of camping out in the lowlands," Trace interrupted. "If you think I'm going to spend the next two days winching my Rover out of bogs instead of relaxing and soaking up some of the joys of civilization while the mountain roads dry out, you're nuts."

"I can't believe I'm hearing this. Susan might be lost and afraid and hurt and all you can think about is having a Scotch?"

"Don't forget a hot shower," Trace suggested softly.

"Why not? You apparently did, along with a shave and clean clothes!" Cindy made a sharp gesture with her hand. "Never mind. There's no sense in appealing to your better nature. I doubt that you have one. Seven hundred a day and we leave right now."

Trace picked up his second Scotch, held the glass against the table light and admired the liquid's fine color. "No."

The refusal was so soft that it took a moment for it to register on Cindy.

"Eight hundred," she said angrily.

"No."

"Nine!"

"Princess, there are some things money can't buy. I'm one of them. If you need my help, ask. Don't wave money."

"Ask? *Ask!* What do you think I've been doing?"

"Demanding or buying."

"Instead of begging?" Cindy suggested icily. "Haven't you learned yet, Tarzan? All begging gets you is sore knees." She pushed away from the table and stood, ignoring the hammer blows of pain in her head. "Fortunately I won't have to wear my knees out on your masculine ego. I don't need you. I'll check out the villages myself."

"How? You don't speak Spanish, much less any of the local Indian dialects."

"Neither does Susan."

"Look where it got her."

"I'm planning on it!"

Trace laughed derisively. "Sure you are." He glanced at Cindy's pallor, at her lips drawn flat with pain and at the fine trembling of her hands. "Go back to your room and lie down, princess. I'll pick you up Thursday morning at your hotel at dawn."

Cindy spun on her heel and walked out, neither looking back at Trace nor aside at any of the interested patrons watching the tall *gringa* stalking away from the bar. She was furious with herself for handling Trace so badly and furious with him for being such an unbending, overweaning SOB, and furious with life for putting her in a situation where her father's money—which she would never have touched for any reason less urgent than Susan's disappearance—couldn't even buy a decent guide.

Smiling coolly, Trace watched Cindy leave. He had been rough on her and he knew it, but it had been a cut-and-dried case of self-defense. He had been caught flat-footed by her, his dropped jaw flapping in the wind. Nothing in Invers's briefing or in the picture Trace had been given of Cindy had even hinted at the real woman. Quick, intelligent, vital, with black eyes whose clarity and enigmatic depths challenged a man. And she had something more, something Trace had dreamed about but never found.

Beneath that cool exterior Cindy McCall burned with the kind of passionate, dark fire that a man would kill for. Or die for.

Trace had felt an answering fire licking through his body. It was still there, burning, urging. He ignored it now as he had ignored it in Cindy's presence, knowing that to give in was to hand himself over to his sensuous combatant without a murmur of protest. He wouldn't allow that to happen.

The smile on Trace's lips curled higher as he realized that he was probably the first man ever to say no to Ms. Cynthia Edwinna Ryan McCall. It must have been a salutary learning experience for her. At the very least, in the future she wouldn't look down her nose at Trace Rawlings with such fine disdain. She needed him. It would be a pure pleasure to hear her admit it.

Smiling, Trace sipped at his Scotch.

He was still smiling Thursday morning when he drove over to pick up Cindy, only to discover that she had rented a Jeep and set off down the highway for Popocaxtil on Tuesday.

Chapter 2

Cindy stared at the smudged, rumpled map again. If she were right, she was definitely on the road to Popocaxtil. If she were wrong, she was one lost puppy.

She looked dubiously through the cracked windshield at the so-called road, which was a raw gash that wound up and down and sideways across the shoulder of a mountain whose top and bottom were hidden in clouds. The dense forest of the uplands had given way to an equally dense cover of brushy plants. The road had remained the same…awful. She hadn't seen a road sign since yesterday.

The one nice thing was that Cindy's headache had finally gone. She didn't know whether she had become accustomed to the thin air or the road had really dropped more in altitude than it had subsequently gained clawing its way back up the mountain. All she knew for certain was that her headache had departed, and for that blessing she was profoundly grateful.

Again Cindy looked from the map to the road. Hers were the only vehicle tracks to mark the rutted, overgrown track since the last rain.

"I'm not lost," she said aloud, wishing it didn't sound so much like a question.

"You're not lost," she answered herself firmly.

She heard the conversation with herself and muttered, "I'm going crazy."

"No, you're not," she retorted immediately. "You just like to hear English spoken after days of incomprehensible Spanish."

"Really? That makes me feel better. Know something? I like you."

"It's mutual."

"Maybe I *am* going crazy."

"No, you're just stalling. You don't want to go back to wrestling with the Jeep."

"You're right."

The paved road Cindy had started out on had been no treat once Quito's environs had been left behind, but compared to the secondary and tertiary roads she had encountered since then, the paved road had been a miracle of modern engineering. Her whole body ached from fighting the Jeep over the rain-greased road.

Sighing, Cindy leaned forward and turned the ignition key. The engine started immediately, a fact that continued to surprise her each time it occurred. To be diplomatic, the Jeep had an aura of experience about it. To be factual, the Jeep looked as though it had been through the wars, all of them, beginning with the Crimean and progressing right on through Iraq.

Despite that, the vehicle seemed quite hardy, if Cindy discounted the tires' distressing tendency to flatten at inconvenient moments. Not that any moment would have been truly convenient. The first flat had occurred yesterday, after only a few hours on a detour to bypass a washout on the main paved road. She had barely begun to wrestle with the jack when a boy who looked too young to be out in the world on his own had walked by, seen her distress and stopped to help her.

The language barrier proved to be irrelevant. A flat tire by any other name was still not round. The boy had simply handed his baggage into Cindy's keeping and had proceeded to whisk off the tire, put on the spare and watch with fatalistic good humor as the tire promptly sank onto its own rim. The spare had been as flat as the other one.

The boy had pried both tires off their rims, patched the inner tubes and pumped them up, using tools from the battered box that was bolted in the cargo area of the Jeep. Then he had put all the pieces together again, giving Cindy two good tires. During the entire process she had stood in the cool drizzle and held the

boy's precious baggage—a burlap sack containing
two monumentally unhappy piglets—and watched
what he was doing very carefully. The patching pro-
cedure was simple. Find the leak, clean the area to be
patched, apply sticky stuff to the patch and the patch
to the tire, hang on tight to everything and count to
fifty-eight thousand while two piglets achieved
operatic heights of despair within the burlap bag.

Even the memory of it made Cindy laugh aloud.
She wished she had a picture of herself holding a
sack with two bouncing pigs in one hand and an
umbrella in the other hand, while rain ran in rivulets
from her chin and elbows as she leaned over and
braced herself against the Jeep in an effort to keep
the boy dry during a sudden shower. But if she had
had that picture she would have traded it for the one
she really wanted, that of a busload of natives
standing in the muck up to their ankles as they
argued and gesticulated robustly about the best way
to free her Jeep from an entanglement consisting of
uninjured but outraged livestock, a pile of kindling
that could have filled a church and enough mud to
build the Great Wall of China.

Still grinning at the memories, Cindy eased the
Jeep from the verge back into the road. And it was *into*
rather than *onto* the road. The ruts were twin and
sometimes triplicate trenches filled with water. The
water looked either brown or gunmetal-gray, depend-
ing on the angle of the sun through the dispersing
clouds.

No matter how hard Cindy tried, it was impossible to keep the Jeep's tires entirely free of the ruts. At least there was a bottom to the ruts, she consoled herself. She wasn't at all certain she could say the same about the puddles of water that lurked in low places along the sides of the road. When there was a side to the road, that is. Sometimes there was nothing but a long, long drop into a valley.

Water was everywhere, trickling from each crease and crevice on the steep mountainside. Early that morning the trickles had been creeks and streams, but the runoff had slowed dramatically as the rains diminished in the highlands. The thought cheered Cindy as much as the sunshine streaming between banks of clouds. Soon it would be actually warm instead of nearly warm. Soon the Jeep's canvas roof would stop drooling water down her left shoulder. Soon she would turn a corner and see a tattered Popocaxtil sunk happily into the mire. There she would be able to find food and water and, best of all, word of Susan Parker.

If this were, indeed, the road to Popocaxtil.

It took every bit of Cindy's concentration to enable her to pick her way over nature's obstacle course at a rate slightly faster than that of a three-legged burro. With every yard she progressed she silently thanked her brother Rye for having forced her to learn unwanted skills. Years ago he had insisted that she learn to drive his rugged ranch road in the Jeep he kept for winter transportation. She would never again tease him about his rustic taste in road surfaces. After her experience in Ecuador she would be able to drive Rye's ranch roads at eighty miles per hour blindfolded.

The Jeep's front tires were grabbed by ruts at the same instant that the wheel was wrenched from Cindy's hand. She downshifted for more power, grinding the gears heartlessly. Rye had neglected to show her the finer points of speed shifting or double clutching, a fact that she regretted now. At the time, however, she had thought it outrageous enough that he had insisted she learn to drive primitive roads in a vehicle that lacked an automatic shift. And then she had had to learn to change a tire in the bargain. She had given Rye a steady line of smart remarks while he tutored her, but the next time she saw him she would gratefully go down on her knees in the ranch yard and kiss his dusty boots in thanks for his foresight.

Crunching and groaning, the Jeep clawed out of the deep ruts. Even on flatter ground, the vehicle wanted to lunge to the right. Cindy found a relatively firm spot, stopped and climbed out to see what was wrong. With a sinking heart she realized that the right front tire was a mere shadow of its former rotund self.

"Damn!"

Swearing at the tire wouldn't get it changed. Nor was Cindy's vocabulary extensive enough to make her feel better. Muttering, she went to the back of the Jeep, unbolted the jack, shoved it under the chassis and started leaning on the jack's lever.

What had taken the boy mere minutes to accomplish took her nearly half an hour. Finally the flat tire rose far enough above the mire for her to be able to reach all the lug nuts holding the wheel in place. She grabbed the lug wrench and leaned. It popped off, nearly sending her face-first into the mud. She put the wrench back over the lug nut and leaned again.

Nothing happened.

Cindy leaned harder and then harder still. She had never considered herself an Amazon, but she couldn't believe that she was too weak to remove a simple lug nut. After all, the boy who had helped her yesterday had been her height and he hadn't had much trouble changing a tire. Finally she jammed the lug wrench in place, held onto the Jeep, and jumped onto one arm of the cross-shaped tool, using the weight of her whole body to force the nut to turn.

Five jumps later she managed to loosen the first lug nut. The rest of them weren't as easy. By the time Cindy had dragged the wheel off, rolled it to the back of the Jeep, swapped it for the spare and gotten the spare screwed into its new home to the best of her ability, she was dirty, thirsty, hungry and exhausted. After she put away the tools she sluiced off the worst of her dirt in a rain puddle. The cool, murky water tempted her almost unendurably.

"Don't be an idiot," Cindy told herself as she licked dry lips and wiped her hands on her dirty jeans. "All you need to really make your day is the local version of Montezuma's revenge."

Wearily Cindy pulled herself into the Jeep's

rump-sprung seat, started the engine and crept forward, praying that no other tire would flatten. She wasn't going to take time to patch the ruined inner tube right now. In truth, she was afraid that she wouldn't be able to pry the tire off the wheel rim, much less put it back together again.

The next hour was uneventful. Then Cindy came to a steep curve where the road had a pronounced outward slant toward the valley, which was a breath-taking two thousand sheer feet below on the right. Suddenly all four wheels began to spin as the Jeep lost traction in the greasy mud and began to slide sideways inch by inch toward the drop-off. She clung to the wheel and fed gas gently, wondering if forward momentum would get her past the slippery spot before gravity pulled the Jeep into the abyss. Just as she reached for the door handle to jump out, one front wheel finally found good traction and pulled her up and around the dangerous curve.

Over the shoulder of the mountain a long, narrow valley opened up. The surrounding forest had been cut or burned fairly recently, giving the valley floor a ragged, mottled look. Only very small trees and modest bushes grew along the road. There wasn't a drop-off or a curve in sight. After what Cindy had been through, the road looked beautiful.

"Hang on, Susan, wherever you are. I'm coming. Not fast, but I'm coming."

Feeling much more cheerful, Cindy drove down the gentle incline into the valley…and sank right up to her bumpers in mud.

* * *

"Gracias," called the man to Trace.

As Trace waved in acknowledgement, the man gunned his rattletrap truck, lifted a rooster tail of dirt into the air and shot around a muddy spot where the main road had washed out. Trace wound the forward winch cable he had used to free the man's truck and climbed back into the big, battered Land Rover. He had covered the distance from Quito to this point in record time, despite the washouts, and every inch of the way he had wondered if he were on a wild-goose chase.

Even after Trace had seen a place on a washout detour where a vehicle had pulled over to change a flat, he hadn't been convinced that the small footprints in the mud had belonged to Cindy. A woman, yes. The disdainful princess? Maybe, but not very damned likely.

Trace hadn't really believed that Cindy had set off alone for Popocaxtil until he had turned off the main road onto the dirt road. At a tiny village where he had stopped for food and water, he had heard the epic of a bus, a Jeep, a mountain of kindling, assorted livestock—and *una Americana muy hermosa* who had black hair, a warm smile and no Spanish to speak of.

Trace hadn't seen Cindy smile, but he doubted that there was more than one beautiful American woman who was traveling the backcountry alone in a Jeep, asking in fractured Spanish along the way for a village called Popocaxtil.

Certainly someone had recently been along the

dirt track he was driving. That someone was getting
a cram course in four-wheel skills, if the abundance
of wallow and skid marks were any indication. At first
the Jeep had hit all the bad spots in the road as though
it were guided by a perverse sort of radar. As the kilometers went by, Cindy—presuming it was, indeed,
Cindy who was steering the Jeep—had learned how
to keep the vehicle from getting high-centered
between the ruts. She had also learned that the rut-
puddle you know is a lot safer than the puddle at the
side of the road. Presumably she had also learned to
feed gas evenly and firmly in the boggy spots to
prevent digging in or fishtailing all over the place.

Now, if only it would rain.

With the cynical eyes of a man who has found
answers to questions most people would rather not
even ask, Trace measured the clouds. If it didn't rain
before sunset he would be surprised. If it did rain, it
wouldn't amount to much.

*Too bad. A good rain would wash her right out
of the game and into my arms.*

The phrasing of his own thought made Trace's
mouth flatten into a hard line. He had spent two very
restless nights thinking about Cindy Ryan's cool intelligence and taut, warm curves. The combination
fascinated him even as it challenged him. It also irritated him unreasonably. He was old enough to know
his own mind and body very well, but the depth of his
response to the lush Ms. Ryan was something new.

And the jungle had taught Trace that new was a
synonym for dangerous.

Frowning, he drove on. A few minutes later the road divided. There were no signs to mark towns or directions. The main dirt road went to the left. The fresh tracks he was following went to the right. In the distance, the road began snaking up the steep side of a mountain.

"She must have been born under a lucky star," he muttered, wondering how Cindy had known to take the right-hand fork to Popocaxtil. Nothing about the road announced it as a likely candidate for anything but a dead-end logging track.

Ahead, lightning danced among the lowering clouds. Suddenly Trace wasn't so sanguine about rain washing Cindy into his arms. If she didn't know enough to pull over, park and wait out the storm, a good rain might wash her right off the mountain. The people who had made this road had neither known nor cared about grading the surface so that an out-of-control vehicle would slide into the mountainside rather than into the abyss. The road had been graded—if it had been graded at all—with rapid drainage in mind. Every slant led downhill. The farther up the road, the longer the downhill drop to the valley below.

As the afternoon wore on, Trace drove the Rover with near-reckless speed. The track became worse with every foot it climbed up the uninhabited mountainside. He paused only a few seconds at the spot where the Jeep had had its second flat. A single glance told him that there was only one set of footprints this time. Any tire changing that had been done had been done by the princess herself. One corner of his mouth curved up at the thought of how muddy she must have been by the time she had finished.

Then Trace wondered which one of Cindy's men had taught her to change a tire, and what else he had taught her to sweeten the lesson.

Trace pushed the thought away and concentrated on the road, which had dwindled until it required every bit of his skill and coordination, not to mention occasional applications of pure strength, just to keep the Rover pointed in the right direction. When the road pitched up suddenly, and simultaneously wrapped out and around a tight curve, he saw the broad marks left by Cindy's Jeep as it had slid sideways closer and closer to the lethal drop-off on the right side of the miserable road.

"Christ," Trace hissed between his teeth as he saw how close Cindy had come to disaster. "It's time someone taught some sense to that high-nosed little…"

Trace's voice died as the Rover breasted the small ridge and he saw the burned-over valley spreading out below. A few hundred yards away, in the center of a deceptively smooth-looking stretch of road, a Jeep was buried up to its fenders in mud.

Smiling rather grimly, Trace let in the clutch and started toward the prey he had finally run to ground.

Chapter 3

Cindy didn't even notice the Rover cautiously working its way toward her. At that particular moment she wouldn't have noticed anything less impressive than a magnitude eight earthquake. She was bent over, panting and red-faced, hopping around on one foot in the muck while she tried to force the broken-handled shovel into the muddy mess with her other foot. The point of the whole exercise was to ladle enough of the goo from the vicinity of the front tires so they could find the traction necessary to pull the Jeep out of the bog.

There was more gluey mud lying in wait than Cindy had the muscle or tools to remove. After more than an hour of shoveling she doubted that she was going to get the job done by herself. Unfortunately, there wasn't much hope of help. The surface of the road hadn't seen a wheeled vehicle since the last hard rain. If there were any native pedestrians about, they hadn't passed her way lately. Not so much as a footprint marred the deceitfully smooth surface of the bog ahead of the Jeep.

With a muttered word of disgust, Cindy watched the hole she had just made with the shovel slowly fill up with goo. She propped the slippery, much-too-short handle of the shovel against the Jeep and decided there was no help for it, she would have to go for more shrubbery. Wiping her hands on equally muddy jeans, she released the cable on the winch that was attached to the Jeep's front bumper. Rye hadn't spent much time showing her how to work his Jeep's winch, but she had remembered enough to get the thing unlocked and started about an hour ago. Trial and error had refreshed her memory after that.

The first time Cindy had wrapped the cable around the skeletal trunk of a burned tree, she had confidently expected to winch the Jeep out of the mud. She had figured it would take a lot of power, so she had given the winch everything available. For a few moments the cable had whined taut and the Jeep had indeed crept forward. Then the tree had exploded into charcoal and the cable had snapped back toward the Jeep with enough force to make the air whistle.

After that Cindy had gone back to shoveling until her hands had stopped shaking. Then she had attempted to use the winch again. All that had been within reach of the cable had been tree skeletons even more frail than the first one she had tried to use. In the end she had settled for the vigorous green bushes and saplings that had grown up since the fire. The first bush she used the winch on instantly leaped out of the mud and bounded toward her. The second and third bushes did the same. None of the shrubbery had held long enough to move the Jeep forward so much as an inch.

The bushes had other uses, however. Cindy had discovered rather quickly that their branches could be beaten into smaller pieces with the shovel and then pushed under the Jeep's wheels to make a sort of rough mat that gave more traction than straight goo did. That was how she had managed to move forward a whole fourteen feet. At the present pace she would be out of the bog by nightfall…of next week.

Putting that unhappy thought from her mind, Cindy slogged over to the nearest shrub with the broken shovel in one hand and the cable hook in the other. Kneeling, using the shovel, she pushed the end of the cable around the base of the bush until she could grab the hook with her free hand, put it over the cable and stand up. As she turned to go back to the Jeep, she spotted movement on the road.

At first Cindy thought that the vehicle slipping and slithering half on and half off the road was a mirage coming toward her. When it came to a halt fifteen feet away—just before the point where her

Jeep's wheels had sunk in to the fenders—she recognized Trace.

He was smiling.

Normally Cindy would have been the first one to laugh over the picture she must have made with mud up to her eyebrows and greenery sticking to unlikely parts of her anatomy. Unfortunately her reaction to Trace hadn't been normal from the first word they had exchanged. Suddenly Cindy was furious with Trace, with the Jeep, with the muddy road, with the world in general and Ecuador in particular; but most of all she was furious with herself for caring that she looked muddy and foolish in front of Mr. Trace Insufferable Rawlings.

When the Rover's door opened, Cindy turned her back on Trace and put the winch into motion with a vicious jerk. The bush fairly jumped out of the soil and raced toward her. She stopped the winch, lifted the shovel and began beating on the shrub until it had flattened out enough for her to release the hooked end of the cable without having to stand on her head in the muck to do so.

"Aren't you a little old for mud pies?"

The deep, amused male voice did nothing to cool Cindy's temper. She turned and slowly looked at Trace from the ground up. His lace-up jungle boots were scarred and clean where they rose above the mud. His khaki pants were clean, dry and tucked into the tops of his boots. Though loose fitting, the pants managed to convey very strongly the masculine power just beneath the cloth. His belt was wide, worn and fastened around a lean waist. An astonishingly big knife—more of a sword, really—was sheathed at his waist. His shirt was khaki, clean, dry, long sleeved, with cuffs rolled up just far enough to reveal tanned skin and a sheen of black hair stretched over sinewy arms. His hands were strong, long fingered and very clean. The black hair on his forearms was thickly repeated in a rich cloud that curled up from the open neck of his shirt. He had shaved since their last meeting. Somehow the clean, heavy line of his jaw was more intimidating than the careless masculine stubble had been.

Cindy looked no higher than the sensual curve of his lips. The triumph and amusement in his smile made her own lips flatten. She told herself that she was a big girl, that she could take whatever teasing Trace dished out without losing her temper and making the situation worse by saying something.

And then she discovered that she was wrong. With a sense of mingled horror and pleasure she heard herself say, "I'm too old for a lot of things, Tarzan."

Cindy's black glance sweeping back down Trace's body hinted that he was foremost among those objects she had outgrown. Without another word she turned her back on him and resumed flattening the uprooted bush and stuffing it beneath the leading edge of her left front tire.

"You know, an intelligent girl like you should have figured out by now not to bite the hand that is going to feed her. But since you haven't, I'll be glad to deliver a little remedial instruction."

"You're too kind," she muttered, chopping viciously at the bush.

"I know. I also know if you'd been reasonable a few days ago instead of being a high-nosed princess who didn't know any more about men than to throw money at them, you could have spent the past two days doing your nails and have ended up no farther from Popocaxtil than you are now."

Cindy went very still. Slowly she released the shovel because she didn't trust herself not to take a swing at Trace with it. Part of her was appalled that she had even thought of it. Another part of her was appalled that she hadn't followed through. Three days ago she would have sworn that she knew herself through and through. Trace, unfortunately, brought out depths in her temperament that had remained blessedly hidden until she met him.

She knelt and began cramming brush around the tire by hand. Trace offered advice on the best type of greenery to use until she lost patience.

"Are you going to help get the Jeep out or are you just going to stand around and make noise?" Cindy asked without looking up.

"I'm waiting for a request. A nice one."

For an instant the world went an odd shade of reddish-black in front of Cindy. Too many memories. Too many useless requests.

"Would you please," she said in a husky voice, *"go to hell?"*

Trace's green eyes narrowed as though he had been slapped. For a minute the only sound was that of soggy brush being rammed into the mud. Then came the distinct sucking sounds of Trace's boots as he walked back to his Rover. Cindy didn't look up. She simply continued blindly stuffing twigs and leaves and stems into the mud, furiously refusing to give in to tears or to memories, telling herself that she had come this far without Trace, she could go the rest of the distance alone, too.

The door to the Rover opened quietly and closed with emphasis. Trace sat back on the comfortable bench seat of the Rover and stretched his legs onto the passenger side of the floorboards. Confident of the outcome, he waited for Cindy to get tired of chewing on her pride, swallow hard, and ask him for the help she so clearly needed. Her learning when to ask for help—and how to ask for it—would make the rest of the trip a lot easier on both of them.

Trace had no intention of fighting Cindy every inch of the way while they "searched" for her crazy friend. Not only would continual fighting be stupid, it could be dangerous. There were times and places in the wilds where questioning instructions was a fast way to get into deep trouble. If he said jump, she would have to learn to jump. If she needed help, she would damn well ask for it. That was the only way to ensure that she didn't put both of them in danger with her foolish stubbornness.

Combat pay. Well, you sure called it, Invers, you SOB.

A curse hissed between Trace's teeth. All fights between Cindy and himself would be won and lost

right here, right now. She had chosen the battle-
ground, the weapons, and the stakes—her pride. The
only thing that remained for Trace to do was to
accept her surrender so that they could get on with
the farce of combing the wild country to find a
woman who wasn't lost.

From Trace's vantage point in the Rover he could
see the churned mess behind the Jeep. Twigs and
slender branches with bruised and shredded leaves
stuck up every which way on the sides of the deep
ruts the Jeep had left. Idly, then with growing understanding, Trace's eyes followed the various trails
Cindy had left through the mud as she had attached
cables to bushes and dragged them to the Jeep.

The shattered remains of a charred tree raised
Trace's dark eyebrows. *I hope that little fool didn't
have the winch at high revs when that trunk came
apart.*

Yet an uneasy prickling along Trace's spine every
time he looked at the ruined tree told him that was
precisely what had happened. Rather grimly he
wondered if the crack in the Jeep's windshield was
old history or if the glass had given way from a
recent hit delivered by a dangerous, whipsawing
steel cable.

The longer Trace looked at the area immediately
around the Jeep, the clearer it became to him that
Cindy had been mired in place for a long time. Incredibly enough, and despite her demonstrable lack
of expertise in such situations, she had managed to
get the Jeep to move forward a few feet. Grudgingly

Trace gave her credit for not sitting with her clean hands folded in her lap, waiting for a knight in muddy armor to rescue her.

Stubborn and resourceful, but that won't get the Jeep out of the muck. Even if it would, there's no way that soft rich girl is going to have enough strength to make mud pies much longer. Hell, it's a miracle she hasn't given up by now. She's got to be exhausted.

Fifteen minutes, Trace reassured himself silently, watching Cindy kneeling in the mud next to the front end of the Jeep. *Half an hour, max. Then she'll wise up and give up and do what she should have done in the first place—ask me for help.*

Trace was correct in his assessment of Cindy's reserves of strength. The past few days had exhausted her. Doing without food or drink so far today had been the final touch. She was running on adrenaline alone, supported by the rushing chemical wave of fury that came each time she looked up through the black, tangled curtain of her hair and saw Trace all dry and clean and comfortable, lounging in his Rover while he watched her crawl around in the muck.

Cindy winched another bush out and began beating on it with her shovel. When it came time to remove the cable from the mangled bush, her fingers were uncooperative. They insisted on trembling and tangling and slipping when they should have held firm. It was a good five minutes before she was able to retrieve and rewind the cable. Finally she picked up the shovel again and used its edge to smash and gnaw the bush into smaller pieces. One by one she shoved those pieces in the mud around the front tires.

Past experience had taught Cindy that she would need at least one more bush rammed into the muck before there would be enough traction for the Jeep. The prospect cheered Cindy considerably. Maybe this time she would get completely free of the bog and get on with looking for Susan. Even though the rational part of Cindy's mind kept insisting that Susan was an experienced traveler who had a positively feline ability to land on her feet no matter what the circumstances, the irrational part of Cindy's mind kept whispering about all the disasters that could befall a woman traveling alone in a foreign country.

For instance, Susan could have hired a guide like Trace Rawlings.

The surge of adrenaline that followed upon the heels of seeing Trace still ensconced within the dry, clean comfort of the Rover served to push Cindy through the mud, cable in one hand and shovel in the other. She was running out of conveniently placed bushes. On her hands and knees, and finally on her stomach, she maneuvered the cable until steel encircled the base of a bush. Slowly she slogged back to the Jeep, fired up the winch and reeled in the bush.

The bruised leaves of this particular bush smelled like the worst kind of swamp. Even more depressing, the five-foot-long branches were unusually springy, which meant that breaking each stick took twice the whacks with the shovel that an ordinary shrub would have. Finally, however, Cindy had the bush beaten and chopped into useable portions. Wearily she set aside the shovel, picked up a clump of vile-smelling greenery and began cramming it into the muck in front of one tire.

Trace looked at his watch for the thirtieth time in as many minutes. A half hour gone and Cindy didn't look much worse off than she had before. Obviously she was tired. Just as obviously, she wasn't going to give in. His lips flattened into a hard line beneath his dark brown mustache as he remembered what Invers had said: *Any woman who could stand up to Big Eddy could teach stubborn to a Missouri mule.*

Teeth clenched as tightly as her hands, Cindy trudged back toward the side of the road, dragging the winch cable in one hand and the shovel in the other. All that kept her from going down on her face in the mud and staying there when she hooked the cable around a bush was a bone-deep determination not to knuckle under to a man again, because once she did, she would lose more and more and more of herself until there was nothing left and she was just a shell standing and watching Jason walk away from her, taking her innocence, hopes and belief in herself with him.

But I learned from that, Cindy told herself firmly. *After Jason left I told Big Eddy to go directly to hell and to take his dreams of a dynasty with him. Then I changed my name, closed all the McCall expense accounts, and left home.*

Since then Cindy had not taken one dime from her father. She would speak to him as long as the subject of men, marriage or babies did not arise. If she didn't like what she heard—and she usually didn't—she would turn around and walk away. The kind of pride, intelligence and courage it had taken for Cindy to walk out on uncounted millions and make a life for herself was often labeled "character" when it occurred in men. When it cropped up in women, the labels applied were a good deal less flattering.

They were nothing, however, to the names Cindy called Trace as she fumbled around pushing more brush into the mud.

Trace looked from his watch to the muddy woman and mangled bush. His green eyes narrowed in a combination of irritation and grudging approval as the time registered.

Forty-seven minutes.

Absently Trace knuckled the hinge points of his jaw, trying to loosen muscles clenched in outright rebellion against sitting and doing nothing while a woman worked herself into the ground right in front of his disbelieving eyes.

She has to learn that I'm valuable to her or we're going to end up in big trouble in the cloud forest.

Somehow the lesson seemed less important to Trace at the moment than it had before.

Yet cold reason told him that the lesson was more important than ever. Cindy simply must give him a measure of control over their lives in the cloud forest. She had proven herself to be far too determined an individual for Trace to even consider fighting with her over every little aspect of the expedition.

If she would drive herself to exhaustion rather than admit that she needed his greater strength, to say nothing of his expertise, what would she do when an important issue arose, such as running for cover from a storm rather than continuing to drive on a road that would go from difficult to dangerous with the first good rain? What if he told her not to question some natives about Susan—and there were some natives in the backcountry who definitely should *not* be questioned—and she went ahead and asked questions anyway, endangering everyone with her stubborn certainty that she could do everything herself, and do it better?

Trace kept repeating that line of reasoning as he watched Cindy through hooded eyes, silently willing her to give in at least long enough to rest for a time.

She didn't. She simply kept after the task of freeing the Jeep with a tenacity he could only admire. Yet the more he watched, the less he could bear it. She was overmatched. He knew it even if she didn't. He found it too painful to see her working her heart out when he knew that eventually she would fail.

But Trace forced himself to watch the uneven contest between woman and bog. If Cindy could drive herself beyond all reason, the least he could do was to witness the brutal cost of her learning this particular lesson.

For both of them.

It would have been difficult to say whether Cindy or Trace was more relieved when she finally fumbled the last bit of brush into the mud and climbed into the Jeep.

At first it was enough for Cindy just to sit behind the wheel. Not to be bent over in the mud was sheer heaven. Besides, in the Jeep she was beyond the reach of the puddles. Their winking, reflective surfaces had been tormenting her with visions of drinking and drinking cool water until she was satiated.

"Not to mention drinking at the same time hundreds of miscellaneous and unpronounceable microscopic beasties that would make you so sick you'd be afraid you *wouldn't* die," Cindy reminded herself wearily. "No water for you until you're out of the bog and have time to boil up a quart or three."

Sighing, Cindy wiped her muddy hands on her muddy slacks and reached for the ignition key. Her hand trembled visibly. She closed her eyes and willed herself to be strong for just a bit longer. The Jeep would get free this time. It had to. She was too tired, too hungry and much too thirsty to do it all over again.

As always, the Jeep's engine fired up the first time. Cindy wiped her palms on opposite shoulder blades— the cleanest patches on her shirt—and gripped the wheel. Carefully she let in the clutch and fed gas. The front wheels slipped, spun, skipped, and finally bit into the mess of mud and shrubs. The Jeep lurched forward a few inches, slewed off to the right, found traction again, leaped and then swerved off to the left side of the road. The vehicle measured its own length in untouched muddy road, bucked, wallowed, whined…

And settled up to its fenders once more in the bog.

The sight of Cindy slumped over the steering wheel was too painful for Trace. After a single glance he looked away. Her posture stated her defeat more clearly than any words could have. He had won, she had lost…and the taste of victory was muddy on his tongue. He reached for the Rover's door, wanting to save Cindy the walk over to his vehicle to ask for help.

The Jeep's door popped open at the same instant as the Rover's. Cindy got out, sank calf-deep, and slogged to the front of the Jeep. It took her a long time to unlock the winch and drag the cable toward a big, particularly lush bush on the edge of the road. Though the bush was on the same side of the road as the Rover, Cindy didn't even glance toward Trace.

He closed his eyes, then opened them again. Nothing had changed. Cindy hadn't admitted defeat.

What is it with you, princess? Why is it impossible for you to give me a fraction of an inch? Would you ask me for help if my bank account was as big as yours?

Since the bitter questions never left Trace's mind, no answers came.

Cindy staggered, slipped and went down on her hands and knees. She stayed that way for a few moments, head down, beaten but unbowed. Slowly she pushed herself to her feet. Trace swore steadily, savagely, but he knew defeat when he stared it in the face. He could not force himself to sit and watch Cindy work until she fainted from exhaustion.

And that was what it would come to.

Nor would the bitter lesson have accomplished anything useful. Quite obviously the princess would drop dead in her muddy tracks before she lowered herself to ask for anything from a peon like Trace Rawlings.

So let her drop.

Trace didn't bother to answer his silent inner snarl. The sentiment was only the last defiant cry of the vanquished, and he knew it. There were some people he could have watched dispassionately while they drove themselves beyond exhaustion, but Cindy wasn't one of them. Bitterly cursing his weakness every step of the way, Trace closed the distance between himself and Cindy, who was almost up to the robust bush she had chosen to sacrifice beneath the Jeep's front wheels.

Just as Trace caught up to Cindy, she screamed chillingly and lashed out with the broken shovel at a snake that had been concealed within the bush.

Chapter 4

An instant later Trace slashed through the snake
with his machete. Even as the big knife flashed past
her, Cindy spun away from the bush in an effort to
flee that was as reflexive as the trapped snake's strike
at her had been. But Cindy went no more than a step
before she discovered that her body was trembling
too much for her to do more than sway on her feet.
Trace held her upright with his left hand while he
finished off the snake with the machete in his right
hand. Only when he was quite certain that the reptile
was dead did he sheathe the lethal blade, grab Cindy
and carry her back to the Rover.

"Didn't anyone ever tell you that snakes don't
make special allowances for stubborn princesses?"

Trace demanded, his voice loud and rough with the adrenaline that was still pouring through his blood. Cindy had come within inches of dying, and while she was probably too naive to know it, he wasn't. "It's a damn good thing you got lucky with the shovel or that big 'two-step' would have nailed you on the first strike and you would have gone two steps and died. Do you understand me, princess? You would be d-e-a-d, *dead*. Where do you think you are—Disneyland? Didn't you even think to look for poisonous snakes?"

Cindy bit her lower lip and struggled to control the shudders racking her body in the wild aftermath of fear. "Rye always t-told me if I made p-plenty of noise, s-snakes would leave before I ever saw them."

"That doesn't mean you can close your eyes and braille your way through an Ecuadoran cloud forest," Trace snarled, wondering who the hell this Rye was. "Use your head! It's too cool, wet, and overcast for reptiles to be particularly lively right now, so the two-step felt trapped by you and it lashed out to protect itself. Thank God the snake was too sluggish to be any more than half-speed on the strike. You were lucky. Very, very damn lucky." Trace's arms tightened around the muddy, womanly weight in his arms. "But don't push it, princess. God has better things to do than to watch out for stubborn princesses."

"G-go to—"

"Hell," Trace interrupted impatiently, finishing Cindy's sentence for her. "You keep recommending the place to me. Perhaps you would like to join me there?"

He yanked open the passenger door of the Rover and slid in, still holding on to Cindy. When she struggled as though to get off his lap, Trace's arms tightened.

"Not a chance, princess. I came so close to putting you at the very top of my private list of midnight regrets that I'm not letting go of you for a while. God, I can hardly believe you're alive," he said in a raw, husky voice as he smoothed his cheek over the tangled silk of Cindy's hair. "That was too close. Much too close." He felt the sudden shudders of her body and shifted her until he could cradle her in his arms. In a much more gentle voice he murmured, "It's all right. Go ahead and cry. You're safe now."

Cindy sensed as much as felt the caress of Trace's cheek over the crown of her head. She didn't cry despite the burning of her eyes and the ache of her throat. She had learned long ago that crying, like begging, was a waste of time and energy. What was going to happen would happen and neither her tears nor her pleas would make a bit of difference in the outcome.

She took in and let out a long, shaky breath and then another and another until she gradually relaxed across Trace's lap, her cheek on his left shoulder, her left hand tucked beneath his chin, her palm resting in the warm nest of hair that pushed up through his open collar. When he began to stroke her hair and spine with slow sweeps of his right hand, she sighed and shut her eyes, absorbing his comfort as if it were a balm.

Close up, the signs of Cindy's fatigue were all too

obvious to Trace. Beneath random smears of dried
mud, her skin was very pale, almost translucent. It
was the same for her lips, nearly bloodless. Her
eyelids showed dark lavender shadows of exhaustion. The slender lines of her hands were blurred by
mud and the random cuts and scrapes that came
from changing tires and winching bushes out of the
ground. Her loose cotton clothes looked as though
she had been packed in a mud bath and left to steam
for an hour. Her blouse clung to her like a brown
shadow. Her hands were smeared with mud, and so
were her feet.

All in all, Trace had never seen a woman half so
sexy to him…nor had he ever felt half such a heel.

The realization shocked him. It was utterly irrational. No sane man would prefer a muddy lap full
of mulish stubbornness to the perfumed, practiced
allure of the women he had known in the past, would
he? No, of course not. No sane man would let
himself in for the kind of grief a spoiled princess
would inevitably deliver to her lover, would he? No,
of course not. No sane man would…

Cindy sighed and snuggled fractionally closer to
Trace's body, distracting him from his interior catechism on the subject of masculine sanity. Her
breath stirred the hair below his throat and the dis-
tinctive, male flesh between his legs stirred in
answer. He fought the nearly overwhelming impulse
to pick up Cindy's hand and kiss her muddy little
palm.

I've gone nuts.

Trace closed his eyes. It didn't help. It just made his other senses all the more acute. He felt the taut, full weight of Cindy's breasts resting against his chest, the rounded sweetness of her hips cradled between his thighs, the delicate touch of her breath and fingertips softly tangled in the hair just below his collarbone. He could also feel with razor clarity the heavy, deep beat of his own blood and the surging heat filling his loins, filling him.

Princess, what would you do if I peeled you out of those muddy jeans and unzipped my pants and fitted you over me like a hot velvet glove?

Trace's heartbeat doubled at the thought. His eyes snapped open. Very carefully he lifted Cindy from his lap and slid out the Rover's door, muttering something about getting her gear from the Jeep. Mud squelched and sucked at his boots all the way to the Jeep. He grabbed the two small suitcases from the back and tucked them under one arm. A folded tarp, mosquito netting and a sleeping bag went under the same arm. There was nothing left in the cargo area of the Jeep but the battered toolbox that had been bolted to the floor.

The front—and only—seat of the Jeep didn't offer much more in the way of supplies. Purse, empty canteen and a paper bag with a few discarded food wrappers were the only things Trace found. He grabbed the purse and canteen and went back to the Rover.

Cindy sat on the passenger side of the bench seat, watching Trace and wishing that he were in the car with her again. She could still feel the imprint of his hard body and the gentle, reassuring sweeps of his hand over her. She hadn't felt so cherished since the months after her mother's death, when Rye would hear his little sister crying in the night and come to her room and lift her into his arms, rocking her until she fell asleep once more.

"Anything else?" Trace asked, looking into the clear, black eyes that watched him with surprising intensity. He felt an urge simply to stroke Cindy's tangled raven hair once more. The effort it took to control the impulse shocked him.

"Just the radiator water and gas cans," she answered.

Cindy's voice was somewhere between husky and raspy, as though her scream of fear had made her hoarse.

"They'll be okay for now," Trace said. "Do you feel strong enough to steer the Jeep while I winch it out of the muck?"

She blinked slowly, trying to focus on his words instead of on the sculpted line of his lips. "That's all? Just steering?"

Trace nodded.

Mentally Cindy took stock of herself. She had never been a tenth so tired. On the other hand, everything still worked, after a fashion.

"I can handle it," she said, as much to herself as to Trace.

Cindy started to climb out of the Rover, only to feel Trace's hard arms sliding beneath her knees and around her back once more. She made a startled sound as he lifted her from the Rover's bench seat and walked over to the Jeep as though she weighed no more than one of her soft-sided suitcases. He looked down at her surprised, mud-smudged, yet still elegant face. One corner of his mouth kicked up slightly.

"I asked you about steering, not walking," he explained.

Trace saw the slow curving of Cindy's lips, felt the subtle changes in her body as she relaxed against him, and wanted to laugh in triumph and howl with frustration at the same time.

"A man of your word, is that it?"

As Trace looked down at Cindy again, all the laughter left his face.

"Yes," he said simply.

For a long moment she stared into his intent green eyes. At that moment he reminded her oddly of Rye, the only man who had never failed her trust. Slowly she nodded.

"All right," Cindy said in a husky murmur. "I'll remember that."

Just as Trace reached the Jeep, Cindy spoke again.

"Trace?"

"Hmm?"

"Thank you."

"For this?" he asked, lifting her a bit higher.

"No. I mean, yes, but...the snake," she said simply. "Thank you."

Trace's mouth flattened out and his arms tightened around Cindy in unconscious protectiveness. "No need to thank me. You got in the first shot."

"Luck. The snake was twice as long as that miserable shovel handle."

Cindy watched as the powerful man holding her closed his eyes, concealing their jungle-green behind a dense thicket of nearly black lashes. They were the only hint of softness in Trace's suddenly bleak face.

"Don't thank me. I'm the fool who nearly got you killed."

"That's ridiculous. You didn't put the Jeep in the bog or the snake in the bush."

"I should never have allowed you to drive out of Quito," Trace said flatly.

"What do you mean, *allow?*" she retorted. "You had nothing to do with it. I rented the Jeep the same way I drove it—by myself!"

"And look where it got you."

Cindy looked up into Trace's narrowed green eyes and swallowed hard. "Into your arms?" she asked weakly.

Unwillingly Trace smiled even as he slowly shook his head. "Up to those sweet lips in mud, that's where," he muttered, outlining the curves of her mouth with a glance that revealed frank male hunger. "I can pull you out of the mud with no problem, but after that you might find yourself in bigger trouble than you were before."

Before Cindy could answer, Trace dropped her into the driver's seat of the Jeep and strode away. She watched with a mixture of envy and admiration as he maneuvered the Rover through the mud and into position with matter-of-fact strength and skill. The

Rover had two winches, one in front and one in back. When the vehicles were roughly lined up Trace used the rear winch cable to attach the Jeep to the Rover.

The bigger, wider tires on Trace's vehicle spun through the fresh layer of storm-deposited silt to the older, more solid road beneath. The Jeep lurched forward, startling Cindy. She did her best to steer, but knew that it was the much heavier Rover and Trace's skill that were doing the real work. Together the two vehicles churned through the low stretch of the road and up the muddy incline on the opposite side.

The whole process took about three minutes.

Furiously Cindy's hands clenched around the wheel, wishing it were Trace's throat. He had barely gotten his boots dirty yanking the Jeep out of the bog, yet he had sat on his rump and watched her work her hands raw poking brush into the mud.

Waiting for her to ask him for help. *Nicely.*

It was just as well that Trace kept on driving rather than stopping to disconnect the two vehicles. Cindy was far too angry to pay much attention to details such as steering or clutch or accelerator. She was too furious to do anything but grit her teeth against the scream of pure rage that was trying to claw its way out of her throat. Her temper wasn't improved when a village appeared no more than ten minutes farther down the road.

"Damn him!" Cindy said with aching force. "*Damnhimdamnhimdamnhim!* If I had known, I could have walked here in half an hour!"

The object of Cindy's wrath divided his attention

between the road ahead and the Jeep behind, towing Cindy to a spot just in front of the local cantina. As he parked, several old men looked up from their comfortable positions around a canted table. Cindy watched Trace walk over to the men before she got out and walked stiffly to the front of the Jeep. Without looking at Trace she began tugging at the cable, trying to release the Jeep.

"Leave it," called Trace. "We're not going anywhere today."

"Speak for yourself," Cindy muttered beneath her breath.

The next thing she knew her hands were being yanked away from the cable.

"I said leave it."

Cindy stared at Trace in mute, seething defiance.

"This is Popocaxtil," he said. "You wanted to come here, remember?"

She transferred her glare to his throat.

"Something bothering you?" Trace asked calmly.

"You. You're despicable. You knew you could get the Jeep out in a matter of minutes, but you let me work until I was cross-eyed."

Trace waited.

"And you knew all along that Popocaxtil was close by!"

It was more of an accusation than a question, but Trace answered anyway.

"Yes."

"But you didn't tell me!"

"You didn't ask." He looked at the high color that

rage had brought to Cindy's mud-smudged cheek-bones and inquired softly, "Anything you want to ask me now, princess?"

Trace waited, but Cindy simply turned away, dragged herself into the Jeep once more and sat with her head resting on the back of the seat and her eyes tightly closed.

"Suit yourself," he said, shrugging despite the anger simmering in his blood. "But then, princesses always do, don't they?"

With that Trace turned and went back to the men at the cantina. Cindy watched through slitted eyes while another rickety chair appeared out of nowhere. Trace sat down. From inside came a huge, thick-bodied woman carrying a heaped plate of food in one hand and a quart bottle of beer in the other. She set both in front of Trace.

Cindy's salivary glands ached in a sudden on-slaught of hunger and thirst. She put them out of her mind. She would rather spit dust and starve to a skeleton than beg Trace for food or water. She would simply rest for a while. In half an hour or so she should have gathered enough strength to gesticulate with the natives until mutual understanding came. And with it, food and water.

"Water…"

She pulled herself into a fully upright position, blinked and looked around with real interest. As did most villages, Popocaxtil had a central well where its citizens drew water and gossiped.

Despite the exhaustion that made her clumsy,

Cindy's determination hadn't diminished one bit. She leaned over the seat, fumbled in the toolbox until her hand finally connected with a tin pot from the mess kit, and pulled herself out of the Jeep. When she stood up she felt light-headed. She waited for the feeling to pass, then set off for the local well. No sooner had she filled the pot with cool, luscious water than Trace appeared like an evil jinni and dumped the water into the dirt.

"You little fool! Have you been drinking the local water all along?" he asked harshly.

Cindy shook her head and looked wistfully at the spilled water. "I was going to boil it."

Trace let out a harsh breath. He took the pot in one hand and Cindy's grubby wrist in the other. "Did it ever occur to you that I might have water in the Rover?" he asked as he hustled her back to the vehicles. "Or did you figure that one peon's water is pretty much like another's, so you'd have to boil it all anyway?" Without waiting for an answer, Trace threw the pot into the back of the Rover and fished out his own canteen. He shoved it under Cindy's nose. "Drink."

She didn't wait for a second invitation. She fumbled the top off the canteen and began swallowing great mouthfuls of the wonderful water, not caring that some trickled from the corners of her lips. She had never tasted anything half so fine.

Eyes narrowed, Trace watched her. When she stopped for a breath he said, "How long have you been without water?"

Cindy looked at him over the canteen. "Not too—"

"How long?" he interrupted flatly.

"I ran out late yesterday," she said, her tone defiant. "I was going to boil some last night, but couldn't even find a puddle where I parked. Then I was so busy making mud pies today that I didn't get around to cooking any."

"And you would have died of thirst before asking for anything from a peon like me, right?"

"After I saw your smug smile when you pulled up and saw me in the mud, you're damned right!"

Trace remembered the paper bag with its few discarded food wrappers. "When was the last time you ate?"

"No problem. I can always live off the fat of the land," she said, smacking her right hip with her palm.

"How long since—"

"Yesterday," Cindy said, cutting across his words.

"And here I thought you were intelligent!" Trace's hands locked around Cindy's upper arms, hauling her up to within inches of his face. "Listen, princess. This is a wild land with mountains taller than God and meaner than hell. The cloud forest doesn't give one tinker's damn whether you're rich or poor, royalty or peon, dead or alive. And it's dead you're going to be if you don't climb down off your high horse. I'm not a bloody mind reader. If you want something—food or water or any other damn thing—*ask*. And when you're told to do something like leave the Rover's winch cable in place, *do it*.

That particular winch has a tricky release. If you handle it wrong you'll lose a finger."

"If you had told me about the winch, I—"

"No," Trace said flatly, interrupting Cindy. He looked down into her defiant black eyes. "What happens when something goes wrong and there's no time for me to argue or explain? Should we both get injured or die because you're too spoiled and stuck-up to follow reasonable instructions? There can be only one leader of any expedition, and I'm the leader of this one. If you can't accept that I'll tie you in the Jeep and tow you all the way back to Quito."

Cindy wanted very much to tell Trace to roast his haunches in hell, but she knew that would be stupid—as stupid as some of the things she had already done. She didn't have the experience or reflexes to be on her own in the cloud forest, and she had proven it over and over. Going without food and water at a time when she needed every bit of her strength hadn't been one of her brighter moves.

But then, her IQ seemed to have been on hold since the first instant she had set eyes on Trace and felt dark fire licking beneath her skin.

"All right," Cindy said between her teeth. "You Tarzan, me Jane. Go for it."

"Are you asking me or telling me?"

She closed her eyes and wished she were twice as strong as Trace. Three times. Four.

"Ask me, princess."

But she wasn't strong. She was light-headed and

tired and her tongue felt like a dirty mitten in her mouth.

"Have you ever," she said huskily, "had to beg for anything?"

"I'm not talking about begging, I'm—"

"Have you?" she demanded, cutting across Trace's words.

"No," he said curtly.

"I didn't think so." Cindy opened her eyes. They were as black and bleak as a night sky with neither moon nor stars. "I have. It won't happen again. Ever. So if you want the job of finding Susan Parker, I'll pay the way. If you want me to say 'pretty please, help me,' I'll find another way to follow Susan— because no matter how nicely I beg, you'll do what you damned well wanted to do all along, and you'll rub my nose in it every step of the way."

The bitterness seething beneath Cindy's matter-of-fact tone was almost tangible. Instinctively Trace's grip on her arms gentled until his palms were soothing over her in a slow caress.

"Is that what some man did to you?" Trace asked softly. "Made you beg and then humiliated you?"

There was a swift blaze of defiance, then nothing. Cindy's expression became as empty as her eyes. She had spent several years learning not to think about Jason's treachery. There was no reason to start remembering now.

"That has nothing to do with finding Susan," Cindy said.

For an instant Trace's grip hardened. Then he

released her. "Susan was here over a week ago," he said, turning away. "She bought weavings and left for San Juan de Quextil."

Chapter 5

"San Juan de…whatever," Cindy muttered, trying to remember the order of the villages from which Susan's cloth came. "That's not far."

Trace paused but didn't turn around. "It's on the next ridge over to the east."

"Good," Cindy said with relief. "We can be there before midnight."

"Not likely."

Cindy looked at the sky. The sun was already behind the flank of mountain but there was probably an hour of daylight left. As always, there were clouds of one kind or another hanging around, but no real rain threatened. "But the weather is fine."

"You aren't," Trace said bluntly. "You need food, a bath and sleep, in that order."

"But—"

"No."

Cindy clamped her mouth shut against her unspoken protests. *You Tarzan. Me Jane.* It was Trace's cloud forest and his rules. Arguing wouldn't change anything.

Besides, she was too tired to argue.

Without looking back to see how his curt refusal had settled with Cindy, Trace walked into the cantina. Once inside he fought a sharp struggle with himself. He lost. Cursing his lack of willpower when it came to one Cindy Ryan, he tracked down the monumental waitress. He had promised himself that he would make Cindy ask for whatever she needed, but the thought of her being thirsty or hungry defeated him. He would get the expedition on some kind of normal footing once she was fed and rested. Until then he wouldn't be able to look at her dirty, wan face without wanting to turn himself in to the nearest police station and start confessing to crimes he'd never even heard of, much less committed.

Ten minutes later, when Trace emerged from the cantina carrying food, Cindy was curled awkwardly in the front seat of the Jeep, sound asleep.

I'll bet if I'd said she needed sleep, food and a bath, in that order, I'd have found her skinny-dipping in the village well, Trace thought in exasperation, looking down at the tangled cloud of black hair fanned across the seat. *Maybe if I tell her to sleep in*

*the Jeep tonight she won't argue about the two of us
sleeping in the only bed in the only room in town.*

Trace reached into the Jeep and shook Cindy
awake. The instant she began to mumble protests at
being dragged into consciousness he shoved a plate
of food under her nose. The effect was immediate
and salutary. Black eyes opened, focused on the
mounds of tiny potatoes and roast chicken and corn
tortillas. Cindy inhaled the fragrance and reached for
the food. The sight of her dirty fingers stopped her
in midreach.

"Your shower won't be ready for a few minutes,"
Trace said in a clipped voice. An impatient snap of
his wrist unrolled the damp makeshift hand towel he
was carrying. He dumped it over her wrists. "I'll be
back for the plate. It had better be clean."

With that Trace went to the Rover and began un-
loading it. Cindy was too busy wiping her face and
hands to notice what Trace was doing. Halfway
through her cleanup, when the soft white cloth she
was using had become irretrievably dirty, she looked
closely at it and made a startled sound. She was in-
dustriously grinding mud into a formerly clean
T-shirt. From its size, it could belong only to one
man—Trace Rawlings.

"Well, it's too late now," Cindy muttered. "I might
as well make a thorough job of ruining it."

She finished wiping her fingers and face clean
before she attacked the plate of food with outright
greed. The flavor of the roast potatoes was unexpected, delicate and utterly delicious. The chicken

had a chocolate sauce that was equally unexpected and not so delicious. The meat was as tough as the tortillas were savory and tender. She ate everything without a pause, deciding that the odd chocolate sauce improved upon longer acquaintance.

When Trace came back half an hour later, Cindy's eyes were closed and her plate was empty of all but a pile of neatly gnawed bones. He hoped having a full stomach would improve her mood. He reached down to awaken her, then stopped, staring at the luminous, fine-grained skin framed by wings of raven hair. She was breathing deeply, easily, and the tiniest crumb of tortilla was tucked into a corner of her full lips.

Slowly Trace withdrew his hand. If he touched Cindy, he would bend down and lick up the small crumb…and then he would slide his tongue into Cindy's warm mouth and kiss her the way he had wanted to since he had first seen her in the smoky Quito bar.

"Your bath is ready," Trace said, his voice deep.

Cindy stirred. Trace watched hungrily while her rosy tongue roved over soft, very pink lips, tasting the recent food and licking up the tiny crumb. She started to sit upright, groaned softly, and curled into another uncomfortable position in the bucket seat.

"Can you walk or do you want me to carry you?" Trace asked finally, hoping Cindy would opt for walking. If he felt her weight in his arms right now he wouldn't be responsible for the kiss he would surely demand of those deep pink lips.

"Mmph."

"Mmph," Trace agreed, sighing, not knowing whether to smile or swear at the opportunity that had just presented itself.

He plucked Cindy from the Jeep's front seat, carried her through a side door of the cantina and into a tiny room. There were wooden slats on the floor, a rusty pipe poking out of the wall and a bar of improbably blue soap stuck to a high window ledge. Her own shampoo, conditioner and comb had been set out near the door, along with a towel bearing the initials TER.

"You awake?" Trace asked softly.

She murmured a sleepy negative.

"Good."

Slowly Trace let Cindy slide down his body and onto her own feet. He didn't let go of her, simply shifted his arms until she fit his body the way mist fit the mountainside, seamlessly, no gaps and nothing in between. He stared down at her lips and wondered if she tasted half as sweet as she looked. With a final, silent curse at his lack of self-control where this one woman was concerned, he bent and fitted his mouth over hers with exquisite care, leaving no sensitive surfaces untouched.

For a few moments Trace moved his head slowly, parting Cindy's lips by fractions, feeling the subtle changes in her body tension as she went from dazed sleep to sensuous half wakefulness. Suddenly he could wait no longer to taste her. He twisted his head hungrily.

Cindy's mouth opened in surprise and response to Trace's kiss, leaving her vulnerable to the velvet penetration of his tongue. She could neither speak nor move, so tightly was she held in Trace's arms. She had no physical defenses against the slow, hot glide of his tongue. Nor did she have any mental defenses against the consuming kiss, for she had never been kissed with a tenth so much heat, even by the man she had once thought to marry.

With a throttled moan Cindy gave herself to Trace's embrace, moving her tongue over his, tasting him more and more deeply with each racing second until they were locked together in a searching kiss that turned her bones to honey.

The abrupt appearance of the floor beneath Cindy's feet came as a distinct surprise to her. So did the sudden feeling of emptiness when Trace's mouth lifted from hers. Slowly she opened her eyes, aware of a distinct feeling that she had just made a mistake. A bad one. She hadn't been the least bit aroused by any man since Jason, her first lover. And—she had vowed—her last. If she were going to make an exception to that particular personal rule, she knew she should have started with someone a good deal less potent than Trace Rawlings. He was way beyond her level of sensual experience.

But he tempted her almost unbearably. The late golden sunlight slanting into the washroom through the high window made his eyes luminous, nearly emerald in color, twin green fires watching her.

"I do believe I've finally found a way to communicate with a high-nosed little princess," Trace said, smiling, bending down to Cindy's mouth again.

Cindy stiffened and tried to ease from Trace's arms. She didn't have the least bit of success. He was even stronger than he looked, holding her effortlessly, hotly. The caress of his lips on her sensitive, flushed skin made goose bumps march up and down her arms.

"Now don't get your ruff up," Trace murmured, nibbling along Cindy's lower lip. "All I meant was that since you have such a hard time with words, it only made sense for me to give you another way to thank me for waiting on you hand and foot."

"Generous of you," Cindy managed through clenched teeth.

"I thought so. Care to build up your account against future maid service?" he asked, running the tip of his tongue along her closed lips.

"No, thanks," Cindy said coolly, feeling like a fool for having responded so completely to Trace when the kiss had been nothing more than a casual joke to him. "I always take care of maid service with a generous tip."

Trace straightened and released her. "Wide-awake now, aren't you, princess?"

"Better late than never."

"Not as far as I'm concerned. The sleepy version is a hell of a lot more woman."

"Woman isn't a synonym for stupid," Cindy retorted.

"I know. I'm surprised you do, though."

With that Trace walked out and closed the door

behind him. His voice came back through the badly fitted slats, warning Cindy that she had only fifteen minutes to get clean. She shut her eyes, got a grip on her fluttering nervous system, and turned on the shower.

A thin, erratic stream of cool water came out of the pipe. She looked at her clothes, shrugged, and stepped under the water. Working quickly she wet down and lathered everything from crown to heels with her shampoo, rinsed, and then peeled down to underwear and repeated the process. By the time her hair had been conditioned and rinsed once more, she was feeling deliciously clean.

She turned off the water, which was down to a trickle by now, shed her clothes, wrung them out and her hair as well, and examined her soggy tennis shoes with a rueful smile. They had been white to begin with. Now they were a kind of ruined beige. It was the same for her blouse and jeans. Though clean, they were randomly stained by brown mud and traces of green vegetation.

"Oh, well," Cindy muttered to herself. "Some women pay a fortune for just that look."

She picked up the towel, dried herself quickly, then rolled her clothes up in the big towel, squeezed hard, and squeezed some more.

Trace knocked on the door and called, "Time's up."

"Wait!" Cindy called, unrolling her bikini underpants and pulling them on frantically. "I'm not dressed!"

"Is that an invitation?"

"Don't you dare!" she said, cringing against the clammy cups of the bra as she fastened it in place with flying fingers.

"A dare is better than an invitation any day," he drawled.

"Dammit, Trace…!"

Cindy knew that pulling the damp jeans quickly over her curvy hips was out of the question. She jammed her arms through the short sleeves of her blouse and pulled the clammy sides together over her full breasts.

"Relax," Trace said, opening the door and walking in, unbuttoning his shirt with one hand, carrying clean clothes with the other. "You've got nothing I haven't seen before, and vice versa."

After Trace hung the clothes on a nail and shut the door, he was no more than a foot away from Cindy in the tiny room. For several frozen instants she stood with damp slacks dangling from one hand and towel from the other as she stared at the bare male chest emerging from the shirt. Technically what Trace had said was perfectly correct. She had seen shirtless men before, and had seen Jason wearing nothing more than a triumphant smile.

But seeing Trace was a whole different order of experience. Jason had been good-looking, but not…compelling. Trace exuded a kind of potent, effortless masculinity that went beyond the swirling patterns of dark brown hair and the supple bands of muscle crossing his chest. He was intensely vital, overflowing with heat and life, and he had set her on fire with a single deep kiss, something that Jason hadn't managed to do with the sum total of all his lovemaking.

Cindy didn't realize that she was staring at Trace until his hands went to his waist. Her breath caught with a small sound that was lost beneath the hiss of his descending zipper. She spun and faced the wall. He laughed.

"You are de…" Cindy said angrily, but couldn't force any more syllables past the breath wedged in her throat.

"Desirable?" Trace taunted.

She made a choked sound. He laughed deeply, enjoying himself for the first time since Quito, when he had sensed the dark fire burning within Cindy. Well, he was enjoying himself for the second time, to be precise. He had enjoyed kissing her far too much for his own comfort. Teasing her was a lot safer, as long as he kept his pants mostly on. "And here I thought spoiled, overcivilized women liked being turned on by peons."

"Says who?"

"D. H. Lawrence," Trace said smoothly.

Cindy's mouth snapped shut. By an immense effort of will she managed to ignore Trace long enough to wriggle into her wet pants.

"Our room is the second door to the left. And don't wander too far in those clothes, princess. They don't conceal nearly as much wet as they did dry."

The door closed behind Cindy with a distinct thump. She looked down at herself, made a stifled sound, and fled to the privacy of the second door on the left. Not until she was inside with the door safely shut did the implication of Trace's words sink in.

"*Our* room?" she asked in a raw voice, looking around.

There wasn't much to look at. The sagging bed was either a generous single or a stingy double mattress lying flat on the floor. There was a blanket but neither sheets nor a pillow. Rugs, curtains, electricity and running water were also among the missing amenities. Not to mention privacy. She couldn't even lock the door for the simple reason that there was no lock in sight, not even a dead bolt or a chair to wedge under the door handle.

And Trace's duffel bag was sitting with her suitcases on the floor, right next to the lone mattress.

Cindy peeled off her wet clothes and pulled on dry ones, moving quickly, not knowing how long she would have before Trace finished his shower. She did know that she wasn't going to be caught in see-through clothing again. Not that it had bothered Trace. For all the response he had shown, she could have been wearing the ratty blanket that was folded haphazardly at the foot of the even rattier mattress.

For his part, Trace spent an unusual amount of time in the shower, trying to forget the picture Cindy had made when he had walked into the washroom. The deep, rich curves of her body had been a shock to him. She must have worked very hard choosing clothes that would minimize the sweet contrast of her small waist with her taut, full breasts and hips.

Graceful feet, long legs, a lush triangular shadow balanced at the apex of her thighs…and nipples gathered into deep, pink pouts by the wet cloth of her blouse.

Trace had wanted her just that way, cold cloth and hot flesh and his tongue shaping her nipples into hungry velvet daggers. Just the thought of it brought a grating sound from deep in his throat. He had seen other women wearing much less, but not one of them had brought his body to immediate, full alert. Cindy had. He was still hard, throbbing, so hot he half expected to hear the water sizzle on his skin.

One bed. God. She's so damned soft and that floor is going to be so damned hard. Maybe she'll take pity on me and let me sleep next to her.

Yeah, sure. And maybe all her money will turn to grass and the cow that jumped over the moon will eat it and give green milk.

By the time Trace had finished his shower and dressed in clean clothes, his body had reluctantly accepted the message his mind was sending: *Forget it.*

For Trace to be stuck on an expedition with a spoiled princess who had taken one look down her nose at him and decided he could be bought out of her petty cash account was bad enough. To let her get the upper hand because he wanted her would be the dumbest thing he had ever done in a long life studded with dumb things.

For God's sake, she can't even lower herself to ask me the time of day, and here I am tying myself in knots wanting her?

I'm nuts. That's all there is to it.
Nuts!

Angry with himself, the world, and the thought of a long night on a hard floor, Trace stalked down the unlighted hallway to the bedroom. After a perfunctory knock he walked in.

Cindy had changed from her wet clothes into a pair of pants that were loose everywhere they could be loose—waist, hips and legs. The top was big enough to double as a pup tent. Trace knew he should have been grateful that Cindy was no longer wearing sexy, water-slicked, transparent cotton, but he wasn't. It was irritatingly obvious that she was making a special effort to be as unappealing to him as she could manage to be.

"You mug the waitress for that outfit?" Trace asked, balling up and tossing aside his dirty clothes.

Cindy looked down at her pants and shirt. Handwoven from hand-dyed natural fibers, the clothes were colorful, unstructured and very fashionable, as well as sinfully comfortable.

"This is one of Susan's designs."

"No wonder she's lost. She can't follow the lines of a woman's body, much less a road map."

"She made it to Popocaxtil," Cindy shot back.

Trace grunted and looked around. "That's no recommendation."

Cindy took a better grip on her temper. No one had ever been able to pull her cork quite so quickly, not even Rye at his most maddening.

Trace glared at her. "You know, for someone

who's so blazing fond of Susan Parker, you sure aren't very curious. You haven't even asked me if the villagers knew anything else about her but the fact that she left."

"You know I care about Susan. If you learned anything else—and if you want to tell me what that is—you will. My asking won't make a bit of difference."

Despite the cool neutrality of Cindy's words, she watched Trace with anxious eyes.

"The villagers sold her some cloth, food and gasoline and went about their own business. They said she was *muy hermosa*, very beautiful," Trace added almost grudgingly, "and that she spoke with her hands and her smile."

Cindy let out a long breath and relaxed, reassured about Susan for the first time since her friend had turned up missing.

"That's Susan," she said eagerly, her eyes alive with laughter. "Cinnamon hair and the kind of slender, willowy body that looks good in everything, and she can make anyone understand anything with that stunning smile of hers and a wave of her elegant hands. If she had turned up covered with mud the way I was, she'd have started a new fashion rage."

"Is this where I'm supposed to gallantly point out that you're hardly a dog yourself?"

The cool sarcasm in Trace's voice took the laughter right out of Cindy's eyes.

"Gallant? You?" she retorted incredulously, thinking of how Trace had sat and watched her struggle to free the Jeep. "Not very damn likely. For instance, the *gallant* thing to do with one mattress, one man and one woman is for the man to—"

"Put a cork in it, princess," Trace said coldly, slicing across Cindy's words. "I'll sleep on the floor tonight but not out of any misplaced sense of gallantry. Sharing a lumpy mattress just isn't worth putting up with your grief."

Ignoring Cindy, Trace began making the mattress into a bed. First he removed the musty wool blanket and dumped it into a bare corner of the room. With an expert flip of his wrist he spread his tarp over the mattress. When he began untying Cindy's sleeping bag she made an involuntary noise. She was too violently aware of Trace as a man to be comfortable sleeping in the same room with him, no matter who was on the mattress and who was on the floor.

Trace looked up suddenly, pinning Cindy with his icy green glance. "Relax. I'm not going to stick my hand up your blouse while you're asleep. I won't crawl into bed with you, either. And crawling is what you'd make a man do to get close to you, isn't it, princess? Well, I just don't crawl worth a damn. The sooner you figure that out, the easier this trip will be on both of us."

With another impatient movement of his wrist, Trace unrolled Cindy's sleeping bag so quickly that the cloth made a snapping noise as it settled over the mattress. She waited until he let go of the bag before she bent over and retrieved it. Saying nothing, she turned and went to the door, grabbing her own tarp along the way. She barely had the door open when Trace's hand shot over her shoulder and slammed the door shut in front of her face.

"Planning on sleeping in the hall?" he asked in a deceptively soft voice.

Cindy wasn't going to answer, but a single glance over her shoulder at Trace's face told her that he would get his answer one way or another. "No. In the Jeep."

"You'll be more comfortable lying in the bed than sitting up in the Jeep."

"I'm used to it. Besides, after a day of making mud pies, I'm tired enough to sleep standing up. As your day has been considerably less strenuous," she added with a cool smile, "I'm sure you'll appreciate the mattress more than I would. And don't worry, Mr. Rawlings. Where I sleep won't have the least effect on your tip."

Trace hissed a searing word under his breath and turned his back on Cindy. He didn't move until he heard the door open and close behind him. Then he stripped off his clothes, turned off the battery-powered lantern he had brought from the Rover and lay on the contested mattress.

He was still awake when it began to rain.

Chapter 6

The luminous dial of Trace's watch told him that he had been lying on the lumpy mattress for nearly an hour. He had counted sheep, goats, llamas, alpacas, mice and raindrops, all to no avail. He was no closer to sleep than he had been when he went to bed. Even worse, he had run out of new ways to curse himself as a fool and the old ways had lost their zing.

"Hell."

In a single motion Trace shot off the low mattress and stood glaring toward the inoffensive bedroom door. It was quite obvious that Little Ms. Rich Britches wasn't adult enough to admit her mistake and come in out of the rain. That meant that he would have to be adult enough to point her mistake out to her and drag her back inside.

Muttering to himself, Trace yanked on the clean underwear and slacks he had laid out by the mattress. He groped around in the dark until he found the tiny pencil flashlight he had put at the head of the mattress. With a tiny clicking sound the light came on. He found and scuffed into his boots before he stalked out the door, making less noise than the softly falling rain.

Though it was hardly late at night by city standards, the cantina building and the village were absolutely dark. Out in the countryside a rooster was the only clock that kept local time. Trace knew the territory, so he never traveled without a variety of battery-powered lights, one of which was the flashlight that was no bigger than his index finger. The penlight generated a very narrow, very sharp shaft of illumination. Rain fell in gentle silver veils through the cone of light. With another exasperated curse Trace stepped into the rain and stalked to the nearby Jeep. The moldy canvas top was up, but he knew that it must leak somewhere. Canvas always did.

As soon as Trace opened the door he knew where the Jeep leaked. Everywhere. Water ran in cool trickles across the ceiling and down the sides of the canvas top, with occasional diversions down his neck as he stared in disbelief at Cindy. She had the tin mess-kit pot underneath the biggest area of drips, which happened to be left of center in the driver's seat. The other leaks were deflected from the passenger side by a ground tarp Cindy had pulled up to her neck. Beneath the tarp was her sleeping bag, which she had opened and used as blanket. Despite having curled herself almost double, her bare feet stuck out from under the tarp. A trickle of water splashed onto her toes every so often. Water dripped into the tin pan with monotonous regularity.

Cindy was asleep.

Trace stared at her, not knowing whether to swear or to take his stubborn princess into his arms. It was a conflict he was becoming accustomed to the longer he was around her.

In the end Trace gave in, a bittersweet solution to which he was also becoming accustomed. There was really no other choice this time, as there had been none the other times. If Cindy stayed in the Jeep, by morning she would be stiff, sore and doubtless sick into the bargain. And Trace had little doubt that Cindy was more than exhausted enough to sleep despite all the running water. After all, he was the gallant knight who had sat and watched her work until she staggered, all in the name of teaching her how to ask for help when she needed it.

Obviously the lesson hadn't been learned.

"Princess," Trace muttered in a low, gritty voice, "what the hell am I going to do with you?"

There was no answer but the hollow sound of water drops running onto the tarp and from there onto Cindy's soft flesh. Swearing, Trace tucked the penlight behind his ear as a makeshift miner's light.

Gently he removed the wet tarp and extricated Cindy from her uncomfortable, leaky bed.

"At least you could have slept in the Rover," Trace continued in a husky, reasonable voice. He arranged Cindy in his arms and tucked in trailing edges of her sleeping bag so that he wouldn't trip. "It doesn't leak and you would fit nicely on the front bench seat. But no, you wouldn't even ask for that much from a peon, would you?"

He sighed a sibilant curse. "One of us is going to have to smarten up a bit, princess, or you're going to keep on being too proud to take a peon's advice and then you'll end up hurting yourself before I can stop you. Then I'll feel lower than a snake's belly and I'll take it out on you and you'll get your ruff up and try to walk on water or something equally stupid and then we'll be back where we were a few minutes ago—me lying awake and you fishing for pneumonia in a leaky Jeep."

Cindy's only answer was a murmured word that Trace didn't catch. Protecting her from the rain as best he could, he carried her to the cantina, then ducked in through the side door and down the dark hallway leading to the small room. He went in and shut the door behind him with his foot, then knelt and put Cindy on the mattress. She stirred again. Her fingers clung to him when he would have withdrawn.

"Rye?" she murmured.

Trace froze in the act of turning off the penlight.

"Rye?" she repeated, her voice growing stronger.

"Yes," Trace lied softly through his gritted teeth.

"It's Rye." He turned off the light and tucked it alongside the mattress. "Go to sleep, love. I'm here. Everything is all right."

Cindy murmured something contented that Trace couldn't understand. Her hands linked sleepily behind his head and her cheek sought the warmth of his naked chest once more. He fought a short battle with his conscience, won, and lay down beside her. He pulled her lightweight sleeping bag over both of them.

With a sigh Cindy curled trustingly against Trace's body and sank into a deep sleep again. His hands clenched into fists as he felt the sweet weight of her breasts against his chest and wondered who the hell Rye was. Who was the paragon of humanity Cindy trusted enough to give herself into his keeping without struggle or hesitation? And why in God's name wasn't dear, no doubt *gallant* Rye in Ecuador with Cindy right now, keeping her out of Trace's hair and—more to the point—out of his arms?

Trace breathed in deeply, feeling the warm, spicy fragrance of Cindy radiate throughout his body. What sane man would let a woman like this go off into the wilds alone?

"You're crazy," Trace whispered aloud, his voice a soft rasp.

He had all night to think just who was crazy— Rye, Cindy, or Trace Rawlings.

The woman in Trace's arms breathed softly, her breasts stirring subtly against his chest with each breath, her warmth tangling with his own. Their bodies were equally tangled. His left arm encircled her narrow waist; her torso lay half on his. Her right arm was stretched across his chest and her fingers were tucked into the warm nest of hair beneath his left arm. Her leg lay between his, her thigh so close to his rigid male flesh that he was afraid to breathe. If she accidentally touched him…

And it would be even worse if she didn't.

Trace couldn't stifle the groan that leaked between his clenched teeth. The hunger for Cindy that had nearly brought him to his knees in the shower yesterday had tormented him all night. He had slept little and had awakened so aroused that he ached from his neck to his knees. He had spent all the long hours of darkness that way. The night hadn't been a total loss, however. He had definitely decided who was crazy.

He was.

Very carefully Trace eased away from the smooth, fragrant woman who had shared the mattress with him in a night of unaccustomed chastity. At least it had been unaccustomed for Trace. He had never spent the night with a woman he wanted and not taken her. Nor had he ever spent the night with a woman he hadn't wanted. At the moment he was too aroused to decide if that made two more rules he had broken for Cindy, or only one.

Why not just smooth her legs apart and wake her up from the inside out? If that kiss in the washroom was any sample, she wouldn't mind a bit.

That is the dumbest idea you've had in months!
Trace told himself savagely as he rolled off the
mattress and stood up.

*Wrong. The dumbest idea was doing Invers a
favor by getting Big Eddy McCall off his back.*

Trace sighed and rubbed his face with his palms,
wishing he could get his hands on Invers. But that was
impossible. The only thing within reach was a
stubborn princess whose eyes and body burned with
dark fires she wouldn't let him touch. Cursing Invers
and Big Eddy and everything but the softly sleeping
woman who was too close and much too far away,
Trace rubbed his face harder. Beard stubble rasped
back. Without stopping to question why he was bothering to shave when he wasn't even in the lowlands,
Trace picked up his shaving kit and silently left the
room.

Cindy awakened moments later. Eyes closed, she
stretched luxuriously. Suddenly she made a startled
noise and sat up, looking around wildly in the semi-
darkness. She remembered falling asleep in the Jeep
and nothing else. Obviously this wasn't the Jeep.

"Trace?"

There was no answer. Slowly Cindy inventoried
her surroundings once more. The room was familiar
enough. Her suitcases were still there. So was
Trace's duffel bag. Ditto for his battery lantern and
sandals and a pencil flashlight tucked alongside the
mattress. She was covered with her own sleeping
bag, which she had opened up to make into a blanket
last night in the Jeep. She was resting on top of

Trace's sleeping bag, which had been similarly unzipped. There was no other bed in sight, not even a makeshift pallet on which Trace could have slept.

The only possible conclusion was that Cindy had spent the night, or at least part of it, sleeping with Trace Rawlings.

Relax, princess. I'm not going to stick my hand up your blouse while you're asleep.

Too sleepy to marshal her usual defenses, Cindy admitted to herself that there was nothing she would have liked better than to awaken with Trace's hand caressing her breasts. Even the thought made her shiver, tightening her nipples until they stood out against the loose cloth of her blouse. The bittersweet irony of her situation made her want to laugh and cry at the same time. She had given up hope of finding a man who would want her instead of her money. She had given up men, period. Then along came Trace Rawlings, a man she found she wanted very much…a man who had kissed her once and apparently had decided that kissing her was more trouble than it was worth.

Crawling is what you'd make a man do to get close to you, isn't it? Well, I don't crawl worth a damn.

A slow, hot flush crawled up Cindy's body as she remembered Trace's icy words. Was that how she seemed to him—a woman whose greatest pleasure was in humiliating men, making them beg for a kiss or a smile?

Teeth scored Cindy's lower lip as she shook her head in silent denial of Trace's indictment. She had once been humiliated in just that manner by a man. She would never make another human being submit to that kind of cruelty any more than she would force herself to crawl for any man again, no matter what the reason. Maybe if she explained that to Trace they could start all over again.

Maybe this time he would want her instead of being angry with her.

"Oh, sure," Cindy muttered, rolling out of bed and standing up. "He's the very soul of understanding and gallant forgiveness. You knew that the instant you looked up from the mud and saw a smug smile plastered on his handsome face."

Gloomily Cindy began packing everything. She had to roll the sleeping bags several times each before she was satisfied that they wouldn't come undone the instant someone picked them up, which was what her own sleeping bag had done the first time she had rolled it. The dirty clothes she had collected without regard for ownership went into the big plastic garbage bag she had packed for just that purpose. Her shoes were still soggy and none too appealing, but a pair of dry socks made it possible to squeeze her feet into the shoes.

With a feeling of foreboding, Cindy pulled her small travel mirror out of her suitcase. A single glance told her more than she wanted to know.

"No wonder Trace couldn't wait to get out of bed this morning," she said, grimacing. "I've seen better looking women riding brooms on Halloween."

A small brush and a lot of patience took the snarls

from Cindy's hair. She looked at her makeup kit, shrugged, and put on a minimal amount, not wanting to call attention to herself by wearing something as useless as blusher in a cloud forest. The result of her sketchy pass with the makeup kit was depressingly less than spectacular. And, to be honest, she wouldn't have minded looking spectacular for Trace, if only to prove to him that she could be a desirable woman.

"Hey, princess. You awake?"

At the sound of Trace's voice Cindy guiltily buried her mirror in the dirty clothes bag.

"Yes."

"Good. Get the door, will you?"

Cindy opened the door and tried not to stare. Trace was wearing an old black T-shirt whose soft knit fitted perfectly over his chest, underlining every powerful shift of muscle and tendon. His slacks were khaki, loose, yet they managed to remind her with every movement he made that there were long, muscular legs just beneath the cloth. His dark hair was glistening from the shower, showing a hint of curl in its thick depths. Clean shaven, his face revealed its uncompromising Scandinavian planes. Beneath very dark, steeply arched brows, his eyes were gemlike in the clarity and intensity of their green color.

Cindy had never seen a man who appealed to her senses more. It was all she could do not to reach up and trace the clean masculine lines of Trace's eyebrows, his lips, his jaw, and then to kiss him as she finally had in the shower. Only this time she wouldn't freeze up. She wouldn't stop kissing Trace until he was trembling as much as she had yesterday. If such a thing were possible.

A thoughtful frown settled onto Cindy's face as she wondered if men ever got so aroused that they trembled. If she asked Trace about it, would he answer her or simply make fun of her obvious lack of experience?

"Hello?" Trace said, wondering why Cindy was staring at him as though he were an utter stranger. "Remember me? Your intrepid guide?"

Cindy stepped back hastily from the doorway, feeling a blush heat her cheeks. "Er, yes. Come in."

"Here," said Trace, holding out a plate on which was balanced a cup of coffee, a mound of eggs and a wad of tortillas. "This will take the cobwebs out of your brain."

Wordlessly Cindy accepted the plate, staring at Trace as though he were a magician. She had been so busy drinking in his appearance that she hadn't even realized he was holding two plates in his hands. And very intriguing hands they were—tanned, long fingered, lean, strong, the backs patterned with the same glossy dark brown hair that curled up from the vee neck of his shirt.

"Coffee," Trace explained, giving Cindy a sideways glance when she made no move to eat or drink.

She didn't notice the glance. She was looking up the bare length of his forearms, tracing the exquisitely masculine textures of tanned skin and very dark, shiny hair, and the flex and flow of muscle with each motion of Trace's body. She wanted to run her fingertips and cheek and lips over his arm, outlining each warm ridge of muscle and tendon. Would he like that? Would it shorten his breath just a little? Would it make him look at her as though she were a desirable woman rather than a useless albatross tied around his neck?

"Are you all right?" Trace asked finally, glancing at Cindy's hands, which were clenched so tightly on the plate that her knuckles were pale.

"No." Cindy closed her eyes and wondered at the turmoil of her mind and the curious, slow tendrils of heat uncurling from deep within the pit of her stomach. "I mean, yes. Just a little…scattered."

Trace looked around the room, expecting to find it as disorganized as Cindy's mind obviously was. To his surprise everything was neatly packed and lined up by the door, ready to be taken to the Rover. Apparently she was eager to be gone from the forced intimacy of the small room and the implications of the single, lumpy mattress.

A thin smile grew on Trace's face. If Cindy thought the room was intimate, wait until she tried the Rover on for size. But he was no fool. He would say nothing. She could discover the dimensions of the Rover for herself.

Chapter 7

The Rover hit a massive tree root, lurched, wallowed and thumped down the other side. Cindy opened her mouth to ask Trace if he was certain that the miserable track they were on was the road to San Juan de Whatsis. After an instant of deliberation, she closed her mouth again. Trace had been either surly or amused with her since the moment they had left the little room and he had calmly loaded everything into the Rover.

"Everything" had included one Cindy Ryan, who had been hustled into the vehicle with slightly less care than had been given to the bag of dirty clothes. Unlike the laundry, she had protested her treatment in a calm, firm voice. Trace had simply looked at her,

called her princess and informed her that he had
arranged for the Jeep to be driven back to Quito.

Cindy had been so stunned that she could think
of nothing to say. She had remained silent since then.
Trace had done the same, except for a few sizzling
exceptions. One of them occurred half an hour out
of Popocaxtil, when a tire went flat. There were
many words then, all of them Trace's and not a single
one of them would have graced the approved list of
a girl's finishing school. When Trace paused for
breath, Cindy spoke.

"Can I help?"

"With the swearing? I doubt it, princess," he said
dryly. "I know more languages than you do."

"With the tire," Cindy said, her voice tight.

"You sure can," he said as he slid out of the Rover.
"You can stay the hell out of my way."

The Rover's door slammed hard behind Trace.
Cindy hung on to her temper and settled in for a long
wait.

As had happened many times since she had come
to Ecuador, she discovered that she had miscalcu-
lated. Despite the uneven, rutted, slippery ground,
Trace had the bad tire off and a new one in place
within fifteen minutes.

"That was fast," Cindy said as Trace climbed back
into the Rover.

He grunted. "Anyone who can't change a tire has
no business on these roads."

"I changed a tire on the Jeep," Cindy retorted.

"Yeah. The right front."

"How did you know?" she asked, startled. The Jeep's tires had been so caked with mud that there should have been no way for Trace to tell which tire was new and which was not.

"The lug nuts were so loose the wheel wobbled." Trace turned and gave Cindy a glittering green glance. "You're damned lucky that wheel didn't come off and dump you over the edge of the pass," he said flatly. "It was a long, long way down to the bottom, princess. Or was your nose too high in the air to see the drop-off at your feet?"

Cindy looked at her hands clenched in her lap and said nothing in her own defense, because there really was nothing for her to say. Trace was right: when it came to rough-country skills, she had none. If he thought her stuck-up into the bargain, she could hardly object. She had been abrupt and impatient with him from the first instant she had seen him sprawled like a huge jungle cat in a warm corner of the Quito bar. His lean, relaxed, yet overwhelmingly male presence had done odd things to her nerves. She had taken it badly. Things had started going wrong between the two of them from that moment.

Blindly Cindy turned and stared out the window at the dense greenery that lurched by in time to the Rover's rough forward progress. *Maybe if I try hard enough, things can go right from now on. Maybe I can put my best foot forward and take the other one out of my mouth. Maybe then Trace will stop looking at me as if I'm just one more thing gone wrong with his life.*

Gradually the view outside the window resolved

itself into separate shades of green reaching up toward a misty, pearl-white sky that was so brilliant it was impossible to look at directly. Leaves of all kinds unfurled to the white sky—leaves short and broad and glossy, leaves long and dark and sword-like, leaves lacy and graceful, blunt and leathery—more shapes and shades of green leaves than the human eye could distinguish or comprehend.

Without realizing it Cindy forgot her unhappy thoughts and became absorbed in the unfolding panorama of the land in a way that had been utterly impossible for her before, when she had been forced to give every bit of her attention to the road and the Jeep. Curious, wondering and finally awed, she began to understand the wild immensity of the country she had blithely taken on with no prepara-tion beyond a dubious hand-drawn map and a rented Jeep of uncertain mechanical soundness.

In places along the narrow track the canopy of leaves closed tightly overhead, putting the road into total shade. In those places Cindy could see into the forest itself. Beneath the dense, leafy canopy, the forest floor was open. Too little sunshine penetrated the layers of leaves for any but the most shade-tolerant plants to survive beneath the tall trees. Where the canopy had been torn by recent tree falls or by the road itself, plants flourished in a solid green mass as they fought a determined, silent, life-and-death struggle for a place in the sun.

Despite the fact that the narrow road pitched up and down as it wound over ridges and through what

Cindy suspected was a pass of sorts, the mountains themselves were rarely visible. Part of the problem was the green canopy of vegetation covering everything, muffling all sensory input, all orientation, leaving at best only a vague sense of up and down. Part of the visibility problem was stated in the name of the landscape itself.

Cloud forest.

Moisture was the cloud forest's third dimension. Mist, drizzle, windblown streamers of fog, water drops of all sizes condensed on every green surface to make tiny clear beads that gave off subtle glints of light when wind stirred through the forest. And every bit of the moisture came from the gently seething presence of grounded clouds. The mountains were dark, invisible sky castles more sensed than seen, land swathed in silent, warm billows as though a giant had exhaled against a mirror, blurring all reflections of reality. Clouds were everywhere, permeating everything, even the breaths that Cindy and Trace took.

Stretching from three thousand to eleven thousand feet along the east-facing slopes of the Andes, the cloud forest was bathed in perpetual moisture that came from thick, sultry tropical air rising up mountain slopes, cooling and condensing into clouds, and in the process creating a landscape that was like nothing else on earth. At times impenetrable, at times parklike, always expressed in shades of green on green, infused with the silver rush of water, the cloud forest lived and breathed, complete within its own immensity.

A searing torrent of language snapped Cindy out of her forest-induced reverie. The Rover lurched to a halt. She looked at Trace questioningly.

"Tire," he said in a clipped voice.

Automatically Cindy opened her mouth to ask if she could help, saw Trace's expectant, sardonic glance and closed her mouth once more, limiting her response to a nod. As the door slammed behind him, she looked at her watch. To her surprise, it was nearly noon. Her lips turned down in a rueful line at this latest underlining of her own incompetence relative to Trace's relentless skill. If she had been driving, the hours would have crawled far more slowly than the vehicle, and she would have been exhausted from wrestling with the steering wheel before she had come half so far.

Gloomily Cindy realized there was simply no doubt about it—traveling with Trace was much better in all ways than traveling by herself had been.

Not quite in all ways, she amended rebelliously. *When I was alone I could talk to myself. And better yet, I could get a civil answer!*

The Rover jiggled rhythmically as Trace jacked up the rear. Cindy glanced at her watch again and decided to risk Trace's wrath by rummaging for lunch. She knew there was something back in the cargo area. The smell of roast chicken and fresh corn tortillas was unmistakable.

Outside the Rover Trace pulled off the wheel, unstrapped the second spare he kept on the top of the Rover, and replaced the bad tire. He hesitated, then decided there was no help for it. He had to patch both ruined tubes on the two spares. If he didn't, sure as hell the next flat would come in pouring rain on the edge of a road that would have given an eagle second thoughts.

Cursing steadily beneath his breath, Trace took the tire iron, levered both tires from the wheel rims, pulled out the tubes and went to work. In both cases the cause of the leak wasn't difficult to discover. Some of the forest trees were very hard. Fallen sticks or branches made very efficient spears, especially when lying concealed beneath a thin layer of mud or moss on top of the road. Usually he was lucky or skillful enough to avoid the hidden traps. Today his skill had been on hold too much of the time because his attention had been divided between the road and his beautiful, silent passenger.

As for his luck…it had been on a holiday since Quito and showed no signs of coming back anytime soon.

Trace heard the Rover's door open and shut. When Cindy didn't approach him, he assumed that she was going to venture into the forest for the obvious reason. He called out to her without looking up from his work on the tubes.

"Don't lose sight of the Rover. And watch out for plants like the one growing near the left front fender. The stems are hollow and are the home of some really vicious ants."

Cindy's answer was muffled but clearly nonrebellious, so Trace gave his attention back to the patches.

He heard Cindy return, but she still didn't approach him. He finished checking the new patches on the tubes, put the tires back together and strapped them to their respective places on the top and rear of the Rover. He wiped down the tools and his own hands, topped off the gas tank, checked the water and decided everything would hold together until the next time he was looking at Cindy's profile when he damn well should have been looking at the road.

What the hell has she been thinking about? What's going on behind those beautiful black eyes? She hasn't said ten words since we left Popocaxtil.

Can you blame her? The last time she opened her mouth you landed on her with both feet.

If I had landed on her, it wouldn't have been with my feet. I've never made love to a woman in a car before, but better late than never, right?

Wrong. All wrong. Don't be any dumber than God made you. Get to Raul's place; show Cindy that Susan is okay; go tell Invers his problems with Big Eddy are solved and then start drinking until you forget the dark fire burning just beneath Cindy's lovely skin.

God, did she really shiver in my arms when I kissed her...or was it me shivering and wishing she wanted me?

Trace swore and tried to put Cindy out of his mind as he washed his hands beneath the trickling spout of the big water can attached to the rear bumper of the Rover. When he was finished he wiped his hands on his khakis and stretched. He was just thinking how wonderful a strong, hot cup of coffee would taste when he smelled the stuff of his dreams on the wind.

Inhaling, wondering if he were crazy, he followed the smell to the front of the Rover. The hood had been transformed into a table. Pieces of cold roast chicken and tortillas were laid out on top of a paper bag. Next to that was a mound of roughly hacked chunks of bittersweet chocolate. The food made his stomach growl in sudden demand, but it was the steaming mug that focused his attention. He reached for the mug, already anticipating the familiar, rich bite of coffee on his tongue.

"I didn't know if you took sugar or milk," Cindy said.

She glanced up from the road where she was crouched over a backpacker's stove that consisted of a single burner fueled by a canister of pressurized gas. A small pan of water was just coming to a boil. Next to her was another mug that wore what looked like a tin hat, which was actually the top half of a single-cup drip coffeepot. The mug itself provided the bottom half.

"This is fine. Much more than I expected," Trace added between sips of the scalding brew. He made a sound of satisfaction. "Good and strong, too. The way I like it."

Cindy smiled in relief. "I wasn't sure about how to use your little half pot," she admitted, "but the color of that first cup looked right. Rye taught me to make it strong enough to stand up to a high-country blizzard."

Trace grunted, suddenly less pleased with the coffee. He couldn't help wondering what other ways Rye had taught Cindy to please a man.

"He even taught me to like drinking it," Cindy continued as she poured water into the tiny pot perched over her mug.

She glanced over her shoulder, hoping that Trace had accepted the coffee as it had been meant—as a peace overture. A single look at his hard features told her that coffee hadn't been enough to get the job done. Unconsciously biting her lip, she turned back to her own coffee. By the time her cup was ready, Trace had finished his. When he put his mug aside to reach for tortillas, she substituted her fresh cup for his empty one and set up the coffeemaker once more.

In quiet horror Cindy watched while Trace tucked chunks of chocolate and chicken into a tortilla, rolled it up and ate it with every evidence of pleasure. She had meant the chocolate as dessert, not as part of the main course.

"It all ends up in the same place, princess," Trace said sardonically, accurately reading the look on her face.

Cindy's lips turned down at the nickname she had come to hate.

He smiled thinly. He knew that she didn't like being called princess. That was why he did it. That, and to remind himself that she was the spoiled child of wealth, even if she would rather die than admit it to him.

You know, you really should quit riding her with

the princess routine, Trace advised himself. *You're not supposed to know who she is, remember? As for you being angry because she doesn't trust you enough to tell you her real name—she'd be a fool if she went around announcing her wealth and you know it. South America has a reputation for being the kidnap capital of the world. That's why Invers was sweating bullets at the thought of having Big Eddy's daughter waltzing around the cloud forest looking for another ditzy, ritzy American woman.*

On the other hand, pointed out the devil's advocate that lived within Trace, *if Cindy hates the nickname princess so much, all she has to do is ask me not to use it. Just ask me. That's all. No big deal.*

Except to her.

And to me, Trace admitted silently. *If it's the last thing she does on this green earth, she'll ask me for something. Anything.*

And I'll give it to her, no matter what it is or who it costs.

With his coffee cup Trace drank a silent toast to his vow. Only after he had swallowed did it register on his mind that the formerly empty cup had been magically refilled. He looked at the mug and then at Cindy, who was just pouring a final measure of water through the tiny pot. He realized that she had given him her cup.

Maybe she drank some while I was cleaning up.

"You like this blend?" Trace asked, inhaling the fragrance rising from his mug.

"Tell you after I've had a sip," Cindy said,

blowing across the steaming surface of her coffee. "But if this is what I think it is, I love it."

Trace started to say something, then stopped. It gave him an odd feeling in the pit of his stomach to realize that she had given him two cups of coffee before she had taken so much as a taste for herself. That wasn't what he would have expected from a child of wealth, especially from one who was too proud to even ask him for the time of day.

But then, Cindy had been unexpected from the start, and in very uncomfortable ways.

"Wonderful," she murmured, closing her eyes as the taste of coffee spread through her in a fragrant, revitalizing wave. "Just as I remembered from my last birthday. Beans so mellow you could eat them."

"You're sure this is the same coffee?"

"Positive. I almost cried when I used up what Dad had sent me."

"Then your father must know somebody who knows Raul."

"Who?"

"Raul Almeda. This is his private blend, grown from his own coffee plants and given to his friends and business partners. Raul owns a vast hacienda up ahead that runs from the lowlands to the cloud forest." Very casually Trace added, "If Susan isn't at the next village, doubtless she'll be with Raul, her feet on an embroidered stool and servants hovering to grant her every wish."

"Sounds boring," Cindy retorted.

"Only to people who have been rich enough, for

long enough, to know what it's like. Most never get the chance to find out. But you wouldn't know about that, would you?"

"Would it make any difference if I did?"

Trace's mouth turned up at one corner in a smile that was as cold as his eyes. "I doubt it, princess. Money just doesn't get some jobs done, and they're nearly always the jobs worth doing."

Cindy made no response this time. What Trace had said was a razor truth that she had encountered too many times not to acknowledge it, and each time she confronted it the truth sliced deeper. Money simply couldn't buy the important things. It couldn't buy self-respect or intelligence or talent or real companionship or laughter or...love.

Love was most definitely one thing money could not buy. Nor could begging. Love was a gift freely given.

But nobody gave gifts to Big Eddy's daughter.

Chapter 8

Cindy watched Trace turn away from the natives he had been questioning. He reached the Rover in a few swift steps, slid in behind the wheel and slammed the door just as the overcast condensed into an odd, dense mist.

"Susan left a few days ago, just before the first hard storm," Trace said. "She was hitching a ride with one of Raul's workers."

Biting her lip, Cindy stared out the side window, not wanting to reveal her worry to Trace.

"Don't look so glum. Raul's *hacienda* is just a few hours down the road. When it started pouring, I'll bet they just made a run for one of the hunting cabins Raul has scattered up and down the mountainside.

They're fully stocked at all times for just such emergencies."

"Do they have phones?"

"The cabins? Hardly. Despite the greenery, princess, this isn't Central Park."

"Really? What an astonishing revelation," Cindy said before she could stop herself. She really did hate that nickname.

"It might be a revelation if you'd think about what it means instead of making smart remarks. No phones means no way to call and tell people you're all right. That's what the Andean cloud forest is all about. Lack of communication."

"Precisely. If something went wrong for her—"

"Quit borrowing trouble," Trace snarled, letting out the clutch and leaving the village behind. "We've got enough of our own without you hunting for more."

Before Cindy could ask what Trace meant, the swirling mist surrounding the Rover changed into true rain.

In the next hours Cindy came to understand rain and Trace Rawlings in a new way. She passed from nervousness to disbelief to admiration and finally to outright awe as she watched Trace negotiate the narrow, melting, liquefying road. She wouldn't have made it half a kilometer out of San Juan de Whatsis and she knew it. It took experience, strength, coordination and coolness to hold the slewing, sliding, slithering Rover to the course. Time after time Trace guided and bullied the vehicle through situations where Cindy knew she would have ended up sideways or topside down or hopelessly mired. Even if she had managed to extricate herself and the Rover, she knew she would have just ended up in trouble all over again a few yards down the road.

If you could call it a road. She no longer did. It was a pathway to hell; a slippery, sliding, greasy brown string unwinding endlessly downward beneath clinging slate veils and between blackish-green walls of vegetation that thrashed like souls in torment. Gray rain hammered down from the heavens without pause or purpose.

Cindy lost count of the times Trace dragged a winch cable into the forest, wrapped the cable around a suitable tree and yanked the Rover out of a mud hole. She lost track of the passage of time as well, and of distance, and of all directions except down.

Despite the rain and the wind, the air wasn't cold. It wasn't even cool. That made sense to Cindy in a crazy way. Hell, after all, was reputed to be warm, and she had no doubt that hell must be where they were headed, slithering endlessly downward, a descent that was underlined by the tropical heat of the air, a viscous warmth that deprived her of any temperature sense at all. Everything she touched seemed to hold the same amount of heat—the window, the upholstery, the rain, her own body.

Numbly Cindy watched as Trace got out in order to investigate a low spot in the road on foot. Being alone further increased her sense of unreality, of being suspended within the endless, elemental drumroll of water that was battering the Rover. Her body was tense and her throat ached out of a futile desire to somehow lighten Trace's burden. Without Trace she would have been helpless, and she knew it to the marrow of her bones.

The realization neither frightened nor irritated Cindy. It was simply a fact like rain or mud or a cloud forest that bowed to no man.

Even Trace Rawlings.

"That's it," he said flatly, climbing into the Rover and turning off the engine.

Cindy blinked as though coming out of a trance. "We're there?"

"If by 'there' you mean Raul's hacienda, no. If 'there' means where we're going to spend the rest of the storm, yes. There's no point in pushing anymore. At this rate we won't reach the *hacienda* before midnight. We'd make much better time going on foot."

"Oh." Cindy peered through the windshield, trying to see where they were. All she saw was rain. Not that it mattered. If Trace said they couldn't go any farther, then they couldn't, period.

"No argument?" he asked sardonically.

Cindy shook her head. "Frankly I don't see where you got the strength to go this far."

"That's easy enough. I didn't want to be trapped for the night with you in the Rover." Trace shrugged. "But here we are anyway."

"Trapped," she repeated, her mouth turning down.

If Cindy had had any doubt about how Trace regarded her, he had just removed it. He had driven for hours over impossible roads in the hope of avoiding the opportunity to spend the night with her again.

Trace saw the unhappy line of Cindy's mouth and said coldly, "Don't worry, I—"

"Yes, I know," she interrupted bitterly. "You won't stick your hand up my blouse while I'm asleep."

Don't bet anything important on it, princess. I want you like hell on fire. That's why I kept driving long after I knew it was a lost cause. I hoped I'd be too tired to get hard every time I looked at you.

It didn't work.

For the sake of his own pride, however, Trace kept his thoughts to himself. Besides, what woman would put up with a man who was covered with mud and smelled as if he had carried the Rover on his back for the past three hours? In fact, Trace was surprised Cindy hadn't complained about him once through the long afternoon. He could barely stand himself in the confines of the Rover.

"I'm going to take a shower," he said abruptly.

"What? Where?"

Trace's laugh was a bark of disbelief. "You've got to be kidding."

Cindy looked at the warm rain pouring down and understood. She watched while Trace stretched over the seat of the Rover and snagged his shaving kit. It was an easy reach for him because there was no backseat. As had been the case with the Jeep, the

Rover's rear seat had been taken out to make more room for carrying equipment and supplies.

After Trace vanished into the rain with a bar of soap in his hand, Cindy rolled down both front windows for ventilation. The rain blowing inside didn't worry her. Trace had been in and out of the Rover so often that everything that could get wet already was. She unclipped the cargo net, crawled over the seat back and began assembling ingredients for dinner.

Given the single burner and the impossibility of cooking outside, Cindy didn't try for anything elaborate. Fresh coffee was first on the list. While the water came to a boil she diced up a small tin of ham and added water to a packet of sliced freeze-dried potatoes. More water went into a mixture that purported to be freeze-dried carrots and peas. Another bar of chocolate turned up. She hid it, afraid that Trace would add it to the stew she was assembling. By the time Trace returned from his makeshift shower, Cindy had made a canteen of coffee, cooked the ham and vegetables together and steamed the remaining tortillas into a renewed flexibility.

"Here," she said, kneeling on the front seat and leaning over into the cargo area until she could grab a mug. Quickly she poured coffee from the canteen and handed the mug to Trace. "The rest of it will be ready in a few minutes."

Wordlessly Trace took the mug. He stared at the darkly reflective surface of the coffee as though he were looking into the future. It was safer than staring at Cindy. In the process of getting the food ready, she had gone close enough to the open windows for rain to dampen odd patches of her clothes. When she leaned over the seat, those wet spots stuck to the curves beneath. When she turned around and sat facing the windshield, her blouse clung to her nipples as though dampened by a lover's mouth.

With an inarticulate curse, Trace forced himself to think about something else. Anything else. Counting raindrops, for instance. Licking them from her body one by one…

"Ready?" Cindy asked.

Trace turned and gave her a smoldering green glance. With a sinking heart Cindy wondered if he would be in a better mood after he had eaten. Silently she handed him a plate of food. She knew it wasn't haute cuisine, but she thought it deserved better than the black scowl he gave it. For several minutes the only sound was that of the rain and the muffled scrape of tin spoons over tin plates.

"More coffee?" she asked finally.

Trace held out his mug. "Yes." Then, softly. "Thank you."

Startled, Cindy looked up from the canteen and smiled. "You're welcome, Trace."

Her smile and the sound of his name on her lips sent streamers of dark fire through Trace's body. Suddenly he knew he couldn't spend another moment in the Rover's enforced intimacy without making a very hard pass at Cindy. That didn't bother him as much as the angry realization that he didn't know what he would do if she turned him down.

And he had every expectation that she would do just that.

"Look," Cindy said, turning toward the window. "It's stopped raining. Well, almost. It's not raining nearly so much."

Trace's head turned. Cindy was right. As suddenly as the hard rain had begun, it had stopped. The end of the downpour was too late to do the road much good, however. Dark would come long before the low places had drained. There seemed to be no help for it—in the next few hours he would get the excruciating opportunity of discovering how long he could hold out before he made a fool of himself, or worse, with Cindy.

A pale flash against the dark green of the forest caught Trace's eye. Slowly he made out a series of blazes on the trunk of one of the bigger trees. Once he had spotted the first blaze he had no trouble at all deciphering the message Raul's workers had hacked with machetes into the tree's trunk. He and Cindy were at the edge of one of Raul's forestry experiments. A few hundred yards down the hill there should be a clear trail used by Raul's men. A few klicks up the trail—straight up—would be the spur road leading to the big house, the main Almeda residence.

And in that residence there would be more than enough rooms to separate two unexpected guests. Trace wouldn't have to see Cindy, much less be forced constantly to brush against her.

Trace finished off his coffee in a gulp. "As soon as you're done eating, we'll walk to Raul's house."

Cindy looked blank. "Walk?"

His eyes narrowed. "That's right, princess. Walk. It's a form of transportation often used by the peons of the world."

It took a considerable effort, but Cindy managed not to say anything more inflammatory than "Is it far?"

"A few klicks as the crow goes. Four or five times that by the road. We'll leave the luggage here. When the road dries out a bit, Raul's men will bring the Rover to the big house."

Without a word Cindy finished her coffee, gathered up the dirty dishes and pushed against the unlatched passenger door. Trace started to protest that she would get wet in the steady drizzle, then realized how foolish that would sound. She was going to get a lot wetter on the way to the big house.

It would make more sense to stay here, Trace told himself.

The hell it would, he snarled in silent, instant response. *I'd be all over her like hot rain.*

Like I said. It would make more sense to stay here.

The door of the Rover slammed behind Trace. Before Cindy could protest he had taken the dishes from her and shoved her purse into her hands. He fired the dishes into the back of the Rover, yanked his machete from the sheath at his waist and stalked toward the blazed tree, hoping that Raul's men had left some encroaching forest for him to hack up.

After a few moments Cindy followed Trace.

There was no path, but the walking wasn't too difficult at first. They were in one of the densely shaded, almost parklike areas of the cloud forest. The only thing she had to watch out for were tree roots and moss. By placing her feet carefully, but quickly, she could keep up with Trace. Barely.

Just as Cindy was congratulating herself on her previously unsuspected wilderness skills, her foot slipped on a mossy root and she sat down hard. Hoping that Trace hadn't noticed, she scrambled to her feet and wiped off her palms on her colorful pants, leaving the first of what would be many such smears.

Beyond the blazed tree a trail of sorts appeared. The footing varied between slick and impossible. Cindy found herself grabbing at branches and bark, bushes and drooping vines, anything to help her keep her balance on the narrow path. Most of the time she stayed upright. The rest of the time she gathered new marks for her clothes and body.

Mist closed in again, swathing everything in hushed moisture. Trace was too busy hacking at intrusive greenery to notice that Cindy was barely managing to keep up with him. He moved forward with the steady, rhythmic body motions of a strong man who was accustomed to the cloud forest's demands. From time to time he glanced over his shoulder to check on Cindy, but could see little more of her than a dark shape veiled in the mist of a grounded cloud.

Halfway up the very steep path he paused, looked

over his shoulder and saw no one. He called out and was answered by a muffled voice. He started to ask Cindy if the pace was too fast, then stopped himself. If he was going too fast, surely she would have the sense to say something. Wouldn't she?

Sure. Right after she finished teaching stubborn to a Missouri mule.

"Everything all right?" Trace asked, cursing himself even as he spoke.

"Just fine," Cindy said through gritted teeth as she pulled herself upright with the aid of the same tree root that had tripped her in the first place.

Trace hesitated, not liking the breathless quality of Cindy's voice. He checked his watch. If they were going to get to the big house by dark, they had to keep going.

"Let me know if you have to stop," Trace said.

Cindy made a sound that Trace took as a response. With a last look over his shoulder, he turned back to the trail that had only recently been hacked from the cloud forest's solid green body. Unconsciously he resumed the unhurried, unbroken rhythm of chop and walk, chop and walk, chop and walk. Trace made it look effortless, but the skill with which he moved through the dense forest was the result of hard experience and an even harder body.

Only when the new forest trail cut the spur road to the *hacienda* did Trace stop. As he stood quietly, breathing deeply and easily, he realized that he had fallen into a pace that might have been rewarding for him but almost certainly had been too hard on a proud princess.

"Cindy?"

No answer came back from the swirling streamers of cloud.

"Cindy!"

There was no response.

Even before the sound of his call was absorbed into the forest's silence, Trace was back on the narrow path, moving with doubled speed, cursing.

Cindy heard Trace coming toward her long before she saw him condense out of the gray-white mist swathing the steep, rough trail. The last thing she wanted was for Trace to find her sprawled out flat on her face, compliments of a tree root she would have sworn leaped up to grab her foot. Hurriedly she tried to claw her way to her feet, but succeeded only in losing her balance once more. Doggedly she pushed herself to her hands and knees.

Trace stopped and stared at the apparition that was kneeling before him in the narrow trail. Relief and anger warred for possession of his tongue. Anger won.

"What the hell do you think you're doing?" he demanded.

Cindy had no problem with conflicting emotions. Her peace overtures toward Trace had been singularly unsuccessful. That left war.

"Worshipping the ground you walk on," she retorted. "What the hell does it look like?"

Unfortunately for her intentions, Cindy sounded

more worn-out than sarcastic, and she knew it. She set her teeth and started to pull herself upright again, hating her own weakness, hating Trace for seeing it, hating herself for caring, for wanting to see something besides impatience and anger in Trace's eyes when he looked at her.

Trace hissed a curse through his teeth and reached out to help Cindy to her feet.

"Don't touch me."

Trace was close enough to see the utter fury of defeat in Cindy's black eyes. She was like a cornered animal turning on its tormentor. Pain lanced through him, drawing his face into bleak lines. He hadn't meant to do this to her. Why in the name of God couldn't she even open her mouth and ask him for what she needed?

"I'm not a bloody mind reader! Why didn't you ask me to slow down or stop?" Trace demanded harshly. And then his expression became even more grim as he heard his own question. "Dumb question, right? I keep forgetting. You'd rather die than ask a peon for the time of day. Better watch it, princess. You just might get your wish."

With a single quick motion Trace sheathed his machete. Another even quicker motion brought his hands around Cindy's upper arms. In an instant he had lifted her to her feet.

"Now, if you had *asked* me not to touch you, I wouldn't lay a finger on you," Trace said in a clipped voice. "But you didn't ask. You did what came naturally. You ordered. A princess to the marrow of your elegant bones. Would you like to ask this peon not to touch you? Nicely?"

The surge of rage that had come to Cindy when Trace had once again found her grubbing in the mud faded, leaving nothing behind but defeat. She turned her face away from him and said nothing.

"That's what I thought," Trace said, disgusted with her and with himself for caring that Cindy disliked him so much that she wouldn't ask him for anything, no matter how much she might need it. He pointed her toward the trail. "Walk. I'll be right behind you."

Cindy started up the trail. Three steps later she would have fallen flat had it not been for Trace's left hand closing around her upper arm in the instant after she slipped. He held her upright until her feet found stable footing once more. When she tripped again a few steps later, he grabbed her again. This time he didn't release her. On the steepest parts of the trail he shifted his grip to her bottom, boosting her along as she scrambled forward. When they came to the muddy spur road that led to the Almeda home, Trace moved up alongside Cindy so that his left hand could keep a firm grip on her right arm.

They were still walking that way when Raul and Susan found them.

Chapter 9

"Susan! Is it really you? Are you all right?" Cindy asked in a rush, hardly able to believe her eyes when she saw the stunning, cinnamon-haired woman sitting at ease in a Jeep.

"You just stole my lines," Susan said, looking at Cindy with real concern. "What in God's name happened to you? Did you have an accident?"

Cindy looked at her friend, who was immaculate in ice-blue silk that perfectly matched her gorgeous eyes. Then Cindy looked at herself. Her unstructured clothes had long since passed beyond the point of fashionable disarray. They were wet, ripped and stained by mud and vegetation to the point that their predominant color was an unappetizing greenish-brown.

Cindy started to explain what had happened but the words wedged in her throat. She had just caught a view of Trace from the corner of her eye. He was staring at Susan as though transfixed. It wasn't the first time Cindy had seen a man respond that way to Susan. It was the first time it had hurt, however.

"Ask Tarzan," Cindy said curtly.

"Tarzan?" Unerringly Susan's wide blue eyes turned toward Trace. "It does rather fit, doesn't it?"

Trace's smile was a scimitar curve in his hard face. "I told you Susan was all right, princess. Raul's very good with women. Aren't you, Raul?"

For the first time Cindy focused on the man sitting in the driver's seat of the Jeep. Her eyes widened fractionally. Raul's hair was silky blond. His skin was a rich, dark gold and his eyes were as black as her own. It was a startling combination, particularly when set against the bold, very masculine bone structure of his face.

Rather cynically Trace watched Cindy's reaction to Raul. She wouldn't be the first woman to fall at Raul's feet after taking one look. Nor would she be the last. That didn't mean that Trace had to enjoy watching it. Somehow he had thought Cindy would have better sense than to be knocked over by a man's looks. God knows she had managed to ignore his own looks without difficulty, and more than one woman had told Trace he was handsome. Not Cindy, though. Not by so much as a sideways glance. The only passion she showed when she looked at him was a desire to commit mayhem on his much stronger body.

"You must be Señor Almeda," Cindy said. "I'm Cindy Ryan, Susan's partner."

Raul's jet-black eyes widened as he looked at the rumpled, muddy, thoroughly disheveled creature in front of him. "It is a great pleasure, Señorita Ryan," he said. "Susan has told me much about you."

"I left out her enthusiasm for mud baths," Susan said, her eyes still disbelieving. Then she added, "You really are all right, aren't you?"

"Nothing a hot bath and a decent bed won't cure."

"But of course," Raul said instantly. "Please, get in the Jeep."

"Thought you'd never ask," Trace said dryly. Before Cindy could object, he picked her up and dumped her in the backseat of the open Jeep.

"We were just checking on the bridge over Orchid Ravine," Raul explained as he drove down the muddy road.

"And?" Trace asked.

"I would not want to attempt the bridge at the moment," Raul said carefully.

Trace grunted and flashed a jungle-green glance at Susan, who was smiling at Raul. Silently Trace conceded that if Cindy were watching him the way Susan was watching Raul, Trace wouldn't be in any hurry to rush his bridges back into civilization, either.

"Then it looks like you're stuck with us for a day or two," Trace said. "We walked overland on the new trail your men cut up the far side of Thousand Springs Divide."

"We? Señorita Ryan was with you?" Raul asked, startled.

"Every step of the way."

"La pobrecita," murmured Raul. "Poor little one. I am a man, yet I would not wish to make that walk with you."

Cindy smiled wanly. "Trace wasn't wild about the idea of having me underfoot, either."

Raul's laugh was low, husky, intimate. "I doubt that very much. My friend has never turned down the company of a charming and beautiful woman."

Just as Cindy found herself warming to the compliment, common sense intervened. At the moment she was about as beautiful as a handful of mud, and as charming, too.

"It is very kind of you to say so," Cindy murmured, "even though it's a gigantic whopper."

"What is this 'gigantic whopper'?" Raul asked.

"A big lie," Trace said succinctly.

Raul blinked, then laughed again. "Now I believe you are truly Cindy Ryan."

"Tongue like a wasp," Trace agreed.

"The hotter the sting, the sweeter the honey," Raul said, smiling with distinct masculine satisfaction.

Cindy bit her tongue and said nothing. Susan winked at her and began fishing for information with all the subtlety of an old, trusted friend.

"What are you doing out here? And how did you end up with Trace?"

"I came to find you. Trace is helping me."

"Why?"

"Because I'm paying him," Cindy retorted.

"Puh-leese," Susan said, calling upon the mist as her witness to Cindy's recalcitrance. "I meant why did you come after me? Didn't you get my note telling you my change of plans?"

"That was nearly two weeks ago. I was… worried."

Susan made a humming sound that managed to sound skeptical and musical at the same time. "Translated that means you left because Rye and Lisa were busy making another baby and Big Eddy was running around trying to buy studs for you again."

"Susan!" Cindy said, appalled.

"What? You know as well as I do that he offered the last hotshot a bonus if he got you pregnant. You see," Susan said kindly to Trace, "her father just recently figured out that a woman only needs a man to get pregnant. Marriage isn't necessary. Even more pertinent, if Cindy doesn't marry, her children will have her last name, which is also Big Eddy's. He was quite pleased by the discovery, because he wants a raft of grandchildren, and he's going to have them if he has to kill his own children trying. Do you blame Cindy for telling the old bulldozer to go to hell and running after me instead?"

"Oh, my God," Cindy said faintly, putting her face in her hands without regard for the bits of vegetation still clinging to her fingers.

Trace looked from Susan to Cindy. He picked over the information for the least incriminating parts.

"Rye and Lisa, huh? Is she the one who beat you to it?" Trace asked.

"To what? Pregnancy?" Susan asked when it became apparent that Cindy wasn't going to answer Trace. "There was no contest. Lisa and Rye wanted kids."

"And Cindy didn't?" Trace asked.

"She's old-fashioned. She wanted a husband first."

"What was wrong with Rye?"

"Same parents, that's what. He's her brother."

Trace digested that. "Oh."

"She sicced me on Rye once, but it was too late," Susan continued. "He'd already seen Lisa."

Raul smiled. "I can't imagine that would make a difference once he saw you, *corazon*."

"You haven't seen Lisa," Susan and Cindy said as one.

"She's small, delicate, has eyes the color of amethysts and natural platinum hair down to her hips," Susan continued, ticking off Lisa's attributes. "And innocent. God above, she was innocent! She'd been raised with the kind of tribes you only see in National Geographic specials."

"I should have sent Lisa after you," Cindy said softly. "Anyone who can make a wicked knife from an antler and a piece of glass would be right at home in the cloud forest. She would have been a help to Trace, not a burden."

"I am sure you were not a burden," Raul said instantly.

"You're very kind," Cindy said, closing her eyes. She smiled sadly. "I'm sure if it had been you doing the guiding, I wouldn't have felt like a burden. But I would have been a burden just the same."

Susan gave her friend a worried look, then glanced toward Trace. He looked back at her with opaque green eyes.

"You're just tired, Cinderella," Susan said gently, leaning over the seat and stroking Cindy's wet, tangled hair. "The world will look different after you're dry and clean and rested."

Cindy made a noise that could have been agreement, but from the down-turned line of her mouth, Trace doubted that she meant it. Frowning, Susan examined her friend's wan face and closed eyes before she turned around and stared out the windshield again.

A few minutes later the Jeep hit a bump. Cindy didn't open her eyes as a lock of her hair fell forward across her face. With gentle fingers Trace stroked the hair back behind her ear. When she didn't move at all, he realized that she had fallen asleep. Just as the Jeep hit another bump, he reached out and lifted her half across his lap. When she mumbled a question that was also a name, Trace knew what to say.

"Yes, it's Rye. Go to sleep, Cindy. Everything's all right."

Susan's head snapped around. Trace looked back at her with eyes that were as green and as impenetrable as the cloud forest itself. One big hand stroked Cindy's hair slowly, gently, while the other hand held her against his chest. Cindy murmured something and burrowed more deeply into Trace's arms.

After a moment Susan spoke.

"When her mother died, Cindy was just a kid. Rye used to hear her crying in the middle of the night. He'd go and hold her until she fell asleep again."

Trace's eyelids flinched but he said nothing.

"What did you do to her?" Susan asked flatly.

"Nothing major. I'm a lousy mind reader, so I tried to teach Cindy to ask for what she needs. That's all."

"That's all?" Susan's eyes widened into deep, faintly tilted pools of blue. "She never asks anyone for anything. Ever. Not me. Not God. Not even Rye. But she'll give you the heart from her body if she thinks you need it…or if you ask her for it," Susan added.

Trace's mouth curled into a thin, sardonic smile. "The only thing she'd willingly give me is a knife between the ribs."

"That doesn't sound like Cindy."

"Maybe you don't know her as well as you thought."

"And maybe I do," Susan retorted. "If you managed to get under Cindy's skin deep enough to get her angry, congratulations. No man has raised her temperature a quarter of a degree since a walking disaster called Jason came into her life. You would have gotten along fine with Jason."

Trace raised a single eyebrow in skeptical query.

"Like you," Susan said coolly, "Jason believed in

making Cindy beg for every little thing from a hamburger to a good-night kiss."

Have you ever had to beg? Well, I have and I'll never do it again.

"There is one hell of a difference between asking and begging," Trace said between his clenched teeth, as though it were Cindy rather than Susan he was trying to convince.

"Try explaining that to Cindy."

"I did."

"Didn't work, did it?"

"No."

"But you didn't give up, did you?" Susan continued icily, looking at Cindy's pale face, her skin drawn by fatigue even in sleep. "You just kept hammering away at her until you beat her down. Like I said. You and dear, sweet Jason have a lot in common."

"Corazon," murmured Raul. "Trace is not like that."

"Not to you, surely," Susan said. "You'd take his head off and make an orchid planter of it."

"You underestimate Trace," Raul said dryly. "And you misunderstand him, as well."

"Said the crocodile's brother to the curious little fish," Susan muttered in disgust. "The only reason a croc has a mouthful of teeth is so he can smile real pretty, right?"

Trace smiled.

Susan threw her hands up and didn't say anything else until the Jeep stopped in front of a stately, multistoried house that grew elegantly in the midst of the cloud forest. Cindy stirred. Reluctantly Trace eased her over onto the seat. Without waiting for anyone else to get out, he vaulted over the side of the vehicle. When a woman's broad, smiling face appeared at the front door, Trace called out in rapid Spanish mixed with hissing, harsh *indio* words. The big woman laughed and returned the bear hug Trace was giving her.

Susan sighed. "I take it that Trace is a friend of the family?"

"He is a member of the family," Raul corrected, smiling. "My cousin."

"Ah, the wonderful taste of raw foot in the mouth."

"I beg your pardon?"

"Never mind," Susan said, pushing a long strand of cinnamon hair aside. "I still think he was too hard on Cindy."

"So does he."

Susan looked startled. Before she could think of anything to say, Trace had returned.

"Tia says we can clean up and eat dinner here, but then I'm to take the Jeep and Cindy to my cabin."

Raul's eyebrows arched upward in an exact echo of Trace's dark ones. "You're not to sleep here?"

"No." Smiling, Trace switched to Spanish. "Tia wants you to have more time to get to know your… guest. Better watch it, cousin. Tia is already making up wedding lists in her mind."

An irritated expression darkened Raul's handsome features. Then he shrugged and answered in

Spanish. "As always, with Tia it is easier to be as the forest and bend beneath the wind, yes?"

"You always were more successful at bending than I was, *compadre*," agreed Trace. He leaned into the Jeep, lifted Cindy into his arms and switched to English. "Wake up, princess, or get kissed by a frog."

"That's not how the fairy tale went," Cindy complained sleepily, turning her face into Trace's neck.

He closed his eyes as he felt the accidental brush of her lips against his skin. It was all he could do to control a shudder of violent response.

"That's the thing about life," he said huskily. "It's always so damned unexpected."

For instance, he hadn't expected to be spending another night alone with Cindy. In fact, he'd dragged her up half a mountain just to avoid the prospect…only to find himself booked into the fragrant, hushed silence of the Cloud Cabin. One man. One woman. One bed.

"One hell of a mess," he muttered.

A night on the hard floor had never looked so unappealing.

Cindy looked from the inky wall of forest rising on either side of the Jeep to the black shadows thrown across Trace's face by the dashboard lights. Neither moon nor stars were visible overhead. Mist seethed in silver streamers through the bright shafts of illumination given off by the Jeep's headlights.

"It's not much farther," Trace said.

His tone was like the line of his mouth. Flat, hard,

unyielding. Cindy sighed. Apparently he was angry at not being allowed to stay at the big house.

"Don't blame Raul," she said hesitantly. "He couldn't have known we were coming, so he could hardly be expected to prepare rooms for us."

Trace gave Cindy a sardonic, sideways glance. "Rooms are always prepared. Raul just needed time to be alone with Susan. He wants her."

"So does every other man who's ever seen her."

"I don't."

"Yeah. Right. That's why you looked at her like you'd never seen a woman before." Suddenly Cindy laughed, remembering how she herself must have looked a few hours before. "Or not for a few days, anyway," she added.

Cindy looked down at herself and grimaced. She was wearing one of Susan's outfits. The fitted blouse and skirt looked smashing on Susan. Cindy, however, had more inches around the bust and hips than her willowy friend. The skirt fit in the waist and was the right length. The same could be said of the blouse. After that the only thing that could be said was that the outfit covered everything required by law.

In all, Cindy felt like a sausage stuffed into somebody else's skin. Every time she took a breath she was reminded of Susan's slender, elegant figure—and of her own, less-than-slender self.

"Fishing for compliments again?"

Cindy's bittersweet smile vanished. She didn't say another word, even when Trace stopped the Jeep long enough to put on its canvas top. The silence grew oppressive long before the Jeep's headlights picked out a small cabin tucked away just at the edge of darkness, bathed in mist and the warm silver rain that had just begun to fall. The sound of water running over the Jeep's canvas roof was soothing, almost caressing.

With a corner of her mind, Cindy wondered how Trace had known that it would rain before they reached the cabin. It was just one more of the many ways in which Trace had proven himself to be supremely at home in the cloud forest. And with each of those proofs Cindy herself had become more defensive, more determined to demonstrate to him that she wasn't simply a burden to be hauled through the wilderness like two piglets squealing in a burlap sack.

But she was a burden. It hurt to admit it, yet it was the simple truth.

Trace pulled up close to the cabin, switched to parking lights and turned off the Jeep's engine.

"In order to save a big scene when you walk into the cabin," Trace said in a clipped voice, "I'll tell you three things right now. One: there's only one bed. Two: you're sleeping in it. Three: I'll sleep on the floor or in the Jeep, whichever I decide is more comfortable."

Cindy tried to think of something to say. Nothing came to her but the intense, unhappy realization that Trace would spend a very uncomfortable night because of her.

"That isn't necessary," she said quietly. "We could share the bed. I know you don't want…that is, you wouldn't…"

"Stick my hand up your blouse?" Trace offered in a cold voice.

Cindy made a helpless gesture. She knew that she didn't appeal to Trace sexually, but she hadn't wanted to state it quite so baldly.

"Exactly," she said, taking a deep breath. "I know you don't want me so there's no reason not to…" Her voice died as she looked into Trace's narrowed, bleak eyes and the savage lines of his face. "I'm doing this badly, aren't I? Trace, I'm not strong enough to carry you off to a comfortable bed after you fall asleep." She took a deep breath and said quickly, "I never even thanked you for that, or for all the other things you've done for me. I should have thanked you. I wanted to. I just…couldn't. Thanking you would have meant admitting that I couldn't have done it by myself, that I needed you. And years ago I swore I would never need anyone again."

The sad, rueful sound of Cindy's laughter made Trace ache to take her in his arms, but he didn't move toward her. If he touched her he was afraid he wouldn't stop with simple comfort. He wanted her until he could barely breathe.

"But I do need you," Cindy continued. "I'm way out of my depth in the cloud forest. I need you the way I've never needed anyone. It's a terrible burden for you to be needed like that and it's very uncomfortable for me. I didn't handle it well at all. You see,

I've been fighting my own battles for years, and losing them when it came to that. Alone."

Cindy made another futile gesture with her hand and then rolled down the passenger window, wanting to touch the rain. The lights of the dashboard illuminated her face and turned the water drops washing over her outstretched hand into molten gold. She brought her fingertips to her lips and delicately licked up the glittering moisture.

"Sweet," she murmured absently. "Why does that always surprise me?"

Trace clenched his jaw against the raw sound of need that had risen in his throat. Her spontaneous, utterly natural sensuality was killing him and she didn't even know it.

"What I'm trying to say," Cindy continued, holding her hand out in the rain once more, watching warm liquid gather and run down her fingers, "is that I'm sorry I was a burden to you. On the way back to Quito, I promise I'll be better at staying out of your way. As for tonight, there's no good reason that we can't share the bed."

"You are dead wrong."

Trace's dark, gritty voice was so close that Cindy turned toward him in surprise.

"What?"

"This," he said harshly.

Trace's shoulders eclipsed the dashboard lights at the same instant that his powerful hands framed Cindy's face. His mouth came down hard over hers, twisting urgently, and his tongue shot into the warm feminine darkness he had been aching to penetrate. For a long minute that was just what he did, repeatedly, claiming her mouth with a searching intimacy that made her tremble. And then she realized that Trace was trembling, too.

Trace tore his mouth away from Cindy and exited the Jeep in one continuous, savage motion. The driver's door slammed so hard behind him that Cindy flinched. Hardly able to believe that she had been kissed with such intensity, she touched her hot, softly bruised lips with fingertips still wet from the rain. The moisture she licked up with the tip of her tongue tasted of more than raindrops. There was passion and hunger, heat and strength.

She tasted of Trace.

The realization made her eyes close as a tremor of hunger and delight radiated through her, changing her body in the space of a breath, two breaths, dark fire burning.

Rich yellow light flared within the small cabin, then dimmed as Trace put the glass chimney on the lantern. The doorway became a golden rectangle that was all but filled by Trace as he left the cabin. He stepped off the porch and walked around to the driver's side of the Jeep, heedless of the warmly falling rain that had dampened his hair and shoulders. He opened the door, turned the headlights completely off with an impatient flick of his hand and reached into the backseat. A single suitcase lay there. The suitcase was Raul's. The contents had been donated by Susan. Trace grabbed the suitcase as though he expected it to fight back, yanked it into the rain and slammed the door behind him again.

Eyes wide, Cindy watched every motion Trace made. There was none of the air of lazy, sensual humor about him that he had shown when he had kissed her in the washroom. There had been nothing languid or humorous at all about the way he had just kissed her. He had wanted her.

And he had trembled with that wanting.

The golden light spilling out of the cabin was eclipsed twice more as Trace went in, dumped the suitcase on the floor and went back out to the Jeep. He jerked open Cindy's door.

"Out," Trace said flatly.

Cindy opened her mouth.

"For your information, princess, I'm not any happier about wanting you than you are about needing me," he snarled. "So I'd advise you to get your fanny out of the Jeep and into the cabin and do it *now*."

Chapter 10

Cindy was too surprised to speak, much less to move. Before she could gather her wits, Trace leaned in, put one arm under her knees and the other behind her back and lifted her out of the Jeep.

"You're a slow learner, aren't you?" he said roughly.

With no more warning than that, Trace caught Cindy's mouth fiercely beneath his own and tasted the soft depths behind her lips once more. This time his passion didn't catch her by surprise. Her arms slid around his hard neck as she returned the deep kiss with a hunger that equaled his. Trace groaned and his arms tightened until Cindy couldn't breathe. She didn't object. She didn't even notice. Trace was filling her senses to the point that there was no room for anything else. She gloried in the feeling, wanting nothing else, only him.

When Trace finally lifted his mouth he was breathing raggedly, trembling, holding Cindy with bruising strength while warm rain fell over both of them. She made an inarticulate sound and turned her face up into the rain, searching blindly for Trace's mouth once more.

"Cindy," he said, then groaned when he saw that light from the doorway had turned the raindrops on her lips into transparent golden gems. "My God, princess, do you know what you're promising me?"

This time Cindy didn't object to being called princess. She knew from the raw need she heard in Trace's voice and saw in his expression that he wasn't baiting her. She whispered his name as she licked raindrops from his chin and the line of his jaw. When the tip of her tongue stroked the corners of his lips, he shivered and made a sound deep in his throat. Her arms tightened around his neck, pulling her closer to his mouth. She was hungry for the heat and taste of his kiss, the sensuous consummation of his tongue mingling with hers while warm rain bathed their bodies.

Cindy didn't know the exact instant when Trace shifted her in his arms, partially releasing her so that her legs and torso flowed down his powerful body. She only knew that suddenly his hands were free to caress the rounded contours of her hips, turning her knees to water, making her as boneless as the falling rain. His long fingers kneaded her buttocks and rocked her against the heated cradle of his thighs, plainly revealing to her the extent of his own arousal.

The honesty of Trace's hunger completely undid Cindy. She had never known anything like it from a man. She gave a husky little cry and moved sinuously against Trace, slowly stroking his body with her own, making the sweet, dark fire within both of them blaze higher. Trace's fingers raked down the back of her thighs, parting them even as he lifted her and held her pressed intimately against the blunt ridge of flesh that was proof of his nearly uncontrollable desire for her. His hips moved once, hard, as though he were plunging into her, and then he moved very deliberately, shaking, listening to her shattered breaths, feeling her tremble wildly as she tried to get even closer to him.

At that instant Trace knew Cindy wanted him as much as he wanted her—and he was so hungry for her that he thought he would die of it. He whispered her name again and again between hard, deep kisses, wanting all of her, wanting to be sheathed within her satin body until she burned out of control, showering both of them with a blazing, incandescent release.

But not yet. Not here. Not this instant.

Now that Trace knew Cindy wanted him too much to refuse him, he was able to control his own violent need. He wanted to share much more with her than a fast tumble in the rain. He needed to know every bit of her skin, to taste her wild hunger, to absorb her into himself. Only then could he begin to ease the raging hunger that had consumed him from the first moment he had sensed the untouched woman smoldering beneath Cindy's aloof exterior.

Reluctantly Trace let Cindy slide down his body until she was standing once more on the soft, moss-covered floor of the cloud forest. She swayed uncertainly, barely able to support herself. Not understanding why he had let go of her, clinging to his hard, bare forearms for balance, she watched him with dazed eyes.

"Trace?" Cindy managed to whisper. "Don't you want—"

The question ended in a husky cry when Trace's hands moved over Cindy's rain-slicked blouse, caressing the nipples that had hardened into crowns beneath wet, clinging cloth.

"Oh, yes, I *want,*" Trace said, his voice deep and as dark as Cindy's eyes. "I want you until I'm crazy with it. I want things with you I've only imagined before, and I want things I've never imagined until right now. You make me wild," he said, shuddering as he fought to control the passion that was burning in the very marrow of his bones, burning through the self-discipline he had always taken for granted.

But no more. Through her he had discovered fierce, nearly uncontrollable currents deep within himself, a need to be one with her that was as old as the cloud forest and as new as each breath he took.

Slowly Trace lifted Cindy, bringing her breasts level with his open mouth. With breathtaking care he bit the tip of first one breast and then the other before he returned to the first nipple, drawing it into the hungry, hot depths of his mouth. Wave after wave of sensation burst through Cindy until she felt as though she were dissolving in hot rain, spinning away, burning as invisible streamers of fire seethed through her.

The sound of Cindy's low, broken moan was the sweetest music Trace had ever heard. His fingers caressed her other breast, drawing more of the husky music from Cindy's lips. He lowered her to the ground once more.

Without lifting his mouth from her breast he began unbuttoning her blouse, working up from the taut navel he longed to kiss. When the buttons parted between her full breasts he ran his tongue over her cloth-covered nipple once more before his mouth released her by degrees, biting gently while the whisper of raindrops absorbed her shivering cries.

Finally Trace drew both hands upward from Cindy's waist until they rested in the warm, deep valley between her breasts. Slowly he spread his fingers wide, peeling the wet blouse away from her body until she wore nothing but rain turned golden by the lantern light. Transparent drops fell onto her high, full breasts and gathered on the twin pink crowns.

He had never seen anything to equal her beauty. His hands trembled as he took the warm weight of her onto his palms. With a murmured, reverent word, he sank to his knees and licked the raindrops from her naked breasts.

Cindy saw Trace's lips part, saw the pale flash of his teeth and then felt the piercing sweetness of his mouth cherishing her. Wave after wave of pleasure washed through her, making her sway. Instinctively she braced herself against her lover's powerful body, holding his head to her breasts with a primitive, fierce pleasure.

Trace's hands shaped Cindy's spine, her hips, her thighs, her calves, kneading and caressing repeatedly, sensitizing her flesh with each sweep of skin over skin. The last time his hands stroked down the length of her body, every bit of her clothing came away and pooled around her ankles. The feeling of warm rain gliding over her skin so intimately was indescribable. She started to say something, but her breath and her thoughts scattered when one of Trace's hands slid up between her legs until he could go no higher.

"Open for me, princess," he whispered, biting gently at Cindy's breasts and belly, caressing her with his tongue, his touches as warm and soft as the rain laving her. "I won't hurt you. I just want to touch you. That's all. Just…touch."

With a stifled cry Cindy kicked free of the clothes that were swathing her ankles. Then she stood trembling, open to the rain and to the sensual caresses of the man who knelt at her feet.

Gently, inevitably, Trace's fingertips combed through the thick triangle of midnight hair until he could trace Cindy's layered softness. He cherished her with exquisite care, memorizing her with repeated gliding touches until he knew her better than she knew herself. She said a broken word that could have been his name, but the word was lost in the husky sound of triumph and need Trace made as he slowly penetrated the hot secrets of her body. When he could go no deeper he withdrew as slowly as he had entered, leaving her empty and trembling.

"Trace," she whispered. "Trace, I..."

Cindy's words became a low moan as his caress took her slowly once more. She shivered with each movement of his hand, each tender penetration and gliding withdrawal, tension gathering within her until it burst sweetly, surprising her even as it drenched her in pleasure. Her trembling legs gave way. Slowly she sank down onto the moss-clothed ground until she was kneeling before Trace, bracing herself on his broad shoulders. He smiled darkly and licked the rain from her lips while he stole into her body once more, caressing her, savoring her exquisite softness, absorbing her intimate shivering as her body changed in anticipation of the much deeper sharing to come.

Cindy clung to Trace with her lips and her body while pleasure washed through her to him. He clenched against a tearing shaft of need as he felt her abandoned response to his caresses. He wanted her until it was agony not to take her. He burned to tear off his clothes and sheath himself inside her with a single hot thrust of his body; but despite the repeated, secret rain of her pleasure, she still was so tight to his touch that he was afraid she wasn't ready to accept him.

And he wanted—needed—to be certain of her pleasure. Since they had met she had suffered too much because of his miscalculations. When he finally slid into her clinging heat, there must be no question that whatever cries came from her sweet lips would tell him of ecstasy, not pain.

Trace's hand moved until his thumb could tease the velvet nub hidden within Cindy's softness. Her eyes closed and her head tilted back helplessly as pleasure splintered through her in shivering waves of heat. Her fingers dug into his shoulders and she arched toward him, her body drawn so tightly by need that she couldn't even form the words to tell him that he must take her or she would die.

Trace understood, yet he did not give Cindy what she was crying for. Instead he slid one powerful arm around her waist, supporting her while his caresses took from her the ability to hold herself upright. Eyes half closed, smiling despite his own violent need, he absorbed her sweet cries, wishing he could drink her essence as well, wanting to take her into himself so completely that he would never again feel the emptiness of being separate from her.

After drawing a final, helpless cry from Cindy, Trace caught her mouth beneath his own. Gently he brought her back to herself, stroking her without demand, holding her, kissing her repeatedly, lightly. The heat and taste of him made her sigh with pleasure. Slowly her hands began exploring the broad shoulders and strong arms that had supported her while sweet fire had consumed her. She had never known pleasure such as he had just given to her so unselfishly. She hadn't even known such feelings were possible.

"You're…" Cindy shivered and looked at the golden light and black shadows lying across Trace's face. "There aren't any words," she said huskily. "Masculine. Hot. Powerful. All true, but not the *truth*. I don't know how to describe you except, perhaps, this…."

Slender hands framed Trace's cheeks. Soft lips brushed his mouth again and then again. The moist tip of Cindy's tongue traced the sensitive outline of his lips and dipped hotly into his mouth, withdrawing before he could even react. Her teeth closed lovingly on his lower lip, holding it captive for her caressing tongue. He groaned her name and tightened his arms around her as though to hold her still for the kind of kiss he suddenly, desperately needed. Her fingers spread wide across his chest, but not in an attempt to push him away. She kneaded his flesh with an open appreciation of his hard body that was as exciting as her tongue teasing him.

Hungrily Trace wrapped his fingers around Cindy's head and took all of her mouth, consuming her with deep, hot strokes of his tongue, feeling her instant, utterly honest response. Her hands moved over his chest, tugging at the buttons on his shirt until suddenly it came apart. Her fingers tangled hungrily in the thick, damp mat of hair that she had wanted to touch since the first time she had seen the tempting thatch curling up from his open collar. She could not touch him enough. Biting softly, tugging, tasting, her hands and mouth roamed over the masculine territory she had uncovered.

With Cindy's help Trace shrugged his shirt aside, letting it fall heedlessly to the ground. Her palms slicked across his wet shoulders and down his arms to his fingertips, then back up again until her fingers curled into the fine hair beneath his arms. She made a murmurous sound of pleasure and stroked gently, savoring the unexpected softness concealed on such a hard masculine body.

Trace's breath caught and stayed as a thick wedge in his throat. He hadn't known how sensitive he could be, nor how arousing it could feel to have a woman slowly, tenderly devouring him. The feel of Cindy's lips and hot tongue nuzzling down his neck, her teeth biting in exciting counterpoint, her breath caressing him in soft bursts of heat—everything about her open enjoyment of his body set Trace afire. When her tongue found one of the tight, small nipples hidden beneath his chest hair, he shuddered and dragged at breath, unable to get enough oxygen to feed the searing currents of pleasure and hunger coursing through his body. He tried to stifle a groan when she circled his nipple with her tongue and then caressed him with the changing pressures of her mouth. He couldn't bear any more without crying out for her to stop, yet he would have died if she'd stopped.

"Cindy," Trace said finally, his voice hoarse. "You are killing me so sweetly…."

In answer her hands kneaded down his muscular

torso to his waist. Turned back by cloth, Cindy's fingers hesitated, then dipped down inside the waistband. Trace sucked in air with a soft ripping sound that was echoed an instant later as his zipper was drawn down by her warm, wet fingers. Her right hand slid inside his slacks, finding him unerringly, rubbing over his rigid male flesh with her palm, loving his heat and the knowledge that it was she who had made him so swollen and hard.

Trace bit off a curse and a plea as Cindy caressed him, moaning even as he did. Finally he caught her hand with his own, trying to stop her, but he couldn't bring himself to remove the sweet pressure of her palm from his throbbing body. He permitted himself to move his hips once, very slowly, letting her know his full length, feeling a groan wrenched from his throat when her fingernails raked lightly, devastatingly over the cloth that still covered his erect flesh.

"Stop," Trace said hoarsely, moving against Cindy in frank contradiction of his own command. "Oh, baby, stop."

"I can't," Cindy admitted, her voice trembling. "Trace, I've never wanted to touch a man before. I've never wanted…this."

Cindy's hand eased away from captivity and slid inside Trace's briefs. The instant their bare skin met, Trace stiffened and shuddered as though lightning were coursing softly, hotly, wildly through him. He could no more have prevented the slow surge of his hips as he gave himself to her than the warm rain could have prevented itself from falling into the waiting forest.

"Cindy," Trace whispered, holding her hand pressed tightly against him, trying not to move, failing, wanting to die of the pleasure her words and touch had given him. "Cindy, I need you so much I can't even…" His words became a groan as her fingers curled around him, holding him boldly captive, learning his masculine textures in the same way he had learned the secret feminine contours of her desire.

"If you want me, take me," Cindy finally murmured, biting a hard ridge of muscle on Trace's chest.

"Not here. Not now. Not in the rain."

"Yes, here. Now. In the rain." Her lips sucked lightly on Trace's biceps, his shoulder, his neck, his dark, sexy smile. She smiled at him in return. "Did you know that rain tastes like wine when I drink it from your skin?"

Trace's whole body jerked with the lightning stroke of pleasure that raced through him at her words. When she lifted her head he was watching her, his eyes heavy lidded, glittering in the golden light, and she knew that he was going to take her there, right there, with the warm rain bathing their naked bodies.

"Undress me," Trace said almost roughly, biting Cindy's lips, making her moan. He felt her palms on his skin, sliding beneath his briefs, beginning to uncover him. "Wait," he said through clenched teeth, half laughing, half groaning. "If you don't start with my boots, I swear to God I'll still be wearing them when I take you."

Cindy's hands hesitated. She looked up at Trace with hunger and laughter and curiosity in her eyes. "Would you like that?"

Trace smiled down at Cindy as he ran his fingertip over one of her nipples, lifted his hand to his lips and licked up the drops of water he had taken from her tightly drawn crest. "I'd rather be like you, princess, as naked as the rain. But if you want me wearing jungle boots, I sure as hell won't argue the point. I'll take you any way I can get you."

Cindy drew in a deep, ragged breath and brought her hand slowly out of Trace's clothes, caressing him lovingly even in the act of withdrawing her touch. "None of my fantasies involve men wearing jungle boots," she admitted, her voice husky, breathless.

"What do they involve?"

"My fantasies?"

"Yes," he whispered.

"Being wanted for myself. Just me."

"That's all?"

"It's the world, Trace."

"Then I give it you," he said softly against Cindy's lips, kissing her slowly, deeply. "I want you until I can't stand up. You, Cindy. Just you." He bit her lips with tender care, making her shiver and reach hungrily for him. He caught her seeking tongue between his teeth and raked the moist flesh very gently, savoring her tiny whimpers of pleasure. "I want you until it's like dying not to have you. But before I slide into that sweet body of yours, you'll be wanting me in the same way. I swear it."

Slowly Trace released Cindy. He sat and began unlacing his right boot. She went to work on the other one, making little progress because every time she looked up the long length of his legs to his unfastened pants and naked chest her fingers shook so much they were all but useless. After a few moments she simply gave up and stared at him, lost in wondering enjoyment of his powerful body.

When Cindy's hands went completely still, Trace glanced at her, saw her looking at him with frankly sensual approval, and asked himself almost wildly how he was going to keep his hands off her long enough to get undressed.

"Close your eyes, princess," Trace said huskily, kicking off one boot and reaching for the other.

"Why?" she said, startled out of her reverie. "Are you shy?"

"Not likely," he said, his voice caught between laughter and raw passion. "But I'll never get this boot off if you keep looking at me like you can't decide whether I'd taste better with ketchup or mustard. The way you lick your lips is distracting and sexy as hell."

There was an instant of silence before Cindy's laughter rippled in musical counterpart to the rain. Still smiling she closed her eyes and began patting air and raindrops until she found Trace's single booted foot. Getting in the way more than she helped, tangling her fingers with his, she loosened laces until together the two of them managed to tug off Trace's remaining boot. Going only by touch from his naked feet to his clothed knees, her hands worked their warm way up his legs.

"I've never done this with my eyes closed," Cindy said, searching blindly, caressingly, slowly, heading in the general direction of the waistband of Trace's pants. "Or open, either," she added absently, kneading the clenched power of his calves, his thighs, testing the strength and resilience of his muscles. "You're very strong." She heard her own words and laughed softly. "That's like saying rain is wet. Of course rain is wet and Trace Rawlings is strong. It's just that I've never felt...and you're so..."

Cindy's voice trailed off into the sound of raindrops falling as her hands caressed slowly higher. Somehow Trace had managed to peel his remaining clothes down over his hips while Cindy explored her way up his legs. Now he watched, frozen, while her slender fingers progressed upward toward his naked, rain-slicked flesh. He felt as though he were being drawn on a rack. When he could bear it no longer, he twisted suddenly, kicking free of the last of his clothing.

"Trace?" Cindy asked.

He watched the widening of her eyes, the parting of her lips, and her fingers reaching toward him, trembling. Suddenly she became motionless and looked only at his eyes.

"Trace?" she whispered.

"Whatever you want, princess," he said huskily.

She smiled almost wistfully. "And here I am without a lick of mustard or ketchup," she murmured.

Trace laughed until Cindy's palms stroked all the way up his thighs and her thumbs traced the deep creases where his legs joined his powerful torso. Then his laughter became a hoarse groan. She jerked her hands away.

"Oh, Trace, I'm sorry! I didn't mean to hurt you!"

At first Trace couldn't believe he had heard Cindy correctly. A single look at her downcast face told him that she had meant every word. The memory of her tight satin depths returned to him. Although there had been no virginal barrier to his searching caresses, it was clear to him now that whatever Cindy's past experience with men might have been, it had been long ago and not terribly illuminating.

"You didn't hurt me," Trace said, his voice gentle and rough at the same time. He took Cindy's hands in his own and pulled them back up his thighs. "It just felt so good that I…ahhh," he groaned, "*yes*, like that, just like that…again, princess. Just once more," he groaned, "then…no more, please, no…"

"You're so hot," Cindy whispered, feeling Trace's vitality radiate through her encircling hands as she caressed him wonderingly, savoring his unexpected response, sensing more than the slick heat of rain on her fingers.

Shuddering with pleasure, Trace gently, inexorably freed himself from the sensual captivity of Cindy's hands. Slowly he lifted her until she was astride his thighs. Raindrops and the lantern light falling through the cabin's open door gilded her breasts and the subtle curve of her stomach and made a shimmering mystery of the lush black cloud nestled between her thighs. He tangled his fingers in that cloud slowly, searchingly, rediscovering the depth of her softness and the hot pleasures of her secret, sensual rain. When he finally withdrew she whimpered deep in her throat.

"Did that hurt?" Trace asked, already knowing the answer, wanting Cindy to know it, too.

"Only when you stopped." Cindy's eyes opened and focused on the harshly drawn lines of her lover's face. "Don't stop, Trace," she breathed. Then she saw the rain glistening on his lips and added huskily, "And a kiss…your taste…I love the taste of you."

Trace's hands were trembling when he pulled Cindy down to him. Even as his tongue thrust between her lips, the taut peaks of her breasts rubbed against the mat of hair covering his chest, sending sensations twisting wildly through her. She moaned into his mouth, tasting him, wanting him, shaking with her wanting. When his hand slid between their bodies and captured one nipple, rolling it, tugging on it, she felt fire radiate out from the pit of her stomach. Instinctively her hips moved, caressing him even as she searched for a way to ease the hungry aching between her legs.

Trace knew what Cindy wanted. He wanted it,

too, wanted it the same way she did, shaking with the wanting. Suddenly his palms slicked over her hips and down the back of her legs. Long, powerful fingers bit sensually into the soft flesh high on the inside of her thighs, easing them farther and farther apart while his mouth mated rhythmically with hers and his tongue promised her pleasures she had never imagined. With his teasing fingertips he encouraged her to abandon all hesitation, arousing her until she wept and opened herself to him and to the hot rain washing over her violently sensitive skin.

When Cindy felt the first blunt probing of his flesh she gasped. Trace caressed her slowly, outlining her, learning her once more, letting her know his own textures, teaching her that for all his hard strength he could be deliciously smooth, like satin stretched over throbbing heat. For long moments he teased her, preparing her with tiny penetrations and withdrawals until she moaned brokenly and moved her hips, instinctively trying to capture more of him.

"Easy, princess," Trace said, his voice soft despite the cruel need that made his body clench as though he were being tortured. Once again he eased into the outer edges of her feminine warmth, parting her delicately, withdrawing, returning. "We're going to take it slowly...sweetly...slowly...."

"Trace," Cindy said raggedly, shivering, wild for more of him yet not experienced enough to know how to manage it. "Now? Like this?"

"Oh, yes. Just like...*this*. You're so tight, so sleek. Slowly, baby, slow..." Trace groaned against her lips. "You're beautiful, Cindy…hot…perfect. Don't let me hurt you," he said raggedly, pressing deeper, feeling her trembling response as though it were his own. "Am I…hurting you?"

Cindy tried to answer but she could not. The slow consummation was taking her breath, her voice, her mind, her soul. She tried to tell Trace how exquisite it felt to be filled so tenderly, so carefully, so completely, but speech was impossible for her. She shivered repeatedly as rings of pleasure expanded up from their joined bodies and burst, drenching her in sweetness and heat.

Trace felt each hidden quivering of her satin flesh, each secret rain of pleasure easing his way. The unexpected, deep intimacy of the sharing took him right up to the edge of his self-control, wrenching a groan from him, unraveling his voice and his breath, unraveling him.

"Dark…fire," Trace groaned, kissing Cindy between each word, biting her tenderly, pressing farther into her with each caress, each word. "So hot…so…deep. Ahh, love, I…"

And then Trace could say no more. He was fully sheathed within Cindy, held tightly, completely, and they were sharing every fragmented breath, every soft groan, hot rain sliding over them, joining their bodies in an incandescent intimacy that was so intense he didn't know if he would survive it.

Cindy felt the shudder that took Trace even as he moved within her. In the wake of his movement, exquisite sensations radiated through her, overwhelm-

ing her. She moaned and moved in instinctive counterpoint to Trace, redoubling the advance and retreat
of his hard flesh within her, crying softly as ecstasy
stole through her again and again, dark fire
blooming, lush flames climbing higher, consuming
her until she called out with something close to fear.

Despite his own violent need, Trace heard Cindy
and went utterly still. His hands shook as he threaded
his fingers through her wet hair, lifting her head
from his chest until he could look into her eyes. Her
face was streaked with tears and rain, her eyes were
wide, nearly wild, and her mouth was swollen by the
passionate kisses she had given and taken.

"Am I hurting you?" Trace asked, his voice ragged.

Cindy's head moved in a slow negative that made
her breasts stir over Trace's hot, wet skin. "It felt so
good…incredible…and then almost…frightening."

"Frightening? How?"

"I don't…I can't…" Her voice frayed. "When
you move…when I feel you inside me…" She
shivered and cried out softly as echoes of ecstasy
stirred within her, urging her to give herself to her
lover once more. "It's the sweetest kind of burning,"
she whispered, "and I'm being consumed by it, each
breath I take, each time you…"

"Do this?" Trace asked, measuring himself
slowly within Cindy, smiling darkly when she
moaned her pleasure.

"Yes," she said shakily, closing her eyes. "Oh,
yes, Trace."

"That's how I want you to feel," he whispered,

easing his hands from Cindy's hair, finding and caressing her breasts, rubbing her nipples until she moaned and he felt again the melting heat of her pleasure as she tightened around him. "I feel the same way when you move. Look at me, Cindy."

Her eyes opened slowly, heavy lidded and almost wild with a combination of passion and hesitation. "Do you really feel like I do?" she asked.

Trace moved again inside her, retreating and returning with excruciating care, pleasuring both of them until they trembled.

"Yes, I feel it. I'm in you so deep and you take me so perfectly…you're in me, too," he said in a gritty voice, sliding into Cindy slowly, feeling her move with him again, wanting to drown in the wild, honeyed rain of her passion. "That's where the sweetness comes, and the fear," he said.

He watched her expression change as ecstasy consumed her softly with each of his motions within her. Seeing his body transforming her excited him almost beyond bearing.

"I've never been this close to anyone before," he said almost roughly, shaking with the restraint he was imposing on himself. "You're burning me so softly, so hotly, it's like dying. Move with me princess. Please. Tell me that it's good for you…." Words died as a low groan was dragged from Trace by the gliding motion of Cindy's hips. "Yes," he said deeply. "Yes, like that. Come with me, love. I need you…with me."

Trace's words and his hands and his heat dissolved all of Cindy's fears. When his fingers closed lovingly around her nipples, tugging at them, hot streamers of sensation overwhelmed her. She arched helplessly into the caress, sliding over him, making both of them cry out with the pleasure they were sharing. Heat welled up within her once more, a shimmering need that could no longer be denied. He thrust deeply into her, taking everything she had to give, giving everything he had in return.

Wonder shivered in Cindy's voice as rapture gently convulsed her, stealing through her body again and again, consuming her. Trace heard the rippling cries of her completion even as he felt the sweet contractions sweeping through her. His own release burst from him, more piercing with each deep pulse, ecstasy pouring through him until he thought there could be no more…yet still the pulses continued through him until he arched like a drawn bow and cried out hoarsely, giving himself to her as he had never given himself to anything, even the hushed mystery of cloud forest and rain.

Chapter 11

Cindy slept long after dawn filled the cabin with a diffuse silver-gold light. She awoke for only an instant when Trace eased from the bed. As soon as he brushed her lips with love words and soft reassurances she slept again. He smiled down at her while he drew the sheet up over her breasts. The temptation to lie down next to her and make love to her in the full light of day was almost overwhelming. All that kept him from giving in were the pale lavender shadows that lay beneath Cindy's eyes, shadows that silently announced her need for more sleep.

Trace lifted his hands carefully from the sheet and turned away from Cindy. He knew if he kept on looking at her, he would touch her. If he touched her, he would make love to her. If he made love to her, he would take her again and again until he lacked the strength even to raise his head, for she was both a wild sweetness in his soul and a dark fire burning in his blood.

Just the thought of joining his body to hers once more made breath hiss between Trace's teeth. Blood pumped through him suddenly, hotly, filling him until he ached. He had never known a lover who suited him half so well. There were so many things he wanted to share with her, so many ways two people could enjoy one another. He wanted them all with her, every one of them, but most of all he wanted to watch her while he pleasured her, to see her skin flush with passion, to taste her, to feel her give herself to him over and over again, sensual fire burning through all inhibitions, all differences, fire burning until nothing remained but two lovers joined all the way to their souls.

If I don't get the hell out of this cabin, I'm going to pull down that sheet and slide into her before she's even awake, before she even knows if she wants me.

And then Trace caught a glimpse of himself in the mirror—stained khaki shirt and pants, beaten-up jungle boots, heavy stubble making his jaw even more square, his dark hair combed by nothing but sleep and Cindy's fingers. He looked rough, primitive, fully suited to the untamed land surrounding him.

Will my princess want me now, in daylight, when she can see so clearly what a peon her lover is?

Frowning, Trace turned away from the mirror and

tried to shake off the feelings of rootlessness and worthlessness that had once defined his life. He and Raul were related, but only because Raul's uncle had felt a sense of responsibility toward a wild American rose whose child probably had not been his. Megan Rawlings had died weeks after giving birth to Trace. Though her passport proclaimed that she had been American, no family could be found in the United States. There was no one to take in the motherless baby.

Finally a priest had picked up Trace and carried him to the Almeda *hacienda*. Once there he had calmly announced that God had answered Esteban Almeda's prayers. A son had been born. Esteban's barren wife had wept, crossed herself and accepted her husband's purported child into her arms and her life with the sweetness of a true angel. Yet despite Maria's love and Esteban's pride in having finally attained a son, Trace had grown up knowing in his soul that he didn't belong. He wasn't a true Almeda. The Almedas were the aristocracy of Ecuador, and he was the bastard child of an American woman who had had neither family nor husband to call her own.

Trace had grown up half in the United States and half in the Andes he loved so well. It had taken him decades of hard, dangerous living before he had accepted his own worth as a human being. It had been many years since he had felt himself less than the equal of any man solely on the basis of family background or personal wealth.

Yet he felt inadequate today. Cindy had given

him so much, surrendering her fears and herself to him, trusting him with her lovely, responsive body…and there was nothing he could give to her in return that wasn't already hers by birth.

Cynthia Edwinna Ryan McCall and a man whose only birthright is a hard body and a skull to match. What a pair to draw to. It's so funny it hurts.

Shutting the cabin door softly behind himself, Trace stepped out into the brilliant mist that permeated and defined the cloud forest. The rain had stopped sometime during the night, leaving behind little evidence of the storm. Only the places where man had carved out roads or fields showed the results of last night's rain in swaths of mud and puddles. The untouched forest took in moisture like an immense, living sponge. Later when the true monsoon rains came, even the forest's capacity to absorb water would be exceeded and the rivers would run brown, but for now the streams were still clear and sweet, gleaming like polished crystal in the diffuse light.

Trace found a nearly invisible trail leading down into the huge, steep ravine that lay just beyond the cabin. He had discovered the twisting, rugged trail years before. It led to a series of waterfalls and pools that were visited only by mist and wild animals. There orchid plants thrived in lush profusion, their extraordinary flowers swaying gracefully in the silence. The orchid garden was a secret place, a hushed landscape where time didn't exist. Trace had gone there often during his wildest years, when he had fought against everything—and himself most of all.

The trail hadn't changed. It was still narrow, easily lost, overgrown, infused with mist. Even so Trace rarely wielded the machete that hung at his belt. He didn't want to make a clear path for any man to use. He wanted the place of orchids and silence to remain as he had found it. Unknown.

He had never taken a single orchid from there, though he knew that even a thousand flowers would not have been missed from the massed magnificence of the ravine's garden. It was simply that there had never been a good enough reason for Trace to make the difficult descent to the hidden river and the arduous ascent out of the ravine simply for a handful of flowers, no matter how rare or beautiful they might be.

But there was a reason now. Down in the ravine's misty silence grew an orchid that had no name, an orchid that had never graced civilized greenhouses or the jeweled breasts of royalty. Of all the orchids Trace had ever seen, that wild orchid was the most superb, as perfectly sensuous and elegant as a pearl. That orchid was something no amount of money could buy, because only Trace knew where the orchid grew and no amount of money had tempted him to tell of the hidden ravine.

It wasn't money that tempted him now. It was the fact that he had finally found a woman worthy of the orchid's beauty.

The morning was half gone when Cindy woke again. The sound of the cabin door opening and closing curled through her dreams, followed by less definable sounds as Trace took off his boots and clothes and walked to the bedside. Cindy murmured and stirred languidly, reaching for Trace before her eyes were even open, wanting to curl up against him and hear his heart beating beneath her cheek as she had before she slept. When her hands met only tangled sheets, she opened her eyes.

"Trace?"

His name spoken in Cindy's husky voice sent a primitive shiver of sensation down Trace's spine.

"I'm right here, princess."

She turned toward the sound and thought she was still dreaming. Trace's nude body glowed with a sheen of moisture as though oiled. Various textures of hair had been slicked by water until curling patterns were created across his thighs and torso. The muscles she had kneaded with her hands and tested with her teeth were no longer concealed by darkness. He was even more powerful than she had guessed, and so compelling in his masculine beauty that she forgot to breathe.

Trace wanted Cindy with a force that he couldn't conceal, a hunger that made an answering heat uncurl deep in the pit of Cindy's stomach. As she looked at his strength and his arousal, she could scarcely believe how gentle he had been with her last night. He could have overwhelmed her, taken what he wanted and given nothing in return…yet he had loved her so tenderly, making her feel as fragile as a virgin, as cherished as a fairy-tale princess.

"But I'm not a princess," Cindy said, her voice

soft, her eyes openly approving of everything she saw in the man who stood naked before her.

"You are to me," Trace said simply. Green eyes searched Cindy's face, hardly able to believe the sensuous elegance of silky black hair, porcelain skin, eyes as brilliant as black diamonds and a mouth whose intense pink exactly matched the flushed heart of the orchid cupped in his hands. As Trace bent down to brush his lips over Cindy's soft mouth, he whispered, "You're too beautiful for a peon, but I want you so much my hands are shaking. Will you make love with me, even though I'm not a prince?"

Cindy's heart turned over at the combination of hunger and hesitation she saw in Trace's haunted green eyes. She reached for him, ignoring the sheet that slipped down to her waist. Slowly she rubbed her fingers over his skin, savoring its satin dampness. He smelled of mist and forest and passion. The combination made her dizzy.

"You're a man," she said huskily, "more man than I've ever known. That's all I care about." A delicate shiver took her as her lips pressed against the taut heat of Trace's navel. "And if I can't hold you inside my body soon, I'll die."

Trace's eyes closed but for a shimmering flash of green as a knife of pleasure and desire turned in his loins. The merest thread of a groan escaped his lips while the tip of Cindy's tongue probed the taut hollow of his navel. When her hands smoothed down his torso, a torrent of desire poured through him, bringing him to his knees beside the bed.

"Cindy, I…" he whispered, but no other words could push past the aching closure of his throat when he looked into the midnight clarity of her eyes. He bent his head until he could cherish her lips with his own. When he lifted his head once more, he could speak. Slowly he opened his hands so that she could see what had been cupped protectively within. "I brought this for you."

For an instant Cindy thought that it was a butterfly poised so delicately on Trace's hard palm. Then she inhaled an elusive, fragile fragrance and realized that the graceful curves belonged to the most extraordinary orchid she had ever seen. The satin petals were long and creamy, with the faintest flush of living pink in the veins. In sensuous contrast was the flower's lush fuchsia lip with its elegant frill. At the edge of the frill the pink color darkened until it was nearly black. The balance of color and shape in the orchid was flawless, drawing the eye unerringly toward the throat of the flower, where vibrant fuchsia again slid down the scale of color into a velvety darkness that was just a few shades removed from midnight.

"When I undressed you, I thought of this orchid," Trace said huskily, bending over Cindy, softly pressing her back into the bed until she was half sitting, half reclining against the heaped pillows. "Your breasts are like the orchid's petals, fine textured, creamy, flawless." He bent his head and kissed one of her breasts, catching its tip in his mouth, drawing the sensitive flesh into a tight peak before he released it. "When you're aroused, your lips and nipples are the same color as the orchid's mouth."

The hand holding the orchid came to a rest between Cindy's breasts. "Yes," Trace murmured, comparing the colors. "Like that. Vivid and alive. It's the same here," he said, easing the sheet down until his hand nestled between her legs. "So perfect. Too perfect for a peon. *Princess.*"

"Trace," Cindy whispered, sensing sadness beneath his words, as though he were retreating from her even while his words turned her into honey and sweetly devoured her. "I'm not a princess and I'm far from perfect. My nose is too long and my eyes are too far apart and my figure went out of style a hundred years ago and I've got broken fingernails and scrapes and bruises all over and my hair—" The tumble of words stopped as though cut by a knife. "Trace?" she asked in an aching whisper. "What is it? What's wrong?"

He released the orchid, letting it settle over Cindy's navel as gently as a breath. For the first time he saw the signs left by the cloud forest on her soft body. With gentle fingertips he touched each small shadow bruise, each tiny abrasion, and he cursed himself in searing silence for what he had done to Cindy when he had forced her to march through the cloud forest simply because he hadn't been able to bear the thought of spending another night alone with her and not having her.

And then the night had come, and they had been

alone and he had taken her waiting softness and
known the beauty of her dark, shimmering fire.

"Does this hurt?" Trace asked, gently picking up
Cindy's hand and kissing a slender finger that had a
scraped knuckle and a broken fingernail.

"No, it's—"

"Does this?" he interrupted, brushing his lips
across a pale bruise on the inside of Cindy's arm.

"No, I—"

"This?" Trace interrupted again, touching his
mouth to a small abrasion on her shoulder.

"No, really, I—" Suddenly Cindy's breath sucked
in and her thoughts scattered as Trace's tongue
gently laved a nearly invisible scrape. Her pent-up
breath came out as a sigh when his mouth moved on,
leaving her hungry for more.

The tender catechism continued as Trace brushed
caresses across Cindy's face and down her other
arm, asking at each tiny wound if it hurt, being reassured that it didn't by her half breaths and shivering murmurs of pleasure before he went on to
explore other satin territory. Then he came to a faint,
rosy mark at the base of her neck and another
matching mark between her full breasts.

"Oh, princess, I'm sorry," Trace whispered. "I
didn't mean to hurt you."

"You didn't," Cindy said in a husky voice, trembling as his tongue and lips caressed the narrow
valley between her breasts.

"Like hell I didn't."

The mattress shifted as Trace flowed onto the bed

and knelt over Cindy, looking for other telltale marks of his passion on her creamy skin. She started to object once more that he hadn't hurt her at all, that he had been so gentle despite his own violent need that it still made her heart turn over just to think about it. The words never got past the breath closing her throat when she saw the contrast of Trace's dark stubble and her pale breasts and the sensuous stroking of his tongue over imagined hurts.

"You're so smooth, so gentle," Trace said, caressing her with each word, "and I'm neither. Cindy... Cindy..." His voice caught as he kissed the taut inward curves of her waist. With each caress he looked for and sometimes thought he had found the barest shadows of the previous night, when his mouth and hands had not been smooth enough, gentle enough for the princess who had trusted him. "So perfect," he whispered, caressing the fine-grained skin below her navel with his lips. "I never should have touched you, princess. God knows I tried not to. And God knows I failed."

Cindy tried to reassure Trace, but all she could force past the aching in her throat was an unraveling sigh that was his name. The sight and feel of his face pressed against her abdomen while the tip of his tongue just brushed her skin, caused heat to uncurl in the pit of her stomach, dark fire rippling out through her body, transforming her.

One large hand closed gently around the orchid, caging the flower without moving it. While the tip of his tongue skimmed the orchid's outlines, his other hand gently stroked the silk of Cindy's inner thighs. With tender thoroughness his tongue traced every curve and fold and indentation of the warm orchid held within his circling fingers. He breathed in the flower's exotic essence even as he ravished it so softly that not a mark was left on its lush surface.

"So delicate," Trace said, his voice deep as he sipped at the orchid's exquisite fringe and at the same time stroked his warm palm along Cindy's inner thighs, coming closer to her most sensitive flesh without ever quite caressing it.

When only the center of the orchid remained untouched, his tongue dipped into the soft fuchsia throat until he could taste the fragrant, velvet darkness hidden within the yielding petals. "So lush," he breathed, skimming just once over Cindy's flushed, aching softness.

Cindy tried to stifle a small sound of pleasure and need, but Trace heard it. Slowly he looked up into her midnight eyes. The hand that had caged the orchid during its tender ravishment opened, leaving the flower nestled in her navel. Languidly he rubbed the back of both hands against her inner thighs, caressing and teasing her legs farther apart, giving her light touches and skimming promises that made her breath catch. When at last she lay before him with nothing between them but the memory of the orchid, he bent down to her. As his breath flowed across her flushed softness she gasped.

"Trace?"

"It's all right," Trace said tenderly, his deep voice

as caressing as his breath. "You're like the orchid. Perfect. And like the orchid, you were made for this. This is what I should have done last night, enjoying you without hurting you, leaving you…unmarked."

"You didn't hurt me last night. You…" Cindy's breath tore softly. "What are…ahhh, Trace, you're making me…"

The ragged whimper of pleasure that came from her trembling lips was all that she could say, the only sound left to her, and she made it repeatedly while Trace caressed her as completely as he had the orchid. The knowledge that he was taking as much pleasure from the intimacy as she was made the gentle ravishing all the more overwhelming. She tried to speak, to tell Trace what sweet wildness he was unlocking within her, but all that came from her lips were rippling cries of passion.

When Cindy moaned and arched against Trace, he fought against thrusting into her, losing himself in her sultry satin depths as she was silently, unmistakably demanding that he do. He wanted that. He wanted it until he felt as though he were being slowly torn inside out, every nerve on fire, his blood burning in savage rhythms that matched the violent hammering of his heart. All that kept him from losing control was an even greater desire; he wanted to bring his trusting princess to shivering completion in his hands. He wanted to know every aspect of her sensual release with all five of his senses unclouded by his own pleasure. He couldn't manage that if he were inside her, for then her sweet fire would burn through his self-control.

When Cindy arched into Trace again, requiring more from him than his relentless delicacy, he shuddered and caged her very carefully in his hands. The words he spoke to her then were unrestrained and elemental in their demands, yet the tenderness of his caresses didn't vary, each touch unraveling her, each word a hushed burning in her responsive flesh, extraordinary sensations radiating up through her body, softly devouring her flesh until only fire remained and she was its center, burning.

Trace shuddered and absorbed Cindy's release with all of his senses, savoring the knowledge that he had given her such intense pleasure. With redoubled tenderness he caressed her, feeling oddly satisfied even as he clenched against his own violent need.

Slowly Cindy opened her eyes, breathing raggedly as echoes of ecstasy rippled through her. She started to speak, but the sight of Trace caressing her so intimately made her tremble. Pleasure burst softly within her once more. In its trembling wake came the knowledge that for all the sweet fire rekindling in her, consuming her, she wanted more. She could hardly believe it, yet she still...*needed.*

"Trace."

The husky timbre of Cindy's voice sent a shaft of raw hunger through Trace. He looked up and saw the orchid she was extending to him on the palm of her slender hand. The flower's scent mingled with the heady fragrance of the woman held between his hands. She shivered within his grasp as he caressed the velvet bud of her passion.

"Trace, I…"

Breath and words came apart in a shower of heat. When Cindy knew the sultry pleasure of his touch again, she moaned softly and pressed against him, twisting slowly. She felt the shudder that ripped through his powerful body, tightening his hands on her for just an instant.

"Trace," she breathed, reaching for him.

The orchid tumbled softly from her hand to his cheek and then to her thigh. He turned and brushed his lips over the flower before he picked it up and gently set it aside.

"You're more beautiful than any orchid," Trace said, bending to Cindy again.

"So are you," she said, her voice husky with the shivering pleasure that was rising in her once more, seduced from the secret places of her body by Trace's elemental masculine sensuality.

Smiling, Trace turned and kissed the slender fingers that were caressing his cheek. "I'm about as beautiful as that mud hole I finally winched you out of, princess."

"You're wrong," Cindy said, her voice breaking with pleasure at Trace's touch. Looking at him was another kind of pleasure, equally intense. He was utterly male, hard with muscle and brushed with tempting swirls of hair, and the sultry heat of his mouth held her in thrall.

"Trace?"

He made a gently inquiring sound as he caressed her with slow pleasure. Cindy started to speak, then stopped as pleasure shimmered and burst within her.

She wanted to tell him what she needed, but the only words she could think of made her blush.

"Trace," she breathed, rubbing her fingers through his hair and being rewarded by a caress that scattered her thoughts. "Come here. I want to whisper…" The words became a moan as he touched her with ravishing delicacy.

Trace closed his eyes and fought a sudden, savage thrust of need at the thought of Cindy's husky voice whispering sensual demands in his ear while he buried his hungry flesh in her softness.

"I'd better stay where I am," he said finally. "If you whisper in my ear, I'll take you slow and deep and hard."

"Yes," Cindy said, sliding down the bed, insinuating herself beneath Trace, discovering that his skin was as steamy as hers and that he shook when her hands found the fascinating combination of satin and pulsing strength that was quintessentially male. "That's what I want," she said huskily. "You inside me. Slow and deep and hard. And then fast, Trace. And hard, very hard."

Cindy's fingertips raked softly, urgently, over Trace's aroused body, measuring with wonder how much he wanted her. Even as his breath fragmented into a groan, her fingertips discovered the single sultry drop she had called from his violent restraint.

"Trace," she said shakily, "take me now." As she spoke she moved her hips slowly beneath him.

"I'll hurt you, princess," Trace said harshly. "I'm too big, too rough for you."

"No," Cindy said, kissing his hot skin as she drew him closer and then closer to her hungry softness. When the blunt heat of him touched her, she shivered eagerly. "You're perfect for me. I need you, Trace. Inside me. Filling me."

He felt the truth of her words in the satin flesh that eagerly parted for him. The hot rain of her passion bathed him, silently begging for a deeper joining. The tangible evidence of her need dissolved his control. His arms swept up beneath her knees as he pressed slowly against her, into her, giving her what both of them so desperately wanted, joining them with a slow thoroughness that was a consummation in itself. She made a broken sound as she felt him taking her, filling her until she overflowed, filling her until she could take no more.

And then Trace gently lifted Cindy's hips as he slid deeper and then deeper still, joining himself completely to her, sealing them one to the other, stopping only when his thighs were cradled against hers and he was fully sheathed within her welcoming fire. Only then did he begin to move, his hips describing slow, sensuous circles against her heated body. She had never felt anything half so intimate, so utterly exquisite. Each time he moved, streamers of glittering pleasure swirled up through her body.

Without realizing it Cindy began to murmur breathlessly, moving in deliberate, sensuous counterpoint to Trace, doubling and redoubling their shared pleasure, until gentle convulsions began to undo her, feeding upon her languidly, sweetly, and she wept with each unraveling ripple of ecstasy. He smiled and rocked slowly in the tight satin cradle of her body as he bent down to sip the tears of ecstasy from her…and still it continued, rocking, shimmering, building and she knew she was going to die of it and she didn't care as long as he was with her, deep inside her, moving, rocking, and flames of pleasure quivering through her, growing, burning.

Cindy called Trace's name as he retreated slowly, unbearably, leaving her empty when she knew she could not live without him. Instinctively her hands slid down to his hips, nails scoring his skin in passionate demand. His breath caught in a deep groan as his whole body clenched. This time he took her in a hard thrust, moving powerfully, restraint slipping away as her nails sank into the flexed muscles of his buttocks at each stroke, nails stinging him sweetly, telling him to withhold nothing of his power.

The urgent caresses inflamed Trace, but not as much as Cindy's husky words shivering against his ear, her body luring him deeper and yet deeper, faster, harder. Her nails scored him with ecstasy, stripping the world away, taking inhibition with it, leaving only the hot pricking of her nails and her passionate words and her fiery softness sheathing him, taking everything he had to give and giving him shattering ecstasy in return.

She caressed him with her hands, her words, her abandoned response, infusing his driving body with more strength, more heat, rapture pulsing from him to her and back again with each breath, each shimmering convulsion deep within her body, and still it was not complete, not enough. He was dying and he couldn't plunge far enough, deep enough, hard enough.

With ancient instinct her hands swept down to cradle and caress the twin sources of his primal need. At the first enfolding touch he thrust into her with a hoarse cry that was her name, abandoning himself to her as completion burst repeatedly from him in an ecstasy that had neither beginning nor end, simply an incandescent pulsing center that was both himself and the woman whose softness called forth and drank the searing pulses of his release.

Racked by ecstasy, Trace held Cindy, knowing that he had touched her soul and she had touched his and nothing would ever be the same again.

Chapter 12

"Well, you don't need to look so happy to see me," Susan said in exasperation, put out by Cindy's frankly dismayed expression when she opened the cabin door and saw guests on the doorstep.

Unsuccessfully, Cindy tried not to look guilty. "Of course I'm glad to see you," she said quickly.

"Uh-huh. Pull my other leg. It has bells on it."

Raul laughed even as he gave Trace an intent, probing look over Cindy's shoulder. "I would have called, cousin, but you know the difficulty."

"Yeah. The phones are still out, right? Or is it the bridge that's keeping the world at bay?"

Trace's sardonic inflection and smile weren't lost on Raul. Nor was the frank irritation that had come to Trace's expression when he had looked over Cindy's head and seen the other couple standing at the cabin door. Trace had known that his time with his captive princess would inevitably end, but he hadn't known how fiercely he would resent that end when it came.

"Tia would like you to come to dinner," Raul said smoothly. "There might be other guests as well, if the roads are dry enough. If that is the case, there might be unhappiness if you were unable to attend."

Though Raul said no more, Trace got to the bottom line very quickly. The outside world was no longer accepting Raul's radio silence at face value. If communications weren't reestablished at the Almeda hacienda, someone from Quito would drive up and "fix" the equipment for them.

That someone would probably be Invers, spurred on by Big Eddy McCall.

Cindy didn't notice Trace's grim expression. She was too busy looking at Susan's daunting physical perfection and remembering how, when Trace had first met Susan, he had looked from Susan to Cindy and then away. Cindy sighed. She didn't measure up to Susan's standard of beauty and she knew it. And even if she tried to forget that unhappy fact, standing around in Susan's clothes—which were a bit loose in the middle and much too tight on top and bottom—was a constant reminder.

Sighing again, Cindy resigned herself to accepting an evening of inevitable comparisons with as much good grace as she could muster.

Trace saw the shuttered look that came to Cindy's face and remembered he had seen that same look once before, when they had first encountered Susan and Raul.

"Cindy?" Trace asked, looking into the enigmatic, crystalline midnight of his lover's eyes. "We don't have to go anywhere if you don't want to."

"It would be best if you did, if only for a few minutes," Raul countered smoothly before Cindy could answer. "While radio reception has been erratic, I suspect that someone is worried about Señorita Mc—ah, Señorita Ryan."

"You suspect?" Trace asked in a clipped voice.

"Um," Raul agreed. "It is only common sense, is it not? Señorita Ryan is a woman alone in a foreign land. Surely her family would be concerned by the fact that she has not been in contact with them for nine days."

"Nine?" Cindy blinked. "Oh, that's impossible. It can't have been that long."

"Forgive me for insisting," Raul said, smiling slightly and giving Trace an amused look, "but it has been closer to ten days than to nine."

Mentally Cindy counted forward from the instant she had left the plane in Quito. First the argument with Trace, then two days on the road, then he had found her and they had slept in the village and then the storm and they had come to the Almeda hacienda and then...

Images of Trace splintered suddenly through Cindy's mind. Trace undressing her, loving her with his words, his hands, his mouth, every part of him, and all around them the cloud forest's sensuous rain bathing their interlocked bodies. Trace standing naked before her with an incredible orchid in his hand and sad shadows in his eyes. Trace joining himself with her slowly, deeply, repeatedly, teaching her so many exquisite ways to touch the shimmering ecstasy that waited within.

"We can't have been staying with you for six days," she said weakly. "It seems more like two, or maybe three."

Raul just managed not to smile. "I am delighted that you have found your stay with us so pleasant. Especially with Trace as your, ah, host. My cousin tends to regard the cloud forest much more highly than he regards mere men."

"Cindy isn't a man," Susan pointed out reasonably.

"But of course," Raul said, bowing slightly, failing to conceal his smile. "That explains it."

Trace grunted. All that kept him from being outright hostile to Raul was the fact that Cindy had barely looked at the other man—that, plus the clear dismay in her expression when she had opened the cabin door and had seen the end of their timeless days of mutual exploration and passion. The knowledge that Cindy was no more ready to rejoin the world than he was satisfied something deep within Trace, something that he had not even known was there.

"Tell Tia we'll come to the big house for dinner,"

Trace said in a clipped voice. "It might be nice if you worked very hard on the radio connections between now and then. Even if you can't *receive* messages, you might be able to send them. Try the American embassy, for instance. They have more powerful equipment than most. Tell them Cindy is doing very well, so no one needs to worry about the fact that she's going to stick around the cloud forest until the roads dry out."

Raul's eyebrows climbed. He turned to Cindy. "Is that the message you wish passed on to your family?"

Cindy turned to Trace, whose vital warmth was even now radiating out to her, touching her, enfolding her. His hard hands reached out and gently cradled her face. He bent and brushed his lips over hers once, twice, three times, tasting the warmth of her breath as it rushed out to him in an invisible caress.

"Is that what you want?" Trace whispered too softly to be overheard, touching Cindy's lips with his own between words. "Just ask me and if it's mine to give, it's yours. I promise you, princess. All you have to do is ask. I'll let you go if that's what you want, or I'll keep you here and make love to you in the midst of orchids and rain."

Sudden tears gleamed between Cindy's thick black eyelashes. She stood on tiptoe and pressed her lips against Trace's hungry, sensual, familiar mouth. His arms closed around her with fierce strength. She didn't object to the possession. She simply closed her eyes and hugged him as hard as she could in return.

"I told you that Señorita Ryan wasn't being held against her will," Raul said dryly, turning to Susan in the manner of someone continuing an argument. "Trace may lack a certain superficial charm at times, but he has more decency in him than a regiment of polished aristocrats."

Susan's skeptical blue eyes went from Raul to Trace. As she looked at her friend nestled within Trace's powerful arms, she sighed. There was no doubt about it. If Cindy was a captive, she was definitely a willing one.

Susan met Trace's blazing green eyes and said distinctly, "She doesn't need another Jason."

"You don't know me," Trace said in a cold, flat voice.

"Does Cindy?" Susan retorted.

"Susan, don't," Cindy said quickly. "It's all right. Trace isn't like Jason. Believe me. You won't have to put me back together after we… I promise. This is different."

"I hope so," Susan said, touching Cindy's arm. "You deserve to be loved more than anyone I know." Susan's smile was both beautiful and very sad as she turned to Raul. "What is it that you Spanish say? *Que sera, sera.*"

"What will be, will be," murmured Raul. "Yes."

"A primitive point of view," Susan said, looking directly at Trace.

"Don't knock primitive until you've tried it," Cindy said quietly, looking at Susan. "I've discovered I'm rather primitive myself. Like my brother.

He spent his life looking for a woman who would want him just for himself. Just a man called Rye. And then he found Lisa and now he spends his days looking like a man who has just swallowed the sun."

Trace heard the complex resonances in Cindy's voice—joy for her brother, wistfulness, hunger—and knew in that instant why Cindy traveled and lived under a different name. It wasn't kidnapping she had feared, it was being wanted for all the wrong reasons. She had hoped to be as lucky as her brother, desired for what he was, not who he was.

"I had given up hoping to find a man who would want me, just me, Cindy Ryan," she continued, pressing her hands over Trace's. "Not my family ties, not any future expectations of wealth or power, nothing but me." Smiling, she brought one of Trace's hard hands up to her mouth. Eyes closed, she kissed his palm and cradled it against her cheek before she said softly, "Now I know how it feels to swallow the sun."

Trace met Raul's enigmatic black glance without flinching while Cindy's words echoed between them. *A man who would want me, just me, Cindy Ryan. Not my family ties...nothing but me.*

Even as Trace's arms tightened around Cindy, he knew he would have to let go of her very soon. There was no hope that she wouldn't find out he had known her real name even before he met her. That kind of secret could never be kept. His only hope was to let her go before she knew the secret. Then, when she learned the truth, she would look back and know that he must have wanted her, just her, for if he had wanted her money he never would have let her go.

When she realized that, she would come to him again in the cloud forest. And he would be there, waiting for her, wanting her with a complex, elemental hunger he had never known before.

"But I'm not going to make Rye's mistake," Cindy continued, turning in Trace's arms, looking at him. "My brother didn't want Lisa to know about his family because he was afraid it would change the way she looked at him. He was afraid she would see money instead of just a man. He didn't trust her, not really, and he almost lost her because of it." Cindy took a deep breath and looked into Trace's shadowed green eyes. "I want you to know that I trust you."

She paused, closed her eyes for an instant and then opened them. When she spoke her voice carried clearly, as though she wanted to be sure that Trace understood every word. "My full name is Cynthia Edwinna Ryan McCall. My father is very...well-off."

"Well off," Susan echoed in an amused aside to Raul. "You have heard, perhaps, of 'filthy rich'? That's Big Eddy McCall. Filthy. Rich. Cindy is his one and only daughter."

Cindy searched Trace's eyes, trying to chart any changes the knowledge of her wealth might make between them. Nothing changed, unless it was the bleak twist of pain that showed in Trace's expression the instant before his mouth kicked up at the corner in his familiar, bittersweet smile.

"I always knew you were a princess," Trace said, brushing a kiss across Cindy's upturned face.

"It doesn't matter," she said almost fiercely.

"No. It doesn't matter," Trace said simply. "Not to me. Believe me. *It doesn't matter.*"

Cindy let out a breath she hadn't even been aware of holding. She smiled at Trace, her eyes radiant. She kissed him softly, hardly able to believe her luck. Trace knew who she was and it had changed nothing. The relief was so great she felt almost giddy. She laughed up at him.

"Now that that's taken care of," Cindy said, smiling, "I'm ready to face dinner in Susan's shade."

"Her what?" Trace asked.

"Her shade. You know."

"No, I'm afraid I don't have the faintest idea," Trace admitted, looking perplexed.

"Remember when we first saw Raul and Susan in the Jeep?"

Trace nodded slowly.

"You looked from Susan to me and then you didn't look at me any more." Cindy shrugged. "That's a man's usual reaction. Susan just puts every other woman in the shade."

Hardly able to believe what he was hearing, Trace looked from Cindy to Susan. "Has she always been this blind?" he asked bluntly.

Susan smiled, but there was no laughter in her eyes. "Big Eddy has been buying men to seduce his daughter into founding a dynasty since she turned eighteen. Little wonder she thinks she's not attractive. The men never saw her for the dollar signs in their eyes. That's why she fell like a ripe peach into the hands of the first man who wanted her body rather than her daddy's bank account."

"It's a damned fine body," Trace agreed matter-of-factly, giving Cindy the kind of loving once-over that made her bones melt, "but it's not why I wanted you."

Her eyes widened in dismay.

"There's a dark fire in you that has nothing to do with your body," Trace said, watching Cindy with eyes that reflected that fire. "That's what drew me, what drove me crazy. I would have wanted you if you'd been short, fat and blond. You…burn," he said, running his fingertip over Cindy's full lower lip. "And while Susan isn't bad-looking if you like skinny women…"

"My, how the man gushes," Susan said dryly.

"The reason I looked away after seeing you next to your wise-mouthed friend," Trace continued, ignoring Susan, "was that I felt guilty as hell for what I'd put you through. You were exhausted, wringing wet, muddy, scraped and your clothes were in shreds, and every time I looked at you I wanted to hire three men to beat me for being such an unfeeling bastard as to force-march you through the cloud forest in the first place. So I tried not to look at you. But I failed. Even looking as if you'd been dragged backward through a muddy knothole, you were still more beautiful to me than any other woman ever will be."

Cindy's eyes widened. "Oh," she breathed.

Trace smiled almost sadly, his lips curving so little that it was barely visible. He touched Cindy's lower lip again, a caress that was both intimate and oddly withdrawn, as though he were afraid to come closer.

"I hate like hell giving you back to the world, princess," Trace whispered. Then he looked up at Raul. "I'll bring Cindy to the big house before dark."

"Ride over with us. One of the men can drive the Jeep back after—"

"No," Trace interrupted, looking back at Cindy. "I have a few hours left with my princess. I don't want to share them, or her, with anyone."

Without waiting for Raul's response, Trace drew Cindy back into the cabin and shut the door. She looked into his eyes and felt tears burn in her own. Before she could ask a question, the silken brush of Trace's lips stroked over her own until they parted on a gasp, permitting the hot glide of his tongue into her soft mouth. He tasted her with aching hunger while he pressed her against himself with slow, powerful sweeps of his hands.

In the space of a kiss Cindy became both pliant and fierce, for she knew that ecstasy waited within the shimmering heat of their joined bodies. And suddenly she couldn't wait for it.

It was the same for Trace, a primal urgency that could not be denied, a stunning foretaste of what it would be to go without the sense of completion that only Cindy had ever brought to him. He groaned and tore open his shirt as her hot mouth slid down his chest. By the time her lips reached his navel he had kicked aside his clothing to stand before her trembling and naked and gleaming with passionate need.

"Love me, Cindy," Trace said hoarsely, reaching for her even as the sultry heat of her mouth bathed him. "Love me as though it were the last time."

Chapter 13

Just as Trace drove the Jeep up to the big house, wind blew over the land, making trees bend and ripple like grass. Mist swirled and disappeared, shredded by flashing knives of metallic gold light. Shadows suddenly appeared as sunlight streamed through the cloud forest, making drops of moisture glitter with alien brilliance.

Trace parked next to the Land Rover, turned off the engine and looked over at Cindy with eyes that reflected both the jeweled greens and the deep shadows that surrounded the Jeep. Cindy didn't notice Trace's silent regard; she was lost in the forest's unexpected transformation. He watched her in aching silence. The unveiled light heightened rather than washed out Cindy's colors. Her beauty squeezed Trace's heart in a foretaste of the bitter loneliness that would come when he let his princess go. He reached out to touch her cheek, needing to feel her warmth.

The front door of the big house slammed open and Susan rushed across the screened porch toward the Jeep. Trace's hand fell back to his side before touching Cindy.

"I thought you'd never get here!" Susan said hurriedly, opening the passenger door for Cindy. "Rye has been calling every half hour since Raul patched up enough equipment to get through to the embassy."

"Rye? What does he want? Is something wrong?" Cindy asked as she got out.

"He said it was a 'family matter' and that everyone's fine but that he had to talk with you as soon as possible to make sure things stayed that way. Does that make sense to you?"

"Not—"

"That's a relief," Susan continued, interrupting. "I thought I was the only crazy one around here. Hello, Trace. You look like your usual cheerful self."

Trace gave Susan a sideways glance as he shut the passenger door behind Cindy.

"Brrr. A look like that would freeze sunlight," Susan said in a stage whisper to Cindy. "Do you suppose he'll ever forgive me for thinking that the only way he could keep you at his cabin was if he tied you to a chair? After all, men with dark beard stubble who look and move like jungle predators are hardly likely to inspire confidence in a civilized woman."

Cindy laughed softly. "I've discovered I'm not very civilized, so don't worry about me."

"I'll try, but after Jason…" The sophisticated mask dropped from Susan's face, allowing her worry and love for Cindy to show through. "I didn't think you were going to make it," Susan said frankly.

Before Cindy could say anything, Raul called from the house. "Señorita Ryan, your brother wishes to talk to you!"

Cindy looked at the blue sky, sighed, and said, "Guess I'd better find out what Dad's up to now."

"Your father?" Trace asked sharply. "What do you mean?"

"'Family matter' is our code for problems with Dad or our third sibling, who takes after Dad," Cindy called over her shoulder as she ran up the steps to the porch. "Since Mom died, Rye and I sometimes think we're the only reasonably sane people left in the family."

Cindy followed Raul to the radiophone. With impeccable manners he waited until he was sure that she needed nothing more, then shut the door behind her, allowing her all the privacy she might require.

"Hello," Cindy said, picking up the phone. "What is he up to now, and which he is it?"

"Hello, Cinderella. Where the hell have you been?"

Rye's familiar voice made Cindy smile. "I've been enjoying a guided tour of paradise," she said.

"Impossible. Lisa and I own it, remember? It's called McCall's Meadow."

"To each his own paradise. Mine happens to be a cloud forest where mountains and orchids hide."

"Is that where Susan was hiding, too?"

"She wasn't hiding, but she was here. She's fine."

"How about you? Are you fine, too?"

"Never better."

"Thank God. I was afraid that Dad had outmaneuvered you for the second time."

"What do you mean?"

"He's been flying in and out of here like Peter Pan, rubbing his hands and smiling and talking about the grandkids he's going to have from you at last. Seems he's paying some stud called Trace Rawlings a thousand dollars a day to keep an eye on you in Ecuador, and double that if you come home pregnant. Now I know you're a big girl and can take care of…"

Rye's voice began fading in and out oddly, like the light in the room itself. Shakily Cindy groped for the chair that was positioned close to the phone. She sank into the leather cushions and waited to find out if she was going to survive.

"Anyway," Rye's voice continued in Cindy's ear, "I got to thinking about it and was afraid you might be more vulnerable in a foreign country than you would be at home. I didn't want you getting cut up again like you were over that miserable son of…"

Sound faded as Cindy dragged air into her lungs despite the knives of pain twisting inside her body.

She barely had the presence of mind to press her palm over the receiver so that Rye wouldn't hear her tearing breath. By the time she had herself under some kind of control again, Rye was beginning to wonder about the lack of input from her end of the conversation.

"Cindy? Hey, sis. You still there?"

Cindy stared at the radiophone. Slowly she reached for the volume control. As she spoke she ran the volume up and down erratically.

"I'm still here, Rye, but the connection is lousy. Can you hear me?"

"I can hear someone fading in and out. Sure as hell doesn't sound like you, though."

"Yes. Well, things are breaking up pretty badly on this end, too. What was that name again?"

"Trace Rawlings. He's some sort of jungle expert according to Dad."

"I can barely hear you." Cindy closed her eyes. "I'm flying out of Ecuador tomorrow. Can I—can I come see you and Lisa for a while?"

"Hell, yes. You're always welcome, sis. You know that. Why do you think I built on the extra suite of rooms after I was married? Lisa loves you as much as I do. She was so excited about having you for a sister that I thought for a while there she would move in with you rather than me."

Cindy gripped the phone so hard that her hand ached as much as her throat. "I love both of you, too," she said as she ran the volume all the way to zero.

Slowly Cindy hung up. She sat in the chair for a long time without moving, not trusting herself to be able to stand, hardly able to think. And then, when she could think, she wished that she hadn't.

How could I have been so wrong about Trace?

The question was painful, but not nearly as agonizing as the knowledge that she had given herself to a man whose body—all of it—was for hire.

Even as Cindy silently screamed that Rye must be wrong, Trace couldn't have made love to her so beautifully if all he had been thinking about was money, she felt herself dying inside. It was Jason all over again, except that Jason had been cruel every inch of the way, making her pay for the fact that his own greed had forced him to pursue a woman he didn't really want.

Trace hadn't been cruel in that way, but the ultimate result was the same. She had trusted herself to a man whose only interest in her was her money. And she had done it twice.

Cindy made a low, choked sound, but no tears came to ease her grief. It was as though Trace had killed even the ability to cry. Yet after Jason had left, she had wept until Susan had been afraid to leave her alone. It would be different with Trace. She couldn't cry for him any more than she had been able to cry at her mother's funeral. She had been a child when her mother had died, and she had felt a child's raw, incoherent sense of betrayal at her mother's absence.

That was how it was with Trace. Cindy loved him as she had never loved anyone. And when that kind of love was betrayed, there weren't enough tears to wash the wound clean, much less to heal it.

"What's wrong, princess?"

Trace's voice came to Cindy as though from an immense distance. Slowly she opened her eyes and looked at the man she had thought was beyond price, only to discover that he was just one more of Big Eddy's greedy recruits after all. Distantly she wished that she could be angry. She wished that she could rage at Trace, releasing the numbing grip of pain on her mind and body. But she could not.

Raging at Trace would be even more stupid than she had already been in trusting him. She needed him for just a bit longer. There were too many miles of rain forest between herself and freedom.

You Tarzan. Me Jane.

But Trace wanted to stay in the cloud forest for a while longer. No big surprise there. He was being paid a thousand dollars a day for his time. Plus the pregnancy bonus, of course.

Cindy closed her eyes and prayed that the numbness would last until she was on the plane out of Quito.

"Cindy?"

She took a deep breath, ignoring the knives sticking into her body, forcing herself to think rationally. If she said she had to leave, Trace would want to know why. There was no way she could tell him. Not yet. Not until she was certain that she could smile and congratulate him on his sexual prowess and then casually walk away from him. She didn't know how long it would be before she attained that level of serenity.

Probably never.

In the meantime she had to get to Quito. She could ask Raul for a driver, but she had seen enough of Raul to know that he wouldn't go against Trace's wishes without a good reason. She doubted that a woman's hurt feelings would even show up on Raul's scale of measuring good reasons.

"Love?" Trace came up to the chair and sat on his heels. Gently he cupped his hand beneath Cindy's chin and lifted her head until she opened her eyes. "Tell me about it. Let me help you."

Cindy looked into Trace's gentle green eyes and found herself believing that he truly cared for her rather than for her father's money. Despite what she knew, despite her past experiences, *she wanted to believe in Trace*. She had no defenses against him even now that she knew what he was.

She was hopelessly in love with him.

The realization panicked Cindy. Ten days ago she would have grabbed the keys to the Land Rover and rushed out of the house and gotten herself stuck in the first bog, where she would have stayed until Trace came along and pulled her out—but not until she first asked for his help. Nicely. And told him why she had been in such a big hurry in the first place.

For a moment Cindy considered trying to buy Trace's cooperation outright, but she knew beyond doubt that he would turn her down flat just the way he had in Quito. Trace did things his way or he didn't do them at all.

She took a deep, careful breath. There was no point in wasting time being more stupid than she already had been. She didn't have the skill or the strength to get herself back to Quito. Trace did. But she couldn't buy his skill. She could only ask for it a few miles down the road when she got stuck on her own—or she could be smart and ask for it right now.

Slowly Cindy's eyes focused on the man she had learned too much about, too late.

"This morning…" Cindy's throat closed.

She cleared it with a sound so tight, so painful, that Trace's eyes narrowed in unconscious empathy.

"You told me…if I wanted something, all I had to do was ask," Cindy continued in a dry voice. "If you could, you would give it to me. That's what you told me, isn't it?"

Trace nodded as he touched her cheek. She flinched subtly at the caress.

"I have to go home," Cindy said starkly. "Will you take me to Quito?"

Trace lifted his hand and looked at her in silence for a few moments. She was far too pale and her eyes were almost wild. Her fingers were clasped together so tightly that her nails were digging into her hands.

"Why?" Trace asked.

"Is that yes or no?"

"Cindy…" His voice died as he looked at her desperately calm face. "Do you really want to leave?"

"Yes."

"When?"

"Now. Right now. This instant. Please, Trace. I'm beg—"

"Don't," Trace said roughly, unable to bear hearing Cindy's pleas. "It's all right, princess," he said, holding her, feeling her lack of response, wondering what had happened, why she was retreating from the cloud forest. From him. "We'll leave right away." His green eyes searched hers. "Can't you tell me what's wrong?"

Cindy closed her eyes and whispered, "Is that the price of a ride to Quito?"

Trace came to his feet in a single savage motion. "We'll be in Quito before noon."

Trace was as good as his word. He took a direct route from the Almeda *hacienda* to the nearest paved road, and from there he drove like a bat fleeing hell. Cindy slept when she could, pretended to be sleeping when she couldn't and said nothing that didn't relate to the necessities of the trip. Trace had little attention to spare from the road in any case. He drove hard and fast, pushing the Rover right to the edge of its mechanical capabilities and holding it there ruthlessly. Driving like that not only made good time, it kept Trace from grabbing Cindy and demanding to know what was wrong. It kept the rage he felt at being cut off from her under control.

And it kept him from asking himself why he felt such turmoil over the end of an affair that was less than ten days old—an affair that he had known must end.

Driving like a bat out of hell didn't, however, keep Trace from sensing at a visceral level that he was somehow the cause of Cindy's pain. There was no other explanation for her distance from him. Assuming he was at the center of her pain, there could be only one reason. Somehow she had found out that he had always known she was Cynthia McCall, not Cindy Ryan.

By the time Trace pulled up in front of Cindy's hotel, he had decided that he was going to put an end to her distance and silence, beginning right then. He shut off the engine and turned toward her. Cindy took one look at his bleak, jungle-green eyes and reached for the door handle. She was too slow. Before her fingers closed around the handle, Trace was holding her in his arms, pinning her back against the seat with his powerful body.

"Since you won't talk to me," Trace said, lowering his mouth to Cindy's, "I'll try another way of communicating with you."

For a few instants Cindy fought against both Trace's superior strength and her own wild desires, but resisting was futile. Her body knew him too well, responded to him too quickly, hungrily reaching for his sensual fire, wanting to burn away the icy grief that was numbing her. With a small, choked cry she stopped fighting against herself, against him, against the need that only Trace had ever been able to arouse and satisfy within her.

When Cindy's lips finally parted for Trace, he sensed the sweetness waiting for him, a sweetness that he needed as much as breath itself. He groaned and took her mouth almost violently, tasting her deeply, wanting something from her that he could not name. When he realized she wasn't fighting him any longer, he tore his mouth away and began sipping tenderly at her eyelids, her cheeks, the corners of her mouth, her lower lip, kissing her so gently that she shivered between his hands, against his body, telling him everything he wanted to know.

"You see, princess?" Trace murmured, nuzzling Cindy's ear, feeling her shiver again, tasting her, biting her with exquisite care. "It doesn't matter that I knew who you were before you came to Quito. After I saw you I would have wanted you if your father was broke and you were wearing rags. Just like it doesn't matter that I'm a peon, a bastard with no real family. You burn when I touch you. I burn when you touch me. That's all that matters. Everything else is just words without meaning."

Cindy's eyes closed as the last flicker of hope that Rye had been wrong was destroyed by Trace's own admission. *I knew who you were the first time I saw you.*

"Cindy?" Trace said huskily, feeling the change in her body, tension draining away, leaving nothing behind. He was holding her but she wasn't there. Not anymore. Not the way she had been, shivering with pleasure at his touch. "Talk to me, princess."

"Thank you for driving me to Quito," Cindy said politely.

"Don't you believe me?" Trace asked, his hands tightening on Cindy's shoulders.

Everything else is just words without meaning.

"Oh, yes," she said softly, opening her eyes. "'Words without meaning.' I believe you. Now, if you'll excuse me...?"

Trace looked at Cindy's fathomless black eyes and felt a chill ripple over his skin.

"Please," she added carefully.

Trace felt a stroke of anguish as he lifted his hands from Cindy's shoulders. He had vowed that he would make Cindy ask him for something, and he had. Twice.

And each time the request had been that he separate himself from her.

"You don't believe me!" Trace said savagely, anger clear in his voice. "You just can't bring yourself to trust a peon, can you?"

Words without meaning.

The only words that mattered were still tolling in Cindy's mind. Trace had known who she was. He had let her make her little speech about trust and had said nothing. Sudden humiliation galvanized her, giving her the strength to leave him.

"I don't know any peons," Cindy said, opening the door.

"You know me," he shot back.

"You're a stud for hire. Studs and peons are two entirely different things."

"What?"

"Big Eddy hired you."

"Your brother was a regular mine of information, wasn't he?" Trace said viciously.

"Did my father hire you?"

"Technically, yes, but what does that—"

The door closed, cutting off Trace's words, leaving him alone in the Rover. He started to get out, then thought better of it. Cindy was angry now. So was he. Much too angry to accomplish anything. It would be better to wait for her to cool down. When she did, she would realize that what they had was too good to throw away just because Big Eddy had been the one to bring them together.

Trace shifted gears angrily and drove away from the hotel, telling himself that he could be patient and understanding about how Cindy felt. From what Susan had said, Cindy had had a rough time with men because of her father. Naturally Cindy would be upset to find out that Trace had always known who she was. But surely it wouldn't take long before she realized that he wasn't some kind of low-life gigolo. He had been hired by Big Eddy to keep an eye on his daughter, period.

When Cindy got past her anger, she would understand that making love to her hadn't been any part of Trace's deal with Invers and Big Eddy. If she just slowed down and thought about it, she would know that the kind of passion they had shared was one of those things that money simply couldn't buy.

Let's face it, Trace told himself. *A man can't fake it in bed. What he wants—or doesn't want—is right out front for anyone to see. Cindy must know that. All she has to do is slow down and think.*

He was still comforting himself with those thoughts

when Invers knocked on the front door of Trace's apartment that night.

"What the hell are you doing here?" Trace asked.

"Delivering mail," Invers said in a resigned voice.

"What?"

"Got some more of that for me?" Invers asked, gesturing toward the glass in Trace's hand.

Trace stepped back into the room. Invers followed. A few moments later he took an eye-watering swallow from the glass Trace handed over.

"Thanks," Invers said after a moment. "At least I'll die with the taste of good Scotch in my mouth."

Trace's mouth lifted slightly at the corner, which was as close as he'd come to a smile since he had walked into Raul's radio room and seen Cindy looking like the world had been jerked out from under her feet.

"Is it that hard to be a mailman in Ecuador?" Trace asked.

"You know what they used to do with the bearer of bad news," Invers retorted. He pulled an envelope out of his breast pocket. "This came to my office by special messenger. I'm afraid it's meant for you."

Trace looked down. The envelope bore the name of Cindy's hotel. Written on the outside of the sealed envelope was: "For Stud Rawlings, the best man money can buy."

Trace said several vicious words as he ripped into the envelope.

Invers finished his Scotch in a single swig and

muttered, "I was hoping it was a case of mistaken identity. Guess not."

A shower of money spilled from the envelope onto the floor. American bills. Big denominations. Big enough to make Invers suck in his breath hard and fast. Trace didn't even glance at the money, much less try to pick it up. He had eyes only for the message inside.

> Big Eddy taught me that a workman is worthy of his hire. The enclosed covers both our original agreement and the days we didn't spend in the cloud forest waiting "for the roads to dry." I've included the pregnancy bonus because if I'm not, it certainly won't be for lack of effort on your part. I doubt that Big Eddy will be so generous but, as you taught me, you never know until you ask.
>
> Too bad I didn't ask the right questions sooner.

The note swiftly became pulp in Trace's powerful hand. He pinned Invers with a savage look.

"*Pregnancy* bonus?" Trace asked with dangerous softness.

A single glance at Trace's grim face made Invers wish himself elsewhere. Immediately. He looked toward the door, wondering if he could make it before he was stopped.

"Not a chance in hell," Trace said succinctly, following Invers's glance. "You're not going anywhere until you tell what you left out when you conned me into getting Big Eddy off your back."

"It's a long story," Invers said.

"So was Scheherazade's. If you're as lucky as she was, you'll survive to finish it."

A long time later Trace sat alone in his apartment, a drink in one hand and thousands of dollars scattered across the floor at his feet. He no longer expected the phone to ring, no longer waited to hear Cindy say that she believed him and wanted to be back in his arms, no longer expected her warmth to fill the aching hollows of his life. She had flown out of Quito hours before, leaving nothing behind but the envelope explaining why she didn't believe in him.

Trace didn't blame her. If he had been Cindy, he would have felt as angry and betrayed as she did.

Wearily Trace leaned his head back against the cushion and thought of all the things that might have been: the woman of his dreams burning in his arms, loving him, and the cloud forest enfolding them....

A draft stirred through the room, whispering over the green bills, herding them across the floor until they gathered around Trace's feet. He didn't notice the money. He never had.

But he didn't expect her to believe that, either.

Chapter 14

Autumn had turned the aspen trees into thousands of yellow torches burning against the coming night of winter. Granite peaks thrust against the cloudless blue sky in saw-toothed magnificence. Dark green pines, silver sage and blazing aspens covered the rugged mountain slopes with a living patchwork quilt that stirred beneath a chill, pure wind.

Cindy noticed none of the grandeur of her surroundings as she stood with Lisa and Rye on the porch of their ranch home. In Cindy's soul she was in the center of a cloud forest swathed in mist and orchids and warmth, and Trace's heart was beating slowly beneath her cheek while she slept in his arms.

"Beautiful, isn't it?" Lisa asked, watching the horizon with amethyst eyes.

Rye stood beside her, looking at the woman, not at the land. He smiled with a gentleness that was at odds with his muscular appearance. It was the same for his hand touching his wife. There was a tenderness that was unexpected in a man who looked as rugged as he did. Slowly his fingers twined in Lisa's long, almost transparently blond hair, which fell in a shimmering cascade to her slender hips. The silken veil was a continuing source of delight to the violet-eyed, black-haired daughter who was gurgling serenely in Lisa's arms. Lisa's hair delighted Rye, as well. With open pleasure he stroked a shining tendril between his fingers while he smiled at his wife and child.

"The view isn't nearly as gorgeous as you are," he murmured, bending down to kiss Lisa. "And you, too," he added, laughing, when his daughter patted his mouth with her tiny hand.

As Cindy watched the others, she felt a combination of sadness and joy. Lisa's and Rye's love for one another welled up invisibly between them, spilling out to enrich everything they touched…and telling Cindy wordlessly just how much she was missing in her own life.

Trace.

Cindy pushed the silent cry into a dark corner of her mind, the same place where she kept the irrational sadness that came every time she realized that she wasn't pregnant. She should have been relieved that there was no legacy of her bittersweet brush with love. But she wasn't relieved. With her period had come a melancholy that could only be lightened by her niece's artless smiles.

The fact that Cindy wasn't pregnant had so depressed her that she had told no one. She was afraid that talking about it would shatter her brittle calm. Besides, as long as her father believed he had been successful, he wouldn't lay any more traps for her.

"Who was that on the phone?" Lisa asked.

"Dad," Rye said, turning reluctantly toward his sister. "Will you call him back?"

Tension tightened every muscle in Cindy's body. "No," she said without looking away from the horizon.

Rye ran a hand through his thick, unruly hair and said, "I don't blame you, sis. If it helps any, when I found out what he'd done, I tore a strip off him wide enough to cover the barn."

"Nothing will change. You know it as well as I do. Nothing either one of us says matters to him. He'll do what he has since mother died—whatever he damned well wants to do."

"What he wants is to talk to you," Rye said bluntly.

"Not really. All he wants to know is if I'm pregnant."

"So tell him."

Cindy fought against the tears welling up inside her, closing her throat. She shook her head in a silent negative and said nothing more. She had refused all calls from her father since she had returned from Ecuador. She had every intention of refusing Big

Eddy's calls until she was too old and feeble to pick up a phone.

"He said that Trace Rawlings is on his way to the States," Rye continued. "Dad wants to know if he should pay the pregnancy bonus. If you don't call him, I'll bet he'll be on the first flight out of Texas to here."

For an instant Cindy felt off balance, as though the earth had hesitated in its turning. Then came a slashing disappointment at this further confirmation that Trace was her father's hired stud.

"He can do what he always does," Cindy said after a long moment, her voice as expressionless as her face. "Whatever he pleases."

Lisa looked at Cindy, hesitated, then said quietly, "If you're pregnant, will you stay with us? Please? We want very much to share that time with you. Babies were meant to be shared."

Cindy searched her sister-in-law's unusual eyes and found the same unselfish love there that Rye had discovered during a timeless summer in McCall's Meadow.

"You may have been raised among Stone Age tribes, but you could teach angels how to be kind," Cindy said huskily.

"Kind?" Lisa laughed and kissed her daughter's tiny, waving fist. "More like selfish. I love seeing new life grow, feeling it kick beneath my hands, knowing that someday the miracle will be complete and another person will be standing close to me, talking to me, seeing a world that is both different from and the same as mine. A new mind, a new laugh, a new smile—even new anger and tears. A whole new person to love and be loved."

"Or hurt and be hurt?" Cindy asked painfully.

"Sometimes that's the only path to love," Lisa said, turning to brush her lips over Rye's lean hand. "It was for us."

"And sometimes there's no path to love at all." Cindy's mouth turned down in a sad curve. "We're told that the road to hell is paved with good intentions. I don't think so. I think it's paved with Big Eddy McCall's money."

Cindy stepped off the porch and walked to the beginning of a trail that led to a small creek. She had spent a lot of time by the creek since she had come back to the States. The crystal dance of water reminded her of the many liquid voices of the distant cloud forest where she had loved…and lost.

Rye started after his sister, only to be stopped by a light pressure from Lisa's hand.

"Let the sound of running water and the turning of the seasons heal her if they can," Lisa said. "We can't. We can only love her."

"I would like," Rye said too softly, "to get my hands on this SOB called Trace Rawlings."

"And I would like to help you."

Lisa's smile was as chill as the wind blowing down from the mountain peaks. Rye lifted his wife's small hand to his lips and pressed a kiss into her palm. Other people judged Lisa by her fragile appearance and spontaneous, radiant smile, forgetting that she had been raised among tribes for whom life was very simple, very direct. Rye never forgot the primitive fires that had forged Lisa's character. She not only loved, but she defended the things she loved with every bit of strength and intelligence she had.

And one of the things Lisa loved was Cindy.

"Too bad we'll never get to meet him," Rye said.

"Yes," Lisa said softly.

She rubbed her cheek against Rye's hand, sending a veil of hair shimmering over her deceptively delicate features.

Trace pulled up in front of the sprawling, recently remodeled ranch house and shut off the engine of his rented car. There were five vehicles parked in the ranch yard. He wondered which one of them belonged to Big Eddy. The Mercedes, probably. It sure as hell didn't belong on the lumpy dirt road that wound from the state highway to the ranch house.

No one came out to see who had just driven up. Trace lifted a small, hand-size box from the seat before he got out. He mounted the three front steps in a single flowing stride and knocked on the door with more force than finesse. It had been a long flight from Ecuador to Texas, where he had been told that Big Eddy had gone to see his son in Utah. Another airplane had brought Trace to a small airstrip, a rented car and a washboard road leading— he hoped—to Big Eddy.

Trace had dreamed of getting his hands on the man who had cost him the woman of his dreams.

The instant the door opened, Trace knew that the person facing him wasn't his quarry. The man was about Trace's age, slightly smaller in height and build, with the kind of eyes that Trace liked in a man—direct, confident, self-contained.

"Rye McCall?" Trace asked.

Rye nodded.

"I'm looking for Big Eddy."

"You've found him. He expecting you?"

"Yes. But not here."

Rye smiled slightly and moved inside. "Come in out of the wind."

Trace stepped into the house and waited while Rye closed the door behind him.

"Been on the road long?" Rye asked.

"Two days."

Rye's dark eyebrows climbed. "Long drive."

"Only for the pilots. I slept from takeoff to landing both times."

Within Rye, suspicion crystallized into certainty. His gray glance raked up and down the tall, powerfully built man who stood just a few feet away, looking both out of place and quietly dangerous in his worn khakis and jungle boots.

"You're Trace Rawlings."

The shift in Rye's tone didn't escape Trace. He wasn't welcome here. At all.

"Don't worry," Trace said coolly. "My business won't take long."

"You have five minutes."

Rye said nothing more. He didn't have to. Trace

knew that he had five minutes to get out of Rye's sight or take the consequences. For an instant Trace wanted nothing more than the violent physical outlet of the fight Rye was offering. Then Trace realized it would solve nothing. It would simply make things worse.

"If you weren't her brother, I'd take you up on it," Trace said calmly. "But she loves you, so hurting you would only hurt her."

Rye met Trace's savage green eyes and knew that Trace meant every word. Curiosity began to compete with anger in Rye. Why should a man like Trace Rawlings care what hurt Cindy? And there was no doubt in Rye's mind that Cindy was the only thing keeping Trace in check. The subtle change in the way Trace held himself while he waited for Rye's reaction told Rye that the other man was both unafraid of and trained in physical combat.

A motion in the doorway at the far end of the living room made both men turn. Lisa stood there, watching and listening to Trace with the intensity of a wild animal searching for danger. Just beyond her was a half-open door and a partial view of a man sitting behind a desk.

"Are you the man who took Cindy's laughter?" Lisa asked.

Trace's flinch was so subtle that only someone who was watching for just such a reaction would have seen it.

"Yes, I guess I am," he said softly. He looked at the shimmering fall of platinum hair and remembered Cindy's description of her sister-in-law. "You must be Lisa, the woman who makes knives out of glass."

As Lisa nodded, her hair shifted and glistened with ghostly radiance. "Are you here to see—"

"Big Eddy," Rye said quickly, not wanting Trace to know that Cindy was at the ranch.

"About the pregnancy bonus?" Lisa asked.

"I don't know," Rye said before Trace could answer. "He didn't tell me."

"Of course," Lisa said. "It's none of our business, is it? It belongs to Big Eddy and this man and whatever passes for a conscience between them."

"You use those glass knives to cut out men's hearts, don't you?" Trace asked softly as he walked past Lisa to the half-open office door.

"That shouldn't worry you."

Trace hesitated, then gave Lisa a green-eyed glance that concealed none of the shadows within his soul. "You're right. I don't have a heart. I gave mine away. But she didn't want it. I don't blame her. Hearts cause more pain than pleasure."

Before Lisa could speak, Trace walked into the office and stared at the man sitting behind the desk. He was the right size, the right age, and his eyes were a faded gray match for his son's. Big Eddy ignored the interruption. He sat looking off into the distance with an air of melancholy that was almost tangible. His daughter had refused to speak to him.

Trace walked up to the desk, pulled a wad of bills from his hip pocket and dropped the money in front of Cindy's father. The bills slithered across the desk in green disarray.

"What's this?" Big Eddy asked, focusing his shrewd gray eyes on the money.

"A refund. Your money and hers. You can sort it out between you. You're real good with money, I hear. You're hell on people, though. If I'd known you were crazy I'd never have taken the job."

"What job?"

"Guarding your daughter in Ecuador."

"Guarding?" Big Eddy smiled. "Is that what Invers told you? Well, it was true as far as it went."

"It didn't go nearly far enough, did it?"

"But apparently you did," Big Eddy said with real satisfaction. "Is she pregnant?"

Very carefully Trace set down the small box he had been carrying. With a good deal less finesse, he spread his fingers and planted his palms flat on the scarred surface of the wooden desk with enough force to scatter money in all directions. He leaned hard on his hands, hoping that would lessen the temptation to throttle Cindy's father. It didn't.

"Old man," Trace said in a low, rough voice, "you cost me the love of a good woman. If you weren't her father, I'd make you hurt as much as you've hurt me."

There was a sudden movement behind Trace, but he didn't turn away from Big Eddy.

"Love?" the older man asked softly, tasting the word as though it were unfamiliar on his tongue.

Trace's only answer was the predatory violence in his eyes as he watched the older man.

"A good woman loved me once," Big Eddy said quietly. "She died and nothing was ever the same...." He sighed deeply. "We all die, boy. The only thing that goes on is the children of our love, and their children, and their children, world without end. With enough children, she isn't really dead. She's alive. And someday she'll look out at me through the black eyes of my grandchildren or great-grandchildren and she'll smile." He nodded to himself. "Enough children, that's the key. Everyone thinks I want my own name and image out there—Edward McCalls down to the end of time." His mouth curved in a sad smile. "I did, once. No more. I'd rather see her face, young and alive, laughing and loving. Love is all there is that matters in life. The rest is just flash and fertilizer."

For a long moment Trace and Big Eddy looked at one another. Then Trace slowly closed his eyes. When they opened once more, the predatory gleam was gone, leaving behind only emptiness.

"Is there nothing of your dead wife in Cindy?" Trace asked quietly.

Bittersweet pleasure lighted Big Eddy's face. "Cindy is the image of her mother."

"Is that why you don't want her to trust any man enough to marry him?"

"What the hell are you talking about! I've moved heaven and hell to get my daughter married. When that didn't work I settled for pregnant."

"Is that what she wanted?"

"Who?"

"Cindy. Your daughter. Remember her? Or are you so busy thinking about your own dreams and needs that you don't know what you're doing to her?"

"Just who the hell do you think you are to—"

"I'm Trace Rawlings," he said coldly, cutting across Big Eddy's protests. "I'm the man who can take Cindy so far into the cloud forest that the twentieth century isn't even a rumor. And that's just what I'll do if you don't leave her alone. I'll take her away. I swear it. You've ridden long and hard on your solid gold horse, but it's over."

"Do you know how wealthy I am?" asked Big Eddy, more curious than overbearing.

"Do you know what I'd do with your money if I had it?" Trace said coolly. "I'd use it for toilet paper."

Reluctantly Big Eddy smiled. "She said the same thing."

"Your wife?"

"My daughter." He eyed Trace shrewdly. "You really think she'd go with you to that cloud forest?"

"Willingly?" Trace's mouth flattened. "Not a chance, old man. You ruined that for us. But I'd take her just the same. She belongs there. Most people hate the mist, hate the dense forest, hate the wildness. She didn't. So think about it and think hard. Leave her alone or lose her to a cloud forest where all your money doesn't mean one damn thing. Take your pick."

"I should have listened to Invers," Big Eddy said, sighing again. "He told me if you didn't want Cindy, no amount of money would change your mind. And if you did want her, nothing but killing you would stop you from having her."

"One thing would. It has. She doesn't want me."

"Thanks to me?"

"And to me," Trace admitted softly. "We could have survived your meddling. My bungling was different. I didn't believe a princess could love a peon until it was too damn late." Trace watched Big Eddy with opaque green eyes. "Have you decided?"

The older man smiled. "She's all yours, son. I decided that when your friend called and told me that you had shown up at the *hacienda*, that you wanted Cindy and that she wanted you. I was as excited as a kid at a birthday party. She hasn't looked at a man since I bought Jason for her, and that was years ago. I'd given up hope of getting her interested in any man. That's why I picked you. I figured if you wanted her, a determined man like you would find a way past her defenses. And you did, didn't you?"

"Once." Trace looked at his big hands and wondered if he would feel any better after he had had another talk with Invers, who had once again withheld more than he had told. "Are you particularly attached to Invers?"

"Who?"

"My 'friend.' The one who helped you set up Cindy."

"Raul Almeda was the one who helped me. Invers damn near scotched the whole deal. Said if it turned out badly you'd use our butts for a boot rack. Raul had to lean on Invers pretty hard before he'd agree. I still don't know how it went wrong," Big Eddy said, shaking his head. "You know, at first I thought Raul would be the ideal man for my daughter. I suggested it and described Cindy to him. He described you to me. I liked what I heard a whole lot. So I told Raul about Cindy's friend buying cloth in South America, and the rest was so easy, I thought it was meant to be."

Trace hissed a harsh word.

"Well, the logistics of getting you two together and keeping you together were easy enough," Big Eddy amended hastily.

"Was Susan in on it?"

"Hell, no, boy. She'd as soon cut my throat as look at me. But Raul kept his men on her all the way from Quito to the hacienda. It went so damned slick." Big Eddy sighed. "Then I had to go and brag to little Eddy and he squeezed Raul's number out of Invers and everything blew to hell and gone."

"Little Eddy?"

"My boy, Rye."

"Cindy would have found out sooner or later. Only dead men keep secrets. Be grateful I wasn't in on the secret sooner, old man. It would have been worth killing to keep."

Trace straightened, retrieved his package and turned to leave in a smooth, continuous motion. As he had expected, Lisa and Rye were standing behind him.

"Relax," Trace said coolly. "I haven't touched a

single gray hair on that slippery renegade's head."
He hesitated. "Do you know if she's pregnant?"

"Would it matter?"

"She was my woman. If she's pregnant, I want to
take care of her. I want the child to be born into my
hands…." Trace looked from Rye to Lisa. "But you
don't believe me and Cindy doesn't need me,
anyway. She has you two." Trace held out the box to
Rye. "She left this behind. Will you give it to her after
I leave?"

"What makes you think she's here?" Rye asked,
taking the box.

"She loves you and you love her," Trace said
simply. "If I had been hurt the way Cindy was, I'd
go to a place where I was loved."

Trace started to walk around the other two, only
to be stopped by a light touch from Lisa's hand.

"Is that where you're going now?" she asked. "To
a place where you're loved?"

Trace looked into Lisa's compassionate eyes for
a long moment before he said, "I don't have a place
like that. I never cared about love until it was too
late." He looked at the box in Rye's hand. "When
you give that to Cindy, tell her…" Trace's voice
faded into silence as he fought for self-control. It was
too long in coming. When he spoke, his voice was
too husky, almost rough. "I'll always look for her in
the mist, even though I know she'll never be there."

Suddenly Trace was moving quickly, brushing
past Lisa and Rye, leaving everything behind.

"Wait!" Lisa said.

Trace didn't even hesitate. Lisa ran after him into the living room and caught his arm with surprising strength.

"I want to talk with you. Privately. Please?" Lisa asked, her hand tightening on Trace's arm. "It won't take long. There's a room in the new wing where we won't be bothered. Please, Trace. It's very important."

Trace wanted to refuse but it was impossible. Her soft pleas had sounded too much like Cindy's. Reading his acceptance before he could speak, Lisa smiled gently and took Trace's hand.

Rye waited only long enough to be sure that Trace was listening to Lisa before he turned and walked swiftly through the kitchen and out the back door. He saw Cindy coming from the barn and waved her over.

"Did Dad finally give up and leave?" she asked.

"Not yet, but this came for you." Rye held out the box to Cindy.

She took it with a puzzled look.

"Open it," Rye urged.

Cindy peeled the tape off the top, lifted the lid and gave a broken cry as she saw an incredible orchid that had grown wild in a cloud forest thousands of miles away. A haunting fragrance drifted up from the flower, enveloping her, wrapping her in memories as she had once been wrapped in mist.

There was no note. Nor was there any doubt as to who had sent her the orchid. Gently she lifted the flower from its mossy nest and let the box fall away.

Feeling as though she were being torn apart, she bent her head over the orchid while hope and fear warred within her.

"He just wants to know if I'm p-pregnant," Cindy said, fighting against hope, knowing she wouldn't survive if hope won only to prove false once more.

"He said, 'I'll always look for her in the mist, even though I know she'll never be there.'" Rye looked at the orchid Cindy was holding and added softly, "His hands were trembling like yours. You can't buy that with money, sis. Not from a man as hard as Trace Rawlings."

Slowly Cindy lifted her head. Tears shimmered like raindrops on her cheeks and on the orchid's creamy petals.

"Is he—here?" she asked huskily.

"If I know Lisa, right now Trace is alone in the new den, watching the fire and wondering how in hell she sweet-talked him into staying when every instinct he has is screaming at him to run back to the cloud forest and lick his wounds in peace."

Before Rye finished speaking, Cindy was running into the house.

At the sound of the door opening behind him, Trace turned away with the primitive masculine grace that had haunted Cindy's dreams. As she walked toward him she saw that he looked older, harder, more alone, and his green eyes devoured her with a complex yearning that said more than words.

"Princess…?" he whispered, afraid to hope.

"I love you," Cindy said, holding out her cupped

hands to Trace, within them the orchid trembling as though it were alive. "I love you."

Slowly Trace cupped his hands beneath Cindy's and bent until he could breathe in the fragrance of both flower and woman. When he straightened, more clear drops gleamed on the orchid's flawless petals. Very gently he took Cindy in his arms, kissing the tears from her eyelashes, whispering his love for her again and again. Then he held her close and hard, trying to absorb her through his skin into his bones, feeling tears like warm rain on his cheeks, on hers.

And he knew all the way to his soul that the next time he looked for her in the cloud forest's swirling mist she would be there, holding her hands out to him, running to him, bringing to him the sweet, dark fire of love.

* * * * *

EXPECTING HIS CHILD

USA TODAY Bestselling Author

Leanne Banks

LEANNE BANKS

is a *USA TODAY* bestselling author who is surprised every time she realizes how many books she has written. Leanne loves chocolate, the beach and new adventures. To name a few, Leanne has ridden an elephant, stood on an ostrich egg (no, it didn't break), gone parasailing and indoor skydiving. Leanne loves writing romance novels because she believes in the power and magic of love. She lives in Virginia with her family. Visit her Web site at www.leannebanks.com.

Prologue

He thundered across the dusty Texas soil on the back of a black stallion like an avenging angel. Panic flooded her bloodstream. Martina Logan quickly backed away from the crowd of wedding guests and hid behind a tree. The guests at her brother's outdoor wedding gasped and murmured. Not many would be able to identify him from this distance, but Martina could. Her eyes didn't need to tell her; her heart did the trick, pounding erratically against her rib cage.

Noah Coltrane.

Noah slowed the stallion and guided the impressive animal to the vacated dance area. He scanned the crowd and Martina tried to make herself shrink.

Her brother Tyler spoke up. "What do you want, Noah?"

"I'm here to see Martina."

Her stomach dipped to her knees and she prayed he wouldn't see her. She wasn't ready to face him. Not yet.

"She doesn't want to see you," Tyler said. "Get off the property. Can't you see we're having a wedding?"

"That means she's here," Noah said, surveying the crowd once again.

"Buy a vowel," Tyler said. "She doesn't want to see you."

Martina closed her eyes during the long pause that followed.

"I will see her," Noah finally said, the hard resolve in his voice giving her a chill. "Give her that message."

Trembling, Martina stole a private moment and covered her face with her hands. A dozen images raced through her mind. Months ago, hearing Noah's Texas drawl on the stalled El in Chicago had reminded her how far from home she was. Hearing his voice had rubbed at an empty spot, and she had turned around to see the most fascinating man she'd ever met.

Noah was not the usual cowboy. Not only did he rope and ride, he also fenced and traded cattle options on the Chicago exchange. When they'd met, Martina had been temporarily assigned to a computer company in the Windy City while Noah was taking a course in commodities. He'd charmed her and made her feel comfortable before revealing his name.

Martina still remembered the regret she'd felt and seen echoed on his face when they'd realized their families hated each other. There was enough bad blood between the two ranching families to fill the Red Sea. It was bad enough that his family and hers had quarreled for generations over the stream their ranches shared. What sealed the grudge was the fact that Noah's great-grandfather had tried to steal the wife of Martina's great-grandfather, and during the course of it all, the Logan bride had died.

Still, Noah had suggested with a wry chuckle that since they weren't in Texas, they could pretend their last names were different.

He was the biggest no-no she'd ever said yes to. It had been all too easy to fall for him, and the memory of the passion and laughter they'd shared still made her weak. But reality and family loyalty had eventually crept in. Their affair had ended as quickly as it began. Martina, however, had been left with the consequences of her temporary insanity called Noah Coltrane.

Martina bit her lip and opened her eyes. She touched her abdomen swollen with Noah's child. She dreaded the day she would have to face him. She knew it was coming. Noah Coltrane would always be her biggest no-no. Her favorite mistake.

Chapter 1

He'd finally found her. Six weeks after he'd crashed her brother's wedding, Noah eyed Martina Logan's condo with a feeling of satisfaction and cynicism. The woman had made love to him like a firestorm for three of the most insane, yet oddly fulfilling weeks of his life, then abruptly disappeared.

Her leaving had stung his ego and he hadn't gone after her. He would forget her, he'd told himself. After all, with so much bad blood between their families, they'd both known the relationship was doomed from the start. But he'd seen a fire of independence in Martina's eyes that echoed in his gut, and he hadn't wanted to resist.

As the days passed after she'd left, Noah was

haunted by her memory. Thoughts of her interrupted his sleep. It stuck in his craw when he made a few small attempts to locate her and couldn't.

Then it became his mission to find her and to exorcise her from his mind. His peace would come from looking into her eyes and letting her see that she couldn't hide from him. His relief would come from seeing that she wasn't nearly the woman he'd thought her to be. Then he would be on his way.

Walking toward her front door, he idly noticed the scrape of his boots against the hot pavement and the deceptively peaceful sound of birds chirping in the late-spring morning. He paused on her doorstep and, pushing aside the feeling that all hell was about to break loose, he pressed the doorbell twice.

"Just a minute," her voice called, and his gut twisted at the sound. He heard her footsteps and voice grow louder as she came closer.

"Yes, I'm keeping my appointments. I'm fine," she said, opening the door. "I'm—" Her eyes met Noah's and her mouth formed an *O* of surprise. Her jaw worked, but no sound came out. He watched her swallow. "I…I…I've got to go," she said, and pushed a button to disconnect.

Noah drank in the sight of her—her dark, tousled hair, shocked blue eyes, worried mouth, long throat, full breasts and fuller tummy.

Much fuller tummy.

The implication of her change in size triggered a dozen questions inside him. Martina was pregnant.

Whose baby?

Could it be his?

How far along was she?

His mind asked the questions, but his gut knew the important answer.

"I've gained weight," she said, smiling brightly enough to almost blind him. Almost, but Noah noticed the protective way she covered her abdomen with her hand. "You know how that goes. Some people just seem to gain it all in one place." She pushed her other hand through her hair and blinked innocently. "I can't imagine what would bring you here."

Noah struggled with the images that raced through his mind. Images where she had been laid bare beneath him, crying out his name. Images where she had looked into his eyes and he had gotten lost in the depths of her. At the time, he could have sworn she'd been equally lost in him.

"When did you start gaining the weight, Martina?" he asked. "About eight to twelve weeks after the last time you were with me? You must be over six months pregnant."

Her smile slipped slightly. "I don't remember when I started gaining weight," she said.

Another way of pleading the Fifth, Noah thought cynically. "And I'll bet you'll lose a lot of this weight suddenly," he said, his emotions roiling like the Galveston beach before a storm.

"The baby's mine, isn't it," he said, cutting through her ridiculous story. He decided this situation was going to require the best combination of his instincts and brain.

She dropped her hand from her hair and clasped both of her palms in front of her abdomen. Her gaze narrowed and her eyes glinted with a mixture of fear and fight. "My baby," she corrected. "Who told you?"

"No one. I looked at you and knew," he said, his entire body clenching with the knowledge that Martina was carrying his baby. "You need to let me in," he said, surprised at the calm tone of his voice. He felt as if she had set off a bomb inside him.

Martina bristled. "This isn't a good time. I'm busy working right now. My company is allowing me to design Web pages from home, but I do have deadlines."

"When is a good time?" Noah asked, baiting her. "Next year?"

Martina's smile vanished and she set her chin. "Next year is too soon."

It occurred to Noah that this woman could have easily inspired the saying Don't mess with Texas. She tried to close the screen door in his face, but he caught it with his boot. "I'm not going away."

Her eyes flashed. "I'm over my quota of pushy, overbearing men in my life. I don't respond well to force."

He nodded. "Good," he said. "I only use force as a last resort when I'm dealing with someone who is being unreasonable."

She looked at him with skepticism, but stepped away from the door.

Martina had dreaded this day. She'd known she would have to tell Noah about the baby someday.

She'd decided an e-mail, fax or message sent by carrier pigeon would be much preferable to a face-to-face confrontation. The time had never seemed right. As a rule she didn't procrastinate, but she'd broken several rules by getting involved with Noah in the first place.

As he walked past her, she remembered some of the silly reasons she'd allowed herself to get involved with him. His height. She'd always been tall, and it had felt good to be held by a man several inches taller. She'd liked the way he smelled—of leather and spicy musk. She'd liked the sound of his voice and the way his mind worked.

After living with a father and two brothers determined to protect, defend and dominate her, being with a reasonable man who treated her as an equal had gone to her head like too much tequila.

Martina had the unnerving intuition that she might not be able to count on Noah to be reasonable right now.

He glanced around her den, then walked toward her. Her heart squeezed in her chest at the formidable expression on his face.

"When were you going to tell me?" he asked in a calm voice at odds with the turbulence in his eyes.

Her stomach fluttered with nerves. "I was going to tell you. I just hadn't figured out how."

"When? After the baby was born? After our child took first steps or went to school? Or reached legal age?"

The sense of betrayal in his voice scraped at her.

She struggled with shame and frustration. "I should have told you. It would have been the right thing to do, but it was wrong to get involved with you in the first place. When I found out I was pregnant, I couldn't believe it was true. I had to come to terms with it on my own."

"If you'd told me, you wouldn't have had to do anything alone," he told her.

Martina's heart hurt as a dozen memories slammed through her. "We knew when we got involved that it couldn't last. You said we could pretend while we were in Chicago. You never talked about a future with me because you knew there wouldn't be one."

He rested his hands on his hips. "The baby changes things."

Her stomach sank at the determination in his voice. "For me and maybe for you, but not for us."

"You should have told me."

"Yes, well, I had to get used to the idea first. And having my brothers find out a Coltrane was the father…" She broke off and grimaced at the memory of that confrontation.

"What'd they do?" Noah asked. "Look at you like you were giving birth to the anti-Christ?"

"At first," she said. "But I set them straight."

"Who did you tell them was the father?"

"I told them the stork did it," she said, but the flip remark didn't work its charm. "When you showed up at my brother's wedding like the Lone Ranger, it became difficult to deny paternity." She took a careful breath. "I have handled this on my own. I got through the shock and morning sickness and everything else on my own. I'm strong. I can handle the rest alone, too."

He gave a wry half smile that somehow looked dangerous. "We never got around to discussing children, but I have some definite opinions on the subject. The first is that the parents should be married. You and I should marry as soon as possible."

Martina gaped at him. If he hadn't been dead serious, she would have laughed. "You must not have heard me. I have put up with three domineering men in my life—my father and brothers—and I am not interested in tying myself till death do us part to another."

"This baby deserves two parents. Both of us will want to be involved in raising the child. I don't walk away from my responsibilities."

There wasn't an ounce of give in his voice, but he struck on one issue she'd been unable to resolve in her heart and mind. Martina wanted the best for her child, but she couldn't marry Noah. "We can work out visitation," she began, trying to pump conviction into her tone.

"That's another thing that's stupid. It's crazy for you to live alone here in Dallas when you can live at my family ranch."

Everything inside her balked. "Now I know you're insane. Have you forgotten that my family home borders your property? Do you think my brothers and your brothers are going to have a party over this? I don't think so. Plus, there is the Logan curse. Women bearing the Logan name have shown an annoying tendency to kick the bucket when they fall in love and get married. I'll admit I never thought the curse applied to me, but on the off chance that it does, I have a pretty powerful reason to stay alive and healthy. My baby."

Noah stood there silently. He looked as if he was reining himself in, processing every word she'd said. Planning.

Martina felt a sinking sensation, but kept her back ramrod straight. She was no sissy, she told herself. She could handle Noah Coltrane.

"We'll talk again," he said, pulling out a pen and business card and scratching some numbers on the back of it. "If you need anything, anything at all, call me. Cell number's on the back." He met her gaze again. "You said your family curse means a Logan woman will die when she marries. You forget. When you marry me, you won't be a Logan woman. You'll be a Coltrane."

"When cows do algebra," she fumed as she watched Noah walk out her door. "I'll be a Coltrane when Texans stop arguing over water rights, when your brothers and my brothers give each other big hugs, which will be *never*," she continued, even though she was only talking to the air that Noah had breathed and the space he had invaded. His presence was still disturbing even though he was gone. "I'll be a Coltrane when the stars fall over West Texas."

* * *

Noah had so much adrenaline pumping through his veins that he could easily have snapped the steering wheel of his Tahoe in half. He had impregnated the most unreasonable, stubborn woman in Texas, and he had a feeling it was going to take everything he had to corral her and bring her and the baby to the Coltrane ranch where they belonged.

A part of him wondered if he had sensed something important had happened to Martina. He wondered if that was what had kept him awake nights. Although Noah knew he was the most modern of the Coltranes, he also suspected the trace of Native American blood in his veins gave him instincts not so easily explained.

He sighed in disgust. It would be nice if those instincts could provide something more useful than a sleepless night, something like an easy way to win Martina over.

To persuade her, he was going to have to see this from her point of view. Noah knew he was more open-minded than his brothers, but he wasn't sure he could think like a woman, God help him. Especially when every drop of primitive protectiveness and possessiveness raged to the surface when he remembered that Martina was carrying his child.

Taking a deep breath, he pulled into the dusty drive to the main ranch house. On a normal day, he felt a sense of well-being every time he came home. Zachary Tremont, former ranch foreman, had always told Noah that if he grew still and quiet, he would hear the voice of welcome when he was in the right place. Zachary was probably the reason none of the Coltrane boys had ended up in prison. Their father, Joe, had been a drunk, a mean one at that, and their mother, a strict churchgoer, had died of cancer. The union hadn't exactly produced a pleasant home environment.

One good thing Joe had done just before he passed away, though, was to hire Zachary. During his time at the Coltrane ranch, Zachary had taught Noah and his brothers the discipline of fencing. More importantly, he had taught each of the boys about honor and the importance of finding and honoring his individual purpose.

Noah missed Zachary and would have traded his most valuable antique sword for a chance to talk to the man now. But Zachary had left when Noah's brother Adam grew old enough to manage the ranch, insisting it was time for him to move on.

Noah glanced at the recently remodeled and expanded ranch house and waited for the feeling of welcome. On a normal day, he felt the warmth of it curl in his stomach and flow through his blood.

This, however, was not a normal day. His brothers were not going to have a party over his news. A riot was more likely.

He waited until everyone had eaten dinner. Adam was downing a third beer, Jonathan was leaning back with his eyes closed, and Gideon was lighting a cigar.

"We need to make plans for an addition," Noah said.

Adam glanced at him quizzically. "Another

one? We've already built bunkhouses for the fencing camps and roundup weekends you want to run."

"We can wait. I don't want anyone touching the house," Gideon said. "I'm sick of falling over contractors. I want to smoke cigars in peace."

"Then take them outside," Jonathan muttered, his eyes still closed. He wasn't fond of Gideon's trendy habit.

"It's not a building," Noah said. "It's a baby."

Complete silence reigned. Jonathan's eyes popped open. Adam and Gideon stared at Noah.

"Whose baby?" Adam asked in a low voice.

"Mine," Noah said, and called to the cook. "Patch, you mind bringing in that good bottle of whiskey and three shot glasses?"

Jonathan, the brother to whom Noah felt closest, had the most even temperament and was by far the most intuitive. "You're not drinking?"

"Not yet," Noah said, and poured the whiskey.

"Congratulations," Gideon said with a sly grin and swallowed his shot. "Does this baby come with a woman?"

"Yeah," Noah said. "Martina Logan."

Jonathan dropped his shot glass. Adam and Gideon stared at Noah in disbelief.

"You better be joking," Adam said.

"I'm not. She's carrying my baby. We met in Chicago. She's not like her brothers," Noah said, then remembered her scorching refusal to his proposal this morning. "In some ways, she's worse," he said with a wry laugh. "But I'm going to marry her, bring her here to live, and we're going to raise the baby here."

Adam and Gideon stood. "You've gone way too far this time," Adam said. "The Coltranes have *nothing* to do with the Logans. We don't date 'em. We don't marry 'em. We don't get 'em pregnant. Hell, we don't speak to 'em."

"Too late," Noah said.

Swearing, Gideon grabbed Noah by the shirt collar. "It's not too late. Tell her to get rid—"

Instinct raged through him, and Noah pushed his brother away. "I don't want to ever hear that from you or any of you again."

Adam shook his head. "You've gone too far," he said. "I'm cutting you out of the ranch. Just leave and don't come back."

Noah glanced at Jonathan and read the distress and disappointment on his face. His gut wrenched at the thought of leaving. "Okay. I guess that means you don't need the money I make for the ranch by trading cattle futures and leasing the hunting rights."

Adam cursed under his breath. "You know that money has bailed us out during a bad year." He shook his head again. "Now how could you make such a huge mistake?"

"I dislike the Logans as much as you do, but I've been dealt a new hand of cards, and I have to do what's right. We've all spent most of our lives living down the bad decisions our father, or his father, or his father made. I'm not gonna keep making bad decisions. This baby's no mistake."

Adam and Gideon glared at him in hostile silence.

Jonathan sighed and broke the angry, tense silence. "I wonder what Zachary would say right now," he mused in a calm voice that was like cool water on flames.

Noah immediately saw the change in his brothers' faces. Adam exhaled and viewed him with grudging acceptance.

Gideon looked away, clearly ashamed. "Sorry I said that about getting rid…" He broke off. "Sorry," he said. True to form, he was quick to anger, but usually quick to apologize. "I'm going for a walk."

"I'm going to bed," Adam said.

Noah stood in the dining room with only Jonathan. Jonathan reached for the bottle of whisky, poured a shot into his glass and held it out for Noah to take. "I like a lot of your ideas and innovations," he said. "When Adam balked, I could see you were going to do good things. I always envied how you could think outside the box. But I gotta tell you— this isn't outside the box. It's not outside the county or the state. It's outside the universe. So what was it? Temporary insanity?"

Noah swallowed the liquor, feeling the fire all the way down his throat and chest into his stomach. "Maybe," he said, and met Jonathan's gaze. "It felt right."

Jonathan shook his head in disbelief. "How could it possibly?"

"I'm not sure I can explain it. The same way it feels right for you to train horses. Why aren't you hollering or taking a swing at me?"

Jonathan covered a faint grin with his hand. "Based on my limited experience with the Logans, I'm just guessing that Martina Logan is gonna torture you more than I ever could."

Noah gave a wry chuckle. "Maybe."

"How does she feel about getting married?"

"She's getting used to the idea," Noah said, thinking that wasn't anywhere near the truth. It must have shown.

"She flat out turned you down," Jonathan concluded.

Noah nodded. "She did. But I've had a lot of practice turning no into yes."

Chapter 2

"Thanks for helping with the groceries, Rodney," Martina said as she pushed the key into her front door.

"No problem," her neighbor said. "I— Excuse me, who?"

"I'm the father of her baby," a familiar voice said from behind her, heating her to the core with the simple statement.

Martina's stomach dipped. She had thought he wouldn't be back for at least a week or two. Wishful thinking. She turned quickly and met Noah's gaze, noting the fact that he, instead of Rodney, was carrying her grocery bags.

"What a surprise," she finally managed.

Rodney eyed Noah with suspicion.

"Rodney, this is Noah." She took a deep breath. She rebelled at using Noah's words. They were primal, possessive and emphasized the connection between them, a connection Martina preferred to diminish. "He, uh, contributed genetic material," she said, and forced a smile. "Thanks again for helping."

"Anytime," Rodney said with a nod and curious glance at Noah.

"What brings you here?" she asked Noah after Rodney left.

"You." Noah caught the door for her and followed her into the kitchen. "You missed me," he said, his voice holding a mix of sexy humor.

Martina's lips twitched and she put her bag on the counter. "Like I miss morning sickness."

"Did you have much of it?" he asked more seriously.

"About three weeks when I lived on saltines, soda and vitamins."

"And now?"

She turned to face him. "Now I'm just really big."

His gaze fell over her, lingering on her breasts, tummy and legs. "Just in a few places," he said. "Pregnancy looks good on you."

The way he looked at her reminded her of the passion they'd shared and the way he had taken her body. The way he looked at her reminded her of how much she had wanted him. Martina pushed the thought from her mind and turned back around to put away the groceries. "You didn't really say what you wanted."

"Yes, I did," he said. "You."

Her heart jumped and she nearly dropped a carton of eggs. "You wanted to talk to me about something," she quickly corrected for his benefit and hers.

"Have you thought any more about my proposal?"

She mentally put on her armor as she put away the groceries. "I don't recall any proposals."

"For you to marry me," he told her calmly.

"You didn't ever really ask," she said. "You ordered."

"Will you marry me?"

"No," she said as quickly as he'd asked.

He sighed and she reluctantly met his gaze. "Do you think you are doing the best thing for the baby to not have me involved at all?"

She opened her mouth to say yes, but a strong inner integrity defeated her. She closed her mouth.

"Do you think the best thing for this baby is to have two parents married to each other living in the same home?"

Martina had admired his insight before. Now it got under her skin. "In general, yes, but we have a special circumstance. Our families have held a grudge against each other for over a hundred years."

"What's more important? A grudge or the welfare of our child?"

Martina shook her head. "There's more involved and you know it. You and I wanted each other temporarily. We knew we weren't looking for anything permanent. There's a big difference between what is good on a temporary basis and what is good forever."

Noah walked toward her, his eyes glinting. "Are you saying I'm not good husband material?"

Each step he took closer packed a wallop on her nerve endings. His intensity, his confidence, his personality, his aura had been and still were entirely too sexy for her own good. She lifted her chin. "Yes, I am. There's a big difference between a lover and a husband. As a husband, I can already tell you'll pull the same kind of caveman routines my brothers do. You'll order me around and tell me what to do and expect me to be a good, submissive wife. I'm too independent for that. While you may have been an—" she took a breath and wished for a fan "—incredible lover, you wouldn't work for me as a husband," she said, "at all."

She needed to make that clear to him, to her, to the entire free world, all Third World countries and any planets inhabited by intelligent life.

He put his hands on the counter on either side of her, crowding her. "You're assuming I'll act that way. You don't know that I will. You really only have your experience to judge me. So tell me, what did I do wrong?"

Martina stared into his eyes and bit her lip to keep from repeating the words that flooded her brain. *You were too sexy. You made me melt. You made me feel more like a woman than I've ever felt in my life. You made me feel like the most desirable woman in the world. You made me fall so hard I almost couldn't get back up. You made me feel so much for you so fast. You terrified me.*

She tore her gaze from his and stared down at his boots. "You have the wrong last name. And you have given signs that you would try to rule me," she told him. "You tried to *order* me to marry you and come live with you."

"What was your reaction when you found out you were pregnant?"

Martina remembered the bloodcurdling scream she'd let out once she'd left the doctor's office and closed herself in her car. "Okay, I'll admit it wasn't a quiet, rational response."

"How many decibels?"

She frowned at him. "I don't know. I just remember wondering if I'd permanently broken my larynx." She smiled. "But as you can see, I didn't."

"The point is, your first response wasn't the most rational. My first instinct was and is to protect." His gaze drifted over her body, warming her. "What's wrong with that?"

"Nothing, as long as you don't go overboard."

"And you don't think you'll go overboard protecting our baby?"

Martina's chest tightened. She was already feeling overprotective of the precious life inside her. "It's my job to protect."

"Mine, too," he said, lifting his hand to cup her chin. "I won't forget it," he told her, and everything about him, his voice, his determined eyes, his posture, made an oath.

Martina felt a sinking sensation. This was why she hadn't wanted to tell him. She had known Noah wouldn't abandon his child, and her life would be intertwined with his for the rest of her days. She just wasn't sure she could see him on a regular basis and keep her good sense intact. Lifting her head away, she steeled her mind against him. "That's nice, but—"

"And it's part of the reason I'm here," he said, dropping his hand to his hip, but still crowding her. "There's a lot I don't know about you, and there's a lot you don't know about me. You may not want to marry me, but we're still having a baby together. In that case, we've got a lot to learn about each other."

Martina hadn't thought her stomach could sink any lower. "What are you saying?"

"We need to get to know each other. We need to spend some time together."

No, no, no, no, no. Sliding past him would have been much easier if she hadn't been seven months pregnant. Martina gently nudged him away. "I hate for you to have to drive so far for something that shouldn't take much time. Don't you think a résumé would work just as well?"

"No."

"We could write each other. E-mail," she said enthusiastically. "Everyone keeps in touch through e-mail these days."

He shook his head. "If this were the Old West, I could haul you off and carry you home. Sadly, in this case, those days are gone," he muttered under his breath. "I know you as a lover. I know what makes you—" his eyes darkened in remembrance "—go," he finished. "But I need to know more than that. I need to know the mother of my child."

His gaze cut through her, and Martina had a terrible premonition that having Noah know her could be more dangerous for her than making love with him had been. His intensity made the prospect feel unbearably intimate. *Oh, hell,* Martina thought, wanting to kick something. How was she supposed to refuse that request?

He moved closer, leaning on his uplifted arm against the wall beside her. "We might as well start with the hard stuff."

Hard stuff, Martina thought. That would be you. "What's that?" she asked warily.

"What's your favorite flavor of ice cream?" he asked.

A rush of relief raced through her. Martina was so relieved she was almost charmed. Almost, but she was determined to stay on guard.

"En garde!" Gideon cried, and lunged toward Noah. Gideon, whose temper flared quickly but cooled with equal speed, had gotten past his anger and was more than willing to try to best his older brother in a duel.

The parry, the clash and scrape of metal sword-play had been one of the best ways for Noah to let off steam since Zachary had taught him and his brothers to fence in the old barn.

"Rough afternoon with the Logan princess?" Gideon goaded him with a smile.

Noah plunged past his younger brother's defense to touch his chest. *He contributed genetic material.*

Every time Martina's flip words played through his mind, his head roared with anger.

Gideon nodded wryly at the point and backed away slightly. "I'll take that as a yes."

"It could have been worse," Noah said with a short nod. "Ready?" he asked, and they began again.

"In other words, she didn't sic her brothers on you," Gideon said.

"Compared to Martina, her brothers are cake. We've at least been able to reason with Brock Logan about wandering cattle and the pond we share. Martina knows what's best—she just isn't being reasonable."

"And what's best is…?"

Noah stated the obvious. "For us to marry and raise the baby here."

Gideon touched his rib cage.

"Touché," Noah said. "Ready."

"Can't blame her for hesitating. We've never been the favored family of the county," Gideon said.

"That's in the past," Noah insisted. It was one of his greatest passions to put the bad Coltrane reputation in the past and to build a new one based on respect. "All of us have worked to put that behind us."

"Yeah, but for Pete's sake, did you have to pick that Logan woman? Why not someone a little more easygoing?"

"You mean a woman who doesn't have the ability to slice a man to ribbons with her tongue?" Noah asked, pushing Gideon closer to the back wall.

"Yeah," Gideon said, swinging his sword for all he was worth.

"Someone more submissive," Noah said, thinking Martina would probably stab them both if she heard this discussion.

"Yeah. It sounds like you might as well be trying to seduce a porcupine," Gideon said. "A pregnant porcupine."

Noah lunged and pressed the tip of his sword to the protective material covering Gideon's heart. Martina might be acting like a porcupine, but Noah had experienced the soft, giving woman behind the quills. He was determined to find that woman again.

"Touché," his brother said with a shake of his head. "Hell, you make a great case for contraception. What are you going to do?"

"The same thing I do in a fencing match. Find her weakness and exploit it." Noah knew he sounded ruthless, but he wasn't playing for fun with Martina. He was playing for blood, his family name and his child.

He found her reclining on a chaise longue in her backyard in the late afternoon. Dressed in shorts and a maternity tank top she'd lifted above her belly while she rested. Her legs were long and lithe, and knowing the baby she carried was his made him want her in an elemental way. Her expression was soft, almost wistful and her gaze was faraway. He remembered how she had once looked at him with passion-drenched eyes, and he wondered what tender thoughts she could be thinking right now.

He walked closer and heard her say, "I look like a beached whale. I can't even reach my toenails to paint them."

Noah saw the bottle of nail polish beside her, and his gaze shot to the next yard. He saw a woman wearing a bikini. He bit back a chuckle. "You still have the best legs in Texas," he said.

She turned her head quickly, and her cheeks turned pink with embarrassment. "I, uh, was just—"

"—feeling sorry for yourself," he finished for her. "I brought Chinese food for dinner. Does it agree with you?"

Martina sighed. "Unfortunately every food agrees with me now. And I wasn't feeling sorry for myself."

"Uh-huh," he said, without an ounce of conviction.

Martina stood. "No, really. I—"

"Martina, you are a very beautiful woman, pregnant or not pregnant. You just haven't had a man around to remind you."

She stared at him for a long moment, revealing a glimpse of the woman he'd known in Chicago. She took a deep breath. "Don't flatter me."

"I won't," he assured her. "I just tell the truth. I'd say something else," he said, allowing his gaze to linger on her full breasts. "But I don't want you to take a swing at me. You might hurt yourself. Are you hungry for Chinese food or not?"

She blinked and paused as if debating whether to hit him, anyway. "I'm hungry, period. Let's eat inside. I didn't expect you," she said, leading him though the back door to the cool kitchen.

"Didn't your mother tell you to always expect the unexpected from a Coltrane?"

Her smile wavered. "My mother didn't get an opportunity to teach me anything about the Coltranes. She died when I was born."

Noah immediately regretted his joke. "I'm sorry. I didn't mean any disrespect."

"That's okay. Besides, my father and brothers gave me an earful about the Coltranes." She plucked the containers of food from the bag.

"I'm sure they did," he muttered, and carefully voiced his next thought. "I realize you descend from Amazons and you could easily harvest an entire field of corn in the morning, deliver your baby at lunch and finish up another field in the afternoon. But do you ever think you might have problems when you deliver the baby?"

She drummed her fingers on the cabinet. "If you hadn't included the Amazon part, I would say no. But the truth is, although I don't worry about it a lot and the doctor says I'm perfectly healthy," she emphasized, "I think about it every now and then."

He saw the fleeting vulnerability and longing in her eyes and remembered how he had felt when his mother died. "You still miss the chance of knowing her, don't you?"

"I would have given anything to know her. I've always missed her and I probably always will. I was lucky to have two brothers who tried very hard and awkwardly at times to make up for the loss." She pushed her hair behind her ear. "What about your parents?"

"I think I miss more of what might have been. My parents weren't happy together."

Martina lifted her eyebrows. "My parents were crazy about each other. My brothers told me that was why my father never seemed happy after she died. Looking at me was too painful for him, because I reminded him of his loss."

Noah realized he had known Martina's mother was dead, but he'd never heard the whole story, and they'd agreed not to speak of their families during their time together in Chicago. It made him see her in a new light. "We had a foreman named Zachary, who taught my brothers and me about being a man. Zachary always said the strongest love survives distance and death, and it always makes you a better man."

She narrowed her eyes. "Are you saying my parents didn't love each other?"

"I'm saying your dad missed an opportunity to love and be loved by a little girl who could have taken away some of the hurt."

Martina looked at Noah for a long moment. He could practically see her mind poking at his statement, examining and pondering, then setting it aside. She glanced at the boxes of food on the counter. "Dibs on the sweet 'n' sour chicken."

They dug into the food, and Martina didn't eat nearly as much as Noah had expected. "I thought you were eating for two. You made it sound like you're eating everything but the living-room furniture."

"I'm not eating for two. It's more like I'm eating for one and one-twelfth. Besides, I wanted to save room for ice cream." She smiled with mischief. "I need my calcium."

"Have you had an ultrasound yet?"

She nodded as she scooped fudge-swirl ice cream into two bowls. "Two months ago. The way the baby was positioned didn't reveal its sex, but I have a feeling it will be a—"

"—girl," he interjected.

"—boy," she said at the same time with a look of surprise on her face.

"I would have thought you'd have some sort of macho expectation about producing a male," she said.

"And I would have thought you'd have some sort of feminist expectation about producing a female," he said. "Both wrong about each other. Looks like we've got a long way to go to get to know each other."

Her face fell. "I still think e-mail is the best solution."

"It hasn't been that bad this time," he said, rising from his chair and walking closer to her. Following an impulse that could get him kicked, bitten or scratched, he lifted her finger to his lips and sucked the ice cream from the tip. Her eyes grew wide and she jerked her hand from his.

"What has made you more reasonable this time?" he asked. "Maybe you like me a little more than you thought you did."

She took a quick breath and a dozen emotions swept through her blue eyes. Noah would swear one of them was desire. Maybe he was getting through.

"Food," she said. "It was definitely the food."

It was definitely not the food that was keeping her awake tonight, Martina thought much later as she threw back the covers on her bed. Every time she closed her eyes, a picture from the first time she and Noah had made love flashed across her mind.

She sat up in bed and sighed, holding her head in her hands and surrendering to the memory for just a moment. They'd eaten Chicago pizza for dinner, then Noah had taken her back to his suite to show her how he traded futures on the Chicago exchange on his laptop. His excitement had been contagious, and after a while, she'd been more caught up in his enthusiasm than his words.

"You're not listening," he said, sitting beside her, his thigh rubbing against hers.

Martina felt her cheeks heat. "I was," she insisted.

"Okay, what happens after the price jumps ten percent?"

"I didn't know there'd be a quiz."

He laughed, and the rich, dark sound curled inside her and heated her down to her toes. He tugged her from her chair and pulled her onto his lap. "If you weren't thinking about futures, then what were you thinking about?"

Bracing herself on his shoulders, she considered dodging the question, but followed another instinct, instead. "I was thinking about you," she said, lifting her fingers to his solid jaw. "You have such a passion for almost everything you do."

His eyes darkened and he pressed her fingers to his lips. "More than one person has called me crazy for my ideas."

"A little crazy is not a bad thing," Martina said, feeling a relentless urgency grow in her belly and blood.

He sucked her finger into his mouth, and she held her breath while he held her gaze. "I'm getting a passion for Martina."

"That could be too crazy," she whispered as he pulled her face closer to his.

"Too late," he said, and took her mouth.

Martina's world spun. He had kissed her before, but tonight was different. She felt it in the air, in his touch, inside her. He made love to her mouth, tasting her, seducing her, savoring her until her heart clamored for more. She sank her fingers into his hair, luxuriating in the soft, wavy texture.

He pulled away and she felt almost as if she was in a dream. Giving her a dozen opportunities to stop him, he slowly, deliberately lifted her sweater over her head and unfastened her bra.

"Do you want this?" he asked, touching the aching tips of her breasts with his thumbs.

Her mouth went dry and she closed her eyes. Her heart hammered a mile a minute. There were reasons, very valid reasons, she should stop, but her brain could not produce one of them at this moment. She had never wanted a man so badly in her life. It wasn't so much his incredible body as much as it was his mind, his very being. The way he thought, the way he acted.

"Yes," she said, the honesty coming from deep inside her. "I want you."

He dipped his mouth to one of her nipples and took it into his mouth.

Fire had raced through her, and Martina had bitten back a moan. He would consume her, she'd thought, and a lick of apprehension had mingled with the heat of her desire. He would learn more about her tonight than any man ever had. She would have to keep a part of herself from him. He must never know, she'd decided, that he was her first.

Distress crowded Martina's throat, and a soft sound escaped, breaking her reverie. Somehow she had been convincing enough that Noah hadn't guessed. He had been so caught up in their passion that he still didn't know he had been her first. Unable to sit still one second longer, she rose from her bed. She needed to leave these memories behind, to exorcise them, if only temporarily, from her mind.

She instinctively walked toward the nursery. She hadn't bought a crib or even painted the baby's room yet. The only piece of furniture in the room was a toy chest full of odds and ends she'd begun to collect. She knelt beside the light oak chest and touched the infant sleepers, receiving blankets, a stuffed bear, then brought out the little box that made her heart contract and expand every time.

Baby booties.

It was the silliest thing, but the tiny, tiny white booties made it all feel real and right to her. Seeing Noah tonight had confused her, and she didn't need to feel confused. Martina knew what she had to do. She had to keep her head together and love and raise this baby. She had to resist the urge to lean, especially on Noah. He made her think. Every time he visited her, there was more to like, more to admire, more to want and, in turn, more to fear.

The thought of knowing him more made every muscle in her body tense. It wasn't just that he was a Coltrane, although heaven knows that was enough. Martina had a feeling in her heart, in her blood, that if she fell for Noah, his being was so big and powerful that he would swallow her and she would simply disappear.

Chapter 3

"Have you heard anything from—" Martina's sister-in-law, Jill, asked, "—your assistant procreator?"

Martina grinned as the two women carried the results of their shopping trip into her condo. "I like that. Takes a lot of the messy emotion out of it?"

"I wouldn't want to upset the mother-to-be."

"By using expressions like former lover, or father of my child, or one of the top five men my brothers most hate." Martina gritted her teeth. "Thank you."

"Hate is a strong word," Jill said, revealing her public-relations background. "Your brothers may not really hate Noah Coltrane. They don't even know one another."

"They hate him," Martina said, stomping upstairs to the nursery. "Brock hates him because he's a Coltrane and one of their bulls jumped the fence and had entirely too much fun with some of our heifers. It made calving season a real pain because the bull was the wrong size and some of the calves were too big, and then there's your husband, Dr. Tyler Logan, who used to get into fistfights with Noah on a weekly basis when they were in their teens. And then there's the small matter that Noah got their baby sister pregnant. Yeah, I would say his name is dirt."

"But people change and they haven't truly sat down and talked since they became adults."

"That's to prevent bloodshed and eventual death by lethal injection. Texas believes in capital punishment."

Jill chuckled and put her arms around Martina in a hug. "Don't you think you're exaggerating just a little?"

"No," Martina muttered. "And I'm not exaggerating when I say how nice you are to check on me and go baby shopping with me." Martina knew Jill was unable to bear children because of an injury from an automobile accident, and her sister-in-law's continued generosity often brought tears to her eyes. Jill hadn't allowed her injury to prevent her from being a mother to a child who needed her. She and Tyler had adopted a son as soon as they got married.

Jill's watery gaze met Martina's damp one and both women laughed. "At least you can blame this on hormones. I'm really okay. It's amazing what marrying your brother and adopting Sam have done for me. I just want you and your baby to be healthy and happy." She sobered. "And I notice you didn't answer my question about your assistant procreator."

Martina made a face. "Yes. He found me." She pulled bumper pads and sheets with a soothing cloud motif from a bag.

"And?"

"And he immediately said we should get married, and I told him never, and he said we need to get to know each other, and I suggested e-mail."

"You must have felt something for him to get involved with him," Jill said.

Martina didn't like being reminded of her initial attraction to Noah. It had been strong and sexual, and she wasn't feeling very sexy these days.

Her doorbell rang, saving her from responding.

"Pizza," a male voice called.

Martina felt a twinge. The voice was familiar. "I didn't order pizza," she muttered, rising from the floor. Although pizza sounded like a good idea.

Jill joined her at the top of the stairs. "Your pizza-delivery guy looks a lot different from mine."

Noah had let himself in her unlocked door. His intense gaze wrapped around Martina and squeezed before he gave a slight grin that made her stomach flip. How had he known she would be hungry? Martina rolled her eyes at herself. When was she *not* hungry?

"What a surprise," she said in a neutral voice, walking down the stairs.

He flipped open the lid to reveal a large, hot pizza with mushrooms and onions. She eyed him suspiciously. "How did you know they're my favorite toppings?"

"It's my job to know," he said in a voice that would melt brick.

Martina tried to ignore the way her heart sped up.

"You're the man who arrived on horseback at Brock and Felicity's wedding," Jill said, her eyes growing wide in realization. "The fa—" She stopped and appeared to correct herself. "The fellow procreator."

Noah's jaw tightened. "Noah Coltrane. I'm the father of Martina's baby. And you?"

Martina ground her teeth. "This is my sister-in-law, Jill. She's married to Tyler."

"A pleasure," Noah said, shifting the pizza box so he could shake hands.

Jill nodded, still neutral. "You come bearing pizza?"

"I understand pregnant women get hungry," he said in the same sexy voice that made Martina feel hungry in all ways. "Satisfying Martina's appetite is my job."

Jill's lips twitched. "Something tells me you're up to the challenge." She glanced at Martina. "I should run and leave you two to your appetites and pizza."

"No. You don't have to go. There's plenty for—"

"I really need to get back." She gave Martina a quick hug and whispered, "Enjoy yourself. It's not as if you can get pregnant."

Shocked, Martina gaped at Jill. *Traitor!* "Tyler would not appreciate that comment."

"He may eventually," Jill said. "Take care and call me for anything."

"Yes, but—" Martina watched her sister-in-law smile and leave. She turned to Noah and scowled.

"Nice lady," he said cheerfully. "How are you?"

"I'm retaining water."

Looking down at her from beneath his black Stetson, he nodded. "I can take care of a lot of things, but probably not water retention. Pizza?"

"Yes," she said, and added dutifully, "thank you."

"My pleasure." He strolled into the kitchen in front of her, giving her an unobstructed view of his impressive backside. A memory flashed in her mind of the time Noah had coaxed her into making love in front of a mirror. The images of her naked body and his and the passion between them were so hot she prayed her thoughts didn't show on her face.

Noah turned and studied her. "Are you okay? You look flushed."

Darn. "Heating for two." Martina smiled and headed for the freezer. She opened the door and stuck her face inside to cool her cheeks as she pulled out some ice cubes.

She dumped the ice into two glasses and grabbed a couple of soft drinks. "How are you managing to get your work done and take time out to visit me?"

"I keep my trading to a minimum on the day I see you and work on my other projects on the weekends. I can handle it," he assured her in that low, sexy voice.

Martina's gaze skimmed over his broad shoulders. Yes, he could probably handle just about anything he wanted. "You don't really need to visit so often," she said.

"Sure I do. You'd miss me," he mocked.

"Oh, I don't think—"

"Have some pizza," Noah interjected. "I have a surprise for you after you finish eating."

"What kind of surprise?" she asked, immediately curious.

"It's little."

"What is it?"

"Now if I told you, it wouldn't be a surprise."

She gave a much-put-upon sigh.

Noah's smile twitched with humor. "Your impatience reminded me a little of my brother Gideon."

"I don't know much about Gideon. Come to think of it, I don't know much about any of your brothers."

Noah simply nodded and ate a slice of pizza.

"Well?" she prompted. "Are you going to tell me about your brothers?"

"I didn't know you were interested in my family."

I'm not, she opened her mouth to say, but immediately knew it wouldn't have been the truth. She was far more interested in Noah and his world than she should be. "I read an article about how a baby shares genes with the sisters and brothers of the mother and father, so it would probably be a good idea, as a mother, for me to know about your brothers."

"Uh-huh," he said, his expression a mixture of disbelief and amusement.

The amusement bothered her more than the disbelief. "You don't take me seriously, do you?" she asked. "You are tremendously amused by me, aren't you?"

His expression immediately turned deadly serious. "You may have a great sense of humor, Martina, but I have always taken you seriously—as a lover and now as the mother of my child."

Martina felt a shiver at the intensity in his expression. She often had the sense that by getting involved with Noah, she might as well be stepping into a hurricane. She was drawn to Noah's dynamic energy and the calm center he seemed to possess, but she always found herself wondering how she could put one foot in and keep her other foot out. She still wondered how she could be involved with him and keep herself.

"But you want to know about my brothers," he said. "Adam is the oldest. He is quiet and traditional. He manages the cattle on the ranch. His temper is more of a slow burn. He's very serious and could afford to lighten up every now and then. My brother Jonathan is the peacemaker. He raises and breaks horses. He rarely gets angry at anyone other than himself. Gideon is a pistol. He has a quick temper, but he doesn't hold a grudge. He loves a good challenge."

"It sounds like all of you stick together."

Noah made a wry face. "For the most part, we've had to, what with our dad's problem. But we've been known to use our fists to persuade."

Martina couldn't help noticing Noah's hands,

which were clasped together. She knew that when he was a young teen, he'd gotten into many fights. Part of what intrigued her about him was the way he had left his anger behind. She wondered how he'd done that. "Your father's drinking problem?"

"Yep. That and some of the other things our fore-bears have done. The Coltranes have a reputation to live down and another one we want to build. All of us want that."

"What was it like being the black sheep of the county?"

"Good and bad. Mostly bad. Teachers, neighbors, mostly everyone expected the worst when a Coltrane came around. So we often lived down to the expectations. That just ended up causing more trouble. Then my dad hired a foreman. His name was Zachary and he taught us how to fence and turned us into modern-day knights."

Martina blinked. "Modern-day knights? I knew all of you fenced. People were always afraid one of you might stick a sword in someone who ticked you off."

"There's that Coltrane rep again. Zachary started us out with wiffel bats. It was a big deal when he let us use one of his swords, and the biggest deal was when he gave us each a sword. We had to earn it," Noah said with a faraway look in his eyes.

"How did you earn it?"

"Grades, self-control, attitude and skill with the sword."

It was difficult for Martina to keep her objections against Noah intact when she pictured his transformation from an angry teen to a man. "I never heard anything about this."

"Most people haven't. Zachary left the ranch a few years ago. He told us we had the tools. We would always know what to do."

"You miss him," Martina said in surprise.

Noah nodded. "Yeah, I do."

"You've described your brothers," she ventured, picking up her second slice of pizza. "How would they describe you?"

"Besides a pain in the ass," Noah said with a wicked grin, "the driven dreamer, the one who is always trying to do impossible stuff."

"Impossible stuff like what?"

"Like trading cattle futures and making money at it. Running weekend roundups and increasing the ranch's revenue. Starting a fencing camp." He paused and met her gaze. "Trying to marry the Logan princess."

Martina felt as if she'd been punched by the look of determination on his face. Her heart hammered against her rib cage. "You want to marry me because I'm carrying your…" She broke off, refusing to use the words that sent her into a spin every time. "Because the baby I'm carrying has some of your genes. You don't want to marry me because you love me. You don't want me to come live with you because you can't live without me."

His eyes flashed with anger. "It would be tough finding that out now. When you left, you didn't give either of us much choice."

Her chest tightened. "I was just a fling for you."

"Martina, you are not fling material." His nostrils flared slightly and he narrowed his eyes. "Was it so easy to leave?"

His words echoed inside her, sending her perspective in circles. She had survived the past seven months by believing that what she and Noah had shared was a fling. She'd chanted it to herself day and night. "One of us had to do it. It had to be done."

"Why?"

Martina fought the jittery feeling spreading throughout her. She stood and tossed her napkin into the trash. "Because of our families. One of us had to stop it before we got in too deep."

She felt Noah behind her. "Did you succeed? Did you stop before we got in too deep?"

His question taunted her heart while his breath teased the back of her neck. She closed her eyes and mentally put her brick wall back in place. She turned and lifted her chin. "I think the general consensus is that I didn't get out unscathed," she said, putting her hand on her abdomen. "You said something about a little treat? Is it a brownie?"

He tilted his head to one side and shook it. "No." He waved his hand toward the chair. "Have a seat."

Curious, she sat and guessed again. "Cookies?"

He shook his head.

"Not cake or pie?"

He laughed. "No more food this time." He knelt beside her, and shock and alarm crowded her throat.

"Oh, no," she said. "You're not going to ask—"

"—for your hand," he finished. "No. I'm asking for your foot."

She frowned. "My foot?"

He slipped her sandal off her foot before she could say, *You are nuts.*

"If you won't trust me with your hand, will you trust me with your foot?"

"As long as it doesn't involve any weapons."

"Just one," he said, pulling a bottle of nail polish from his pocket. "But it won't hurt."

Chapter 4

"Are you crazy?"

Noah held fast to Martina's foot as she tried to pull it back. "Not at all. You were crying over the fact that you couldn't reach your toes. What's a former lover good for if he won't paint your toenails every now and then?"

Martina gasped, her eyes wide with shock, her mouth moving, but nothing coming out.

It was a nice change, Noah thought. He liked her off balance. There was something incredibly sexy about the color in her cheeks, the spark in her blue eyes and the tremble of her full mouth. He knew how that mouth tasted.

She shook her head as if to shake herself out of her state of shock. "I wasn't crying," she said.

"Okay, whining," he corrected.

She opened her mouth again, then snapped it shut and glowered at him. "I don't like being called a whiner."

Noah pulled a chair over to sit down and prop her foot between his legs. "Good thing I didn't do that."

"You said whine."

"Big difference. Whiner is a noun that suggests a person who whines frequently. Whine is a verb that could indicate a one-time or infrequent occurrence." He opened the tiny bottle and lifted the brush. "Any tips? I've never done this before."

"First you wipe the excess off the brush inside the bottle. Why are you doing this?"

He painted her big toenail. "I told you. You," he said, dipping the brush again, "expressed unhappiness over not being able to paint your toenails."

"Why didn't you just pay for a pedicure?"

He glanced up at her and smiled. "That wouldn't be nearly as much fun. I bet a man has never done your toenails."

"Yes, a man has."

Noah paused, feeling a surprising slice of jealousy. He glanced up at her. "Who was that?"

"Tyler," she said, and smiled. "He always had a steady surgeon's hand."

A surge of relief trickled through Noah when he heard her brother's name. He wasn't at all comfortable with the range of emotions Martina generated inside him. As much as she should be his, she wasn't. He continued to paint her toenails in silence.

"Nice color," she said after he started on her other foot.

"I did research," he murmured, thinking that even her feet were sensual—long and delicate.

She jerked slightly. "Research?"

"Don't move," he warned. "You don't want azalea pink all the way up your foot. Yes, I did research, but I won't reveal my sources." Martina's sister-in-law Felicity had asked him as many questions as he'd asked her the day they'd shared coffee.

"But I want to know."

"Fine," he said, not missing a beat as his gaze met hers. "Let me stay the night."

She blinked and he watched her swallow. "I can't imagine why you would want to stay the night with a woman who is seven months pregnant."

"I can think of some reasons," he said, holding her gaze. "Would you like me to tell you them?

"I'd like to see you naked in the moonlight with your belly swollen with my baby. I'd like to touch you with my hands and mouth. I'd like to—"

"No!" Martina shook her head and put her hands to her ears. "No. I don't want you to tell me reasons, and you don't need to tell me your source because you're not staying the night."

"Why not?" he asked, applying a second coat of polish. "Has pregnancy made you chicken?"

"No," she said. "It's made me more sensible."

Noah silently pondered her response as he

finished the second coat. Then he skimmed his fingers up the sole of her foot and looked up at her. "You have pretty feet."

Her toes curled and he grinned. "You're welcome."

She looked at him with flashes of wariness and wonder, sensuality and seduction in her startling blue eyes. "It would be easier for both of us if you would just be yourself, instead of being so…" She broke off, her finely arched eyebrows furrowing.

"So what?" He linked his fingers around her slim ankle.

"So kind," she said. "It would be better for you to just be yourself."

His lips twitched. "And that would be?"

"Domineering, pushy, superior, overprotective."

"Is that who I was in Chicago?"

She faltered and looked down. "No, but I'm sure the prospect of fatherhood brings out buried qualities in a man."

He sighed, wondering how he was going to get through to her. He had known her when she was soft and open to him. He remembered that Martina and knew she was still inside. Her softness and openness were just locked away from him.

He stood between her legs and leaned forward, nudging her chin upward with his finger so he could see her eyes. "I wish I knew what you were afraid of."

Bingo. Her eyes widened and she sucked in a sharp breath. The air between them seemed to thicken and crackle. "I'm not afraid."

Noah didn't believe her and although she might be mad as hell at him, he wasn't backing down. "Keep saying it, Princess Logan." He dipped his head close enough to brush his lips over hers, close enough to remind both of them what they'd once shared. "Maybe you'll believe it." He grabbed his hat from the table. "Sleep well."

Martina sat in her kitchen fuming as she waited for her toenails to dry. Noah Coltrane was an egotistical jerk, pretending that he wanted to seduce her, then insinuating that she was *afraid*. Not just afraid in general, she suspected, but afraid of him. She made a scoffing sound that only her goldfish could have heard if it had had ears.

She glanced down at her azalea-pink toenails and felt herself soften. The man had painted her toenails. If she tried to explain this to anyone else, she would sound like a nut. But the experience had been oddly intimate. Her foot resting between his legs, brushing his strong inner thighs, had reminded her of the passion they had shared. His determination to do a perfect job had reminded her of his determination to push her to the heights of pleasure.

She wasn't afraid. She was terrified.

What if she couldn't resist Noah? What if she fell in love with him? What if she fell so helplessly in love with him that she gave in and married him and spent the rest of her life trying to make him love her? She knew he didn't love her. He liked her and perhaps in some strange way desired her, but her primary value to him was the fact that she carried his child. His motivations for marrying her were all admirable and honorable, but they didn't involve love.

Martina didn't like the idea of being the only one in over her head here. If she was going to be vulnerable and head over heels in love, then she wanted Noah to feel the same way. It seemed fairer that way. Plus, she'd spent too many years trying to gain equal ground with the men in her life; she didn't want to spend the rest of her years doing the same thing.

Martina shuddered, then stood and walked gingerly toward her computer room. She'd had very good reasons for running from Noah seven months ago, and those reasons were still valid. She put her hand on her abdomen and sighed. Unfortunately, she had an even bigger reason she could no longer run from him. She just wondered how she could keep from falling in love with him.

Martina wasn't exactly sure how it happened, but Noah managed to join her for her first childbirth-preparation class. As they pulled into the parking lot of her doctor's building, she turned to him. "If anyone asks, we are not married. I don't want anyone misinterpreting your presence."

He ignored her and got out of the truck. Martina followed his lead and started to get out of her side. Her foot slipped and she started to fall. A thin slice of panic cut through her.

Noah's arms closed around her and he pulled her against him. "Don't do that," he said.

"Don't do what?" she asked, hiding her own jittery nerves. "I had to get out of your truck."

"Just wait for me to help you," he said irritably, his jaw tight with tension. "Don't let your mile-wide independent streak end up hurting you or the baby."

His accusation stung. It felt so good to be held by him at the same time that his words hurt her. "You don't really think I would do anything to hurt the baby."

He loosened his grip and the fierce glint in his eyes faded. "I don't think you'd do anything to hurt the baby. I want you to be careful with yourself. I'm not around as much as I'd like to make sure you're okay."

"I'm okay," she insisted as much for herself as for him. "I'll be okay."

He released her, but stayed close as they walked into the doctor's office. The lobby was used as the classroom and several couples were already seated. A nurse approached Martina with a folder.

"Hi, I'm Emily Ross and I will be your teacher for the next several weeks. You are?"

"Martina Logan and—"

"And you must be Mr. Logan," Emily said with a smile.

"No," Martina and Noah said at the same time.

"His name is Noah Coltrane," Martina said. "We aren't married."

"But I plan to change that," Noah said.

Emily's smile broadened. "Oh. Well, welcome to the class."

Martina frowned at him. "Did you have to tell her that?"

He shrugged, momentarily distracting her. She wished he wouldn't do that. The simple movement conjured up images of nights when she had traced the contours of his shoulder muscles with her hands and mouth. *Stop it,* she told herself.

"Would you rather I tell her you were the best lover I'd ever had and I have every intention of making you mine for good?"

Martina blinked and her stomach filled with butterflies. "If that were true," she said, "then you would have sought me out before seven months had passed."

"I did," he said. "Your employer said you were doing Web design from your home, there was no forwarding address or phone number from your previous apartment, and no one in West Texas seemed to know where you were. And for some reason your brothers weren't inclined to discuss your whereabouts with me."

Martina stared at Noah, feeling an odd knot of emotion form in her throat. Looking into his eyes, she could almost believe that her leaving abruptly had mattered to him. But that couldn't be, she told herself. He'd been so light about their relationship, so firm about not discussing the future. He'd teased her out of her clothes and into his bed so quickly it had made her head spin. Every time she was around him, it seemed he made her head spin.

Gulping over her tight throat, she shook her head.

"You told me one of the things you liked most about our relationship was that neither of us had any long-term expectations. You told me that the last night we spent together."

He narrowed his eyes. "Neither of us knew what we had, what we could have."

Her heart ached, but she needed to remind him and herself. "And we'll never know now," she said firmly, and looked around for a seat. "Time for class."

Throughout the session, Martina felt Noah's gaze on her, but she tried to concentrate as the instructor gave a brief overview of the warning signs and stages of labor, and instructions on sex during pregnancy. When Martina looked at her full abdomen, she wondered if she would ever have sex again. When she thought about the warning signs of complications, she thought about her mother.

She wondered if her mother had felt a premonition about her pregnancy or if she'd been eagerly looking forward to the birth of her third baby. Martina knew her mother's death had been a complete shock to her father and brothers.

A familiar longing swept over her. Lately, not a day passed that Martina didn't wish she could talk to her mother. Noah touched her arm, shaking her out of her reverie.

"You're supposed to be breathing," he whispered.

"I was," she told him.

He shook his head. "Deep breathing for relaxation. First stage of labor."

Martina glanced at the teacher and put aside her distracting thoughts. If she didn't focus on the class, Noah was going to know more about going through labor than she did, and she would *never* live that down.

After class, they drove home in silence. He pulled into her driveway, but didn't get out. "You're quiet."

She smiled. "Rare, isn't it?"

He nodded. "What's on your mind?"

She shrugged. "Lots of things. Labor, delivery, wondering what it was like for my mother."

His gaze turned thoughtful and he squeezed her shoulder. "Worried?"

"Not really," she automatically said. "There's no reason—" She broke off and smiled at the sensation of her baby's movements.

"What is it?"

"I think we've got a rodeo rider." She pressed her hand against her belly and saw the look of curiosity and longing on Noah's face. The expression moved her. Impulsively, she put his hand on her belly.

His eyes widened. "Hell, she's active!"

Martina laughed. *"He,"* she corrected.

"She," he corrected, then cradled her belly with both hands. "Does she do this all the time?"

The fascination in his voice did strange things to her heart. "Not all the time. He sleeps some, but sometimes it feels like he's gearing up for a rodeo."

Noah stroked his fingers over the blouse covering her. The gesture was oddly tender and sensual. "I know this has been happening for centuries, but it still feels like a miracle. You and I made this magic happen."

With dark eyes, he held her gaze for a long moment, a moment where something inside her seemed to creak and shift.

Martina wasn't sure there were words for what his eyes were saying to her. Noah leaned closer and she held her breath. He dipped his head and slowly, softly rubbed his warm lips over hers.

Martina felt the caress electrify her nerve endings from her head to her toes. He kissed her and a hundred emotions tumbled through her. All the passion they'd shared and something more powerful jerked at her like a game of crack the whip.

Alarm shot through her. She pulled back, staring at him, waiting to breathe. Martina lost herself in his changeable eyes. Sometimes green, occasionally blue and in rare moments gray like a storm-tossed sea, his eyes truly seemed to mirror the inner man. He was one man, yet had such diversity, a diversity that had fascinated her from the moment she'd met him. Strong, rugged, intelligent, intuitive.

Perhaps too intuitive, she thought. Sometimes she feared he could see everything going on inside her. "I need to go," she whispered, and turned away from him.

She didn't make it out of the car before he appeared by her side. He cupped her elbow, and though she felt the urge to wrest her arm from him, Martina knew it would have been childish. Still, just his touch set off a riot inside her. She'd run from the intimacy they'd shared, but his closeness stirred up images of his hands exploring and pleasuring her.

"You haven't forgotten, have you?" he asked in a low voice as they reached her porch.

"Forgotten what?" she returned, digging for keys in her purse.

"What it was like when you were mine."

Her heart slammed into overdrive. "I was never yours."

Noah boldly lifted his hands beneath her cotton blouse and touched the bare flesh of her belly. "Yes, you were. There's plenty of proof. Here," he said, then skimmed his hand up between her breasts. "And here. You were mine."

Chapter 5

You were mine.

Noah's words echoed through Martina's head as she fell into a fitful sleep. The images seeped inside her, at first hazy around the edges.

He set her on the desk in his hotel room with a playful, yet intent gleam in his eye. Martina's heart fluttered and she wondered what was next. He was always surprising her.

He skimmed his finger up the inside of her stocking-clad leg all the way to her knee. "I've always thought the man who invented panty hose should have been horsewhipped."

She grinned. "And why is that? Do you think it would be better for women to freeze?"

"No," he muttered. "But there are better ways to keep warm." He continued to slide his finger up the inside of her thigh. When he encountered bare skin, surprise flickered across his face and he met her gaze. "The person who invented thigh-highs is due a thousand thank-yous." He lowered his mouth to hers and said against her lips, "You keep surprising me."

Martina swallowed all her doubts and lost herself in his kiss. She was totally out of her depth with this man and could only hope she was concealing that fact. He slid his tongue over hers, teasing her to give him what he wanted. Her entire body clamored in response. Her breath grew short, her nipples tightened, and she grew moist and swollen.

Back and forth Noah rubbed the exposed sensitive skin of her inner thigh. He thrust his tongue into her mouth, mirroring the way he had taken her more intimately at other times. Hot and restless, Martina suckled his tongue deeper.

Noah shuddered and pulled back slightly. "Everything about you is one big tease for me." He pushed her skirt farther up her legs and dipped his fingers beneath the edge of her panties. "You're the apple I'm not supposed to eat, but tasting you isn't enough. I want all of you."

The mixture of overwhelming frustration and desire in his voice echoed inside her. Although neither she nor Noah ever spoke of their families, the long-standing grudge stood between them, a silent, strong barrier that prevented them from getting as *close to each other as they wanted. Martina wanted him. She wanted to drink his words and endlessly explore his mind. She wanted to make him ache the same terrible delicious way he made her ache.*

Whenever he kissed her, the air around them seemed to grow thick, just as it did before a storm. She felt that same impending sense that something powerful was going to happen. When they made love, it always did inside her. Martina struggled with the strange feeling that her premonition represented something larger than this moment, but her mind grew cloudy with passion.

Impatient with the obstacles between them and the restraint that kept her from being with him fully, she pushed all thoughts of her family and his aside. She ruthlessly banished everything but him from her mind.

Tugging at the buttons on his shirt, she pulled it open and ran her hands over his warm, solid chest. Instinct driving her, she slid her fingers down to the top of his jeans and pulled his belt loose. She brushed her open mouth against his, then slid her lips down his throat to his chest. She dipped her hands beneath his jeans to where he was hard and aroused.

He sucked in a sharp breath, and his eyes narrowed. "What do you want?" he asked, his fingers exploring her soft, damp secrets. "Do you know what you want, Tina?"

The tension in her core and mind tightened, and she felt hot inside and out. Had she ever wanted this much? Staggering desire and fear mingled. She swallowed, shoving the fear away. "I want you," she said, hearing the telltale huskiness in her own voice. "I want everything."

Her words seemed to make him combust. He pulled her panties away so that she was bare beneath him. Gazing at her naked femininity with a carnal, claiming expression, he lowered his mouth to the inside of her thigh and kissed.

Martina gasped. The near intimacy made her feel incredibly vulnerable. "I…I…"

"Hang on," he said, and took her with his lips.

Flexing her fingers in his hair, she felt consumed and utterly possessed. His tongue laved the pearl of her femininity, creating a tender, delicious friction, sending her over the top once, then again.

Martina cried out, and Noah pulled back. He lowered his jeans, fully exposing his huge arousal and drawing her hand to touch him. She stroked his hard shaft and he closed his eyes as if torn between pleasure and pain.

Trembling, she pulled herself up and tentatively pressed her lips to him. She opened her mouth over him and tasted the heady flavor of his passion.

Noah swore under his breath. "Not this time. I want to be inside you," he muttered, and eased her back on the desk.

In one swift thrust, he took her, and Martina knew she would never be the same.

She awakened with a gasp and bolted upright. Her heart pounding, her body hot, she took deep breaths and tried to gather her composure. Her cotton gown rubbed against her sensitive nipples. She was aroused, Martina realized in surprise. She closed her eyes against the sensations. She had been dreaming about Noah, and the dream had felt an awful lot like the one time she and Noah had made love and forgotten about contraception. The time, she realized, that their baby had been conceived. She'd heard there was a thin line between dreams and memories.

She rubbed her cheeks in dismay. Martina had tried so hard to run from Noah. First in Chicago, then in her mind and heart. She had only succeeded in delaying the inevitable. Now he was walking in her dreams.

Martina stared at the Web page she was constructing on her computer screen and heard a knock at her door. Actually, banging was a better description.

"Surprise!" called the familiar voices of her brothers and their families.

Smiling, she clicked "save" and hurried to the front door. Her two brothers, their wives, and her niece and nephews stood on her front porch.

"Aunt Martina, we've got presents for the baby in your tummy!" yelled Sam, Tyler and Jill's newly adopted son.

Martina swung open the door and gave the little boy a hug. He had been one of Tyler's patients, and the way the three of them had become a family still moved her. "Hurry up and bring them to me, so I can open them all."

Sam looked at her with huge brown eyes. "Why? Is the baby gonna pop out right now?"

Martina laughed and shook her head at Tyler and Jill. "Not yet. I just love presents."

She stood and hugged the rest of the crowd, amazed at the number of gifts. "Y'all did too much. My goodness, what possessed you?"

Brock, her oldest brother, hauled in a bassinet. "We kept hoping you would see reason and move back to the ranch with Felicity, Bree, Jacob and me."

"Or in with Jill and me," Tyler said pointedly.

Martina sighed and her heart swelled with love for her brothers. "I guess you two are never going to stop looking after me."

Brock and Tyler glanced knowingly at each other, then back at her. "No," they both said at once.

"You need a keeper," Brock said.

"And it takes both of us to do the job," Tyler added.

Unbidden tears filled her eyes, catching her off guard. She gave a muffled sound of dismay and swiped them away.

Tyler immediately looked concerned. "You're crying? You'd rather eat glass than cry. What's wrong? Is something wrong with you or the baby?"

"No, I'm fine. Darn pregnancy hormones," she said quickly. Martina felt a twinge of the old frustration she'd felt as long as she could remember. Her brothers still didn't believe she could take care of herself. Even though she was twenty-four, gainfully employed, single, pregnant… She sighed. The single and pregnant part probably hadn't helped her case.

She smiled and kissed each brother on the cheek. "I'm not going to argue with you today. I'm too delighted with your visit." She glanced at her nephew Jacob. "Is that a swing?"

"My idea," Bree, her niece, said. "I babysit for the Walters, and the only time their baby stops screaming is when I put her in the swing. I have to keep cranking theirs, but the one we got you has a setting for infinity. That means it never stops."

Martina had a fleeting frightening image of her baby spending the first year of his life in a swing. Her dismay must have shown.

Brock's wife, Felicity, laughed. She put her arm around Martina. "She's exaggerating. Mrs. Walters usually asks Bree to keep the baby during colic time."

"If you moved in with us, Aunt Martina, I could take care of your baby during colic time," Bree said, slyly glancing at her father.

Brock gave a wink of approval.

Although she smelled a conspiracy, Martina's heart swelled at the obvious love between Brock and his daughter. The closeness they shared was the exact opposite of what Martina and her father had shared, and she thanked the Lord her precious niece wouldn't spend her childhood trying to make her father love her.

"That's tempting," Martina said, giving Bree a quick squeeze. "Maybe you can come stay with me awhile after the baby is born."

"I will," Felicity offered.

"So will I," Jill said.

Brock and Tyler exchanged a look of dissatisfaction. "It's bad enough that you won't move in with us," Tyler said.

"Where you belong," Brock added meaningfully.

"Now you're going to make us live without our wives."

"Temporarily," Jill said, still a newlywed. She shot a flirty smile at Tyler. "The reunion could be enjoyable."

Tyler plastered a stern expression on his face.

"There she goes doing that PR thing again, trying to tell me a sow's ear is a silk purse."

"It's like what she did with you," Martina said with mock innocence, referring to the advertising campaign Jill had used to help Tyler raise money for the new pediatric wing at his hospital. "Got a great photographer, featured you in fundraising ads and turned you into the state's most wanted doctor."

He slid his arm around Jill. "That ad campaign turned out to be costly, since she paid for it by becoming my wife."

"Best thing I ever did," Jill said.

Martina could see the love flowing between Tyler and Jill and felt a twinge of envy. They were practically glowing with devotion. It was disgusting. "Stop. This is so sweet I could throw up. Neither of you look as if you're suffering. Let's all go into the den while I get a good look at all the goodies you brought me."

Martina served lemonade while her brothers assembled the swing, a bassinet and a changing table.

Her nephew Jacob presented her with a dozen pacifiers.

He had flourished under Felicity's care. Who would have thought a boy could become more of a man by getting a Manhattan heiress for a stepmother? Martina glanced at her well-dressed, warmhearted sister-in-law. Felicity had worked magic for everyone at the Logan ranch. Sighing, Martina supposed the Logans had been due a change of luck in the romance department, and she was glad love had found her brothers, even if it hadn't found her.

"Thank you," she said to Jacob, bewildered by the variety of pacifiers. "But why so many?"

He shrugged and hooked his thumbs in his belt loops. "Bree said babies don't always like the first pacifier, so I thought I'd give the baby a choice just in case he hollers like Dad says I did when I was little."

Martina's lips twitched. "Babies don't cry *all* the time."

"I know," he said. "They sleep and poop, too. That's why we filled up the backseat with diapers. I'll bring 'em in."

Martina opened her mouth to respond, but the doorbell rang, interrupting her. She walked to the front door and opened it to a man dressed in a mechanic's uniform. "I'm Jimmy Steen with Lone Star Auto Service Center, and I'm here to check a car that belongs to Martina Logan."

Hearing her brothers approach behind her, she shook her head. "Why? I haven't had any problems."

"We got a call from—" he pulled a folded paper from his pocket "—Coltrane," he said. "Noah Coltrane called and asked us to make sure your vehicle is in perfect running condition."

"Coltrane," Brock ominously echoed behind her. "I thought he was staying away from you."

"He better be staying away from you," Tyler said.

Martina's stomach twisted. "This isn't a good time," she said to the mechanic and turned to face her brothers. Even though they had almost suffocated her by overprotecting her, Martina loved Brock and Tyler with all her heart. Brock still wore a scar on his cheek from rescuing her from an unbroken horse when she was a toddler. Tyler had done things for her most brothers wouldn't dream of, such as painting her nails and braiding her hair. They had tried to make up for her father's lack of attention and love.

This was why she and Noah could never be together. This and the fact that Noah wasn't truly in love with her.

She swallowed over a tight feeling in her throat. "Noah found me," she said quietly. "He knows I'm having his baby."

Tyler's jaw hardened. "He hasn't tried to hurt you in any way, has he?"

"No, not at all." She bit her lip. "He, uh, wanted me to marry him, but of course I said no."

"Of course," Brock said. "He should know better. You'd never marry a good-for-nothing Coltrane."

Felicity joined them, catching Martina's gaze. "He might not be totally good-for-nothing," she said. "After all, Martina must have seen something in him."

"That was a fling," Tyler said.

"A big mistake," Brock said. "She was vulnerable and homesick and he took advantage of her."

Felicity raised a fine eyebrow. "You could be underestimating both Martina and Noah."

"I *know* Noah Coltrane," Tyler said. "I traded punches with him throughout high school."

Felicity bristled. "I'm a little sensitive to the idea that zebras don't change their stripes, because I did. Are you the same person you were in high school?"

"No, but…" Brock narrowed his eyes. "Why are you taking up for Noah? You know the problems the Coltranes have caused."

The possibility of her brother and sister-in-law fighting filled Martina with distress. "This isn't necessary," she began.

Felicity locked gazes with her husband. "Circumstances are different now. We have to think about what's best for Martina and her baby."

"That doesn't include Noah Coltrane," Brock returned.

"That's not for you to decide."

"Please stop," Martina said, feeling close to tears. "If ever a man didn't need someone to defend him, it's Noah. He's quite capable of defending himself. And this discussion is moot because the stars will have to fall on Texas before Noah and I get married."

Both of her brothers visibly relaxed, but Felicity still wore a look of concern. "Jacob tells me you brought me diapers," Martina said to her. "Why don't you bring them in while I go up to the nursery?"

Martina walked to the nursery and tried to gather her wits. The one thing she hated most about pregnancy was this completely foreign but overwhelming urge to cry. Feeling pulled in opposite directions at once, she bit her lip to get her emotions under control.

"Martina," Felicity said from the doorway.

Martina stiffened her backbone and turned to find both sisters-in-law watching her. "You really don't need to defend Noah."

"I've talked with him," Felicity said.

Martina gaped at her and lifted her shoulders in confusion. "How? When?"

"I ran into him at the bookstore one day. Actually, he saw me and remembered me from the wedding. He asked me to have coffee with him. He was so polite and so hungry for information about you that I couldn't refuse. I felt guilty afterward, but Brock and Tyler are so unreasonable about the Coltranes."

"I second that," Jill said.

Martina felt confused and exposed. "What did he ask you?"

"Little things. Your favorite food and color. Between you and Brock, I've gathered enough about you that I could answer most of his questions. I told him if he hurt you I would cut out his heart. His reply is what made me think that everyone needs to give Noah Coltrane a chance."

Martina almost didn't want to hear what Noah had said. She was having a difficult time holding fast to her determination to keep him at arm's length.

"What did he say?" Jill asked.

"He said if he hurt you, he would supply me with the sword."

A chill ran through Martina.

"I know what it's like to be underestimated. I think you do, too," Felicity said. "Don't underestimate Noah. Do what is best for you."

"I am. Noah doesn't really love me," she said, forcing the words from her mouth as much for herself as for Jill and Felicity. "This is some kind of male, family-honor thing for him."

Jill looked undecided. "We just want you to know we're here for you whatever you choose to do." She brushed her hands together as if dispensing with the conversational topic. "Speaking of choices, what would you like to do now?"

Sit down and cry, Martina wanted to say. Instead, she swallowed her emotions and said, "I'd like to decide where to put everything you brought." She pretended to focus on the task at hand, but in her mind, she felt Noah's presence. The strange connection she'd felt with him in Chicago and buried when she'd left wrapped around her like a silken rope. Soft but deceptively strong. Felicity and Brock's argument played through her mind in stereo, however, reminding her that she couldn't give in to crazy fantasies about Noah.

For her family. For herself.

Chapter 6

Martina glanced at her cuckoo clock for the fortieth time and scowled. She was getting used to his calls and his visits. When he'd called last night, he'd told her he would see her tonight around seven. It was after eight. What if he'd been in an accident? Her heart stuttered at the thought. Had he forgotten? She struggled with pure liquid fury.

She'd been reviewing the same part of a Web page for the past thirty minutes. She shouldn't care. It shouldn't matter. In fact, she should be relieved. After all, Noah had become an unwelcome intruder in her life.

The doorbell rang and she sprang from her chair and ran to open the front door. "Where in hell have you been?" she asked, searching Noah's face. "You look tired."

"A tractor-trailer turned over on the highway, spilled oil over the road. I had to take a detour."

"Oh," Martina said, and took a careful breath. "Did you forget your cell phone?"

He rubbed the back of his neck. "I tried a couple of times, but I must've been in a dead zone." He met her gaze. "Are you pissed off or upset?"

Martina felt a surge of conflicting emotions and the terrible, overwhelming urge to cry. "Oh, damn," she muttered. "Damn. Absolutely not," she sternly told herself.

"Huh?" Noah reached out to lift her chin so he could see her face. "Are you okay?"

"I'm not," she insisted.

His brow wrinkled. "Then what's wrong?"

Martina shook her head and took several quick breaths. "I'm fine. I'm not going to cry."

He looked at her in shock. "Cry?"

"I'm not going to cry," she said, closing her eyes and feeling a tiny tear escape the corner of one.

She felt his warm, long finger on her cheek. "You were worried about me," he said in astonishment. "You're upset because you didn't want anything to happen to me."

Martina opened her eyes. "Don't read anything into it. It doesn't mean anything," she told him. "It's those ding-dong pregnancy hormones."

He pulled her against him. "You missed me."

"I did not," Martina said, relishing the comfort of his arms.

"Okay, then I'll leave."

She tightened her hands on his arms. "Don't," she whispered, a request she couldn't stifle.

"Admit it," he said. "You care for me."

"I care for every human being on the planet except ax murderers and very mean people."

"But you didn't worry about every human being on the planet tonight. You worried about me." He lowered his head putting his mouth inches from hers. "Admit it."

You can't make me. You can't make me, she thought, zipping her lips.

"Shy?" Noah asked in a gently mocking voice. "I'm surprised. You're many things, but I've never thought of you as shy."

"I'm not!" Completely out of sorts, she felt as if her composure had taken the last train to Beaumont.

Startling her, he swung her up into his arms and carried her into the softly lit den. "What are you doing?" she exclaimed. "Trying to give yourself a hernia?"

"There you go again—worrying about me. Careful, Martina, or I'll start thinking you truly care about me."

"Oh, that's ridiculous," she muttered, relieved when he set her down on the couch. She started to rise, but Noah put his hands on either side of her, trapping her.

"I would be just fine if you would give me a little space," she told him.

"Maybe later," he said, pulling her into his arms and lowering his head.

He took her mouth, and Martina's composure left Beaumont and headed for Mexico. He kissed her intently, as if to reassure her that he was very much alive. His mouth, a seductive combination of supple and soft, nibbled at hers, sucking her lips, and his tongue slid over hers.

The low, sexual murmur rising from his throat lit a hidden flame inside her. She could almost believe he wanted her. His breath and hers mingled, her heart pounded, and he continued to kiss her.

One of his hands wandered to her tank top, lifting it, and his slightly callused palm touched her bare belly. His fingers caressed her while his mouth grew hungrier with each passing moment.

Martina's temperature shot to sweltering, and she felt her breasts throb with need. As if he knew the way her blood flowed through her body, Noah skimmed his fingers upward to the underside of her breasts. Lifting her bra, he rubbed his thumb over one breast, getting close to, but not quite touching, her nipple.

Unchecked desire licked through her, and she suckled his tongue, craving the way he made her feel. His thumb glanced over her nipple, and she shuddered.

"Like that?" he asked in a taunting sexual voice against her lips. Giving her no opportunity to answer, he took her mouth again and began to rub her turgid nipple between his thumb and forefinger.

The caress tightened her nether regions with shocking speed and force.

"Oh." The helpless sound escaped her mouth.

"You feel incredible," he told her, lifting his other hand to her other breast, stroking and teasing her.

Martina felt as if he was stimulating her intimately. Each tug of his fingers on her nipples squeezed a coil deep inside her. Unable to remain still, she undulated against him.

He groaned and lowered his hand, replacing his fingers with his warm, wet mouth. The sight of his dark head against her pale breast was too erotic to bear. Closing her eyes, she fought the escalating pleasure. This couldn't be happening, she thought.

Noah's tongue cupped her nipple, sucking, sending her over the top and crying out. A shocking, intense climax rocked through her. "Oh, my!"

She bit her lip as his terrible, wonderful mouth continued, sending her into another spasm of pleasure. Helpless and vulnerable, Martina felt a well of emotion that swelled in her eyes.

"Oh, damn, not again," she whispered, distressed.

Noah pulled back and looked into her eyes. She looked away, swiping at hers.

"Come here," he said, pulling her into his arms.

"This is crazy," she wailed. "How do you…" She broke off, feeling a fresh threat of tears. "This is insane. We're wrong for each other. You don't really want me. You want the baby and your honor and—"

Noah moved her hand to his very hard masculinity, abruptly cutting her off. She savored the intimacy of touching him for a few seconds. She savored the hope that he truly did want her for a few seconds. Then the baby kicked and so did reality.

Martina drew back. "You can't want me."

His eyes dark with desire and challenge, he nudged her gaze upward to meet his. "Why not?"

"Because I'm very big," she said.

"With my baby," he said, rubbing his hands over her full abdomen. He lowered his mouth to kiss the bare skin. "This makes you the sexiest woman in the world to me."

Martina searched her brain for a response, but found none. He almost made her believe it. Almost.

"I want to make love to you."

Panic shot through her. "Oh, no." She pulled back and shook her head. "Not a good idea."

"Why?" he asked, his slight grin belying the serious glint in his eye. "It's not like you'll get pregnant."

"It's just not a good idea."

"You really have no idea how sexy you are to me right now. Your body is so responsive, your breasts full. Do you have any idea how much of a turn-on it is knowing I can bring you to climax just by touching your breasts? Imagine what else could happen if—?"

"—I had no idea I would." Martina shook her head adamantly. She didn't need to imagine. Reality was clouding her head enough.

"Never before?" he asked.

"No," Martina said, feeling her cheeks heat self-consciously. "I think I may have seen something about it in one of the pregnancy books I read."

"Really! What did it say?"

"I don't remember much. I think I skimmed that part, but the point is—"

"What *do* you remember?"

Martina sighed, wishing she could transport herself to Anywhere-elseville. "It just said something about how women's breasts are sometimes more sensitive during pregnancy and some women have been known to have orgasms just by…" *Help!*

"By touching," he finished. "With hands or mouth."

Martina felt his words like a touch and her body remembered his recent caresses. She shook her head. "This is crazy. You've got to stop."

"Why?" he asked in an irritatingly calm voice.

"Because we're not right for each other, and—"

"Why?" he asked again.

"Well, there's the fact that your family hates mine and mine hates yours."

"But I don't hate you, and you don't hate me," he said. "So why are we not right for each other? What don't you like about me?"

Martina blinked. He'd taken her off guard again.

"You don't like the way I look?"

Her gaze helplessly fell over his strong body and chiseled facial features. "I, uh…" She swallowed. "I don't not like the way you look."

His lips twitched at her grudging response, but he continued. "Do I not turn you on sexually?"

She cleared her throat. She couldn't very well deny he turned her on after the way she'd just responded to him. "I, uh…" She exhaled in frustration. "Yes, of course you turn me on. I don't think I'd be pregnant if you didn't."

He nodded. "Then it must be my personality, the way I think and act."

Unable to bear the riot her emotions were causing inside her, Martina stood. "No, I like…" She trailed off, confused and frustrated. Noah's personality was what never failed to bowl her over, but she couldn't tell him that. "Yes, that's it. You're just too damn smart," she said angrily. "And intuitive. You're too intuitive. And you argue with me too much."

Noah stood. "You would have no use for a man who didn't meet you head-to-head and toe-to-toe. You're too strong a woman not to demand strength in your man."

Frustration roared through her and another spate of tears threatened. Martina bit her lip, refusing to cry. Heaven help her, this man knew her better than she'd realized. What in hell was she going to do?

He gave her an assessing gaze. "You look like you could use some time to yourself."

He was right. And wrong. But she latched on to the offer. "Yes, thank you."

"Anything else?" he asked.

"Anything else what?" she asked, still confused.

"Is there anything else you need?"

Martina refused to think about what he said anymore. If she did, she feared her brain would explode. "Cheesecake," she said. "I need cheese-cake."

He gave her an odd look, then shrugged. "Okay. I brought something for the baby, but I left it in the truck. I'll be back in a minute."

Curious but wary, Martina followed him to the door.

Remaining on the porch, he opened the door and gave her a CD. "It's Mozart," he said. "There've been studies done that suggest listening to Mozart can increase a child's intelligence."

Touched, Martina scanned the CD. He was thinking about the baby even when he wasn't here with her.

"I don't want to try to make Super Baby, but if a little music will make life nicer for her…" He shrugged.

"Him," Martina corrected.

"We'll see," he said with a knowing grin. "G'night. I'll call you."

"G'night," Martina echoed, and fought a hint of a bereft feeling as she watched him leave. Closing the door and locking it, she opened the CD and put it on, allowing the music to wash over her. Too restless for sleep and leery of the dreams she might have, she poured herself some fruit juice and returned to her computer. She needed to lose herself in her work. She needed to lose herself in something besides Noah.

Mozart played and moments passed. The doorbell rang, surprising her, dragging her from her work. She eyed the clock and wondered who could be at her door. Staring outside her peephole, she saw no one, but heard the sound of a car engine. She checked the peephole again and saw no one.

Irritated, she opened the door and saw a vehicle disappear around the corner. She frowned, wondering if the ringing doorbell had been a product of her imagination. She happened to glance down and spotted a brown paper bag.

Picking it up, Martina peeked inside.

A slice of cheesecake.

Her heart turned over. *Damn him. Damn him. Damn him.*

He was getting to her. Satisfaction pumped through Noah at the thought as he drove to the Coltrane ranch. Martina was starting to face the fact that she wasn't immune to him. Soon she would face the fact that they should marry.

Noah wasn't worried about love. Their passion and their child was enough to bind them to each other. He didn't want love clouding the more important need for them to get married.

Noah had always doubted that romantic love was in the cards for him. His mentor, Zachary, had always stressed how important it was for a man to find his purpose and perform it. Noah had quickly learned his purpose was to bring innovations to the Coltrane ranch to increase revenue and secure his and his brothers' future. In the back of his mind, he'd vaguely believed he was securing the future of the next generation of Coltranes. That belief was no longer vague.

It held a distinct picture in his mind of Martina and his child.

His purpose, also, was to bring honor and integrity to the Coltrane name. God knows, after his father's reputation, the Coltranes needed every drop of honor they could produce. He felt a sliver of discomfort. In that respect, Martina was correct. He had a passion for her, but the bottom line was that this was a matter of honor. She would eventually adjust to that fact, he was certain.

Turning in to the long drive to the house, Noah relished his progress. Soon, Martina would be where she belonged. With him. He tried looking at the ranch through her eyes. Since she had grown up on a ranch, many of the sights, sounds and smells would be familiar. The flat Texas terrain and the dry heat would come as no surprise.

He pulled his truck to a stop and glanced at the large two-story wood-frame house that stood like a stubborn weed on dry rocky ground. Although the Coltrane home showed little in the way of feminine influence, it was freshly painted and renovated, and boasted most modern conveniences.

Mounting the steps, he thought Martina would approve of the rebuilt porch and refinished oak floors. He walked through the downstairs, taking inventory. She might want to add some rugs or pictures, he thought, looking at the clean bare walls, but she would like the modern appliances in the kitchen. She might want to add some lamps. Sometimes the rooms seemed dark. He would clear out a room for her to do her Web page design. With a few minor changes, he decided she would adjust. She would like it, he thought, following the sound of his brothers in the TV room. No problem—

Noah stopped short at the sight that greeted him. Adam and Gideon lay sprawled on the sofa and recliner in their boxers. With a book propped in his lap, Adam chugged a beer and Gideon sucked on a cigar, his newsmagazine abandoned on the floor beside him.

Wearing headphones, Jonathan sat on the floor watching television while he hummed off-key.

"Be quiet," Gideon said.

"He can't hear you," Adam said, and turned up the volume on the wrestling show.

No-woman's-land.

Gideon glanced up. "Yo, brother, how goes the taming of the shrew?"

Noah sighed and raked his hand through his hair. "Progressing," he said, and sat down on the sofa. He stared unseeingly at the television screen, his mind busy.

"No bite or claw marks?" Gideon asked with a smart-aleck grin.

Noah shook his head.

"What are you doing to cut down on the battle scars?"

"I feed her," Noah said, his lips twitching as he imagined Martina's enjoyment of the cheesecake he'd left her.

Still wearing headphones, Jonathan glanced up at him and nodded, yelling, "Hi."

Noah pulled back one of the earphones. "I gave her the Mozart CD for the baby."

"What'd she think?" Jonathan asked.

"I don't know, but she didn't look like she wanted to slap me. That's an improvement."

"Any chance there'll be a wedding soon?"

Noah felt a burning determination. "Damn straight." He looked at his oldest brother, who he'd noticed hadn't said anything. "Talk," Noah said to him. "Front porch."

Adam glanced at him and slowly rose from his easy chair. "Okay." Setting Homer's *Odyssey* aside, Adam joined Noah on the front porch. In his boxers, he was an incongruous picture of a "good ol' boy" traditional cattleman with a closet appreciation for literary classics.

"What do you want now?" he asked, as he had asked Noah dozens of times before. Although Adam gave the impression of being reluctant to change, he offered a steadiness that had provided a balance to him and his brothers.

"When I walked into the house tonight, it occurred to me that a woman considering moving into our home might find the prospect difficult."

Adam propped his beer on the porch rail and glanced down at his skimpy attire. His mouth quirked in an ironic grin. "I don't know why."

"Oh, something about the combination of the *World of Wrestling* full blast on the TV, men sitting in their underwear drinking beer, smoking cigars and yelling at each other."

Adam shook his head. "You're gonna have a hard time changing our habits."

"I'm not planning on it."

Adam took another drink of beer. "Then what?"

"You know that building we've been putting together for offices?"

"Yeah."

"I was thinking about using some of my own money and making it into a house, instead."

Adam let out a long breath. "Has she agreed to marry you?"

"No, but—"

"Don't you think you're gambling against the house? You keep forgetting her family hates us."

"I haven't forgotten it," Noah said. The reality of the grudge burned like a hot poker in his gut every waking minute. "But Martina is going to marry me."

"She and her brothers just don't know it yet, right?"

Noah appealed to his brother's sense of the bottom line. "I'll take it out of my own pocket," he said. "I've done pretty well with some of my day trading."

Adam scratched his head and shot him a glance mingled with doubt and respect. "Good luck. You're gonna need it."

Chapter 7

A ringing sound jerked Martina from her sleep. Disoriented, she sat up in bed. The ringing continued and she shook her head, trying to clear it. When she realized the sound was coming from the phone, a dozen thoughts flew through her mind.

If this was Noah, she was going to give that man a piece of her mind. He hadn't just been late this time. He hadn't shown up at all. She'd paced the house the entire evening watching the clock and then had a difficult time going to sleep.

What if it was someone else, though? Brock? Tyler?

She reached across the bed and snatched the phone from the cradle. "Hello?"

"Martina Logan?" a male voice said.

"Yes."

"Sorry to call so late. This is Jonathan Coltrane. Noah won't be able to make it tonight."

Martina glanced at the fluorescent-blue numbers on her alarm clock. "Since it's after 2:00 a.m., that thought had occurred to me."

"Yeah, well, he was in an accident on his way to see you. The doctor says he's gonna be okay, but—"

Martina's heart sank to her knees. "Doctor?"

"Yeah, the ambulance took him to the hospital. His truck is totaled. He's gonna be real pissed off."

Martina swallowed over her racing panic. "How is he?"

"Broken ribs, punctured lung, concussion and one of his legs is bruised pretty bad. He'll be sore and cranky the next few days."

Wide-awake now, she clenched her hands to keep them from trembling. "Which hospital is he in?"

"County Hospital. We'll bring him home in the morning. The doctor would've let him go except for the punctured lung and the concussion. They wake him every so often and ask his name. I was in there one of the times they woke him, and he muttered something about needing to call you right before he fell asleep again."

"Thank you for telling me," Martina said, her mind whirling.

"You're welcome," Jonathan said. "G'night."

He hung up and Martina listened to the dial tone for a full minute before she returned the phone to the cradle. What if Noah had been hurt worse? A chill ran through her. What if he had died? For a moment, the darkness felt as if it had closed in around her, suffocating her.

Throwing back the covers, she rose from the bed and flipped on one light, then another and another. She walked to the hall and turned on that light, followed the steps downstairs and turned on nearly every light until the house was bright enough for Christmas.

"It's not as if I'll be going back to sleep anytime soon," she murmured to herself, and tried to deal with the terrible fear and pain she felt at the thought of Noah being hurt or dying.

Pacing into the kitchen, she poured herself some orange juice and gulped it. Lately, it seemed as if she was always thirsty. She kept picturing Noah in his truck and the crashing, grinding sound of metal. In her mind, she saw him against white sheets in the hospital. Another more insidious image flashed of Noah dead.

Her heart raced double time and panic coursed through her. She didn't want her baby growing up without Noah. For all her uncertainties about him, she believed he would be a wonderful father, a far different father than the one she had experienced. Noah would not ignore his child. Although Martina tried not to focus on it, when her mother died she might as well have been orphaned. If not for her brothers, she wouldn't have experienced any love as a child.

The thought tore at her, tugging fiercely at her

sense of loyalty, as it always did. Martina closed her eyes and shook her head. She couldn't deal with that right now. Right now, she had the edgy, overpowering need to see that Noah was all right.

Noah awoke to the sound of loud voices outside his hospital room and winced at the pain in his chest. At the moment, it hurt to breathe. The only thing he wanted was blessed sleep. If that nurse poked him and asked his name one more time, he was going to tell her he was an alien. Or the president. Or, he thought with a pained grin, a woman. Maybe that one from the Zorro movie. Martina looked a lot like her.

"If you're not related to Mr. Coltrane, I can't allow you in," the nurse said firmly.

Noah opened his eyes at the mention of his name. His gaze encountered Jonathan and Gideon.

"What?" Gideon rose and cracked the door.

"This is ridiculous. All I want to do is see Noah. I have no interest in even talking to him." Martina's voice carried into Noah's room.

Gideon turned an accusing gaze on Jonathan. "There is one very pregnant, very upset woman out there. Why in hell did you call her? Adam said we shouldn't."

Jonathan shrugged. "Adam left."

"He's gonna fry your butt."

"Not if he doesn't find out," Jonathan returned. "Not unless the baby of the family snitches on me."

Gideon scowled. "You son of a—"

"Would you two shut up so I can hear Martina?" Noah demanded. "I want to hear this."

"What is so—" Gideon began.

"Shut up," Jonathan and Noah said in unison.

"You haven't given me an acceptable reason to allow you into Mr. Coltrane's room. This patient has experienced head trauma and shouldn't be disturbed."

"This is not the first time Mr. Coltrane has acted as if he has experienced head trauma, but that's another matter," Martina said. "Mr. Coltrane is…"

"She's not going to be able to say it." Noah shook his head, then winced at the pain.

"Say what?" Gideon asked in exasperation.

"You'll hear."

"He contributed genetic material," Martina said.

"Pardon?" the nurse said.

"He supplied necessary chromosomes," Martina continued.

"A sperm donor!" the nurse exclaimed. "You think I should let you in there because he was your sperm donor?"

"He was not my sperm donor," Martina hotly denied. "Noah Coltrane donated his sperm the old-fashioned way, I'm expecting his child, and he has asked me to marry him."

Noah started to chuckle, but it hurt too much.

"Oh, you're his fiancée," the nurse said. "Why didn't you say so? You can go in."

"Thank you," Martina said in a cool voice, then

muttered, pushing open Noah's door, "that's right. I did not say I was his fiancée."

"I'm asleep," Noah whispered to his brothers and closed his eyes.

At her entrance, Noah heard both his brothers rise to their feet. Not surprised she had that effect on them, he thought. She'd probably made more than one man think about kneeling.

He smelled her sweet scent and felt her gaze as she paused for a long moment at his bedside. He was struck by an overpowering urge to see her, and it took surprising willpower to keep his eyes closed.

"Is he really okay?" she whispered.

"Yeah," Jonathan said. "He's just—"

"—sleeping," Gideon finished.

"Which of you is Jonathan?" she asked, her voice like honey over his pain.

"I am," Jonathan said. "You didn't have to come."

"Yes, I did. I, uh…" She cleared her throat. "I needed to see for myself that he was okay."

Her simple statement soothed his jangled nerve endings and abused body. Her presence both stimulated and relaxed him, and he felt himself drifting again. Martina was here and she cared. Everything wasn't all right, but it was a damn sight better than it had been.

The next time Noah awakened, it was to an empty room, and he wondered if he had dreamed her into his room, wished her there in his state of concussion.

His door whooshed open and Martina appeared

with a cup of steaming liquid in her hand. Her gaze met his. "You're awake," she said.

"Yeah."

"How are you feeling?"

"Okay," he automatically responded, busy drinking in the sight of her.

"Okay," she echoed in disbelief.

"Well, as long as I don't breathe or move, I feel okay."

She smiled at his light response, then her expression shifted. If he didn't know better, he would say she looked worried.

"I'm sorry about the accident," she said.

"Yeah, the truck's a goner."

"I wasn't talking about the truck," she said. "I was talking about you."

A tiny drop of hope trickled through his blood. "You didn't want me to croak?" he asked.

"No. I didn't."

"You might miss me," he said.

"The baby would miss having a pretty wonderful father."

Life wasn't worth living if a man didn't push his luck every now and then, Noah thought, so he pushed. "Then maybe you should marry me like you told the nurse you would."

Martina stopped and stared at him for a full moment. "You heard that?"

"Most of it," he said.

"But you were asleep," she said, distress creeping into her voice.

"Well, after you whispered with my brothers, I fell asleep, but—"

Her eyes lit with anger. "You eavesdropped and pretended you were asleep. What a slimy—"

"Just a minute, Princess Logan." Noah held up his hand and winced at the pain. "You were practically having a catfight with the nurse right outside my room. That's not eavesdropping."

"But you pretended—"

"Not for long. With the way I've felt since my truck rolled, I'd rather sleep through the next few days than win the lottery."

Her skin paled. "It rolled? Your truck rolled?"

Reluctant to alarm her, he bit back an oath. "It was just a little roll."

Martina sank onto the corner of his bed. "There's no such thing as a little roll. Your brothers hedged on the severity of the accident."

"They were just following instincts. Good instincts," he said. "No need to unnecessarily alarm a pregnant woman."

"I don't need to be protected."

"Yeah, you do," Noah said. "It's okay. This is one of the times in your life you need to be protected. You can't run as fast as usual. You can't lift as much as usual, although I suspect you try," he added with a frown. "You need to be protected, and it's okay. It won't always be that way. It doesn't mean you're not as strong. It just means your body is busy doing something else at the moment. It's busy getting our baby ready for the big entrance."

She looked at him and he could see she half-agreed and half-disagreed. Her eyes rounded slightly and she put her hand on her belly. "Sometimes I wonder if he already knows."

"Knows what?" Noah prompted.

Reluctance shimmered in her vibrant blue eyes. She hesitated. "Sometimes I wonder if the baby already knows your voice."

Noah's gut tightened. "Is the baby moving right now?"

Martina nodded, paused a few seconds, then moved closer to him. She put his hand on her abdomen, and Noah immediately felt a jab and a kick. He met Martina's gaze and saw the wonder in her eyes, the same wonder that burst inside him. The moment was a magical sliver of time. "Amazing," he said, lacing his fingers through hers over her abdomen.

He watched Martina look at their intertwined hands. She bit her lip and eased backward.

Her retreat annoyed him. His patience had been stretched to the limit. He wanted her to admit that she belonged with him. He wanted her to agree to marry him so they could raise the baby together. He wanted to throw her doubt, uncertainty and torn loyalties into a bottomless pit, and then throw her over his shoulder and take her home.

He felt a dull throb in his chest, leg and head, and reluctantly admitted he probably wasn't in the best shape for hauling anybody over his shoulder. He deliberately tamped down his impatience. "Where are my brothers?"

"They went home," she said. "They said—"

The door swung open and the doctor appeared. He flipped through the chart. "I see you made it through the night without too much trouble," he said. "Although the nurse said you objected to the frequent checks."

"She objected to the idea of me throwing a bedpan at her if she woke me once more before 5:00 a.m.," Noah said.

The doctor put his stethoscope to Noah's chest. "Breathe normally," he said, then put the stethoscope to his back. "Again.

"Rest for the next few days. You can sit up, but no physical exertion until your lung and ribs begin to heal. I suspect you won't feel like doing much, anyway. Plenty of fluids." He nodded in Martina's direction. "He's all yours, Mrs. Coltrane."

Martina's eyes rounded. She opened her mouth.

"Thank you very much," Noah said before she could voice her denial.

The doctor left the room and Noah reached for the telephone. "I need to call one of my brothers to pick me up."

Martina put her hand over his, preventing him from picking it up. "That's not necessary. I'm taking you to the ranch," she said.

Surprised, he raised his eyebrows. "Really?"

Her eyes flickered with brief uncertainty, but she took a breath and seemed to gird herself with determination. "I'm going to stay," she said. "For just a few days," she emphasized.

He opened his mouth to tell her he wasn't that

hurt, that he didn't need her to care for him, but the notion of Martina at the Coltrane ranch was so tempting it made his mouth water.

"I feel somewhat responsible for your accident," she said. "After all, you were coming to see me when it happened."

"You aren't responsible. It could have happened to me anytime. You can't predict when another truck driver has had too much to drink and his vehicle goes out of control and strikes yours."

"I can accept that mentally," she said, lacing her hands together. "But…"

"But?" he prompted.

"But I just feel responsible. Your brothers are busy and you will need someone to help you for the next few days. It feels right that I should do it."

Noah wished like hell that it would feel right to Martina to be with him because that was where she belonged. He could push her to confess deeper feelings for him, he thought. Another time, he promised himself he would. He stifled a sigh. "So this is about your honor," Noah said slowly.

She met his gaze, then looked downward. "I suppose you could say that."

"Honor's not bad. It's not a bad place to start at all."

She met his gaze again and lifted her chin, the emotion in her blue eyes inscrutable. "For some things."

Noah was still sleeping when Martina pulled into the Coltrane driveway. She felt uneasy. This land had been forbidden to her since before she was born, and it felt very uncomfortable not only to drive on it, but also to know she would be here for the next few days. If her brothers found out… Her stomach plunged. She slammed the door on those thoughts.

She took in the lay of the land and decided something about the Coltrane ranch seemed more primitive to her. Perhaps it was the buildings under construction, or the fact that no white fence or bluebonnets lined the drive.

Or perhaps it was the house, she thought, as she slowed to view it. Painted brown with no shutters and no vegetation surrounding it, the house reminded her of a barn without the warmth.

She slid a glance at Noah. He must have noticed the difference in speed, for he shifted. Despite his denial, she was sure he felt terrible. His color was off, and dark circles rimmed his eyes. Beneath his denim shirt, she knew his chest was taped. Given Noah's mile-wide macho streak, he would probably forbid her to help him up the front steps. Martina decided to leave the car running while she enlisted the help of one of his brothers.

As she opened the car door and eased out, then headed for the house, it occurred to her that no Logan had ever set foot on Coltrane land without being armed. She lifted her chin and firmly pressed the doorbell.

A tall, unsmiling, unfriendly-looking man opened the door and looked at her suspiciously. This must be Adam, the oldest Coltrane brother, she concluded. She hadn't met him at the hospital. Martina felt the power of generations of distrust flow between them. Her unease grew.

Stiffening her back, she reminded herself that she was armed. Inside the small purse slung on her shoulder was a tiny silk envelope of something that gave her courage. Her secret talisman. Oh, yes, Martina was armed. With baby booties.

Chapter 8

"I brought Noah home from the hospital and I know he's going to try to overdo, so I need someone to help him up the stairs."

Adam Coltrane looked at her as if she were an alien, which, in a way, she was.

She heard the scrape of Noah's boots on the steps behind her. "I'm fine on my own."

She rolled her eyes. "And he complains about my independence."

"I can handle him from here," Adam said. "Thanks for giving him a ride."

"She's staying," Noah said.

Adam's face froze. "She's what?"

"Just for a few days," Martina assured him.

"Believe me, I'm just as uncomfortable with this as you are, but Noah will need some extra help the next few days, and it's not fair for you or your brothers to tend to him when the reason Noah crashed was because he was coming to see me."

She felt Noah's hand at her back. "You look terrible. You need to lie down," she said.

"Thank you," Noah said in a dry tone. "You're not going to turn into a fussy, demanding woman who tries to order me around, are you?"

Martina smiled brightly. "Of course not. I'll be an assertive woman who reminds you of the things you need to do to heal quickly. The quicker you heal," she said, "the quicker I leave."

"No need to rush," he said in a voice that made her nerve endings ripple with sensual possibilities. "If someone lies down with me, maybe I'll rest better."

Martina felt a rush of warmth and a tinge of embarrassment, but she refused to show either. "Then we'll have to see if we can round up a teddy bear for you."

Noah chuckled, then winced and grabbed his ribs. "Oh, Lord, if you have any pity, don't make me laugh."

"Then don't try to seduce me when you can't do anything about it," Martina said as gently as she could.

"Sweetheart," Noah said with a dangerous light in his eyes, "don't say I can't. That's like waving a red flag."

Martina struggled with the awareness that always

seemed to shimmer between them. "I definitely don't want to bring out the bull in you," she murmured, then turned to Adam. "I think we need to get him into bed. Will you help?"

Adam blinked, his eyes still wary.

Martina's impatience climbed up the scale. "So what are you worried about? That I'll knife you all in your sleep? Unfortunately, I'm not as light-footed as I usually am, so I'm sure you'd hear my approach."

"I'm more concerned about what your brothers will do when they find out you're here."

So, this Adam wasn't a dummy. Martina had wondered the same. "They don't know I'm here. My brother Brock and his family have gone to New York City, and Tyler lives in Fort Worth. Besides, they're mostly civilized. I can't believe they would…" She broke off, recalling some recent heated conversations with her brothers. "Well, they don't know I'm here," she said, and walked through the door.

"And you're not worried that the evil Coltranes would do anything to hurt you?" Adam asked.

"Adam," Noah said in a stern voice.

She gave a short laugh. "As if Noah would let you," she said, then met Adam's gaze. "Besides, if Noah is any indication, all of you are into this honor thing in a big way. I'm willing to risk it." She turned back to Noah. "What can I bring you to drink?"

"I'm not thirsty."

She looked Noah in the eye. Heavens, he was

going to be more difficult than a two-year-old. "I didn't ask if you were thirsty. I'm sure you remember the doctor said you needed to drink a lot of fluids. Would you like me to choose for you?"

Noah gave a slight groan. "Whiskey," he muttered under his breath. "Lemonade. Okay, bring me lemonade. Kitchen's straight ahead and to the left."

Noah watched her leave and took a moment to relish the sight of Martina in his home. Her dark hair bounced against her shoulders and her long, coltish legs made short work of the hall to the kitchen. From behind, he could barely tell she was pregnant. Her back was straight, her buttocks tight and round, and her legs still as sexy as the day he'd first met her.

"C'mon, I need to get you into bed. You have lost your mind," Adam said, shaking his head and acting as a crutch on the stairs. "Bringing Martina Logan into our house. Are you sure that concussion hasn't impaired your judgment?"

"My judgment's fine. It's these damn ribs and my gimpy leg." Accustomed to nearly unlimited energy, he despised his current weariness. "I feel like a toddler who needs a nap. I've been trying to get Martina out here since I found out she was pregnant. When she volunteered, did you really think I was going to refuse her?"

"Only if you were thinking straight," Adam said.

"Absolutely not. Martina Logan has just fallen into my lap, and I may not be in the best condition, but I plan to take full advantage of the situation. If I have anything to say about it, she won't be leaving."

Adam helped Noah around the corner to the bedroom. He rubbed his face with his hand and looked at Noah with an expression that mixed admiration and pity. "If she's gonna stay, you'd better get that house finished. The boys won't know what to do with a pregnant woman in the house. A Logan at that."

Martina spent the day bringing Noah beverages, encouraging him to stay away from the computer, intercepting telephone calls and telling him to rest. Before today, she'd had no concept of how busy his plans for the ranch and trading on the stock market kept him. Keeping him from the computer and the phone presented an ongoing tug-of-war. By afternoon, she was tempted to spike his drink with a sleeping pill.

She glanced at the clock—11:00 p.m.—and gazed again at Noah. He was the most driven man she'd ever met in her life. All that passion drew and excited her at the same time that it repelled her. The thought struck her that he was so hard-driven, so much harder on himself than anyone else, that he could use a soft woman in his life.

In that case, Martina wryly thought, he didn't need her. She couldn't help but notice that the Coltrane home needed a woman's touch the way a flower needed rain, but adding a woman's touch to a bunch of rogue brothers in West Texas had never been her life's aspiration. Martina had always prized independence, respect and autonomy. In secret moments in the dark, she had wished for a special love with a man, but she'd never been able to meld her need for independence with her longing for love.

Looking at Noah with his mussed dark hair, black eyelashes against his tanned skin, and broad shoulders, she was struck anew by how complex he was. He was so strong it was difficult for her to imagine him needing anyone, especially her.

She lifted her hand to touch his forehead, then thought better of it and lowered her hand to her lap.

His eyes flickered open, and for a moment she wondered if he'd read her thoughts.

"You're supposed to be asleep," she whispered.

He glanced at the clock. "So are you."

"What do you want to drink with your pain medication?"

"No…" he began, and his lips twitched. "Just water."

Martina filled his glass in the bathroom that adjoined his bedroom to hers and brought it to him. He grimaced as he turned, but quickly downed the pills and water. "Thanks. Did you get anything to eat?"

"Yes, your brothers kept bringing me sandwiches. It was almost as if they thought I was a hungry animal and I'd get nasty if I didn't get fed."

His lips twitched again. "Can't imagine where they got that impression."

Realization hit Martina. "What did you tell them about me?"

"Just that feeding you tends to keep you in a good

mood. You gotta remember we haven't had a woman around for a long time, so they don't really know what to do with you."

"You didn't seem to have that problem." The comment heedlessly popped out of her mouth.

His eyes darkened with sensual awareness. "I always thought it was important to learn what gives a woman pleasure."

"That sounds like you've had quite a bit of practice," she said.

"I've had a few relationships," he conceded. "No woman got me anywhere near the altar. Except you."

Martina opened her mouth to remind him of the very obvious point that the reason he wanted to get married wasn't that she had bowled him over. It was that she was pregnant with his child. He still had circles under his eyes and she could tell his ribs were hurting, so she didn't want to argue with him. He needed to sleep.

"I wasn't your first, either, Martina," Noah said quietly.

She closed her eyes, torn between revealing the truth and keeping her mouth shut.

"You didn't love me like a virgin would."

His assumption irritated her. She opened her eyes and looked at him. "How many virgins have you been with?"

He paused, rubbed his chin, then narrowed his eyes. "None."

"Then I guess you wouldn't know, would you?"

He looked at her in disbelief. "I can't believe you made it into your twenties without having a lover."

"Well, you might be forgetting my two older brothers, who pretty much threatened to cut off the genitals of any man who dated me longer than a month. I graduated from a women's college and I like my independence."

"But you made love to me like a woman who knows how to please a man."

"I didn't want you to know how inexperienced I was."

"Why me, then? Why me for your first lover? A man your family would hate. A man you couldn't share a future with."

"I think knowing I couldn't share a future with you was part of it. It made you safe. You wouldn't want to marry me any more than I would want to marry you."

He pinched the bridge of his nose as if his head was aching. Concerned, Martina touched his shoulder. "Do you need some headache medication?"

"No, I just want to make sure I understand this. The entire reason you got involved with me was that you knew we wouldn't get married?"

Martina pulled away. "Well, no. That wasn't all of it. I was very attracted to you. I was probably even fascinated," she grudgingly revealed. "I loved the way your mind worked."

He glanced at her with a predatory glint in his eye and tugged her down onto his bed. "Still very attracted?"

Martina's heart stuttered. "You need to go to sleep."

He skimmed his finger down her bare arm. "You didn't answer my question. Still very attracted?"

She felt a shiver. "You really do need to rest."

He leaned forward, his lips a breath away from hers. "If you love the way my mind works, why do you fight me so much?"

Martina's mouth went dry and she tried to swallow. "You're a little overwhelming."

"Not for you," he said, rubbing his mouth against hers, creating a delicious buzz. "You're strong, sweetheart. You can take me anytime you want, so why don't you?"

Martina's stomach tightened. His mouth played over hers, teasing, taunting and inviting. He lifted her hand to his shoulder, as if offering his smooth skin and hard muscle for her pleasure.

He made it so easy to touch him and to want him unbearably. He made it so easy to believe at this moment that he would not deliberately bend her will to his.

He slid his hands to the underside of her breasts and gave a sigh that mixed desire and frustration. "I want to make love to you."

A dozen yes and no replies stuck in her throat. She swallowed hard. "You're still recovering. Your ribs are broken, your lung—"

"You could have a healing effect on me," he murmured, his thumbs moving closer to the tips of her breasts.

Martina shook away the thick cloud of wanting. "That's a ridiculous line," she whispered.

"Maybe we should stop talking."

His thumb glanced over her nipple and Martina felt herself begin to melt. She fought it. "Maybe we should start thinking," she said, and forced herself to push away from him.

Standing, she resisted the urge to fan herself. She felt hot from the inside out, and she knew the air conditioner was running full blast. Filled to the brim with such wanting, she feared she would turn into a pillar of salt if she dared even to look at him.

"I've dreamed of making love to you in my bed."

Martina looked at his big bed with the golden oak headboard and royal-blue coverlet. It was easy to visualize him naked and wrapped around her. She squished her eyes closed and banished the images from her mind. "Go to sleep, Noah. You need your rest."

And Martina needed her sanity.

By the following Friday, Noah wanted to fight. Cooped up in the house with his ribs hurting, sitting up in bed every night, blowing into that damn lung machine every hour and having Martina in his house but not in his bed and not to stay made him want to kick down a few doors. To make matters worse, he couldn't even engage his brother Gideon in a good frustration-reducing fencing match because he wasn't supposed to raise his arms.

Martina appeared at his bedroom door with

lemonade and more painkillers. He shook his head. The painkillers might fool him into thinking his ribs didn't hurt, but the inactivity they induced wasn't worth it.

"I'm not taking any more," he said, rising from the bed.

Martina gaped at him. "But—"

"But nothing. I'm not taking any more of those pills during the day." He bent down to pull on his boots and bit back a grimace.

"Wait a minute," she said. "I can help you—"

"I can put on my own boots," he told her.

"Cabin fever?" she asked with far more sympathy than he deserved at the moment.

He scowled, brushed past her and stomped down the stairs. Squinting his eyes against the late-afternoon sun, he headed for the horse barn. He'd almost broken a sweat by the time he reached it, and he swore under his breath at how his body wasn't performing. Accustomed to pushing himself physically and mentally, he had little patience for sluggishness.

He broke the doctor's rule about lifting his arms and saddled his black horse, Thunder. Riding, he knew, would clear his muddy head. He guided the horse out of the barn and mounted him, liking the feel of his feet in the stirrups and the leather reins in his hands. Something inside him eased at the familiar sensation of horseflesh beneath him, and he took off in a trot that quickly turned into a gallop.

He was still sore from the automobile accident, and it occurred to him that he could have used a few spark plugs for this ride. But the wind in his face erased the comatose feeling he'd been fighting.

Riding toward the south pasture, he slowed when he caught sight of cattle. He rode a little farther until he saw the stream that joined Coltrane property with Logan property. The water represented one of the ongoing sources of conflict between Noah's family and Martina's. Their child, he feared, could be the greatest source of conflict the two families had ever experienced.

Not if he could stop it, he thought, determination coursing through him. He swung off his horse and looped the reins over a tree, then strolled toward the stream. He gazed at the Logan land on the other side. The grass had always looked greener, the cows fatter, and everything in general had appeared easier for the Logans.

He thought about Martina and what a powerful mix of woman she was, strong, beautiful, vulnerable. She didn't know the impact she'd had on him from the moment he'd looked into her eyes. He wouldn't call it love, because he'd long ago decided a man shouldn't place his bets on romantic love. His passion had been improving his family's situation.

Although he wouldn't deny his passion for Martina, he didn't want his emotions to get in the way of persuading her to marry him. It was right for them to be together. He knew it in his gut and in his bones. He knew he wanted her more than he should. The idea of losing her made him break into a cold sweat. She was the woman who carried his child, the woman who filled his mind with dreams and tested his mind's ability to rule his heart.

Remembering how his life had been without her, he felt his gut clench and he scowled. She was too important for him to let his emotions get out of control. She kept him on his toes, yet made everything inside him click. Later, after they had married, maybe he would be able to trust her enough to let go a little. But not now, he thought. Too much was at stake.

Martina glanced past her laptop computer screen out the window, searching for Noah. She shouldn't care. She certainly shouldn't worry. "He's a grown man," she muttered. "He can take care of himself."

"He'll come home twice as sore as he was when he left, but three times happier," a male voice said from behind her.

Martina turned and saw Jonathan in her open doorway. The brothers had been scarce around her, almost as if they were afraid of her. Martina knew that couldn't be true. "This is one of those self-destructive patterns men sometimes exhibit?" she asked.

Jonathan nodded, remaining in the doorway. "Yeah, but it's also a survival thing. Get out or go crazy."

Martina slid her glance toward the window once more, then back to Jonathan. "You can come in. Despite the stories I'm sure you've been told, I don't bite."

"I don't think I heard anything about biting,"

Jonathan said in a noncommittal tone, his mouth twitching as he slowly entered the room. She noticed his slight limp again and wondered what had caused it.

"What did you hear?"

He shrugged. "I don't know. Something about a pregnant porcupine."

Martina chuckled. "Well, that would be true. This pregnancy has definitely brought out my quills."

"What are you going to do with my brother?"

Martina blinked at the directness of his gaze and his question. It was the same kind of question she might have expected one of her own brothers to direct at Noah. "I'm not sure. I didn't plan to get pregnant, so I never planned anything permanent with Noah." A subconscious delusional dream perhaps, but she'd never planned.

"He's not a bad guy. Well educated, he's the only one of us to get a master's degree. Of course, everything he got, he got with scholarships. He's smart, honorable and he would protect you with his life."

Yes, but would he love me with all his heart? Martina's heart squeezed at the same time that she was touched by Jonathan's comments. "Are you his PR man?"

"He doesn't need one," Jonathan said. "Sometimes people get themselves in situations where they don't see straight."

"Are you suggesting that I can't see straight?"

"I'm suggesting that you're in a situation where it might be hard for you to see Noah clearly."

She took a careful breath. "I know he's a good man. He's probably a wonderful man, but your family and my family…" She lifted her shoulders.

Jonathan nodded. "Yeah. Bad music between the Logans and Coltranes for a long time. Of course, us Coltranes have been fighting our bad rep since we were born. That black-sheep stuff gets old when all you want to do is ask a girl to dance, let alone try to court her. Gideon says we're all going to have to import brides like they did in the Old West," Jonathan said. "Gideon has a great imagination. We were able to send him to college, and he has a decent head for business, but we're beginning to think he majored in girls and frat parties."

"Why didn't you go to college?" Martina asked.

"I did the rodeo." He cocked his head to one side. "That's how I got the limp. Adam would give his eye teeth for a degree. He's always reading. We call him Abe Lincoln when he's not around."

This was the first extended conversation Martina had ever had with any of the Coltrane brothers, and she found herself hungry for more information. "Why doesn't Adam get his degree?"

"He can't leave the ranch. He's the cattle expert."

"But he doesn't have to leave. He could earn a degree online." Martina pointed to her computer.

Jonathan raised his eyebrows. "Is that so?" He walked closer to her. "We had this foreman who taught all of us how to fence," he said.

"Zachary," Martina said.

Surprise shot through his eyes. "Yeah. He kept us

from ending up in jail, and he was always telling us that we should never stop learning."

"And how do you keep learning?"

He looked self-conscious. "I like music. I listen to classical stuff a lot."

"Do you play piano or…?"

"I never had lessons."

"Me, neither. My mother played and taught both my brothers, but she died when I was born, and my father didn't want anyone touching the piano after she was gone." Martina stopped, surprised at how easy it was to reveal something so personal to a stranger. A Coltrane, at that.

He looked at her with a hint of understanding in his eyes, then shook his head. "We always thought the Logans had it perfect, but I guess everybody has their problems." He glanced beyond her out the window. "Here he comes. He's gonna feel like a piece of tobacco that's been chewed and spit out."

Martina looked out the window, spotting Noah walk, with a slight limp, toward the house.

"He's a good man, Martina. You could do worse for your baby."

Her heart tightened. "I know, but there's more to it than the fact that he's a good man."

"The Coltranes and Logans have been making bad music for a long time. Maybe it's time to change the tune."

Martina remained silent and torn. Even if they

could put all the bad blood between their families in the past, Martina wasn't sure she could spend the rest of her life trying to make another man love her.

Chapter 9

"I need you to stay," Noah said the following night just as Martina started to leave his bedroom.

She turned back to face him, wishing for the hundredth time that he would wear a shirt so her gaze wouldn't wander to his broad shoulders and muscular chest. She was never unaware of the physical power of his masculinity. She was beginning to feel as if she was fighting a landslide by fighting her involvement with Noah. How could she remain close to him and continue to tell herself she didn't want him, mind, body and heart?

Keeping her gaze above his throat didn't help, she thought. His eyes did things to her. They always had. "Why?" she asked, trying to keep the edginess from her voice.

A wave of self-consciousness flashed across his face. It was so rare an expression for him she almost didn't catch it.

"I need to read," he said.

Puzzled, she frowned. "Is this a late aftereffect of your concussion? Do you need me to read to you?"

"No. I need to read," he said, shoving his hands in his jean pockets, "and you need to be in the room. Close by."

Still confused, she walked closer. "Okay. Where should I sit?"

"The bed's fine," he said.

Martina glanced at him sideways.

"This isn't a seduction," he said. "It sounds a little hokey, but Adam read this article about how reading to babies while they're in the womb increases their intelligence."

Amused, but mostly touched, Martina sat on his bed. "You want to read to the baby."

He shrugged and nodded. "Yeah."

Her heart contracted. "Okay. What did you have in mind? Not stock reports."

He chuckled darkly. "No. Adam suggested *War and Peace,* but I told him that might be kinda heavy for a baby."

"So what did you choose?"

He picked up a book from the nightstand. *"The Hobbit,"* he said. "I figure between the two of us this child will get plenty of adventure genes, so we might as well let her get started."

And so Noah sat next to her on his big bed and began to read the wondrous story of how boring, respectable and comfortable Bilbo Baggins got suckered into a wild and dangerous adventure.

And with each passing word of his baritone voice, Martina fell for him a little more. Noah had lied when he'd said this wasn't a seduction. It was a seduction of the most secret places in her heart. Although she'd occasionally badgered her brothers into reading to her when she was a child, her father had never read to her. She would have given up ice cream for a year just to have her father read the sports section of the newspaper to her.

When Noah finished the first chapter, he put the book back on the nightstand and gazed at her in an assessing way. "You're very quiet."

"I was listening." *And feeling too much. Wanting too much.*

"You're thinking I'm crazy."

No, I'm thinking I am crazy. "Not at all," she said. "Did your father read to you?"

"Never," Noah said. "I will be a better father than my father was."

She watched him rub the back of his neck and could tell he was tired. "Why don't you get ready for bed and let me rub your neck for you?"

Surprise chased near refusal chased quiet curiosity across his face. "Okay," he finally said. "Give me a couple of minutes."

He washed up in the bathroom and returned wearing briefs and nothing else. Martina suspected he'd kept on the briefs in deference to her, but they hid little. The air grew thick as she breathed. "I'll sit behind you since you can't lie down," she offered, and moved farther back on the bed to make room for him.

He sat down and she tentatively lifted her fingers to his corded neck. She kneaded the tight muscles and massaged his shoulders. His tension showed in the knots she rubbed.

Noah made a rough sound of appreciation. "I don't remember you being such a good masseuse."

"We didn't have a lot of time," she said, "for taking time."

He caught her hand and brought it to his lips. "That was wrong."

Her heart tripped over itself. "You're tired. You should go to sleep."

"You should stay with me tonight," he murmured.

"Maybe I will." The words popped out of her mouth, but originated in her heart.

She felt him stop breathing. He turned carefully and eased back against the pillows propped in front of the headboard. He chuckled and covered a wide yawn. "You would pick a night when I can barely keep my eyes open."

Martina smiled to cover her nerves. "I'm ornery that way."

He held out his arm. "Then be ornery next to me."

She moved to his side and reached to turn out the light. A suspended awareness seemed to swell in the very air around her. In the darkness, she lightly pressed her cheek to Noah's chest and felt the beating of his heart. She pulled back slightly and he stopped her by curling his hand over her cheek.

"Stay," he muttered.

"I can't lean on your ribs. I might hurt you." She entwined her fingers through his and slowly lowered her cheek to a pillow. "Go to sleep," she whispered.

Too tense, too aware of him to relax, Martina lay stiffly beside him absorbing the rhythm of his breaths and the sensation of his strong hand in hers. A score of emotions tugged at her—anxiety, tenderness, desire, uneasiness. But through them all, she had the odd sense that she was where she was supposed to be. Her mind and her brothers and the rest of the world could argue with her until sunrise, but Martina felt she was where she belonged.

If only until sunrise.

Hours later, she awakened to the sensation of Noah's hands on her bare belly. "What?"

"It's okay," he said, his voice both sensual and reassuring. "It's just me."

Just me, Martina thought. When had Noah ever been *just anything?*

"I keep having this dream where I'm touching your belly and the baby is moving." He brushed his finger over her lips. "And you're kissing me."

Martina licked her lips, her tongue glancing over his finger. His eyes lit like twin fires, and he slid his finger into her mouth. The small sensual invasion kicked the doors off her denial of the past months.

This man could make her want like no other. She suckled gently on his finger and he groaned, then urged her onto his lap.

Lifting her shirt, he splayed his hands over her bare belly and held her with his gaze. "Kiss me."

His words were a combination order and plea she couldn't refuse. Martina slowly leaned forward and rubbed her mouth against his. He darted his tongue over her lips and inside, tasting her, taking her. His warmth and passion moved over her like a wave of heat on a hot Texas afternoon. Her heart pounded against her rib cage and her body temperature soared. She touched his chest and felt his heart pound against her palm. Could he really want her so much?

Noah pulled her shirt upward, stopping at her neck as if he was loath to pull his mouth from hers. With a reluctant sigh, he pulled away slightly and tugged the shirt over her head. He gazed at her bare torso and pushed her panties low on her belly. "Oh, Martina, you have no idea what seeing you like this does to me." He shifted and lifted his dark, frankly sexual gaze to hers. "But you will. Up on your knees darlin'," he told her.

Martina complied. "Why?"

"Closer," he said, wrapping his large hands around her bottom and bringing her belly directly in front of his face.

Then he ran his hands all over her abdomen and followed with his mouth. His mouth on her ripe midsection was the most erotic sight of her life. She felt herself turn to liquid in all her secret places.

As he rubbed his cheek against her stomach, he lifted his hands and unfastened her bra. He ran his hands lightly over her breasts, finding her nipples already hard. "I would never have thought I could have wanted you more than I did in Chicago, but I was wrong," he said, and drew her lower so he could take her breast into his mouth.

Dispensing with her panties, he slid his fingers between her thighs and gently stroked her. Martina had never felt so voluptuously desirable. He made her ache for his possession. Each stroke of his tongue over her nipple and each flick of his finger over her femininity drove her closer to a frenzy of need. She tried, unsuccessfully, to bite back a moan.

Noah pulled back, his eyes nearly black with sexual intent. "What do you want?"

She shuddered as he continued to stroke her. "You in me. I want you in me."

He swore. "I don't want to hurt you."

She shook her head. "You won't."

"Are you sure?"

She nodded, swollen with wanting.

He quickly ditched his briefs and drew her hand to his full erection. He kissed her mouth as she stroked him. Touching wasn't enough, so she pulled back and lowered her mouth to kiss him intimately.

Noah let out a low groan. His thighs taut as bands against her breasts, he allowed her to take him into her mouth, but only for a moment. "I can't last, baby. Come to me."

On trembling knees, she mounted him, and at his

deliciously full invasion, her moan mingled with his. For one powerful moment, they gazed into each other's eyes, joined at last. The evidence of their previous passion for each other, her ripe belly, served as yet another erotic, emotional reminder of their bond. Filled with Noah in the most basic way, she felt her landslide of emotions tumbling her more deeply toward him.

It was more than want, more than need, something terribly close to love. Closing her eyes against a shot of fear, she undulated slightly and heard his groan of pleasure.

"Come here," he said, and drew her mouth to his as he cupped his hands around her bottom and led her in a mind-bending rhythm. Everything but Noah faded from her existence.

Lifting one hand, he stroked her jaw as he consumed her with his mouth and tongue, echoing their deeper intimacy. Swollen with anticipation, Martina felt her body tighten around his shaft. The combination was too much. She shattered around him, her climax shuddering through her in fits and starts.

Noah gave a low groan that vibrated through her mouth, through her very being, as he spilled his pleasure into her. Martina felt her bond with him in every pore of her body.

The first sliver of dawn's pale light woke her the next morning. She blinked her eyes and was immediately aware of Noah. Her cheek rested against his arm, her belly against his side. She was naked and so was he. Although he was propped against the pillows, she could still see the peaceful rise and fall of his chest.

For a moment she wondered what it would be like to wake up in his bed and arms every morning. The forbidden image of looking into his eyes at the start of every day taunted her.

What about their families? And what if he only wanted her and never grew to love her? Her stomach tightened with fear. The baby moved inside her and she felt so torn that tears sprang to her eyes.

She had to get away from Noah, Martina thought. She needed to clear her head, and with him so close she didn't stand a chance. Not bothering with her clothes, she eased out of the covers and carefully slid out of bed, then tiptoed to the bathroom that connected Noah's room with hers. She closed the door, locked it and breathed.

Although he had been gentle, her nipples were tender and a few pink marks colored her skin. She had been completely enveloped by him, and she struggled with a sense of being overwhelmed. Much was at stake.

Biting her lip, she turned on the shower jets and stepped inside the bathtub. *A clear head,* she told herself. *I need a clear head.*

As the commodities exchange would have it, Martina successfully avoided Noah throughout the morning. She had left early to go to the grocery store, and when she returned been told that he had asked for her. Since then, he'd been engrossed in taking advantage of a volatile day on the market.

Martina was no less confused. Making love with Noah had solved nothing. They still had the same problems. The only thing making love with him had shown her was the power of their passion for each other and the incredible bond they shared.

But how long would that bond remain if they didn't truly love each other? Martina feared she was fooling herself with that question. It was frightening to admit to herself, but she loved Noah Coltrane. She could hide it from everyone else, but she couldn't dodge it herself any longer.

She was wise enough to know that one-sided love didn't work. How long would their bond remain if Noah never loved her?

Pensive, she paced the downstairs living room. She didn't know which was the most blah room in the house, but this one came close. Beige walls, beige sofa, brown chair. The house desperately needed some color. It desperately needed a woman, but not her, Martina thought. She was far too independent and opinionated for the Coltrane brotherhood. She would drive them all straight up the wall.

The phone rang. Martina knew Patch, the cook, was out in the garden and everyone except Noah was outside. She hesitated to answer on the off chance that one of her brothers might guess her whereabouts. It continued to ring, and since she knew Noah was glued to the monitor and refused to talk on the phone when he was trading, she picked up. "Hello?"

There was a silent pause. "Is this the Coltrane residence?" a female voice asked.

"Yes, it is," Martina replied, her curiosity growing.

"I'd like to speak to Noah Coltrane, please."

Martina felt a sinking sensation in her stomach. "He can't come to the phone right now. Can I take a message?"

"This is Wendy Holden, and Noah and I had dinner a few months ago in Dallas. I own a travel agency and I'd like to discuss his fencing camp. Tell him to give me a call, and this time, I'll give him a home-cooked meal in my home. That way we can avoid interruptions," she said in a smoky voice.

Martina felt the ugly scrape of jealousy. Fierce, intense possessiveness coursed through her. She took a careful breath. "I'll give him the message. Does he have your number?"

Wendy, whom Martina was certain was blonde, thin and had no problems with swelling ankles, happily recited her number and hung up. *Wendy* probably had no problem seeing her toes.

Martina nearly broke the pencil lead as she wrote the message for Noah. She was so upset she could pop. When had he seen her? Who else had he courted and seduced during the time they'd been apart?

While she'd been heaving with morning sickness, he could well have been seducing half of Texas. Make that Texas and Chicago.

Martina knew she wasn't being rational, but the inviting tone in the woman's voice pushed all the wrong buttons. She stared at the beige wall and decided she couldn't stay in this house one minute longer. She heard the back door slam, signaling Patch's return.

She made tracks to the kitchen and placed the offending message on the kitchen table. "I need to go out for a while. Please make sure Noah gets this message."

"Where you going?" the small, older man called after her.

"Out," Martina replied as she stepped through the front doorway and headed for her car. She needed to think.

As he watched his last trade of the day fill, Noah finally took a breath. The market had been especially volatile today, and since he'd been out of commission several days this week, he'd wanted to take advantage of his opportunities. He felt stiff and sore, and he wanted to see Martina.

She had made love with him with such abandon last night. It had been better, more powerful than he remembered. She had the strange ability to satisfy him completely at the same time that she made him want more.

He stood and resisted the urge to stretch, knowing it would hurt more than it would help. He could tell his lung was better. He didn't feel the damn rattle every time he breathed. Sick of babying his ribs, he figured he'd still have to put up with sleeping upright a while longer.

Noah couldn't deny he was improving, but he was determined to find a way to keep Martina with him. Last night was a start. He wondered where she was. "Martina," he called, whipping open his door. "Martina."

"She's not here," Patch said, appearing at the bottom of the steps and waving a piece of paper. "She told me to make sure you got this message, then she left."

Noah frowned as he made his way down the stairs. "Left? Where'd she go?"

Patch shrugged. "When I asked her, she said, 'Out.'" He raised his bushy gray eyebrows. "You might want to read the message."

Noah scanned the piece of paper and felt his gut sink. Wendy Holden was a man-eater and proud of it. His only interest in her had been her suggestion to promote the ranch's fencing and roundup weekends through her travel agency. When Wendy had indicated she wanted more, Noah had sought other avenues for promoting the ranch's expansion activities. Martina didn't know any of that, though. He could easily imagine what had gone through that pretty head of hers. "Damn," he muttered. "She didn't say anything about where she was going?"

"Out," Patch repeated with emphasis. "That was the last word I heard before the door slammed behind her. She took her car."

"Damn," Noah said again, and took the steps two at a time. If she was leaving permanently, she might have left her clothes, but would have taken her computer, he thought, swinging open her bedroom door to view her room. Her laptop was still on the small desk. He gave a small sigh of relief.

He stood in her room and stroked his chin, thinking. *If I were Martina and I was upset as hell, where would I go?*

An answer immediately came to him. An answer that did not please him. His gut twisted. "Damn," he said for the third time, and headed for his brother Adam's truck.

Chapter 10

Noah spotted Martina's blue Mustang just as the Logan house came into view. He felt an odd mix of relief and ingrained wariness as he looked at the large, impressive home. Damn. Sometimes he hated being right.

The pretty house, the pretty flowers and the pretty life represented the exact opposite of what the Coltrane ranch had to offer. He narrowed his eyes as he pulled the truck to a stop. That was in the past. If they wanted, the Coltranes could plant flowers with the best of them.

He swung out of the truck and headed for the front door, stiffening his spine in preparation for battle with Martina's family. He punched the bell and glared at the door as he waited.

The housekeeper answered the door, casting a suspicious look at him. "Good afternoon, Mr. Coltrane."

"I need to see Martina," he told the woman.

"She's in the library. I'll have to ask if she's receiving visitors," the housekeeper said with a sniff.

Noah made a face at the woman's back and didn't wait for an invitation. "I'll announce myself," he said, brushing past her.

"If she shoots you with one of her daddy's rifles, don't say I didn't warn you. She ain't in a pretty mood."

He paused at the wry tone in the housekeeper's voice and offered his own wry grin as he tipped his hat. "Thank you very much, Miss..."

"Addie," she said with a look of pleased surprise at his politeness. "The library's at the end of the hall. Good luck."

He took in the comfort and beauty of Martina's childhood home and felt his gut tighten. A woman could feel at home here, whereas at the Coltrane ranch... He stopped just outside the last open doorway.

Martina stood, shredding the stuffings of a pillow. Small wads of the stuff clumped around her feet. She made a whimpering sound that clutched at his heart. "I wish you were here," she said. "A million times I've wished it, but never more than now."

She must have sensed his presence because she looked up and saw him in the doorway. She shredded another piece of stuffing. "Go away."

"Like hell I will," he said, walking into the room. "What do you think you're doing taking off and not telling anyone where you're going? You're pregnant. You can't do that."

"Addie would have helped me handle any emergency. She still will." Martina frowned. "I can't believe she let you in," she said, shooting him a look of disdain.

"If this is about Wendy…" he began.

"Ah, yes." She smiled sweetly. Too sweetly. "Wendy, Wendy, Wendy. She sounded like she very much enjoyed the dinner you two shared a few months ago—"

"Nothing happened," he interjected.

"—while I was spending every morning hugging the porcelain bowl," she continued as if he hadn't spoken, "and you were apparently sowing your seed all over Texas."

Noah narrowed his eyes and moved closer, crowding her. "You just hold on to that knife you call a tongue. The only thing I was sowing with Wendy was the possibility that her travel agency might promote my fencing camps and roundup weekends. You may have forgotten the fact that I just learned I was fathering a child a month ago, but I haven't. You haven't given a tinker's damn what I've been doing by myself, let alone with another woman, for the last seven months, so why do you care now?"

He held her laser-sharp blue gaze. "You walked out on me with no warning. If you expect me to live like a monk just because you made love with me, then left me like yesterday's garbage, then…" He took a deep breath. "Then you'd be right."

She blinked, her eyes shiny with tears. "Oh, I can't believe you lived like a monk."

"Believe it." His heart swelled with such confusing emotions that he looked away to gather his wits. His gaze landed on a portrait of a woman who looked exactly like Martina. "Is it you? Is that—"

"My mother," she said, sniffing. "I'm told I look a lot like her."

Blinking, he stared at the picture and shook his head. "The resemblance is incredible." When he realized she had been talking to the portrait when he'd first seen her, his chest grew tight.

Martina hugged the shredded pillow to her chest. "That's what everyone says. That's why he couldn't stand to look at me," she said, nodding toward the portrait beside her mother's.

Martina's father. He had been a hard man, Noah concluded from the picture and what he'd heard of the man's reputation. Losing his wife hadn't softened him.

Noah gazed at Martina and saw the look of an orphan in her blue eyes. He put an arm around her shoulders. "Why'd you come here?"

"I needed to go somewhere that I belonged," she said.

Noah gritted his teeth at the surprising stab of pain her words caused. "Haven't you learned you belong with me?"

She drew in a deep breath and sighed. "I'm not sure about that."

Impatience tore at him. "What's not to be sure? I'm the father of your child. I will be good to you and the baby. You can count on that."

She stepped away from him. "I want more than that."

"What do you mean?"

"I mean, I spent my whole childhood trying to get my father to love me. I don't want to spend my whole adult life trying to get a husband to love me."

Noah felt caught between a rock and a hard place. "You mean a lot to me," he said, but the words sounded insubstantial to his own ears. He tried again. "I want you more than any woman. You know I care about you."

"But you don't love me."

He shoved his hands in his pockets. "I've always thought love was unpredictable at best, not something a man with any sense bets much of his gold on. Other things like family and commitment are more important." He could tell he wasn't getting through to her. Frustration raked across him. "There are some things too important to let emotions mess up. You are one of them."

Her eyebrows furrowed in confusion and indecision. Although Noah firmly believed in allowing each individual his or her freedom to choose, at this moment, he wished he could choose for Martina.

"You don't believe in love?"

"I didn't say that," he asserted. "I just don't bank on it. Here's an example. What if I had decided I'd fallen in love with you when we met in Chicago? After you left me, what was I supposed to think?"

Quiet for a long thoughtful moment, she seemed to have stepped outside herself. "Did it hurt you when I left?"

Noah immediately felt a barrier go up inside him. He looked away and struggled to answer her question honestly. "Yeah," he finally said. "It did. And it hurt even more to find out you were pregnant and hadn't gotten around to telling me."

"How much did it hurt?" Martina asked, shredding the stuffing of the pillow again.

He remembered the pain that had dulled only when he'd lost himself in his work. At night, however, he'd been unable to escape it. "I couldn't sleep," he reluctantly revealed.

She bit her lip. "This is a mess," she said in a broken voice.

"Yeah, you've mutilated that pillow."

Martina glanced down at the pillow and made a sound somewhere between a sob and a chuckle. "I wasn't talking about the pillow. I was talking about us and our situation. I don't see how it can work."

The hopelessness in her eyes cut like one of his swords. "Let me take care of it. I'm known for my innovative solutions."

"This is going to take a miracle."

"I've never let that stop me before. What are you afraid of, Martina?"

"That I'll never know what it feels like to have a husband who loves me. That I'll disappoint my brothers if I stay with you. That the Logan curse will cause a lot of heartbreak."

"You don't really believe in that curse, do you?"

"It's hard not to believe when I heard about it all the time from my father. There's a lot at stake here, Noah."

"I know, Martina. You can count on me."

Doubt shimmered in her eyes. He longed for her unswerving confidence, but understood he had yet to earn it. He had time, he told himself. Not as much as he'd like, but he had time.

She walked toward the baby grand in the center of the room. "My mother played this piano. She taught my brothers, but I never learned."

"You're still carrying on her tradition," he told her.

"How?" she asked skeptically. "I can't even play 'Chopsticks.'"

"You play a different kind of keys," he said. "Computer keys."

A slow smile lifted her lips and subsequently his heart at the same time. "I never thought of it that way."

He crossed to her and pulled her into his arms. "Come home with me. You want to hear chapter two of *The Hobbit*."

She looked torn. "I can't stay with you much longer," she said. "My brother Brock and his family will return from New York, and I don't like concealing my whereabouts from him or Tyler. I owe them that much."

"What do you owe them, Martina?" he asked.

"Now that you're a grown woman ready to give birth to our first child, what do you owe your brothers?"

She bit her lip and shredded more pillow stuffing. "I don't know, but I do know I hate feeling disloyal to them." She shook her head as if she wanted to shake off the discussion. "Addie has homegrown tomatoes for me. And I crave homegrown tomatoes so much I would probably trade my body for them."

Noah tucked that vivid image-inducing comment in the back of his mind and took the pitiful-looking pillow from her arms. "Is surgery possible, or should we go ahead and dig the grave?"

"We can always send it to Wendy," she said in that too-sweet voice again as she turned and walked from the room.

Watching her, Noah wasn't offended by the dig. If Martina was the tiniest bit possessive, then perhaps she could be possessed.

Martina listened to the second chapter of *The Hobbit* and fought the lulling seductiveness of Noah's voice. She remembered the way he'd touched her the night before. She remembered how right it had felt, so right to be possessed by him, to possess him. But she was fooling herself because although she might have a piece of Noah's heart, she would never have all of it. Would that be enough to last her the rest of her life?

Her stomach twisted and desperation tightened the back of her throat. The whole situation felt like a no-win for everyone involved, even the baby. That thought tore at her.

She needed to go back to her condo in Dallas. She needed to think clearly. This was too important. Noah was right about that. In the meantime, she wished Noah would stop going shirtless and get laryngitis.

Her heart and body softened just hearing him read. Which showed how insane he was making her. She bit back a sigh of disgust at her reaction to him. Looking at him in the glow of the lamplight, she knew he would make it so easy to fall into his arms and bed, but she'd learned making love with him would just confuse her further.

As he finished the last words of the second chapter and closed the book, Martina sprang from the bed. "Well, I'm beat and I'm sure you are, too. Good ni—"

Noah stood and took her hand. "No need to rush," he said, pulling her to him.

Oh, yes, there is, she thought. "I need to go to bed," she said, trying very hard to ignore the way her heart raced and the fact that he stood before her nearly naked. "Without you."

He toyed with her hair. "Why?"

"Because making love with you isn't a good idea," she said.

"You didn't like it?"

His gaze wrapped around her with a combination of warmth and seduction. "I didn't say that. You told me that you didn't want emotions getting in the way of your thinking, that this situation is too important. I think you're right, so we shouldn't make love."

"How do you know that making love with me doesn't make you see everything more clearly?"

Because my brain turns to mush when you are within five feet of me. His fingers in her hair had a drugging effect on her. It was all she could do not to lean into him and put her hands on his bare shoulders. She could easily drown in his eyes.

"I just know," she said. "So I'll go."

"Just one moment," he said, and eased his hand under her shirt to her bare belly at the same time that he lowered his mouth to hers. "I want to say good-night to both of you," he murmured, and kissed her and caressed her abdomen.

Martina willed herself not to melt, but his hands were both soothing and arousing, his mouth both gentle and seductive. His clean, musky smell and the promise of all the sensation and emotion he stirred in her drew her. Noah made her feel everything in 3-D Technicolor. She could have kissed him and let him touch her all night.

And if she didn't move away, she was going to dissolve into a puddle on this very spot.

Her heart and body protesting, she moved backward unsteadily. Noah's arms shot out to stabilize her, sending her emotions into another tailspin. She lifted her hands and took another step backward. *G'night, Noah.*

When Martina awoke the next morning, she opened her eyes to a bowl of fully ripe homegrown tomatoes on her dresser. On them perched a note in Noah's bold handwriting. "Tomatoes for you every morning. You with me every evening. Fair trade? Yours, Noah."

Martina didn't know whether to laugh or cry. She had no intention of telling Noah he left homegrown tomatoes in the dust even if it *was* an absolute fact. If he wasn't so nearly perfect, she'd kick him. She had to leave soon or she would give in to him.

That evening, Noah was edgy as hell. He was getting better and he couldn't fake it, and Martina was going to leave. He could feel it in his bones. Why couldn't he get through to her?

After dinner, he reviewed some stock charts, then returned downstairs. He heard Martina and Jonathan laughing in the living room. The sound drew him. He walked closer and heard her voice.

"One, two, three. One, two, three," she said. "See? You can do it. Who told you that you can't dance?"

"My leg isn't helping much, but it's not as bad as it would be if it were raining. This is the waltz? Damn, I never thought I'd see the day I'd be waltzing."

"With a very pregnant lady, no less," she said with another chuckle that made Noah's nerve endings crinkle.

"We're some kind of pair. The limping horse whisperer and…"

"The pregnant porcupine?" she suggested.

"I wasn't gonna say that."

"No." Martina's voice bubbled with amusement. "You were just thinking it."

Noah felt his gut twist with an emotion he

couldn't immediately name. If Martina was going to *pair* with anyone, it was going to be him. Jealousy? Shock raced through him. He was jealous of his brother? He must be losing his mind, he thought, but the feeling didn't fade as he heard their continuing banter. Why was it so easy for Martina and Jonathan? Why did she smile and laugh with Jonathan when she avoided Noah as if he were the evil dragon from *The Hobbit?* Why? he wondered as he listened.

"Let me know if you get tired," Jonathan said. "Are you sure pregnant women are supposed to dance?"

"Pregnant women can do anything their doctors tell them they can do."

"You're sure about that?" Jonathan said.

"I'm sure. Are you afraid I'm going to have the baby in the middle of the living room just because I waltzed with you?"

Jonathan blanched and stopped midstep. "You wouldn't do that, would you?"

Martina shook her head and laughed. She had learned that Jonathan was the most easygoing of the Coltrane brothers. He provided a welcome break from all the tension she felt with the other brothers, including Noah. "I imagine it's going to take more than a waltz to pry this one out of me. You have to remember this baby has inherited stubbornness genes from both Noah and me."

"You and Noah are gonna have your hands full," Jonathan warned her.

"I didn't know dance lessons were on the schedule," Noah said, entering the room. "Where do I sign up?"

Martina stiffened and stepped on Jonathan's foot. He winced.

"Oh, I'm sorry. Maybe I'm not the best teacher."

"The best I ever had," he said.

From the corner of her eye, Martina saw Noah's frown deepen.

"The best you ever had," Noah echoed in a deceptively mild voice.

Jonathan did a double take. "Best *dance* teacher," he said to his brother, and slowly stepped away from Martina. "Thanks for the dance lesson." He shook his head at Noah. "I think I'll get a beer."

He left and an uneasy silence descended. "Would you like to go out on the porch?" Noah asked.

Confused and uneasy, Martina shrugged. "Okay."

She followed him outside, not standing too close. It was a warm, cloudless night, but the breeze made it more bearable. She drew in a deep breath and gazed up at the big Texas sky. "I like being able to order pizza and Chinese food and have them delivered in Dallas, but I sure do miss the stars. The city lights detract. Every now and then it's nice to look at a sky full of stars."

"Are you a city girl or country girl, Martina?"

"Both," she said. "I enjoy the conveniences of city life, but I need the quietness of the country at times."

Noah was in an odd mood. She could sense it, and it made her tense and uncomfortable.

After a long silence, Noah finally spoke again. "You and Jonathan seemed to get along well."

"He talks to me."

"What do you mean?" Noah asked, studying her.

"Your other brothers don't speak to me. I know they wish I wasn't here. Especially Adam. I can't say I blame them, but Jonathan doesn't mind talking to me, and he doesn't really expect anything of me."

"I saw you laughing in his arms when I came downstairs," Noah said.

Realization and surprise raced through her. "You can't think there's anything going on between Jonathan and me. Not if you have half a brain."

He leaned against a railing. "Maybe I don't where you're concerned," he muttered. "He's just a man. He could fall for you."

Martina stared at Noah in disbelief. "Do you have a screw loose? Look at me," she said. "Really look at me and tell me, what do you see?"

He looked at her for a long time. He looked at her so long Martina resisted the urge to squirm. "I see a beautiful woman pregnant with my child," he said quietly.

Martina groaned. "I appreciate the beautiful part. That's very nice, but the truth of the matter is, I have a lot in common with the *Titanic* at the moment. I am not *gently* pregnant. Most men who look at me are either filled with horrified curiosity or fear that I'm going to give birth any minute. I can tell you they are not looking at me with lust. And the only reason you might have any lust is because you are the fa—"

She cut herself off, not wanting to say the words, not wanting to reinforce the connection between them.

"Because I am the what, Martina? Finish what you were going to say." Noah moved closer to her.

Her heart jumped. "I…I was just going to say something about you donating genetic material."

"No, you weren't," he said, gently backing her against the wall. "You were going to say something else. Tell me, Martina."

"I…I…" She swallowed at the fierce expression on his face.

"What were you going to say?"

Trapped, she glared at him. "Okay, I was going to say you're the father. It doesn't change anything for me to say it. I'm still leaving tomorrow."

Chapter 11

"This cigar sucks," Noah said, tossing the stub of one of Gideon's cigars over the porch railing.

"I coulda told you that," Jonathan said, strolling onto the front porch. "Gideon could see you were miserable as hell and in his ignorance he thought a cigar would make you feel better."

Noah knew Jonathan and Gideon were holding an ongoing battle over Gideon's cigar usage. Ever since Jonathan had permanently hurt his leg in the rodeo, he'd become a different man, leading a cleaner life and taking more pleasure in simple things. More than ever, he was the peacemaker among Noah and his brothers. In fact his battle with Gideon was conducted with a more mild, verbal reproach, rather than stinging insults.

Noah longed for the easy, reassuring relationship he'd always shared with Jonathan, but at the moment, he wasn't sure if his brother was carrying a mile-high crush on Martina.

Jonathan joined him at the railing and inhaled the night air. "You've come up with some harebrained ideas before, but this one takes the cake," he said as if he could read Noah's mind.

Noah glanced at his brother in surprise. "What do you mean?"

"You don't really think I'm after the woman you intend to marry, do you?" Jonathan asked.

Noah shrugged. "Martina's a beautiful, challenging woman. It would be hard for a man not to fall for her."

Jonathan shook his head. "You must be so gaga over her that you can't see straight."

Noah resented the implication that he was out of control. "I can see just fine. You were dancing with her, and you two were laughing. Sounded pretty damn cozy to me."

"Gaga," Jonathan repeated. "Totally gaga. For Pete's sake, Noah, the woman is so pregnant with your baby she looks like you could say boo and she'd have the child on the spot."

"So?"

Jonathan groaned. "Can't you see that she feels totally out of place here in no-woman's-land? If one of us doesn't talk to her a little, she's gonna think we all hate her guts. Adam is convinced her brothers are going to ride over here and try to burn down the house, and Gideon is convinced she's got some kind of voodoo power, since she's able to make you act so crazy."

"Crazy," Noah echoed. "I'm not acting crazy."

"Thinking I'm after the woman who's carrying your baby isn't crazy?" Jonathan asked. "Think about it."

Noah reconsidered and felt a trace of foolishness trickle through. He glanced at Jonathan. "I don't know what to say."

"You don't have to say anything. Love makes fools of us all."

Noah shifted uncomfortably. "For the most part, I've kept a clear head about Martina. I'm committed to her, but I wouldn't say I'm in love with her."

Jonathan laughed aloud. "Well, you'd damn well better be, because nothing else is gonna work with her."

Noah frowned. "What do you mean? You know I've never gotten too worked up over the idea of being in love with a woman. I'm not even sure I believe in it." He felt an odd twinge at his words, as if they didn't adequately cover his feelings on the matter as well as they once did. "Besides," he continued, "Martina and the baby are too important to let emotions cloud what I need to do."

"Hate to tell you this, bro, but your emotions already have. Maybe your problem is you've been trying to keep your heart out of this."

Noah fought a wave of uneasiness. "I still don't know what the hell you're talking about."

"Do you really think Martina's the kind of woman who is gonna respond well to a calculated play for her?"

"Well, no." Noah rubbed the back of his neck in frustration. "Maybe not."

"You know her a lot better than I do, but I've always thought women were a little like horses. With some of them, you follow every rule in the book and it all works out fine. But if you've got a Thoroughbred, the regular rules won't necessarily cut the mustard. Sometimes you've got to follow your gut, your instincts, your heart. It sounds to me like you've been leading with your head. If you're gonna get Martina, you might just have to lead with your heart."

Noah prized intellect and passion and held little faith in human emotion. He'd watched too many people get hurt from too much feeling and not enough thinking. Jonathan might as well have told him he would have to jump off a cliff in order to win Martina.

There'd been no more chapters read from *The Hobbit* last night, and Martina had tossed and turned before she'd fallen into an uneasy sleep. When she awoke this morning, she felt lost. Determined to get back control of her life, she showered and began to pack. Midway through her task, a knock sounded at the door.

Martina opened it to Noah. "I'm leaving today," she blurted before she fell under his spell and found another reason to stay with him.

His expression inscrutable, he nodded. "Okay. If you don't mind waiting until lunch, I'd appreciate it. I've got something I need to show you."

Surprised at his lack of protest, she agreed and felt her sense of loss deepen as he left her room. She sank onto the bed and fought the urge to cry. She looked out the window onto the Coltrane ranch and saw a land that needed flowers, a home that needed a woman's touch. Surely she couldn't be that woman, she thought. Not with all the history between her family and Noah's.

She closed her eyes and the truth pounded her like a relentless tidal wave. Although she had fought it, she was in love with Noah Coltrane, and her love for him was going to hurt her and her brothers. It was right for their baby to have two parents and to experience the privilege of having Noah as a father, but it was wrong for Martina to betray her brothers. Her brothers had loved her when her father had not. Logan loyalty ran deep, and she feared that if she stayed with Noah, she would feel guilty for the rest of her life. More confused than ever, she knew she needed to return to Dallas to make her decision.

By lunchtime, Martina was ready to bolt, but she made herself bide her time. Noah met her in the living room and led her out the front door. "Patch, make sure you hang around for the delivery," he called. "I'll be back in a little while."

He turned to Martina and offered his arm as they walked down the steps to the truck. "It occurred to me," he said, "that whatever happens between you and me, our child will spend some time on the ranch, and that means you should know a little about it, too."

His acceptance of her plan to leave rubbed at a raw spot inside her. Had he given up? she wondered. She should be relieved, she told herself. Wasn't that what she had wanted?

She listened as he told her about the various buildings and pastures as he drove throughout the ranch. He showed her the new bunkhouse for the fencing and roundup weekends. Although the Logan ranch possessed a more finished look, Martina was impressed with the size and layout of the Coltrane ranch. The unpolished nature of the ranch held the promise and excitement of fresh possibilities.

Noah pulled to a stop in front of a building under construction. "Let's take a look," he said, and helped her out of the truck.

The spacious two-story building boasted a large number of windows and an elegant, but casual Southwestern-style exterior. Walking through the front doorway, she nodded at all the light from the windows. Martina had always preferred plenty of light in her living quarters.

"It's lovely," she said. "What is it going to be?"

"It was originally going to house a new office, but plans change," he said thoughtfully. "Come upstairs."

They climbed the stairs to the second level, which

boasted five rooms and large closets. Two of the rooms featured skylights with shades. Noah led her into one of the smaller rooms. "I thought this could be the nursery. When I found out about the baby, I wanted to make a place for both of you here."

Martina's heart stopped. "Oh, Noah, I can't. I...I..."

He pressed a fingertip to her lips. "You can stay and you can go. It won't change what's between us. If we didn't lose it when you left Chicago and stayed away all those months, it's not going to disappear now, no matter how hard you may want it to." He stroked her cheek and held her gaze. "No matter how inconvenient and scary it is for you, I'm not going anywhere."

His words cut through her confusion with sword-like precision. But Noah didn't understand the war going on inside her, jerking her from one side to the other. "I still need to leave," she said in a voice that trembled, despite her best intentions.

"Okay," he said. "Let's go back to the house."

They rode in silence and Martina's tension grew with each breath she took. When they arrived, she noticed an unfamiliar car parked in front of the house. "Visitor?"

"Yep," he said, but didn't explain.

Lost in a sea of conflicting emotions, Martina got out of the truck and went back into the house with the intention of quickly gathering her belongings so she could leave.

Patch met them in the hall with a broad grin.

"Delivery was made and your guest is in the den chatting with Jonathan."

"Good," Noah said, and glanced in the living room. He chuckled.

Curious, Martina peeked into the room. "What was the deliv—" She gasped in shock when she saw a baby grand in the middle of the room. "Omigoodness!"

"Yeah, those suckers are pretty big considering they're called babies," Noah said. He glanced carefully at Martina. "What do you think of it?"

Surprised, she walked closer to the piano and shook her head. "It's beautiful. Just beautiful. I didn't know you played."

"I don't," he said, his jaw ticking with discomfort. "But I thought if you wanted to learn, it would be nice to have one available."

Overwhelmed, she gaped at him. "You bought this for me?"

He shrugged and leaned over to touch one of the ivory keys. "I thought it might be a way to make you feel a little closer to your mother."

Martina's chest filled with emotion. Her eyes burned with tears. "But don't you think this is a bit much?"

"I didn't get the impression you'd take a ring," he said, lowering his gaze to hers. "Try it out."

She was so moved she was incoherent. Sitting down on the bench, she tinkered with the keys. "I don't know how to play. How could you do this?" she asked in a voice wobbly to her own ears. "Why?"

"This was an illogical, emotional decision," he said. "You miss the mother you never had. I can't bring her back for you. But maybe I can do something that will make you feel like she's not so far away." He stepped into the hallway. "Hey, Patch, would you bring the visitor in?"

"Visitor?" Martina said, still overwhelmed.

An elderly lady with fluffy white hair entered the room and gave a soft little gasp. "Stars! You look just like Anna."

Confused, Martina looked to Noah for help. "Pardon?"

"This is Helen Lowry and she was your mother's piano teacher when your mom was a little girl. Helen is still teaching piano and she'd be happy to take you on as a student."

One moment ago, Martina hadn't dreamed she could be more overwhelmed, but he'd topped her. "You knew my mother?"

"Most of her life," Mrs. Lowry said with a smile. "She was a sweet girl who occasionally got into mischief. When she first started taking lessons with me, her mother would dress her in the prettiest little dresses. But Anna liked to climb trees and she was always showing up with skinned knees. She hated the finger exercises I assigned, but soon enough she made friends with the piano. By the time she met your daddy, she had received a scholarship to attend a music conservatory."

Martina felt as if she'd traveled across a desert and found a fountain of the sweetest water on earth.

She'd known so little of her mother because her father hadn't wanted to speak of her, and her brothers only knew what little they remembered.

"Did she go?" she asked. "Did she go to the conservatory?"

Mrs. Lowry shook her head. "No. Your daddy bought her a piano and she was as crazy about him as she was her music. When the babies started coming, she was crazy about them, too."

Martina's throat grew tight. "I really don't know if I have any musical ability, but even if I can't learn to play, I would love for you to tell me about my mother."

Mrs. Lowry's eyes softened. "Now don't you worry. I've taught kids who were tone deaf." She patted Martina on the shoulder. "And I'll be happy to tell you all kinds of stories about your mother."

Martina glanced up to find Noah, but he was gone from the room. She needed to talk to him. She needed to thank him. But how could she possibly?

"We really should begin, dear," Mrs. Lowry said.

Martina blinked. "Begin what?"

"Your first lesson, of course. Let's start with middle C. It's right here," she said, hitting a key. "Now, the proper position for your hands is…"

Martina gamely tried to accept instruction from Mrs. Lowry, but her head was in a whirl. In the past thirty minutes, Noah had delivered one surprise after another. And now, heaven help her, she was attempting to learn to play the piano. Another thirty minutes passed and Mrs. Lowry left, and Martina was staring at the beautiful piano.

"How'd it go?"

Her jaw worked, but no sound came out. She took a calming breath. "I don't know. I may not have my mother's patience with this. Then again, I don't have much patience with anything." She stared at him. He was leaning casually against the doorjamb as if he hadn't just given her a miracle. "Where did you find her?"

"I've known Mrs. Lowry for a long time. I used to cut her lawn. She was one of the few people who gave one of those bad Coltrane boys a chance. When I saw your mother's piano the other day, though, it clicked that Mrs. Lowry might have known her. I gave her a call this morning and…" He shrugged.

She stood and walked toward him. "Do you have any idea what you've given me?"

"A big piano," he said.

She closed her eyes and her heart just overflowed, and so did her tears.

Noah made a sound of alarm and pulled her against him. "Mrs. Lowry didn't smack your fingers with a ruler when you hit a wrong note or something, did she?"

"No," Martina said, laughing through her tears at the ridiculous notion. "She's the kindest woman." Martina shook her head and met his gaze. "Noah, don't you realize you've just given me a piece of my mother? A piece of her I would never have known without you? I just…" Her voice broke and she sobbed.

Noah winced. "Are you sure this is good?"

"Yes!" she wailed.

"Okay," he said in a doubtful voice, and held her as she cried. No one had ever given her such a gift. Although he'd captured pieces of her heart when he gave her little things for the baby, this gift was truly just for her. She would never be the same because of it, and she would never feel the same toward Noah because of it, either.

"I hate to see you cry," he muttered into her hair.

"I hate to see me cry, too," she said ruefully, and sniffed. "But if there's such a thing as a good cry, this is it."

"Maybe Jonathan was right, after all," he said more to himself than to her.

"Jonathan?" she asked.

He shook his head. "I'll tell you about it another time. Now I need…"

"…for me to kiss you," she said, lifting her mouth to his.

His arms tightened around her. "Something I always need."

Martina kissed him with all the feelings in her heart, all the joy and sorrow for her mother, all the love and desire she had for him.

Through the haze of that long, searching, scorching, wanting, needing kiss, Martina heard the sound of an exaggerated cough. Noah reluctantly drew away and Martina saw all three of his brothers standing in the hall and staring.

"I take it she liked the piano," Jonathan said with a devious grin.

"Don't y'all have anything better to do than watch me?" Noah asked.

Arms crossed over his chest, Gideon looked at Adam. Chugging a canned soda, Adam looked at Jonathan, who grinned hugely. Then all three of their gazes connected with Noah's. "No," they said in cheerful unison.

Noah groaned. "Let's go," he said, urging Martina toward the front door.

"Where are we going?" she asked.

"For a walk."

He led her a short distance away from the house to a small stand of trees where they could enjoy the shade. He tugged her down in the grass to sit between his legs. Martina had the strong, undeniable feeling that she was where she belonged. Not wanting to fight it any longer, she turned in his arms. "You have made it very difficult for me to leave," she told him.

"How?" he asked, his gaze intent.

"By the way you…" She hesitated, not wanting to use the word *love* because he hadn't said he loved her. The knowledge still pinched a vulnerable place deep inside her. But she had never received a more loving gift than what Noah had given her this afternoon. "By the way you care for me."

He ran his hands through her hair and down her arms as if discovering her for the first time. "I will always make it difficult for you to leave," he said, lifting her shirt and baring her pregnant belly to the sun. "Always."

By unspoken agreement, there was no talk of leaving that night, and Noah breathed easier than he had for days. He pushed aside the niggle of discomfort that everything could fall apart in an instant and simply inhaled Martina.

They took their dinner upstairs in his bedroom away from the prying eyes of his brothers. Tonight he didn't want to share. Noah allowed himself to drown in her blue, blue eyes. He drank in her laughter and couldn't stop touching her.

When he read the next chapter of *The Hobbit,* he persuaded her to lift her shirt so he could read against her tummy.

She laughed. "Your voice is vibrating against my skin."

Her laughter was such a turn-on he had a tough time focusing on the story. "I'm giving you a buzz?" he asked, meeting her gaze and wondering how one woman could be so seductive.

"Yeah, you are," she said, the expression in her eyes cranking up his internal temperature.

Noah resisted the urge to toss the book and dive into her. Barely. By the last few paragraphs he was stealing kisses at the end of every other sentence. The book slid to the floor as he rubbed his hands over her belly and felt the movements of the child they'd made.

Martina drew back breathlessly. "I do not understand your fascination with my belly."

"Well, you should," he said, taking her mouth and taunting both of them. "There's a little bit of me and you in there, and it's incredibly sexy knowing I helped put her there."

"Him," she corrected, sliding her hands over his shoulders and chest.

"Her," he argued, removing her shirt in one smooth motion. "I'm fascinated with more than your belly." He unhooked her bra and lowered his head to her breast. Her soft gasp was an intimate velvet stroke. He cupped the turgid peak of her nipple with his tongue, savoring the sensation of her delicate arousal.

He undressed her and dragged his tongue down her belly to her feminine secrets.

"What are you doing?" she asked in a shocked whisper, then, "Omi…ohhh."

He gently took her with his mouth until she was crying out his name. The sound of his name on her lips made him so hard he wondered if he would burst. Moving back up her body, he kissed her and she slid her hand to his erection to stroke him.

Noah sucked in a sharp breath at the pleasure/pain sensation. He tried to still her hands. "You're going to make it hard for me to—"

"That's the idea, isn't it?" she asked in a smoky voice that nearly undid him.

He growled and urged her onto her side. He lay behind her, with his hardness nestled against her bottom, and stroked her breasts.

"What are you…"

Noah pushed against her swollen femininity and she moaned, shifting to ease his entrance. He thrust inside her and they both made sounds of satisfaction.

She arched her bottom against him and he pumped inside her silken recesses. "So tight," he muttered, holding on to her hips. "So good."

She clenched around him, and his climax roared through him, taking him by surprise. Her intimate shudders milked his release so that it went on and on, robbing him of breath.

Finally she stopped and, utterly spent, he wrapped his arm around her. After a moment, he felt her begin to cry. She was trying to keep it from him, he suspected, and the knowledge clutched at his heart.

"Martina," he said, rising a little and turning her onto her back. "What's wrong?"

She closed her eyes, but tears still seeped from the corners. "It's nothing. Darn, I've cried more in the last eight months than I've cried in my entire life."

He wiped her tears with his fingers. "What is it?"

She gulped. "I am in such deep doo-doo."

Her distress tore at him. He wanted to fix it. He wanted to spend his life keeping Martina out of deep doo-doo. "Why?"

The power of her gaze shook him. "Because I love you."

Noah pulled her close, wanting to absorb the love she emanated, wanting also to push away the glimmer of fear he saw in her eyes. He slept, embracing her the whole night through. The next day her smile outdid the sunshine and he told her so. The day was so magical he allowed his brothers to share her only at dinnertime.

She surprised him when she talked cigars with

Gideon. "How do you know so much about cigars?" Noah asked her.

She shot him a guilty look, but smiled. "I tried a few in college on a dare."

Noah did a double take. "I'm trying to picture this."

"Don't," she said. "I was about as smooth as gravel. Coughed the entire time."

"That's a nasty habit for a woman," Noah said, wondering what other surprises were in store for him.

"It's a nasty habit for anyone," she said sweetly.

"Touché," Jonathan said.

Gideon just threw him a grumpy look.

"I understand you're the best self-educated man in West Texas," she said to Adam, who had been silent and watchful during the entire meal.

"I like to read."

"Did you know there are several programs where you can get a college degree online?" she asked.

"No," Adam said, perking up, despite his caution.

"There are several, and many are self-paced, so you can work them around your schedule. I know of a man who completed his law degree in two years."

Adam's eyebrows shot up in surprise. "What's the address?"

"I'll write a few down for you and you can check them out."

She was winning them over, Noah thought, and took her hand beneath the table. No surprise there, he thought, catching a private smile she saved just for him. His heart squeezed tight at her revelation last night.

The doorbell rang, and Patch yelled that he would answer it.

"How was your first piano lesson?" Jonathan asked.

"This is going to take some work," she admitted wryly. "I asked her if she would mind fitting in two lessons when she visits."

Jonathan looked confused. "You want longer lessons?"

"No," Martina said with a sly smile. "I thought she could start teaching you."

Noah roared at the poleaxed expression on Jonathan's face. Jonathan stumbled over his protest, but Martina just laughed.

In the middle of her laughter, an angry male voice rang out. "Where's Martina?"

Chapter 12

The sight of her brothers' angry faces stopped Martina's heart. "Brock," she said, standing, then wondering if her legs would support her. "Tyler."

Brock glanced at the Coltrane brothers with undisguised loathing. "Get your things," he said to her. "We're here to take you home."

"But—"

"But nothing," Tyler said, disdain oozing from his voice. "It's obvious the Coltranes have tricked you again. You just can't see straight when you get around them."

Noah stood in front of Martina in a protective posture. "Now wait just a minute," he said.

"We don't have to wait a second for you. You're

the one who caused this trouble from the beginning. If you hadn't gotten her pregnant—" Brock said.

"It takes two to get pregnant," Martina interjected.

"You had to be insane at the time," Brock told her. He looked at her, his face full of disappointment. "You know better."

"Don't give her a hard time," Noah said, his nostrils flaring in anger.

"A little late to be protecting her," Tyler said. "You should have been protecting her when you got her pregnant."

Adam stood. "That's pushing it, Logan."

"Yeah, well, I've just started," Tyler snarled.

Martina's stomach roiled with nausea. She had never seen her brothers so angry. Every nasty quality was coming out now. "Stop it!" she cried. "You're making me sick. You're not even listening."

"This has been coming for a long time," Brock said. "You go get your stuff and we'll take you home."

"Martina may not want to go with you," Noah said.

Brock narrowed his eyes and moved toward Noah. "When it comes to Coltranes, she doesn't know what's best for her."

"You weren't invited on our property," Adam said. "I think you'd better be leaving."

"We're not leaving," Tyler said as he stood toe-to-toe with Adam, "until we take Martina."

"This could get messy," Noah said to her. "I don't want you to see this. Go upstairs."

"I can still hear from up there," she said.

"Let me handle this," he told her.

"There's no *handling* my brothers when they're like this," she whispered, growing more nauseated by the second. "Maybe I should leave."

"Go upstairs," Noah said firmly.

One too many orders for Martina. If her brothers and the Coltranes were stupid enough to come to blows over this, then she wasn't going to stop them. Too upset for words, she left the dining room, grabbed her purse from the end table where she'd left it and headed outside to her car.

The sky was cloudy and angry-looking just like the atmosphere in the house. Martina climbed into the Mustang and secured the convertible top. She started it, then gunned it down the driveway.

She'd known the Waterloo with her brothers was coming, but she hadn't expected it tonight. She couldn't believe the hate on their faces. Since she'd lived with the Coltranes the past few days, she'd gained a new perspective on the family. They were every bit as honorable as her brothers. They struggled to produce more with less. They cared about each other, and she cared about them. Nothing could make her stop loving her brothers, but she still cared about the Coltranes. She just wished her brothers could accept that. She wished they could accept Noah. She wished…a lot of things. Her stomach tightened at how mean her brothers had been.

Tumbleweed rolled across her windshield. She gave a start and glanced at the sky again. The clouds were even angrier, and it was obvious, from all the flying debris, that the wind was picking up. Not the best time for a drive, she thought, and turned on the headlights. She considered turning around, but the thought of returning made her stomach roil again. She couldn't bear to hear her brothers' angry voices.

Tightening her hands on the steering wheel, Martina continued to drive until visibility all but disappeared. Wind whipped up, violently stirring dust and dirt. Her already low spirits sank to her feet when realization hit her. She was in the middle of a dust storm. She pulled to the side of the road, stopped and told herself to stay calm.

"Take a breath," she told herself. "Relax."

She inhaled, then felt the distinct sensation of water gushing down her legs. Alarm shot through her. "Oh, no. Houston," she muttered, "we have a problem."

Tyler took a break from hurling insults, and Noah heard the sound of dust and sand striking the window. He frowned, stepping closer to the window. "What the—"

"Noah Coltrane, I want you to stay away from Martina," Brock said.

"No," Noah said, frowning at the gray weather outside. "Not unless Martina tells me to stay away from her, and that won't happen because she's in love with me."

Sudden silence descended on the room. Then Tyler demanded, "She's *what?*"

"She's in love with me," Noah said impatiently.

He had a sinking feeling Martina had not done what she'd been told to do. He rushed to the front door, and although the visibility was poor, he could see that her car was gone. His gut twisted into a knot. "The woman does not take direction well."

"What the hell are you talking about?"

In the distance, Noah could see a fierce dust storm, and Martina was probably right in the middle of it. "Listen," he said, his patience and tolerance shot, "you two might have the time and energy to keep a hundred-year-old grudge going, but I've got more important things to do. Damn," he muttered, feeling his skin grow damp with a cold sweat.

Tyler stepped in front of him and gathered the neck of his shirt in his hands. "What the hell are you talking about?"

Noah felt his brothers move in unison. He gestured for them to stay back. He removed Tyler's hands. "We're not teenagers anymore, Ty. We're not going to fight. There's a dust storm out there and your sister's probably in it."

Alarm widened Tyler's eyes. His gaze shot to the window, then back to Noah. "What do you mean?"

"I mean her little blue Mustang convertible is gone from the driveway and she's probably stuck in a dust storm."

"But we told her to get her stuff," Tyler said.

Noah laughed without humor. "When did Martina follow instructions?"

Realization crossed Tyler's face. "Oh, hell!"

"I'm going after her," Noah said.

"You won't be able to see a damn thing," Adam warned him.

"She's upset. I can't leave her out there by herself when I know she's upset. Anything could happen to her. She's pregnant, for God's sake."

Silence descended again.

"Why didn't she listen?" Brock asked. "I *told* her."

"I think she did listen," Noah said in a dark tone, "all too well. We all gave her an earful, didn't we?"

Her brothers had the grace to look ashamed. Maybe there was hope, Noah thought, but he was too concerned about Martina to give a damn at the moment.

"Take my truck," Adam offered. "But be careful."

"I'll check the opposite direction," Brock said, his face creased with worry.

"Don't get yourself hurt," Noah told Martina's brothers as he grabbed his hat. "She couldn't bear it if either of you got hurt." He ran out the door.

Noah barely cleared the driveway before the dust whipping against the windshield forced him to adjust his speed to a snail's pace. Noah hated that he hadn't protected her from the ugly scene at the house. He should have found a way to circumvent it. He should have confronted her brothers before now. Seeing their families at each other's throats had probably torn her up inside. The idea of her suffering hurt so much it took his breath away.

With each foot he crawled forward, he prayed she was okay. What if she'd gotten hurt? What if she'd lost control of the car? He began to sweat with outright fear again.

Why hadn't he told her she was the most important person in the world and he didn't know how he could live without her? Why hadn't he told her that he loved her?

Noah knew with every beat of his heart that he loved Martina. Why hadn't he told her?

Berating himself, he continued to drive forward. The wind slowed for a moment and he saw a flash of blue. His heart raced. Her car. He pulled over and got out of the truck, shielding his eyes with his hands. The wind whipped around him in a fury. He reached Martina's car and pounded on the window. The door opened and he quickly scooted inside.

"Noah!" she said, leaping into his arms. "I've been so frightened."

"*You* have been frightened!" he said, holding her tightly as he scolded her. "You should never have gone out in this weather."

He felt her tense. Her breathing quickened. Noah pulled back slightly and studied her. "Are you okay?"

She continued taking slow, shallow breaths. "Yes and no," she finally said.

Noah took in the flush of her cheeks and the strain around her eyes. "Explain that answer."

She gave a weak smile. "My water broke and I'm in labor."

Alarm shot through him. He swore. "We need to get you to a hospital."

Martina shook her head, her face tightening again with another contraction. "I don't think we're going to have time."

Noah fought panic. "You have to slow down."

She looked at him as if he'd lost his mind. *"I can't."*

She couldn't have the baby in the car, he told himself. She couldn't. "How close are the contractions?"

She grimaced and cried out in pain, digging her nails into his palm.

"Close," he said. "Damn." He looked outside. Visibility was zero. He had never felt more helpless in his life, but he had never been more needed in his life.

Martina stared at him, taking quick short breaths. "I'm scared, Noah. What if something bad happens? What if the Logan curse is at work again?"

Her fears scored his heart. "Nothing bad is going to happen. You're going to have a baby girl and I'm going to be with you every contraction and you and her are going to be fine." He said it as much for himself as for her.

Her contraction passed and she drooped against the door. "I read about this in one of my pregnancy books. Some women have very short labors and get caught off guard. It's rare the first time." Her face contorted in another grimace and she began to breathe rhythmically. She held tightly to his hand. "I wish I had practiced my breathing more. Oh, Noah, it hurts!"

He felt her pain like a knife in his side. "Focus," he said. "Open your eyes and pick a focal point."

She squinted her eyes and stared into his. "Promise me," she managed in a ragged voice.

"Promise you what, Martina? I'll promise you

anything," he assured her, still holding her hand, wanting more than anything to take away her pain.

"Promise me that if I die, you will always love and cherish this child."

"Honey, you're not going to die," he told her, his eyes growing wet with emotion. "Dammit, you're not going to die."

"Promise me," she implored him.

"I promise," he said, then made another oath. "I love you, Martina. I'm not going to let you die."

Her eyes rounded at his words. "You—" She moaned. "I want to push."

Noah alternately swore and prayed. "It's not time, is it?"

"I've got to push!" she yelled, and Noah wasn't inclined to argue.

Two contractions of pushing passed and Noah positioned his hands between Martina's legs. A little head crowned. "She's coming," he said in wonder.

"He," Martina cried. "He's going to look like you." She closed her eyes and pushed again, and the baby's head emerged. The tiny red-faced infant screamed.

"Omigod, she's already yelling," Noah said, trembling at the first sight of his child.

Martina gave one more push and the baby slid out in a whoosh.

"Oh, Lord, it's a girl!"

Martina gaped at him. "It's a girl?"

Noah nodded, tears flowing down his cheeks. "We have a girl. We have a baby girl. Damn," he said, holding her. "What do we do with her?"

Martina sank back against the door. "Put her on my stomach while we decide."

Noah looked around the car for a blanket, but there was nothing, so he stripped off his shirt and wrapped the baby in it. "I don't know what to do with the umbilical cord. Damn, I wish I'd read something about this."

"Even though he's a hardheaded jerk sometimes, this is when it would be handy for Tyler to show up," Martina said. She gazed at their child and touched the baby's tiny fingers. "Oh, Noah, she's beautiful. Isn't she beautiful?"

"Almost as beautiful as her mother," he said, staring with wonder at both of them.

Martina pointed out the window. "Look, the wind has died down."

"Figures," Noah said. "I'm getting you to the hospital."

A Jeep and Gideon's truck pulled alongside them and stopped. Brock and Tyler jumped out of the Jeep, and Noah's brothers rushed from the truck.

Noah opened the window. "You're all officially uncles," he said. "You have a niece."

All five men stared at him dumbfounded. The baby started to cry, and they looked at one another.

Gideon cracked a broad grin. "I'm armed for the occasion," he said, and pulled out cigars.

One week later, on a hot, sunny day, Martina's brother Brock gave her away in marriage to a good-for-nothing Coltrane, who had turned out to be good-for-everything for her. The small gathering included just the two families, who had made peace with the birth of Anna Logan Coltrane. Adam and Brock were discussing cattle, and Tyler expressed an interest in learning to fence with Gideon.

Since last week, Martina had learned a small meteor shower had precipitated the dust storm. That might not have been stars falling over West Texas, but it was close enough to be a sign for her. More importantly, she couldn't imagine not being with Noah Coltrane for the rest of her life. Martina chose a long, ivory, silk empire dress, and Jill had put flowers in her hair. Felicity held the baby while Noah took Martina's hand and said his vows.

"With this ring, I thee wed," he said, his heart in his eyes.

Martina still couldn't believe it. She repeated her vows, then whispered, "Pinch me."

His eyebrows lifted in disbelief. "What?" he whispered back.

"Pinch me," she said. "I can't believe this is happening."

"I can do better than that," he said, then pulled her into his arms and kissed her deeply.

The minister gave a long-suffering sigh, and his lips twitched. "Most people wait, but I can tell you two aren't much on waiting. I now pronounce you husband and wife," he said.

Noah kissed her again, sealing his vows. "I love you," he said.

Her heart turned over. "I'll never get tired of

hearing you say that." Noah would never quite un-understand how his love had healed her of the empti-ness she'd felt because her father had been unable to show his love. Martina was determined to spend a lifetime reminding Noah how important he was to her. She glanced around at the happy faces of their families. "I think we've finally done it," she said. "I think we've learned how to beat the Logan curse."

Tyler and Brock nodded in agreement and walked toward her. They kissed her on opposite cheeks. "I think you sealed it," Brock said.

"And buried a grudge at the same time," Tyler added.

It never failed to bring tears to her eyes knowing that the three men she loved most had made amends.

"How's that?" Noah asked.

"You should know. You're the one who taught me," Martina said, lifting a hand to his cheek. "Love hard, always."

"Always," he promised.

And they always did.

* * * * *

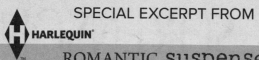
Maddie barked and moved closer to Remy, protecting her.
Remy stepped outside and the dog did, too. Remy was tempted
to run.

Wade, appearing at the open door, aiming his gun, stopped
her. Maybe Maddie would go next door, or her barking would
alert Lincoln.

She reentered the house and closed the door before Maddie
could follow. Her heart wrenched with the sound of frantic
barking.

"In the living room," Wade ordered her.

Maddie's barking stopped. She was running next door.

"You've been sneaking around again," Wade said, stepping
close to her with dangerous eyes. "What were you doing at my
store three days ago?"

"What are you talking about?" She played ignorant, the
same as she'd done the last time he'd come accusing her of
spying on him and his friends. That time she'd followed him
when he'd met some men she hadn't recognized. Nothing had

been exchanged, but she suspected he'd gone to discuss one of his illegal gun deals, deals that he expected her to execute for him.

He leaned close, the gun at his side as though he didn't think he needed it to keep her under control. "You know damn well what I'm talking about. You're supposed to be working with me, not against me."

"If working with you means breaking the law, I'll pass."

With a smirk, Wade straightened. "You've already done that. And if you don't start doing what I tell you, the cops are going to find out."

Because he'd tell them. Soon, he wouldn't be able to threaten her like this. Soon, she'd be able to call the cops herself and have *him* arrested. But for now she had to be patient.

Remy spotted Lincoln at the back door. She'd left it unlocked for him, hoping he'd retrace Maddie's path. Sure enough, he had. Wade's back was to him. Careful not to shift her eyes, she used her peripheral vision to watch Lincoln enter.

"I'm only going to ask you once more," Wade said.

Before he could repeat the question, Lincoln put the barrel of his pistol against the back of Wade's neck. "Put the gun down."

**Don't miss
ARMED AND FAMOUS
by Jennifer Morey,
available February 2014 from
Harlequin® Romantic Suspense**

⊞ HARLEQUIN®

ROMANTIC suspense

Love leaves no one behind

Black Hawk pilot Sarah Benson was born brave.
A survivor from the start, Sarah is known for her
risky flights to save lives, and
SEAL Ethan Quinn is just one more mission.
But when *she* needs rescuing, it's Ethan who
infiltrates enemy territory—and her heart.

Look for the next title from *New York Times*
bestselling author Lindsay McKenna's
Shadow Warriors series
RISK TAKER

Available next month,
wherever books and ebooks are sold.

Heart-racing romance, high-stakes suspense!

www.Harlequin.com

HRS27857